The Calling of
Clemo Trelawney

The Calling of Clemo Trelawney

Christopher Herbert

gatekeeper press™

Columbus, Ohio

The Calling of Clemo Trelawney

Published by Gatekeeper Press
2167 Stringtown Rd, Suite 109
Columbus, OH 43123-2989
www.GatekeeperPress.com

The editorial work for this book is entirely the product of the author. Gatekeeper Press did not participate in and is not responsible for any aspect of this element.

ISBN (paperback): 9781662914294
eISBN: 9781662914300

Library of Congress Control Number: 2021938539

Contents

Dramatis Personae

Clemo Trelawney: main character.

Agnes Trelawney: mother of Clemo.

Richard Trelawney: father of Clemo.

Joan (Trelawney): Clemo's older sister.

Isabel (Trelawney): Clemo's second sister.

Annie: maid at Hadnock Manor Farm.

Antonio di Venezia: Junior Clerk, London.

Brother Adam: Tintern Abbey.

Brother Anton: St Bernard's College, Oxford.

Brother Guy: St Bernard's College, Oxford.

Brother Illtyd: St Bernard's College, Oxford

Brother Jacob: Master Cellarer, Waverley Abbey

Brother Romuald, Novice Master, Waverley Abbey

Marguerite Blake, St Mary Bowe, housekeeper

Alice Blake: St Mary Bowe, maid

Edward Blake: son of Marguerite Blake

Father James Burley: parish priest, Dixton.

Eustace Chapuys: Imperial Ambassador, London

Laura Davies: Clemo's girlfriend and later, wife.

Gwyn Evans: apprentice moulder, Redbrook, later married to Issy Trelawney.

Mistress Fielding: Housekeeper to Father Burley.

Huw Griffiths: Farmer, Agnes Trelawney's second husband.

Rufus Hack: Waverley Abbey gatekeeper.

Harry of Bruern.

Mistress Jenkins: layer-out and midwife, Monmouth.

Brother John of Waverley

Nathanael Johnson: Under Steward, Ambassador's Residence, London

Harry Jones: Moulder: Redbrook.

Herman Keller: High Steward of Eustace Chapuys.

Father Mossman: St Mary Bowe.

Dai Parry, husband of Joan Trelawney.

Evan Prosser: Carter, Redbrook.

Pablo de Roma: Head Groom, Ambassador's residence.

Tom Saunders, servant of Eustace Chapuys.

Giles Thomas: Master of the Guild of the Five Wounds, Monmouth.

Ifor Young: 'The Boss', Redbrook Foundry.

Will: blacksmith and gatekeeper of Bruern.

William: Abbot of Waverley

Chapter 1: Early Life

Clemo Trelawney was born in 1509 at Hadnock, on the eastern side of the River Wye, near Monmouth. It was a tiny hamlet, dominated by the river on one side and encircled on the other by wooded hillsides that clambered up into the dense high ground of the Forest of Dean.

He had two distinct and contrasting memories of his early childhood. His first memory was of lying under a beech tree one Spring day and looking up through the fresh green leaves to the blue of the sky. He was too young to know what the word 'beauty' meant, but he felt enfolded by the wonder of what he was seeing, as though he, the tree and the sky were somehow melting together and sharing a bright happiness. The image stayed with him for the rest of his life.

His second memory was altogether darker. He was asleep in his bed in the room above the kitchen when he was woken by a piercing scream and he heard his father calling out, 'Run! Run!' He was so terrified that he climbed trembling into the bed next to his, shared by his two older sisters, and whispered, 'What was that, Joan?' She too was awake, as was Issy. 'It's our father having one of his nightmares. Go back to sleep. And don't tell anyone what you heard.' He cuddled down between them and noticed that they too were trembling just as he was. He was puzzled by Joan's instruction about not saying anything and could not understand why Joan had been so insistent.

During those earliest years of his life, he mooched around the cottage, playing with stones, building imaginary castles, throwing sticks into the river, and watching them float rapidly away. He sometimes sat near the kennel close to his house where a dog called Patch was chained up, and, if he was lucky, he went with his mother or sisters, to move the cows from one meadow to another. The small-holding was the responsibility of his mother, Agnes, though if it was light when his father returned from the Foundry, Clemo would help him with what his father called 'odd jobs'. He enjoyed that but always remained wary of his father, knowing that his father's temper could flare up at the slightest provocation.

On his seventh birthday he was taken by his older sisters to a small Dame School on the other side of the wooden bridge in Monmouth. It was run by Mistress Hughes, a buxom woman who stood no nonsense and of whom Clemo was a little afraid. He made friends with some of the other children, was taught to read and write and made such rapid progress that Mistress Hughes suggested to his mother that it might be better if he went for lessons to Father Burley, the parish priest of Dixton.

Clemo was thrilled by the idea. Having gone to Mass at Dixton regularly with his mother and father, he had become very fond of the white-haired priest. It was a joy just to be in that church with the sun pouring through the windows and pooling on the flagged stone floor, and the smoke of incense drifting upwards as Father Burley elevated the Host, and hearing the sacring bell ring. He didn't understand the words of the Mass, but there was something so holy in those early summer mornings in that church that moved him deeply. He felt that he wanted to stay there for ever.

When Agnes Trelawney asked Father Burley one day after Mass if he would be willing to take Clemo on as a pupil, he said he would be delighted. And in the days that followed, he introduced Clemo to some of his most valuable books. Clemo was intrigued by a Psalter which had painted illustrations scattered alongside the text and huge red, glittering initials which began the opening word of each psalm. He particularly loved the tiny scenes involving rabbits and hounds; some of the scenes even had monkeys cavorting down the page. It became his favourite book.

Father Burley sensed Clemo's pleasure in that Psalter, for he got into conversation with Clemo one day and asked if he would like to learn Latin so that he could read the words of the Psalms for himself and follow the Mass more closely. The idea of learning Latin seemed so impossible to Clemo that he hardly knew how to reply but thanked the priest for his suggestion. When he got home, he talked with his mother.

'Mam?'

'Yes.'

She was washing clothes in a bowl. Her hands red in the swirl of the cooling, grey water, her sleeves rolled up.

'Father Burley has offered to teach me Latin.'

His mother stopped pummelling the soaked clothes and pushed a hank of hair from her forehead with the back of her hand. What might the offer mean? Was Clemo really that clever? She had always thought he was, but….

'Did Father Burley say why?'

'No, but I'd really like to…'

'You had better see what your father says when he comes home.'

Clemo guessed that that would be his mother's response. She would do nothing without consulting her husband, but she also had a knack of knowing when to broach difficult subjects.

'Could you speak to Dad first?'

'We'll see.'

It was another of his mother's standard responses. And Clemo knew that the conversation could not be pushed any farther. He would just have to be patient.

That same evening his mother did not speak about Clemo's proposal to Richard, her husband. He had returned from work in a miserable, sullen mood and would not say what the problem was. Sometimes he said things; sometimes he didn't. That night was obviously not going to be one for conversation. He slumped by the fire, took his cap off, and in the warmth drifted to sleep. Isabel came rushing through the door but was greeted by her mother with a rough hand placed across her mouth and a whispered, 'Sh! Be quiet. Your father is asleep'. Isabel pulled a face but went quietly to her favourite stool and sat there, fuming. There was something she was bursting to tell her mother and now she would have to wait. And she had so wanted to tell her without Joan or Clemo hearing. Why wasn't their house bigger? You could never say what you wanted to say. It was always their father they all had to circle around. It wasn't fair. She grabbed a bit of cloth and began sewing, jabbing the needle through the fabric with venomous energy. And when he did wake, they would all have to be quiet because you never knew what his mood would be. He had never been too angry with her but when her father lost his temper, it was always poor Clemo who caught the thunderous outburst.

Joan, the older sister came through the door, saw that her sister was sewing, and her brother was gazing out of the window and immediately guessed what was happening. She looked at Isabel who raised her eyes and jerked her head towards their father. There was no need for words. Joan crept in, gave her mother a kiss on the cheek and quietly asked if any help was needed with preparing the vegetables for their supper. The household waited.

A burning coal rattled out of the fire basket, landing with a dull click on the stone floor. Clemo went to pick it up with a shovel. His father woke with a start, 'Who made that noise?' His eyes were wide and staring. He flung out his hand and caught Clemo on the side of his head. 'Did you wake me, boy?' he shouted. Clemo ignored him and continued to pick up the burning coal and replaced it in the fire. 'Well…was it you?'

'No, Father, I was just putting a coal back into the fire after it had fallen out'. His head was smarting from where his father had hit him, and although the shovel trembled in his hands, he was determined not to show that he was in pain. If he did, he knew that his father would hit him again. His sisters and his mother had retreated to the other side of the room waiting for the storm to subside, as it usually did. His father's mood then switched rapidly, his eyes returned to their normal shape, the muscles in his face relaxed and instead of roaring at Clemo again, he asked him what he had been doing at school that day.

Clemo replied that he had been learning things with Father Burley.

His mother and sisters, standing close together, were terrified lest Clemo say anything about learning Latin, but he didn't.

'And what did Father Burley have to say for himself?', asked Clemo's father.

'Nothing much.'

The women waited for another outburst but Clemo continued by explaining to his father that he and Father Burley had talked about some ancient troubles in the country, 'Centuries ago, when the Romans left…'

'And what does Father Burley know about that? I expect he got some of it from them old books he keeps reading.'

The emotional temperature in the room was beginning slowly to subside. And Clemo knew what would happen next. His father would stand up, look around him as though nothing had happened and ask whether supper was ready. His mother and sisters would quietly put wooden bowls on the table. His mother would spoon out the broth and life would go on.

Clemo was bewildered by his father. There were days when he was kind, and other days when he was like an enraged animal. It was a question of living with it. But why his father was so unpredictable was a mystery. He had once asked Father Burley why some people had hot tempers. 'Maybe, it's their yellow bile,' Father Burley had replied. 'They produce too much of it and it makes them fiery'. Father Burley did not go on to say that Clemo's father was of that type, he knew that it was better if Clemo worked it out for himself. But Father Burley had noticed that Agnes Trelawney had once come to Mass with bruises around her face which she tried to hide with a scarf. Life in that Hadnock cottage could not have been easy, and yet, Richard Trelawney was a hard-working man and probably wanted the best for his family. But his temper, oh! his temper! Everyone knew that Richard Trelawney was a man not to be trifled with, especially when he was in one of his dark moods.

It was when Clemo was nine, after he had got used to the occasional night-time screams, that he asked his mother why his father shouted out at night. She explained, like Joan, that he must tell no-one about what he heard. His father, she said, had once had an awful experience which he sometimes relived in his dreams. Clemo sensed that there must be something more lying behind what she was telling him and so asked what his father's awful experience had been.

'I suppose you are old enough to know now,' she said, 'but you must promise me by the Holy Mass that you will never tell anyone what I am going to tell you.'

He promised faithfully that he would tell no-one. She sat him on her lap and hugged him. 'It's quite a long story, so sit still and don't interrupt me.' He nestled against her and gazed dreamily at the fire blazing in the hearth.

'Your father was born in Cornwall, in a place called Perranporth, a very long way from here. When he was ten, just one year older than you are now, he was sent to work as a tin miner. It was a hard and dangerous job, and he became a fire-setter. That meant that when the rocks in which the tin ore was found had been heated, it was his job to throw a bucket of cold water against the rock to split it. Sometimes the rock would split in ways that were unexpected and bits flew off in all directions.'

'Is that why Dad shouts 'Run! Run!' he asked.

'Clemo, I told you not to interrupt.'

'Sorry,' he said, nestling in closer to his mother.

'It might have been one of the causes of his nightmares, but then something happened which changed his life completely. The tin-miners were a tough lot, proud and very independent. One day, the King gave an order that the miners could no longer have their own courts of law, called Stanneries. The miners were really angry about this, and they became even angrier when King Henry VII, who was always greedy for money, said that they could have their Stanneries back, provided they paid him £1,000. The miners were determined that they were not going to give up their rights, and a man called Thomas Flamank and a blacksmith called Michael Joseph, decided to lead a revolt of the tin-miners against the King. Hundreds and hundreds of tin-miners walked up to London from Cornwall carrying whatever weapons they could lay their hands on. Your father was on that march, and on the way they received lots of help from the villages and towns they walked through because everyone was angry about being taxed so heavily by the King. After many days of walking, the miners arrived at a place just outside London called Blackheath. Someone must have warned the King that the miners were coming because he had his army drawn up ready to meet them.

All of this happened twelve years before you were born.

Well, although they were tough and brave, the miners were no match for the King's army, and as the battle raged there came a moment when the miners realised that they were being beaten. So, they turned tail and fled. Your father was held in reserve in the back lines but the next thing he saw was all his friends rushing towards him chased by soldiers waving swords and axes and pikes, and his friends shouted to your father, 'Run! Run! Run for your life!'

'But couldn't Dad have fought the soldiers? I would have done.' Clemo made imaginary sword thrusts against the imaginary enemy.

'No, he couldn't. There were too many of them, so he had to run. He and a friend hid in a ditch outside a churchyard until it was dark, and when they felt it was safe enough, they walked on. They didn't have much money. They were hungry and thirsty but fortunately a kind person gave them some water and bread, and they walked and walked until they found a barn where they could sleep. They knew they couldn't go back to Cornwall because they would have been hunted down as traitors, so they decided to walk to Bristol. They knew it was a big port because some of the tin ore they had dug in Cornwall was off-loaded there. So, that was their plan.

When they got to Bristol, your father and his friend split up. Your father's friend found a ship skippered by a Cornishman that was going to France and he volunteered as a sailor. Your father did not like the idea of becoming a sailor, and instead, he found a boat that was carrying tin ore and was about to cross the Bristol Channel bound for Llandogo. He asked if he could be a passenger. The Captain of the trow agreed, but wanted to be paid, so your father gave him the last of his money, and that's how he ended up in Llandogo. He didn't know anyone, and he had no money. But fortunately, he got into conversation with a man who had a horse and cart which he was loading with tin-ore from the trow. Your father explained that he was a tin-miner and asked where the ore was going. The man answered, 'Redbrook Foundry' and your father asked if the foundry might have work for a tin miner.

'It's your lucky day,' said the man. 'The owner of the foundry is my brother-in-law and if you know about tin, he might be able to give you a job.' And so, your father hitched a ride on that cart and that's how he came to Redbrook.'

The fire in the hearth was burning low. Clemo got off his mother's lap and she fed the fire with coal. Clemo watched her, and then asked, 'So, why can't I tell anyone about his nightmares?'

'Because there are nasty people who would like to get your father into trouble with the King for being a Cornish rebel. But so long as no-one says anything, we are all safe. Do you understand?'

'Yes,' he replied, though he knew it would be hard to live with that secret locked away in his heart. It also meant that from that moment on he could never feel completely safe. In fact, whenever he left the cottage, after that conversation with his mother, he looked left and right to see if any strangers were approaching; the innocence of his childhood had been destroyed. But at the same time, he felt strong because his mother had entrusted him with something of such importance. She was kneeling by the hearth sweeping up the ash and he bent down to kiss her cheek.

'What was that for, Clemo?' she asked, smiling.

'Nothing,' he replied, and skipped outside into the warm sunshine to play.

Chapter 2: Work at the Foundry

Clemo continued his learning with Father Burley until, two days before his eleventh birthday, his father announced, 'Last day with Father Burley tomorrow, Clemo. On your birthday you are coming to work at the Foundry with me.' Clemo had been half expecting it, so the announcement did not come as a surprise, but he was saddened that his education was now coming to an end.

The following day, he went as usual to see Father Burley and explained that his father had ordered him to begin work at the Foundry and that this would be his last day as a pupil.

'It was bound to happen, Clemo', said Father Burley, 'but I have so enjoyed being able to teach you. You have been a fine pupil, and if you can continue to stir up your curiosity and your intelligence, who knows what the future might bring?' He reached up to his bookshelf and handed a small, calf-skin-bound prayer book to Clemo: 'Please accept this, use it, and when you do, remember me.'

Clemo thanked him warmly and promised to pray for him every day.

He woke early the next morning and felt proud but apprehensive as he walked beside his father to the Foundry. Once there, he was introduced to the other men, who greeted him with smiles. Then his father showed him some of the tools that were used and warned him never to go near the furnaces, and never to touch metal even when it looked cool because it might not be. He watched as the men in heavy leather aprons ladled molten tin into moulds to create ingots and was fascinated by their combination of strength and vigilant dexterity.

For the next few years, he learnt the crafts and skills of the foundry until he was regarded as sufficiently trained not to need any further supervision. He had his own leather apron, his own rough wooden peg on which to hang it, and he enjoyed the break from work at lunch time when he could sit in a dark corner of the foundry eating the bread and cheese which his mother had provided. The voices of the men, their banter, their humour, the nicknames they used for each other (he was called 'Tich', being the youngest and smallest) became a part of his everyday life. But as he grew up and developed his muscles and his craft, he began to feel restless. Was this to be his occupation for ever? Might there not be better ways of organising the foundry?

He kept his thoughts to himself until one day, when the Boss asked him how he was doing, he felt bold enough to risk a conversation.

'I've been thinking...,' he said.

'A dangerous occupation,' replied the Boss with a grin. 'And what have you been thinking?'

'I have been thinking about what we do here...'

'Oh yes?'.

'Each week the ore comes in, we smelt it and make ingots and the ingots are then taken away.'

'Yes?'

'Suppose instead of shipping the ingots to Bristol, where they are turned into pewter, why don't we import some lead ourselves, mix it with the tin and make pewter things right here.?'

The Boss paused and then answered. 'We haven't done it because we don't have the skills. Better to stay with what we are good at. Jack of all trades and master of none...'

And with that, the Boss walked away.

A few days later, just after the lunch break, he called Clemo to see him. 'I've been thinking about what you said; perhaps we should give it a try. I know a good moulder who could make the moulds for a pewter plate. I have found some bits of lead...now, see what you can do. The moulder's name is Mr Jones. I've asked him to come and see me tomorrow. Mind you are here earlier than usual, and you can spell out your ideas to him, and if he agrees, I shall leave it to you and him to create the best pewter plates this side of London.'

Clemo was stunned and on the way home that night told his father about the proposal. He expected his father to be delighted, instead of which his father fell into one of his rages. 'Who do you think you are to tell the Boss what his foundry should do, eh? Why can't you keep your head down and get on with things instead of dreaming up hare-brained schemes. The cheek of it…it's outrageous…. It's mad… it's completely stupid.'

They walked the rest of the way in silence.

The following morning, Clemo left for the foundry early. He had lain awake much of the night turning his pewter-making idea over in his mind but then wondering whether he was, as his father had said, 'stupid'.

Harry Jones, the moulder, was an old man with huge, bony hands. He was slightly stooped at the shoulders and when Clemo arrived was deep in conversation with the Boss.

'Here comes young Trelawney,' said the Boss. 'I'll leave you two to work out what you are going to do…'

It turned out that Harry Jones had a slight stammer and so conversation, from Clemo's point of view, was more difficult than he had expected.

'Ever seen a mould?' asked Harry.

'No'

'Right. Ccccome with me…' They walked together to an old shed at the back of the foundry. There on a bench was a large ball of clay, some calf-hair and two identical shallow wooden forms.

'Ssso, what's your idea, young man?'

Clemo explained and Harry replied, 'Well. We'd better see what we can do.'

He began the slow and careful process of mixing the clay and calf hair together and then placed the resultant mix in one of the shallow wooden forms. Then, when he was satisfied with the consistency of the mix, he used some hand-made brass tools to create a plate-shaped hollow with a rim. Running from the top edge of the mould towards the plate-shaped hollow he created a smooth, gouged-out, half-channel down which the pewter would be poured ('It's called a "sprue"' he told Clemo) and from the top of the mould he carved some very fine lines out of the clay.

'What are they for?'

'To let the air out when we pour in the pewter, otherwise it will bubble and distort and in the worst case it will blow back in your face.' Clemo was intrigued by Harry's skill and level of concentration. Harry looked at the mould, stood back, regarded it from all angles to ensure that everything was as it should be… and then said, 'And now we have to make the top of the mould'.

Clemo watched as the second wooden form was filled in with the clay and calf-hair mix. Again, a half-channel to match and line up exactly with the first mould was created, but this time the mixture in the top mould at its centre was raised proud so that it was a mirror image of the mould underneath. Harry sprinkled lamp-black on the images in each mould, carefully applying it with a fine brush. He placed the moulds one on top of the other, squinted at them to make sure that the moulds were truly symmetrical ('Don't want a wobbly pppplate, do we?') then fastened the moulds together with some metal clamps.

'And now the pppproof of the ppppudding…' They walked to the main foundry where a small amount of hot tin and lead was waiting to be poured from a ladle into the mould.

Later that day, Clemo and Harry returned to the shed, with Harry holding the wooden forms. It was cool enough now for the clamps to be released and the pewter plate to be turned out.

Harry clipped off the rough edges with a shears, rubbed it down with a piece of soft sandstone and a rag, then held it out for Clemo to admire. It had a dull but shining surface.

'It's marvellous,' said Clemo, 'the colour seems so deep…'

'And that's our first ttttry…,' said Harry. 'We had better see whether we can do better ttttomorrow…'.

'But it looks perfect to me', said Clemo. 'Not quite it isn't,' replied Harry and pointed out a couple of tiny blemishes. 'We shall have to have another go at making some better moulds. All we need is patience.'

Over the next week Harry and Clemo worked easily together until by the end of the week Harry was satisfied with the finished plate. 'Ccccall the Boss'; he said. Clemo went to find him and brought him to the shed.

He looked at the plate, held it up and squinted across its surface to see if there were any marks, tapped it with his knuckle, paused, and then said, 'Congratulations…that's really good. All we have to do now is to turn out enough of these as fast as we can and then try to sell them.'

So, the Boss had admired the plate, but it was a question now of speed. It was a problem Clemo had not thought about. He was downcast. If it had taken Harry and himself one week to make just one really good plate, what could be done to speed up the process? It wasn't the smelting that was the problem, that was easily solved, it was making enough good moulds. And for that there was just Harry Jones.

'What's the problem, Tich?' asked the Boss.

'I can't see how we can make enough moulds for each plate and do it in such a way that we can produce enough…'

'Perhaps then, young Trelawney' replied the Boss, 'you can now see why I said we should stick to doing what we know.'

'But suppose we asked all the other foundrymen for their ideas?'

The Boss had a soft spot for Clemo and his enthusiasm, and said, 'OK…but you can only have two or three days. Whilst you are playing about with moulds, we are losing orders for ingots, and we can't afford to do that for much longer. So, three days and only three days. No more.'

At the lunch break the next day Clemo explained the problem to the other foundrymen. Most of them said that they would rather stick to what they knew, but a couple of the younger ones asked further questions because the problem had piqued their interest. Clemo noticed that his father was not contributing to the conversation but was obviously taking part, though silently.

As they were finishing their break, Clemo reminded everyone that the problem was speed. They needed to devise moulds which could be used time and time again.

The following day when the men were having their second breakfast, the younger ones came up with two ideas. One said that he could carve a mould from stone; the other said that perhaps they could make a bronze mould from copper and tin. Clemo thanked them and reminded them that the Boss had only allowed one more day to get the moulds made. It was a tall order, but the younger men had caught the excitement and promised to return on the following day with their moulds ready, 'even if it takes all night.'

The next day two new moulds were ready. Harry Jones had been called in to offer advice. He looked at the stone mould and declared that it was a good attempt, but the carving was too rough to be useful. 'The plates would come out uneven and wobble all over the ppplace'. The young foundryman, Michael, who had tried his hand at stone carving looked a little sad. He had spent the previous night chipping away at two blocks of stone. It was no wonder he appeared so tired. The second man, Gwyn Evans, held up a small bronze mould. 'I stayed behind last night and scrounged a bit of copper...'. He handed the mould to Harry for it to be inspected. Harry congratulated him on his work and said that they ought to use the mould as a trial, but he thought that the mould would not be sufficiently robust to create many pieces. Nevertheless, cheers erupted from the enthusiasts who had gathered round as the moulds were revealed. And then Harry suggested that whilst the pewter was being prepared for the bronze mould, he, Clemo and Gwyn, should go to the Moulding Shed and consider the bronze mould carefully. 'We've got to make sure it's right. You can't get mess about with hot mmmmetal'.

Whilst they were looking closely at the bronze mould (Harry held it in his great hands with real tenderness) Clemo mentioned that his father had also expressed an interest in creating a mould.

'Did he?' asked Harry, 'And what did he intend to use?'

'I heard him chiselling away at a block of wood last night and he carried it with him when we came into work. I think he's going to try it out this morning.'

Harry's voice suddenly became fearful and angry. 'Stop him!' he shouted. 'Stop him now! Wood is too dangerous for a mould. If he pours the pewter in, it will explode.'

Clemo rushed out of the shed, closely followed by Harry and Gwyn. He looked around the foundry, and by the flames emerging from the furnace, he could see his father standing bent over his wooden mould. He was holding the mould which rested on a block of wood with his left hand and in his right hand there was a ladle of hot, liquid pewter.

'Dad!' Clemo shouted as he clattered across the stone floor in his heavy boots. 'Stop!'

The sight of Clemo rushing towards him shouting, startled Clemo's father. He knocked over the the mould with his left hand and spilt the pewter from the ladle on to his boot.

His scream rent the air. Work stopped. The men looked up and saw Clemo's father writhing on the floor. Harry and Gwyn arrived. They quickly lifted Richard Trelawney and carried him to the water trough where Harry took the damaged leg and plunged it into the cold water. The water hissed. Richard Trelawney was hardly conscious. They laid him on the floor. Harry eased the sodden boot from the burnt foot and in doing so some of the charred and raw flesh came away still attached to the inside of the boot.

One of the other men hurried towards them carrying an earthenware pot of honey. And with great care Harry smeared the honey over the burnt foot. Clemo, standing by, was deathly pale, tears streaming silently down his cheeks. He bent over and smoothed the hair back that had fallen across his father's forehead.

Harry shouted for someone to bring some bandages. Strips of cloth were rapidly produced and were bound around the foot.

'Clemo', said Harry, 'You need to get your father home'.

They heard a horse and cart draw up in the yard; someone had already alerted Evan Prosser to bring it.

Gwyn and Harry bent down and placing their arms under Richard Trelawney's body carried him to the cart. A workman was placing hanks of straw in the bottom of cart. One of the other workmen pulled off his leather apron and laid it on top of the straw, and once Richard Trelawney was laid with rough and tender gentleness on the apron, another workman placed his old coat over him. The entire foundry work force had gathered round in silent shock.

'Where are we going?' asked Evan.

Clemo whispered the word 'Hadnock', and the horse and cart set off at a steady pace with Clemo walking beside it. Behind them at the foundry the men watched until the cart was out of sight and then in twos and threes slowly made their way back to work.

Chapter 3: Home

As he trudged beside the cart, Clemo only had one thought: 'It was my fault. If I hadn't suggested making pewter, none of this would have happened'. The guilt grutched at his innards. And in his despair, he kept repeating to himself, under his breath. 'It was my fault…my fault.' In the cart, his father continued to groan.

Evan looked at Clemo: 'So, what happened?'.

Clemo explained and having finished his account, Evan, a grey-haired man with several day's growth of beard and a piece of heavy, rough fabric over his shoulders to keep off the rain, just said 'Burns is terrible things'. And that was all he said during the three-mile journey.

When Evan and the cart lumbered down the lane close to the family cottage, Isabel saw Clemo, and ran towards him. 'Clemo, what's happened?'

'It's Dad,' he replied, nodding towards the cart. Isabel looked over the side of the cart and saw her father's white and agonised face, streaked with dust and sweat. 'There was an accident at the foundry. Dad got his foot burnt.'

As Evan pulled up with the cart next to the cottage door and shouted 'Whoa' to the horse, Clemo's mother came out to see what was going on.

'It's Dad,' said Isabel frantically, 'he's had an accident at work.'

'Oh, Holy Mary!' she exclaimed, crossing herself. 'Let's get him out of the cart.'

Clemo went to the side of the cart, reached out his arms, placed them beneath his father's body and with Evan's brawny help, lifted his father out. His weight was almost too much for Clemo to bear but he managed to get his father through the door and into his parents' bedroom which was on the same level as the kitchen. There he laid him gently on the bed. His father looked wild with pain. Isabel fetched one of her own pillows from the room she had shared with Joan and placed it under her father's head. Agnes stood there wondering what to do next, her hands held up to her mouth.

'I'll get Dad something hot to drink,' said Isabel, rushing out of the room. She returned a moment later carrying a tankard of soup which she had scooped out of the cauldron that was always standing near the fire.

Agnes, recovering from her shock, knelt by the bed and cradled her husband's head. 'Richard, Isabel's brought you some soup...'

He opened his eyes, tried to hoist himself up in the bed but screamed again as he dragged his foot up a little way. Blood had oozed through the bandages. Agnes could smell the honey the foundrymen had used to dress the burn. Richard said that he couldn't move anymore: 'I can't drink the soup lying down. You'll have to dribble it into my mouth'. Isabel ran to fetch a spoon and passed it to her mother who began very gently to pour tiny portions of the soup from the spoon into her husband's mouth.

And all the while, Clemo stood by the door watching, still numb, and only moved when he heard Evan turning the cart around and urging the horse to 'walk on'. He strode outside and shouted his thanks to Evan who responded with a wave of his left hand but didn't turn his head.

'He's had as much soup as he can manage,' said his mother coming out of the bedroom. 'But the pain is terrible. Isabel, you'll have to run into town and get some poppy-water from Goody Phelps.'

'Yes, Mam.'

She was racing to the door when her mother reminded her that she would need money for the poppy-water. 'Go to Goody,' she said, handing her a groat, 'Tell her what's happened to your father. She'll know what's best.' Isabel tore out of the house, her feet clattering up the lane.

Clemo stood by the fire, his head bowed. His mother slumped exhausted in the chair.

'Clemo, have some soup yourself, you'll be tired. And take some bread. And there's ale.'

'Can I get some for you, Mam? '

'No, thank you, *cariad*. I'm too tired to eat. It's such a shock. Tell me what happened.'

Clemo spooned some of the soup into his mouth, bit off a piece of bread and then told his mother the whole story which ended with him saying, 'And it's all my fault...'

'But you were trying to save him from getting even worse burns.'

'I was. I know that, but in trying to save him, I caused him to spill some of the molten pewter.' He hung his head and began quietly to sob.

His mother put her arm around his shoulder, but as soon as she did so, her husband called out from the bedroom. She walked quickly to see what he wanted. He was lying just as she and Isabel had left him, but there was a thin film of sweat on his brow, which she wiped off with a small linen towel.

'What do you want, Richard?'

His hands plucked at the blanket. 'Agony' he said, 'I'm in agony.'

'I know, but Isabel will be back soon; she's gone to Goody Phelps to get some poppy-water.' And with that she heard the cottage door burst open and Isabel arriving, closely followed by her sister, Joan.

'Whilst Goody Phelps was making this,' she said, breathlessly, indicating the bottle of medicine, 'I ran to tell Joan. And she's come back with me.'

Richard Trelawney stretched out his hand and clasped Isabel's hand in his. 'You are a wonderful daughter, Isabel...'. Joan looked at her mother. Their eyes spoke, though no words left their lips, but Agnes stepped closer to Joan and put her arm around her waist.

Clemo waited in the kitchen. And from there he heard his father say: 'Clemo almost killed me. He is a fool. A dangerous, dangerous fool. He'll have to leave.' The mixture of pain and anger was terrible to hear, it trembled around the cottage like a bell tolling.

Clemo walked out of the kitchen and stood by the bank of the river. Within a few minutes he heard the door open behind him and his sister Joan came to stand near him. He turned to look at her, his eyes wracked with despair.

'It was my fault.'

'No, it wasn't,' replied Joan. 'It was an accident.'

'But if I hadn't started on this pewter idea, Dad would not have been hurt. What's going to happen now? You heard him say that I have to leave.'

'He doesn't know what he's saying. He's in pain. His mind is befuddled. So, don't listen to him. In any case, if you leave home, how is Mam to survive? Where can she get money from? She needs Dad's wages. Come on,' she put her arm around his shoulder, 'Come back into the house. You can't do any good standing out here. Besides, it's getting cold.' She led him into the house.

In the kitchen, Agnes was sitting by the fire, her elbow resting on the arm of the chair, her head propped up with her hand.

'Oh! Clemo…oh! Clemo…', she sighed.

'What can I do, Mam?' he responded, the anguish clogging his throat.

'Nothing for the moment. We can perhaps work something out in the morning. Isabel's still with him. You go to bed, Clemo. Recite your beads and try to sleep.'

Clemo climbed the ladder to his room above the kitchen, and there he lay down on his bed staring at the ceiling. No prayers emerged from his lips. The rosary beads hung loosely in his hand, but he was beyond prayer.

He must have eventually slept because the next thing he knew was that daylight was seeping through the shutters.

He heard movement in the kitchen and made his way down the ladder and found his mother on her knees tending the recalcitrant fire. *Had she slept, at all?* he wondered,

'Clemo, you must go to work this morning. After breakfast I shall go to see Father Burley to ask if the Guild can help us.'

Richard Trelawney had been invited to join the Guild of the Five Wounds some years earlier. He had always paid his dues in addition to attending the annual Feast and going to Mass with his fellow members each week, though how much it all really meant to him, Agnes did not know.

'That's a good idea, but how is Dad this morning?'

'He's sleeping now but he's had a bad night. Isabel is asleep as well, and Joan's gone home. But I shall have to bathe your father's foot later this morning. Getting that bandage off is going to be purgatory for him, and for me. But Clemo, you really must go to work. Go on. We can manage.'

Clemo had a drink of ale and a piece of bread and tying up his boots he slumped out of the cottage and trudged along the path to the foundry. All the way he wondered what kind of reception he might get. He neither noticed the river, which was normally the centre of his attention, nor did he see Evan coming towards him when he was within half a league of the foundry gates.

Evan, still with the heavy fabric over his shoulders, stood in the way of Clemo so that he was noticed.

'How's your father, Clemo?' he asked.

Although Clemo was surprised to see Evan, he was in such a depressed state that the surprise hardly showed. 'He's had a bad night.' The words stumbled out of his mouth. 'And where are you going, Evan?'

'I thought you might want a bit of company, so I decided to walk towards Hadnock to meet you.'

Clemo's face relaxed. 'Did you? That is really kind, Evan. After yesterday I thought no-one would speak to me.'

'Don't leap to dark conclusions,' replied Evan, turning and falling into step beside him. 'Some of them might be a bit quiet this morning, but only the most bone-headed will blame you for what happened. You were trying to save your Dad, weren't you? And what's wrong with that?'

They walked on in silence.

When they got to the foundry entrance Evan said, 'Look, Clemo. Just walk in and see what happens. They're mostly a good lot and they will have seen exactly what you were trying to do. Accidents happen. The world isn't perfect, and neither are any of us. You're not, nor am I.' And with that he walked off to get the horse and cart ready for the morning's journey to the wharves at Llandogo.

Clemo took a deep breath and walked through the gate. In the foundry some of the men who had helped yesterday were already at work. A couple of them looked up and said nothing, but Gwyn came across the floor to greet him and to ask how his father was, and then said, 'The Boss wants to see you.'

It was the sentence Clemo had been dreading. He expected a dressing-down and probably instant dismissal.

Ifor Young, the Boss, saw Clemo walking towards him, shoulders hunched, head down.

'Good morrow, Clemo. We need to have a talk. We must go somewhere that we can't be heard.'

He led the way outside. Clemo followed, aware that all the eyes in the foundry were surreptitiously watching the solemn procession.

In the yard, Ifor Young stopped and turned to face Clemo. 'How's your father?'

'I haven't seen him this morning, but he didn't have a good night.'

'You wouldn't expect him to. That was a terrible accident yesterday, Clemo,' he said. 'You haven't worked in a foundry long enough to know that from time to time these things happen. Why do you think we always keep that pot of honey handy?'

'I don't know, Mr Young.'

'Because in foundries, burns happen, Clemo, burns happen; accidents happen. You were trying to save your father from a much worse fate. I've seen wood explode when molten tin has been poured into it. The water in the wood turns to steam, the wood bursts apart and the molten tin catches whoever is in the way. I've seen men so badly burnt that they were scarred for life, and sometimes, God forgive me saying this, if they are lucky, they die.'

Clemo did not know how to respond. 'But it was my fault, Mr Young. If I hadn't had that stupid idea about pewter, this would not have happened.'

'True, Clemo, but progress is only made by people who make mistakes and learn from them. You are not to blame. Listen as I say it again: you are not to blame...but you will have had a terrible shock yesterday, which means that I'm not going to allow you to work in the foundry.'

Clemo had expected Ifor Young's next words to be, 'So, you are to go home now and never come back'. But that was not the Boss's response. 'Instead' said Ifor Young, 'you are going to work in the moulding shop with Harry. I've arranged for him to wait for you there. So, go, and let time heal your eyes and your soul of all that you saw and heard yesterday…'

Ifor Young walked away. Clemo, head still bowed, walked slowly through the foundry to the Moulding Shed. There, Harry was waiting for him.

'Ggggood to see you Clemo. I hope your father will recover soon. How is he?'

Clemo gave the same answer that he had given to Ifor Young a minute earlier. 'Well, time will tell. Now, the Boss and I have had a long chat and we have decided that you have what it takes to become a good iron mmmmmoulder'

'But think about what happened yesterday, Mr Jones'.

'Do you think that I haven't thought about it?' His tone was sharp. 'And I realise that I am as responsible as you. Perhaps even more responsible. I was caught up in your enthusiasm and the challenge. At my time of life, I never expected that kind of challenge. And I made a mistake.'

Clemo moved as though to interrupt him.

'Don't interrupt me, Clemo. Let me finish. We should have started with smaller pewter things. A plate was too big for a first go. So, you and I are going to make some small bits of pewter and work our way up. Now,' he continued, 'What do you see on the bench?' Clemo looked. He could see a number of flat, grey, oblong stones.

'That is soap-stone, Clemo; it's the best stone you can use for making moulds, because it's easy to carve. Look. I'll show you'. And with that he picked up a sharp knife and sliced a sliver from the stone as though it were cheese. 'See…And from now on that's what we're going to use.' He picked up a piece and looked at it lovingly, running his thumb along its surface. 'Beautiful stuff, just feel it Clemo.'

'Where does it come from?' asked Clemo, running his fingers along the smooth surface.

'With a name like Trelawney, you should know the answer to that. It comes from Cornwall, from a place called Kynance.'

'How did you get it, Mr Jones?'

'One of the things you will learn as you grow up Clemo, is that if you really commit yourself to a craft, an older craftsman will teach you, just as I am about to do with you. And when that person becomes too old to carry on, if he is a good man he will pass on his tools and bits and pieces to you. This stone was given to me by my teacher, may God have mercy on his soul. He's long since gone.' Harry cleared his throat. 'Now, come on, there's work to do…and, by the way, that knife was his as well.' He took a rag from his pocket and blew his nose.

Chapter 4: Return to the foundry

The day went better than Clemo had dared to hope. The men were quieter than usual at their break, and a couple of them looked at Clemo from under their eyebrows, but when one of them left he laid his grubby hand on Clemo's shoulder and squeezed it. It was a gesture stronger than any words.

It meant that the afternoon flew by as Clemo was instructed further in the art of moulding. At the end of the day, he and Harry turned out two pewter crosses from the moulds. The pewter needed a bit of sanding with the stone and buffing with a rag, but it looked good.

'Not bad,' said Harry, 'not bad. Let's see if we can do better tomorrow. Now, young man, help me clear up-- a good moulder is always tidy, and then you must go home and see how your Mam and Dad are.' He took one of the pewter crosses and handed it to Clemo. 'Give that to your Mam. She might need it.'

Clemo walked back along the path towards his home, the pewter cross in his pocket. Sunlight was glistening on the eddying water. He stopped for a moment as he watched a swan glide imperiously past him and noticed that a couple of moorhens were dibbling amongst the sedges on the edge of the riverbank. His spirits lifted, though he rather dreaded the situation he might find back at the cottage.

As he drew nearer, he slowed his pace and saw his mother throwing some dirty water from a bucket into the river and wringing out a wet cloth. As she turned, she saw him.

'How did you get on, *cariad*?'

'Not too bad', he replied looking at her face to detect how she might be, 'and how has Dad been today?'

'Thank heaven for Goody Phelps,' she replied, 'Your Dad's still in a lot of pain but I think he's a bit better. The trouble is, when he does sleep, he has awful nightmares and shouts out, but I don't understand what he is saying.'

'Did he talk anymore about me leaving?' Clemo asked.

His mother flicked her eyes to the ground for a second and when she looked up, said, 'He doesn't know half of what he's saying, Clemo.' But Clemo knew his mother well enough to know that she was concealing the truth from him. His heart sank. They walked into the cottage together.

'Who's that?' shouted Richard Trelawney, hearing Agnes and Clemo come through the door.

'Clemo, Richard. He's just come back from work.'

'And how many others has he burnt today?' The fierce question trembled in the air, followed by silence.

'Should I go in to see him?' asked Clemo, tentatively.

But before his mother could answer, the outside door burst open and Isabel rushed in carrying a small bunch of wildflowers. She ran past her mother and Clemo and entered her father's bedroom. Clemo heard his father say, 'Isabel, you are a sweetheart. Thank you.'

Clemo sat on the stool by the fire turning his cap over and over in his hands. His mother bustled around, inventing things to keep her distracted.

When Isabel re-emerged, Clemo asked her how their father was. 'Fair', she replied in an off-hand way, 'he wants Joan to come and see him', she said to her mother, avoiding all eye contact with Clemo. 'I'll just go and tell her to come.' She banged the door as she left.

'I can see that I'm not wanted in this house anymore,' said Clemo, clenching his fists, 'I'm not allowed to see my father. He just wants Isabel and Joan…but he certainly does not want me….'

'Give him time,' replied Agnes, 'He's probably still in shock. Be patient.'

'I am being patient. I did not mean to hurt him. I was just trying to save him.' He hung his head. The flames illuminated the beginnings of lines in his young face.

His mother did not reply.

'All I want is to see how he is,' he continued.

'But he's forbidden you from seeing him.'

'Ah…', replied Clemo, 'but he hasn't said that to me. I've only learnt that he doesn't want to see me through glances and overheard words. You and Isabel are acceptable to him; Joan, slightly less so…and me, not at all. So, he has forbidden me, has he?'

His mother remained silent, looking away towards the fire.

'Mam, please, I asked you a question. Has he forbidden me to see him and has he said again that I must leave?'

'Yes,' she replied, in a barely audible whisper. She took her rosary beads out of her pocket and sat in the chair passing the beads through her fingers.

'And so, Mam, answer me this. If I have to leave, how are you and Isabel to live if I don't go to work until Dad gets better and can earn some money himself?'

His mother replied, 'Father Burley said he hoped that the Guild would be able to help.'

'Alright, I understand. The Guild can help but his only son can't. What a mess. What an insult. Why do you let Dad dictate everything?' His voice rose in controlled anger. He twisted his cap in his hand. 'Why?'

'You know why, *cariad*. Men are the head of women, isn't that what the Church teaches? Women were born from Adam. Adam was first, so women have to do what their husbands want. It's been like that from the beginning.'

Clemo threw his cap on the ground and in an outburst of rage stamped on it. His mother looked ashen with worry, her maternal instinct fighting with her matrimonial vows.

Clemo made for the door.

'I'm going out…and incidentally, I made this for you today.' He threw the pewter cross towards her, slammed the door and walked up the cinder path to try to find some kind of consolation amongst the flowers and vegetables growing in a patch of garden his father had created near the house. The family dog, a black and white terrier called Toby, which had replaced Patch, came rushing towards him as far as the tethering chain would allow, his tail wagging. Clemo knelt next to him and stroked the dog's head. 'Oh! Toby, what should I do?'. Cuddling the dog salved his misery, and his temper began to subside. Eventually, he eased himself away from the dog and returned to the cottage. His mother was nowhere to be seen, but he could hear her talking to his father in the bedroom. He sat on the stool. The outside door opened. Joan and Isabel arrived.

'Hello, Clemo,' said Joan, 'How was work today?'

'Not too bad.' He was grateful for Joan's thoughtfulness.

Isabel did not speak to him but tapped on the bedroom door and beckoned Joan to enter. Joan cast a backward glance at Clemo, her eyes filled with quiet concern.

As soon as the girls entered the bedroom, their mother came out into the kitchen.

'I've been speaking with your father, Clemo. He's a bit calmer now and after we had had a chat, he agreed that you can stay here until he's better but once he is up and about, you will have to leave home.'

It was a victory, of sorts, and it would give Clemo a chance to think about what he should do. He imagined that his father would need two or three weeks before he would be well enough to walk and then perhaps a further week before he could resume his work at the foundry. In that three- or four-week period perhaps the future direction of his own life might become clearer.

His mother ruffled Clemo's hair and said, 'Look, Clemo,' as she pointed to a long leather bootlace which she had threaded through the loop of the pewter Cross now nestling on her neck.

Clemo thought it looked lovely, glistening in the firelight, but it prompted a question.

'Did you wear it when you were chatting with Dad? Did he see it?'

'Yes, I did. He said how fine it looked and asked me where I had got it from.'

'And what did you say?'.

'I told him the truth, that you had made it and had given it to me when you came in from work.'

'Did he say anything else?'.

'No. But that was when we began our talk about how long you could stay at home. He blustered for a bit, but I think he was almost proud of your craftsmanship, though he'd never say that to you.'

Clemo turned over in his mind what his mother had said and thanked her for her peace-making efforts.

'One day, Clemo, you might begin to understand how women think and work…but come on, call Joan and Isabel for supper, there's enough meat and bread for us all.'

That evening, warily, the conversation got going. Joan talked about some new blue fabric she had bought at the market. Isabel tried but failed to join in; she was trying to understand why she had been so nasty to Clemo earlier but couldn't solve the problem. Clemo simply ate his meat and bread and drank his ale in silence whilst Joan and his mother conversed about people Joan had seen that day, what they were wearing, where they were going, who was ill, who was getting better. The conversation drifted on; the tension eased. Isabel felt a pout beginning to develop around her lips, left the table and climbed the ladder to her room where she laid out the rag dolls on her bed that she had thought she had finished with ages ago.

• •

The next couple of weeks followed the same pattern. Clemo went to the foundry each day and continued to learn the moulding craft. Joan popped by the cottage every now and again, Isabel took little treats into her father, Agnes continued to cook and run the house but in addition, took up a few dairying duties at the next-door farm where she made butter and cheese.

Clemo spent the hour walking to and from the foundry turning over in his mind what he should do. And one Saturday he went to see Father Burley. He knocked on the oak front door, which was opened by Mistress Fielding, the priest's housekeeper.

'Good day, Clemo. '

'Good day, Mistress Fielding. I wonder if Father Burley might be willing to see me. I should like to have a talk with him.'

Mistress Fielding looked at him quizzically. Her long, thin, heavily lined face peered at Clemo. She was notoriously protective of the priest and so Clemo was uncertain whether he would be granted an audience.

Mistress Fielding ordered him to stay on the doorstep whilst she went back into the house to make enquiries.

She returned almost immediately.

'Father Burley will see you now', she announced, and led Clemo down a long passageway to the priest's study. It was a dark room, smelling faintly of incense. A large grey cat was curled up on a carpet near the fire.

'Clemo,' said the priest, 'how good to see you. Ever since you began work at the foundry, I have missed our Latin lessons.'

'So have I, Father. I really enjoyed them, thank you. I am sorry that the time I have to spend working has meant that there isn't time for anything else…but I do miss them'.

The cat stirred, stretched, raised its head a fraction and then went back to sleep.

'Don't you sometimes wish that we humans could live as lazily as cats?' said Father Burley, smiling, 'Now, what can I do for you today?'.

Clemo blushed and then launched into an account of the previous two weeks. He began with a description of the accident at the foundry and concluded by explaining that he was about to be turned out of his parents' cottage.

Father Burley, his heavy eyebrows almost concealing his dark eyes, sat quietly for a moment after Clemo's description, and then said, 'So, you must feel downcast?'

'Yes, I am. I really don't know what I am going to do.'

'And your father is still not speaking to you?'

'No. He uses my mother as a go-between. It isn't right. I really do want to see him myself.'

There was a long silence and then Father Burley poked at the fire to stir it into life.

To Clemo's surprise, Father Burley asked him, 'What do you know about foxes?'

'Not a lot. They are a pest when they take a chicken, but...'

Father Burley interrupted him. 'So, you have never seen the dog fox chase the young male cubs off his territory?'

'No. Not really.'

Father Burley paused and waited for Clemo's response.

'Are you suggesting that my father is doing the same and that's why he wants me out of the house?'

'What do you think, Clemo?'

'I hadn't thought of that.'

'Now tell me something else, Clemo. Has your father ever been asked to train as a moulder?'

'No...he was a tin miner originally.'

'And he ended up in Hadnock only a couple of weeks after that terrible battle against the King's forces at Blackheath.'

Clemo was completely thrown by the comment. He had thought that that episode was a family secret. His face must have registered surprise because Father Burley continued, 'I imagine you are surprised that I guessed why your father came here, aren't you? Let me tell you, your father has never once told me what happened and of course, I have never mentioned my suspicions to another soul. So, the only people who know the true story are your family and no one else. But I imagine that your father went through the mill as a young man in that battle and afterwards. Experiences like that leave deep wounds in a person's soul.'

Clemo bent down to scratch the cat's neck to give himself time to think. Father Burley waited.

'I hadn't thought of all that still affecting him,' he replied, 'though it does explain things. But what should I do, Father?'

Clemo was expecting some sage practical advice. But Father Burley said, 'You should make your confession, that's the first thing to do because I guess you have been storing up quite a bit of anxiety about what happened at the foundry and, if you are honest, you will realise that you have hated your father and the decision he announced; that mixture of anxiety and hatred can eat into a man's soul. Once you have made your confession, we'll try to sort something out... Now, kneel for a blessing.'

Clemo knelt then rose to his feet, thanked Father Burley warmly and having arranged to see the priest the following Sunday before Mass to make his Confession, walked home feeling unaccountably lighter but sadder. He was trying to come to terms with the new perspective he now had about his father. And, to his own surprise, he was strongly convinced that he should leave home and strike out on his own. It was time.

Chapter 5: An auspicious meeting

O nce he reached home, he went into the back garden to greet
the dog and knelt beside him as the dog licked his hands and
face. When he had to leave, he would miss Toby terribly.

He made his way into the cottage where his mother said to him,
'Did you have a good time with Father Burley?'

'Yes. He was very helpful.'

'Good,' she paused, and then announced, 'Clemo, your father
has asked to see you.'

'Really? When?'

'I'll go in to see if he's awake and call you if he is.'

Clemo waited. The nerves in his stomach were fluttering.

He heard his mother call from behind the door, 'Clemo, come
in.'

He peered around the door and tiptoed in. His father was lying
on top of the bed with a rough blanket covering his legs.

'Good evening, Father.'

'Hello, Clemo. You and I need a talk. Agnes, you must leave us.'

Clemo's mother walked out of the room closing the door quietly
behind her.

'You know that you nearly killed me, Clemo.'

Clemo wanted to say in his own defence that he had had no such
intention but decided to remain quiet. There was no need to anger his
father by disagreeing with the first words he had said to him in weeks.

'Your mother and I have been chatting, and we think that you are
now old enough to leave home' ('*Was his mother in league with his father*

or was this a half-truth, a way of sharing the blame equally?) He decided to not say anything. 'There comes a time when every boy has to leave his home,' said his father. 'So, you can't put it off much longer. Have you anything to say for yourself?'

What was his father implying? Did his father really believe that he had been angling to leave home for some time but had stayed on purpose to rile his parents?

'But I love living here,' he replied, 'And I love my work at the Foundry!'

'No doubt', replied his father, 'but you are growing up and you need to make your own way in the world, tough though it will be. If you stay here, you'll get soft. Go on…out into the world with you. And for goodness' sake, find yourself a girl.'

The next sentence shocked Clemo and was completely unexpected. 'You've been a fine son.' Clemo noticed tears start to his father's eyes but the emotion was camouflaged by his father grimacing, saying that his foot hurt, and he told Clemo to leave the bedroom so that he could have a nap.

On going into the kitchen, he saw his mother shelling peas in the outside doorway. She did not turn to look at him but told Clemo to bring a stool and sit beside her. He noticed that she was still wearing the Cross he had made for her.

He began to speak but his mother interrupted him. 'Your father's right, Clemo. You will have to think what you are going to do and where you are going to live.' She pushed her hair back from her forehead and then turned to look him in the eyes. 'And before you say anything at all Clemo, you need to realise that that was your father's way of saying 'sorry."

Clemo gazed at the river flowing past on the other side of the lane. He was in turmoil. Whilst he was amazed by what his father had said and recognised the truth of his mother's explanation, it left him stunned. He knew he would have to decide what he wanted to do. But leaving home, leaving home, that was such a huge step. If he could stay around for a while longer…

'How much time have I got?' he asked.

'It depends on your father's progress. He expects to be up and about in a week or two, and after that he hopes to be able to go back to the Foundry.'

Everything seemed to be pressing in on Clemo. Could he really come to such a momentous decision about his own life within a fortnight?

'Now, I suggest that you walk into Monmouth, find Joan and have a chat with her. She is very fond of you, you know, and perhaps she will have some ideas for you to think about.'

Clemo kissed his mother on the cheek and walked along the lane to the wooden bridge over the Wye. He paused for a moment to watch the water swirling underneath, and then continued to Joan's house. It was a tiny house with a narrow shopfront. He pushed open the door and saw his sister behind the counter where she was arranging a few millinery and haberdashery things on a shelf.

'Clemo, how lovely to see you,' she said, as she turned to face him. She was wearing an apron and her hair was piled up and held in place by a fabric kerchief.

'Hello, Joan… do you know why I've come to see you?'

'I think I can guess…Dad has told you that you have to leave home.'

'How did you know?'

'When I last saw Mam, she told me that our Dad had made a decision about you and that you should think about leaving.' She opened a drawer and began to tidy its contents. Clemo watched her.

'But Joan, what am I going to do?'

'I really don't know Clemo, but you're clever, you'll think of something. Don't forget you learnt all that Latin from Father Burley. Perhaps you might become a clerk somewhere.'

The shop door opened, and a pretty young girl, aged about fifteen, entered. She looked at Clemo and a blush stole across her cheeks.

'Hello, Laura,' said Joan, 'come through'. She beckoned Clemo to follow them into the parlour behind the shop and then explained to Clemo that Laura would be starting work with her in the next week, learning the millinery trade. 'She's very good with her needle,' she explained, 'and will be a real help to me. I'll just go and get some cordial for you both.' She slipped out into the kitchen and Clemo could hear her clattering jugs and pots.

Clemo had taken his cap off and was twisting it gently in his hands. He had seen Laura at Mass but had not met her formally before. They both stood on the stone floor, heads bowed, not looking at each other. It seemed to be taking ages for Joan to re-appear.

Clemo thought that he ought to break the silence and so, rather awkwardly, said, 'I think I've seen you at Mass a few times, Laura.'

'Yes, I expect you have.'

The silence between them seemed to expand. But it was Laura who broke it. 'I go to Mass each Sunday.'

'I know,' replied Clemo, still twisting his cap.

'And I hear that you have been learning Latin with Father Burley. You must be clever.'

It was Clemo's turn to blush. He stammered his reply, 'I don't know about that, but I do love Latin. But who told you that I was learning Latin? I thought no-one knew.'

'I can't remember,' said Laura, hoping that she'd be forgiven for a white lie and willing Joan and the cordial to arrive, but all she could hear was yet more clattering coming from the kitchen. 'But you work at Redbrook Foundry now, don't you?' she asked.

Clemo was bewildered, did everyone in this town know everything about him?

'I was sorry to hear about your father's accident.'

Would Joan please arrive soon.

'Thank you' replied Clemo, but he could now sense an opening. 'Is that what people are saying, that it was an accident?'

'That's what I heard,' replied Laura.

'Well, it's true,' said Clemo, 'I was trying to save my father from something worse happening, but I rushed to warn him, and he spilt some hot metal on his foot. He's been in bed ever since.'

'I know' said Laura.

How did she know?

At that moment, the door from the kitchen opened and Joan came in with two earthenware tankards filled with cordial. 'Now, would you like some of this cordial?' she asked Laura, 'I made it myself from the elderflowers down by the river.'

Laura reached out to take the tankard, but it was slippery with moisture and to her embarrassment she spilt a little of the cordial on her dress. 'I'm so clumsy, Mistress Joan,' she said, 'Sorry.'

'Don't worry. I'll get a damp cloth and you will look as right as rain in a jiffy.' Joan left the room.

Clemo pulled a clean piece of fabric from his pocket and offered it to Laura. She thanked him, stretched towards him to take it and in doing so touched the end of Clemo's fingers. Something like a pulsating shock hit Clemo. And as Laura began to mop her dress, Clemo steadied himself by having a sip of his cordial.

'Oh! you've already found a kerchief', said Joan.

'Yes, thank you. Clemo lent me his.' Her eyes looked up and she gave Clemo a half-smile. Another pulsing shock hit him. He took another sip of the cordial.

'This is lovely, Joan. Thank you,' he said, as he took another sip and found that he had to hold the tankard with two hands because for some reason he could not understand, he was trembling.

Joan affected not to notice. 'You must have seen Laura at Mass, Clemo? Laura lives with her mother in a house quite close to the church'. Laura still had her eyes averted.

'Now, Clemo,' continued Joan, 'If you have finished your drink, I expect you have some things to do in the town. Laura and I need to have a chat on our own about when she will begin here and there are some things I need to show her. So, if you go for a wander Clemo, and come back in about half an hour, then we can continue our conversation.'

Clemo stood up, said goodbye to Laura and promised that he would return. Laura blushed, her downcast eyes carefully following his departure.

'I'm glad you've met my brother,' said Joan, 'He's a little bit shy, but he's a good boy, well, a good man, actually.' She chose her words with care. 'Now, let me tell you all about the shop.' For the next half an hour Joan introduced Laura to the details of shop work but had the suspicion that Laura was not completely concentrating. She smiled to herself, asked Laura if she had any questions and arranged to see her the following Monday, to begin work.

Laura thanked Joan and made her way out of the shop, her head thinking about the new world she was entering and her heart meditating with delight on Clemo. 'Those eyes…those muscular shoulders…that gorgeous dark hair…'

Clemo returned to the shop. Joan greeted him with a question: 'Well?'

'Well, what?'

'Oh Clemo, let me spell it out for you; firstly, what do you think of Laura? And secondly, what are you going to do for work?'

'Ah…,' he replied, 'I think Laura will be a great help to you. And as for work, I am not much clearer.'

Joan beckoned him to sit with her in the parlour where there were two chairs next to the fire. He still had his cap in his hands. 'I think Laura is really lovely,' she said, 'and, in case you are wondering, she has taken your kerchief home with her to wash it and will give it to you at Mass on Sunday.'

'That's very kind,' he said, and if truth be told, his heart leapt at the possibility of seeing Laura again He had wandered around the town in a distracted manner and with an unexpectedly warm glow deep inside as he thought about Laura. In fact, Laura was the only thing on his mind. He had noticed her at Mass before and thought she was really pretty but had not expected her to be interested in him. But when she had touched the tips of his fingers in Joan's house, was that an accident or was she trying to give him a message? He simply didn't know, but he was thoroughly enjoying being in a happy, confused and restless state. Those emotions in that combination had never been experienced by him before. It was all rather lovely.

Joan felt pleased with the way the meeting between Laura and Clemo had gone and was thrilled that her match-making skills seemed to be bearing fruit so rapidly. When her mother had alerted her to their father's ultimatum about Clemo having to leave home, and had added that it might be good if Joan could think about a possible girl for Clemo, she had begun to study the young women at Mass. She had spotted Laura glancing in Clemo's direction once or twice, though of course, Clemo had not noticed. The more she considered it, the more she thought Laura was exactly the girl for him, and although, in any case, she had intended Laura to work for her, providentially it gave her the excuse she needed to bring about an introduction without either of the parties being conscious of her manoeuvres. At least, she thought Clemo had not suspected a thing, but she wasn't so sure about Laura. She guessed that her plans had been rumbled and, she had to admit, Laura's decision to take the kerchief home to wash was a subtle masterstroke. Yes, she thought to herself, it had been a promising afternoon and she bent to stir the fire with a poker, smiling.

Clemo restated his problem. 'Joan, what am I going to do about work. I can't go back to the foundry, I'm sure Dad wouldn't allow that, but I must get a job. What should I do?'

'Go and talk to Father Burley. I expect he will be able to think of something.'

Clemo assented, not least because it would give him an opportunity perhaps to see Laura again, living as she did, close to the priest's house.

What a lovely late afternoon it had turned out to be.

He took his leave of Joan and sauntered home back across the river bridge and down the lane thinking how beautifully vibrant the leaves on the beech trees were this year.

Chapter 6: A dying man

He wandered into the cottage trying to supress a smile and saw Isabel sitting on the stool by the fire, her head in her hands. His nose was assailed by an unpleasant smell.

'Issy, what's that smell?'

'It's dad's foot,' she said, staring at him angrily. 'Haven't you noticed the smell before?'

'What do you mean?'

'Clemo, why are you so hopeless? If you would only notice what's going on. The wound on Dad's foot became worse last night, and the smell has been getting bad ever since.'

'But he seemed fine to me when I left a couple of hours ago.'

'He might have looked fine to you, Clemo. But it seemed to Mam and me that he wasn't as good as he had been. We changed his bandages just after you left and then I noticed when I took him a drink over an hour ago that he was feverish. His face was covered in sweat. Mam bathed his forehead, but the smell had become much, much worse. We took the blanket off his legs and saw that the bandage around his foot was soaked with pus. Mam and I eased the bandages away, but the smell was terrible. His toes were red and the place where he had been burnt had changed colour to a brownish-black and was weeping horrible stuff. It was awful. His foot was cold and had begun to turn black. Mam's with him now.'

Agnes quietly came into the kitchen from the bedroom looking desperately worried.

Clemo moved towards her. His face lined with anxiety.

'How's Dad now?'

'I've changed the dressings again but he's feeling really hot and is shivering. I touched his foot and the skin crackled like paper. It was awful. And he keeps shouting 'Run! run!'

'Is he having his nightmares?' asked Isabel.

'No, they're not nightmares because his eyes are open but he's so hot, so hot'.

'Can I go in to see him?' asked Clemo.

'Of course. You should.'

His father's face was white, twisted in pain. Sweat was pouring down his face, and the smell in the room was pungent and sickly. It was as much as Clemo could do not to gag.

'Dad?'

There was no response. Clemo knelt by the bed and clumsily tried to wipe away the perspiration on his father's face with a piece of cloth. His father moaned and reached out to hold Clemo's hand. But his eyes remained staring, not seeing anything. His hand squeezed Clemo's hand and then let go.

Clemo stayed kneeling for a while looking at his father's face then rose slowly to his feet and returned to the kitchen.

'He's very sick, Mam.'

'I know, *cariad*. I've sent Isabel to Goody Phelps to ask her what we should do.'

She gazed into the fire, her hands wringing each other with such force that her knuckles showed white.

'I just don't know which way to turn. We changed his bandages just after you left, and he asked us to put some bramble leaves on the wound because he said that that was what they did when he was a child in Cornwall. Issy went to collect some bramble leaves but I noticed that his toes were red and very swollen and most of his foot was brown and black. He slept for a bit but then when I next went in to see him, the smell had become terrible. Issy and I changed the bandages again, but the stench had become so strong; even with the shutters open we could hardly stand it. And that's when you returned.'

She paused and then asked, 'How was Joan?'

Clemo replied that Joan was fine but didn't mention that he had met a girl called Laura. They sat together in silence. Clemo reached out to hold the hand of his mother. She held it for a moment then released it as she pushed her hair off her forehead. They sat together in silence.

'It's the smell of death,' she said after a while, 'I think we're going to lose him, Clemo.'

'We can't', he said, the tremor in his voice preventing any further words.

'Clemo.'

'Yes?'

'Go and get Father Burley. Tell him that we think your Dad is dying'.

There was a sudden and decisive urgency in her voice which meant that Clemo leapt to his feet and ran out of the door. Just before he reached the bridge, he saw Isabel hurrying towards him carrying a small pot of poppy-water.

'This is all that Goody Phelps could offer,' she said, 'She told me that when the toes swell and turn red and wounds begin to smell badly, there isn't much to be done, but the poppy water might ease his pain. And where are you going Clemo, shouldn't you be at home looking after Mam?'

'She's sent me to get Father Burley. She said that she recognised the smell. She called it the smell of death.' His voice choked. 'You run to Mam and I'll get Father Burley.' And with a wave of his arm, he tore across the bridge and down the lane to Dixton.

Laura was in the garden and saw Clemo running down the lane. 'Hello, Clemo,' she called, 'what's the matter?'

He paused to catch his breath and explained that his father had suddenly taken a turn for the worse and he was going to get Father Burley to bring the Sacrament to him.

'Oh! Clemo. I'm so sorry. Can I do anything to help?'

He began to run but called back over his shoulder, 'Would you please go and tell Joan to go home as quickly as she can; explain what's happening.'

Within two minutes he was at the Priest's house and hammered on the door. He heard footsteps coming towards him. Miss Fielding peered out.

'Please Mistress Fielding, we think my Father is dying. Can Father Burley come at once?'

She called out the message to Father Burley who came hurrying to the door.

'Clemo, this is bad news. I shall come immediately.'

He slipped on his robes which had been hanging on a peg by the door, gathered a set of huge keys out of a brass dish on the hall table, and asked Clemo to accompany him to the church. There, he and Clemo genuflected in front of the altar before he took the Sacrament from the Tabernacle, retrieved a small bottle of holy oil from the aumbry, placed a stole around his neck and pointed to a Processional Cross. 'Take that and carry it in front of me,' he said to Clemo, 'and don't rush. Don't forget we are taking Our Lord to your father, so set a properly majestic pace.'

Clemo had never been asked to carry the Processional Cross before and felt a terrible weight of responsibility as they set off steadily along the lane. When they passed by, people stopped, crossed themselves and genuflected; then, after Clemo and Father Burley had gone past, speculated quietly about who might be dying.

They crossed the bridge. Out of the corner of his eye Clemo could see the river flowing strongly towards the sea. Ahead of him he saw Joan running towards the cottage.

Still the procession made its solemn way along the lane on the other side of the river.

At the door of the cottage, his mother, Isabel, and Joan were waiting; their eyes filled with sorrowing wonder, watching as Clemo and Father Burley came nearer. Clemo stopped briefly at the threshold, Father Burley greeted Agnes Trelawney and asked her to lead him into the bedroom. There, Richard Trelawney lay, his skin cold, white, and clammy; he was hardly conscious, (the poppy water had done its work) and by the bedside, with Agnes, Joan, and Isabel kneeling, and Clemo standing upright still holding the Processional Cross, Father Burley began the service. After saying prayers, he anointed Richard on the forehead with Holy Oil. Then, having said further brief prayers, he took a Host from the Pyx he had been carrying, placed it on Richard Trelawney's tongue and waited as the small disc of unleavened bread dissolved and was swallowed, and said more prayers. The family joined in the service by reciting the *Pater Noster*.

Father Burley then leaned over the bed and gently touched Richard Trelawney's nose with the back of his hand. The nose was cold. And having confirmed to himself that Richard really was close to death, he pronounced the words of the Blessing. The family, with anguished tears streaming down their faces, aghast at the speed and suddenness of Richard's dying, crossed themselves. The smell in the room pervaded everything, seeping into their clothes, and stealing into their nostrils. It was like a thick miasma that oozed its way into every pore of their bodies, and into every room of the cottage.

Father Burley assured Agnes, Joan, and Isabel of his continuing prayers for them and for Richard, and ordered Clemo to process steadily in front of him carrying the Processional Cross for the return journey to the church. Clemo was caught in a binding anxiety. He wanted to walk as quickly as possible so that he could return speedily to his father's deathbed but realised that carrying the Processional Cross was a sacred responsibility. He therefore walked at a steady pace.

When they arrived at the church porch, Father Burley, recognising Clemo's worry, told him to carry the Cross into the church, place it in its holder next to the altar and then get home as fast as possible. Clemo deposited the Cross in the stand, thanked Father Burley warmly, and ran out of the church. Laura, to his surprise, was waiting for him at the church-yard gate. Dusk was beginning to fall.

'Come with me,' she said, 'I guessed you would be desperate to get back to your father, so I organised my uncle. He has his boat tied up on the river and he can get you across faster than you can run to your house.' She held out her hand, grabbed Clemo's hand and ran with him to the riverbank.

Seated in a small rowing boat was a burly, muscular man. 'Uncle,' said Laura, 'This is Clemo who I told you about. Get in Clemo.' He stepped into the boat and Laura stepped in after him. He sat on the seat in the stern and Laura sat next to him. He could feel the warmth from her body creeping through her clothes to him. Laura's uncle pulled on the oars, rowed upstream briefly, and then let the current take the boat down and across to the opposite bank where there was a set of rickety steps. Clemo scrambled out.

'Thank you very much, Laura, and Laura's Uncle,' he shouted.

In his haste to get to the cottage he didn't look back. Laura and her uncle watched him and then the uncle said, smiling, 'He seems like a nice lad, Laura.' She punched him on his arm, he grinned and rowed upstream again. When they landed by the church Laura looked across the river but Clemo had already arrived home.

As he opened the door, he heard a wail from the bedroom. He pushed in…his mother was distraught kneeling by the bed holding her husband's hand; Joan was sobbing, dabbing at her eyes with a twisted handkerchief and Isabel was on her knees by the bed holding her dead father's other hand.

'He's gone,' said his mother, crossing herself, as she stood up, her face grey with grief. 'He died just as you came through the door, Clemo. Now *cariad*, you have another duty to carry out. Go to Mistress Jenkins as quickly as you can. She lives next door to Goody Phelps and ask her to come here as soon as possible. She will lay your father out.'

Clemo left, his head swirling with a welter of images and feelings. He had so wanted to be with his father, but the honour of carrying the Cross was immense and it had been his duty to accompany Father Burley. On the other hand, could not Father Burley have walked back to his house on his own and Clemo could have taken the Cross back to him later? And his father was dead… the shock of its finality hit him with the force of a sledgehammer. He was now the head of the household. He rushed on. And then there was Laura. He couldn't get the warm closeness of her out of his mind, but it seemed almost blasphemous to be thinking such thoughts when his father had just died. He determined to put the thoughts to one side. He had duties to perform. He knocked on Mistress Jenkins' door, easing his breath after his run. He had expected a middle-aged woman, but Mistress Jenkins was not much older that his sister, Joan.

'Good evening, Mistress Jenkins. My mother wonders if you could please come and lay my father out. He has just died.' The words, so formal and so polite, did not do justice to the situation.

'Of course, Clemo.' (*Did everyone know him?*). 'Run back to your mother and tell her I'll be with her shortly, once I've got all my things together.'

He thanked her and walked home slowly across the wooden bridge. He needed to get the idea of his father's death straight in his mind. His father really was dead. Dead. Which meant that there would be a funeral to arrange. How did that happen? Questions tumbled over each other. He walked on but stopped for a moment to watch the water flowing beneath the bridge. Life seemed to be continuing, but he felt it shouldn't, not after his father's death. Could there not be a miracle when just for one minute, the water ceased to roll onwards, in honour of his father? The water surged relentlessly on. Could God not grant him a miracle? Was God not all-powerful? Hadn't he made the waters of the Red Sea stand up like a wall when the Israelites were fleeing from Egypt? So, why not now? How could things just go on as though nothing had happened when actually everything had happened. His father was dead. Was there no sympathy to be had from the Creation, from the river and the trees and the grass? How could things he had always loved, now be so indifferent to his numbing, aching grief?

His mother and sisters were gathered around the kitchen fire and asked when he came in whether Mistress Jenkins would soon be there. A large iron cauldron of water was warming by the stove.

'She said she had to get her things together and she would then come immediately.'

There was a gentle tap on the door. Joan opened it, thanked Mistress Jenkins for coming so quickly and asked her to step inside. She went straight to Agnes and hugged her. 'O Agnes, my poor, poor love,' she said. And then she hugged Joan and Isabel and offered them her deep sympathy. She smiled wistfully at Clemo and he felt that he had better leave the women to do whatever they had to do. He went out into the back garden and Toby the dog came rushing towards him, wagging its tail. Clemo knelt, put his arms around the dog's neck and burying his face in the dog's soft coat, sobbed uncontrollably. He realised it was not very brave to behave in such a way, but his loss was huge, and he felt a weight of responsibility settling itself on his shoulders. He nuzzled Toby for a few more minutes, dried his tears on his sleeve and slowly made his way back into the house.

His mother, Mistress Jenkins and his sisters were standing by the door.

'Mistress Jenkins has washed your father and laid him out, Clemo. Perhaps you would like to go in to see him?'

Whilst the women were saying their goodbyes, Clemo tiptoed into the bedroom. His father looked so at peace. Clemo wasn't expecting that. When he'd last seen him his face was contorted with pain. But now, apart from his eyes being closed, and a strip of white cloth tied around from the top of the head to the jaw, keeping the mouth shut, his father looked so normal. So normal but also so absent. He was no longer there. Not there anymore. It was as though his father had sloughed off his body and had become like a bird leaving its roost and flying away. He stared for a long time at his dead father, said 'thank you' under his breath and '*Requiescat in pace*', crossed himself and returned to the kitchen.

'Mistress Jenkins will come back on Monday with the shroud,' said his mother, her voice choking on the words. 'So, the funeral will be then…'.

Joan put her arm around her mother's shoulder. Isabel was stirring broth in an iron pot on the fire. Clemo said nothing. He felt so bewildered, so numbed by everything. It was as though this were a dream, and he would wake up and life would be back to normal. And yet, having seen his father's corpse, he knew that his father would never come back. He had gone. As simple and as impossible as that. He dragged a chair close to the table and slumped down on it, his head in his hands. His father was no longer there. Clemo had never realised until that moment, the sheer enormity of death. It was everything and yet, impossibly, it was nothing. Death was an absence. That was what it was, an absence. It was life which was the intruder, the welcome and unexpected stranger, the mystery, and was all the more precious for that. And just for a second, Laura came into his mind. He looked out of the window. It was beginning to get dark.

Chapter 7: Saturday morning

Clemo's mother was already up by the time he came down the ladder for breakfast. 'I couldn't sleep,' she explained, 'I have so many things on my mind. You will have to go to Redbrook this morning to tell Mr Young that your father has died and ask him if you can have Monday off for the funeral. And I shall have to let the Guild know…and Isabel will have to help me make a few things for anyone who comes back to the house after the funeral.'

He didn't know whether she was talking to herself or to him. So, he took a piece of bread and some cold cuts of meat that she had put on the table and began his breakfast. His mother was bustling around looking distracted and continued with her monologue. 'Isabel will need to go out the back and make sure the sheep are alright and let the chickens out, then there's the ale to check. If we don't have enough, once you are back from Redbrook you might have to go into Monmouth and ask Joan if we can have some of hers. And then there's the tankards. We won't have enough for everyone…'

'But won't the Guild supply the ale and the tankards, Mam?'

Agnes ran her hand across her forehead. 'You're probably right. Come to think of it, go to Giles Thomas, the Guild Master, before you go to Redbrook, that will give him time to organise things and he can only do that if he knows your father has died. Come on Clemo, don't just sit there, get a move on…' She sat down heavily in the chair.

Isabel clambered down the ladder, her hair untidy, her clothes dishevelled.

'Oh, Issy, what a sight you are,' said her mother, 'you look as though you have been up most of the night.'

'I couldn't sleep,' she said.

'That wasn't what I saw earlier,' said Agnes, 'you were fast asleep when I got up.'

'I was pretending...'

'Issy, how can you tell such fibs when your father is lying dead in the next room?'

'Sorry'. She slumped towards the table for breakfast, rubbing the sleep from her eyes and yawning.

'Clemo's just off to see the Guild Master before he goes to Redbrook.'

'And I'm going to take Toby with me,' he said. 'He needs the exercise.'

'But I wanted to have Toby with me, today,' said Issy in a whining voice.

'Well, Issy, just for once, you can't have your own way. I'm taking Toby...and remember, Issy Trelawney that I am now the head of the household.' She threw a piece of bread at him.

He ran his hands through his hair, tidied his tunic and left the house to collect Toby.

The dog was, as always, delighted to see him. Clemo released the chain from the hasp on the kennel and with Toby close beside him, set out for Monmouth to see Giles Thomas.

He knew the house he was aiming for. It was the largest one in the square, half-timbered with the two upper storeys jutting over the street. It dominated its surroundings.

He knocked on the door. A maid answered.

'I wonder if I might see Master Thomas,' said Clemo, 'My name's Clemo Trelawney. My father was a member of the Guild, but he died last night, and I should like to talk with Master Thomas about the funeral.'

The maid nodded and asked Clemo to wait by the door until she returned. He looked about him. The town was just waking up. A few market stall holders were setting out their wares. One was arranging cheeses on a table, another was placing bolts of cloth on his stall, smoothing out the wrinkles as he did so, yet another was laying out some heavy ironware, pots and pans and a couple of hefty fire irons.

Clemo tied Toby to an iron foot scraper next to the door. 'Stay there.'

The maid returned. 'Master Thomas will see you now,' she said, her eyes lowered.

Clemo followed her into a large room at the front of the house which had tapestries on two of the walls. There was a large oak sideboard on which stood two silver candle sticks, and a long, polished dining table surrounded by eight oak chairs. There were two more oak chairs either side of the fireplace.

'Master Trelawney,' said a heavy voice, as Giles Thomas entered the room. 'I am saddened to hear your news. Your father was a fine member of the Guild.'

Giles Thomas was a strongly built man with the features of a wealthy, retired butcher, red cheeks, bulbous eyes and an air of solid, mercantile authority. 'Sit yourself down.' Clemo did as he was bidden. 'Now, what can you tell me?'

Clemo rather nervously rehearsed the events of the past twenty-four hours and concluded by saying that he thought the Requiem Mass and burial were likely to take place on Monday.

'I'm afraid I have never had to organise a funeral before so I should be grateful for your guidance, Sir,' he said.

'You have come to the right place, young man,' said Master Thomas. His confident manner left Clemo feeling uncomfortable.

'Let me explain to you what has to happen. I take it that you have already been in contact with Mistress Jenkins?'

'Yes, Sir. She came last night to lay my father out.'

'Good. Have you alerted Father Burley about your father's death?'

'No, Sir, not yet.'

'You must do that as soon as you have left here. He will need to know the time of the service and will then organise his sexton to dig the grave.'

'Yes, Sir.'

Clemo's heart lifted. If he were lucky, on his way to alert Father Burley he might chance to see Laura again.

'If we assume that the Requiem will be at about two o'clock, the Guild will arrive at your mother's house at just after one o'clock. We shall bring the bier and the pall with us and that will give Mistress

Jenkins time, earlier that morning, to place your father in his shroud, and it will give our pall bearers time for a sip of ale, hey?'

He smiled a fat, knowing smile.

'Of course, Sir.'

'The Guild will lead the procession to the church following the crucifer. There will be four acolytes, two each side of the bier, and you will walk behind the bier with your mother and sisters. Once we arrive at the church the pall bearers will carry the bier into the church; that will be followed by the Requiem, then we shall take the bier out to the graveyard. Now, I have a question for you. Will you want to receive your father's body when it is placed into the grave?'

'I'm sorry, Sir, I don't quite understand.'

'It is the tradition that after the Requiem, when the corpse is removed from the bier, it is placed into the waiting arms of the son of the family. So, if you are going to do this, you will need to have climbed down into the grave (don't worry, the Guild has a small ladder for the purpose), the body will be passed to you and then you can place your father reverently on the soil at the base of the grave….and then you climb out.'

It was not a process to which Clemo had given much attention before. Did he really have to man-handle his father's dead body? He shuddered.

'If you would rather not do this on your own, one of the Guild will join you in the grave and help you.'

'If that is possible, that would be a help, thank you.'

'Is there anything else you need to know?'

'Yes, Sir. After the funeral will you all come back to our house, if so, does the Guild supply the ale and can everyone please bring a tankard?'

'Good question. And the answer is that all the Guild members will meet afterwards in the Guild Hall, and because your father was a member of the Guild, you and the family will be able to join us there, plus any friends and relations. We only do this for our members, you understand.'

'Thank you very much, Sir, my mother will be very relieved.'

'And you need to tell your mother that if she has any money concerns in the future, she can always come to the Guild. By the way, the Guild will pay all the fees due to the church for the funeral.'

'That is really kind, Sir.'

'Not kindness at all. It is all met by the fees the members pay.' He stood up, the meeting over. 'And once you have completed your apprenticeship at Redbrook, you might want to consider joining the Guild. We shall be having our own Guild Mass on Tuesday at 5pm. It would be good to see you there to represent your father. He was a good man, your father, though he did not always enjoy the best of health. I imagine that he had been through a lot before coming to Monmouth, but we never enquired too closely.' It was said in such a way that Clemo guessed they actually knew his father's story.

'The maid will see you out. Good day, Clemo.'

'Good day, Sir, and thank you.'

He felt surprisingly tired after that encounter and explained to Toby as he knelt to unfasten him that they would go to see Joan for a drink before going to Dixton. 'She might even have something for you.' The dog wagged its tail.

Clemo pushed open the door to Joan's small shop and called out to her. She came hurrying through from the back parlour, her eyes dark with grief.

'I've just been to the Guild Master to arrange the funeral details,' he explained, feeling rather pleased with his grown-up comment, 'and now I have to go to Dixton to see Father Burley to check that 2pm can be the time of the funeral and then I have to go to Redbrook to see Mr Young to ask if I might have the day off.'

'Clemo, you are going to be worn out. Look, I'll get Dai to look after the shop for an hour, though he hates doing it, and I'll come with you to see Father Burley. At least we can have a chat on the way.'

Dai Parry, a ginger-haired man with a trim beard and a round, freckled face, came into the shop from the back parlour. Joan explained that she and Clemo had to go to see Father Burley and asked him to keep an eye on the shop. His face fell. 'It's not a man's job', he said, a tinge of anger in his voice, 'but I'll do it for you Joany, just this once.'

She grabbed a shawl which she threw around her shoulders and joined Clemo on the walk to Dixton.

It was a bright, late-Spring morning, the sun sparkled on the river, and Joan and Clemo fell into an easy conversation saying how they were astonished by the speed of their father's death and how very saddened they were for their mother. Clemo also explained about all the arrangements that the Guild would make for the funeral.

'I guess,' he continued, 'now that father's dead I won't have to leave home for a while, so I can help Mam.'

Joan agreed, and as they came closer to the church she pointed out where Laura lived.

'I know her house,' replied Clemo, finding himself blushing, 'I saw Laura when I came to fetch Father Burley yesterday. Her uncle rowed me home afterwards.' And then the thought struck him that Laura hadn't returned his kerchief. He expressed his concern to Joan.

'I'm sure she will give it to you at Mass tomorrow,' said Joan, 'and if I know Laura, it will have been washed and dried and ironed.'

They saw Father Burley, (he answered the door himself. Miss Fielding whose normal duty it was to open the door had gone to market) and asked his permission to have a Requiem on Monday afternoon with the burial to follow. He was only too willing to oblige, he said. And addressing Joan, he expressed his sympathy and reminded her that Dai had missed Mass the previous week and therefore he was most certainly expected on the morrow.

'Yes, Father,' said Joan, bowing her head and almost curtseying.

They made their way back towards the town.

'Why didn't Dai go to Mass last week?' asked Clemo. 'He'll get himself into trouble.'

'That's what I told him myself, but he won't listen. He's a good man but very stubborn. He went to hear one of those Lollard preachers in the fields out towards Mitchel Troy a couple of weeks ago and was troubled and excited about what he had heard. He reckons that the Church has had it far too easy for too long and that soon the Holy Father himself will be toppled.'

Clemo looked around to see that no-one else might have heard Joan's comments.

'That's really dangerous stuff,' he said, 'Please…he mustn't get himself muddled up in all that. One of the men at work told me he had heard that a Lollard had been burnt to death in London recently, for heresy.'

'I've told Dai it's dangerous,' said Joan, 'but he says that he's old enough and wise enough to do his own thinking, and he doesn't have to believe all that Father Burley says.'

'Oh Joan', replied Clemo, standing still for a moment, despite Toby wanting to press on, 'that's awful. It's heresy. Father Burley is a good man. He wouldn't teach us things that aren't right. Dai is living very recklessly, he really is.'

Joan too had stopped. She put her hand on Clemo's arm and asked him not to breathe a word of what she had told him to anyone, not even their mother and certainly not to Issy.

'Of course, I wouldn't Joan, but if others get a whiff of Dai being involved, they will blame you as well. You know what people are like.'

They walked the rest of the way in silence. When they reached the shop, Clemo asked Joan if she could tell Giles Thomas that the Requiem, had been arranged for 2pm on Monday.

'It would be much better if you did that, Clemo. I would rather not talk to him.'

'Why not?'

'I'll explain one day,' said Joan and distracted him by saying that she would pop to see their mother and tell her about the funeral arrangements and assure her that she didn't need to worry about ale or tankards or much food. She waved Clemo goodbye.

Clemo was beginning to wonder if his family might have had more secrets than just the one concerning his father's part in the Cornish rebellion.

He went across the square, delivered his message to the maid about the time of the Requiem and then set off back across the bridge and headed towards Redbrook.

Chapter 8: Redbrook and back

In normal circumstances, the walk to Redbrook along the river with Toby would have been pleasant. But today it was not. He thought continually of his father; he wondered about his mother and how she would cope with her loss; he thought of Issy; she would miss their father dreadfully, and he recalled the morning's encounter with Giles Thomas (he really did not like the man but could not work out why) and remembered the walk to Dixton with Joan. It was her final comment about 'telling him one day' that troubled him. What might she have meant? And then there was his brother-in-law, Dai; what was he doing going to a secret Lollard gathering?

His father's death had been like a landslide; some of the certainties of his everyday world had slipped from beneath his feet, and the ground which had always seemed so stable, was now riven with large and hazardous cracks. He was not quite sure of anything, except he was sure of Father Burley and the Mass. He loved the church, and he loved the Mass, especially the moment when Father Burley elevated the Host, and the tinkling bell rang. Of course, he had never seen Jesus in the bread, tho' that simple girl, Annie Harris, told him once that she had. 'I saw the blood coming out of our Lord's hands and side,' she had said in a conspiratorial whisper. He didn't know whether to believe her or not. But Father Burley had taught him that at the Elevation the bread became the real body of Christ. It was a miracle. And he certainly believed in miracles. If you were a foundryman (which he was) was it not a miracle that something as rough and solid as tin ore could be turned by fire into a golden-red liquid? And he'd once seen one of their sheep giving birth to a lamb, and even though it was messy, just watching the lamb being licked into life by its mother, tottering unsteadily on to its legs and immediately nuzzling for milk, well, that was a miracle, wasn't it? And looking up at the endless stars at night, wasn't that a miracle? The stars seemed to go on for ever and ever. It seemed to him that miracles were everywhere if you knew how to look.

As he turned these ideas over in his mind, he realised that in addition to Father Burley, he loved his work-colleagues, tho' not in the way he loved the Mass. But as he was thinking of the beauty and mystery of the Mass he suddenly thought of Laura. Did she like him? Or was she just flirting? Did he like her? Yes, he did. The unexpected strength of his feelings for her amazed him. Just a few days ago he wouldn't have taken any notice of her, yet here he was now, walking by the river, and the picture of her in his mind was an aching joy. And then, as he smiled with happiness, another more sombre set of feelings hit him: his father was dead. He repeated it to himself, 'Father is dead; Father is dead,' as if by repetition the horrible truth would sink into his soul. He would never walk this path with his father again. His loss was acute, and so painful that tears sprang to his eyes. But at the same time, to his amazement, he realised that they were not only tears for his father, but tears of thankfulness for Laura. 'Laura'. He said her name aloud and twirled around like a dancer. Toby looked at him with a perplexed, dog-like frown.

He was soon at Redbrook. He knew where the Boss lived and went to his stone-built house just up from the river. He tied Toby to a tree in the garden and knocked on the door.

The door slowly eased itself open, and a small, elderly, white-haired lady looked out at him. She was leaning on a walking stick. Her knuckles and fingers were large, shiny and twisted. 'Yes?' she asked.

'Good Morrow, Mistress; my name is Clemo Trelawney and I wondered if I might speak with Master Young?'

'I shall see if he's in,' she replied and hobbled away, the stick tap-tapping on the stone floor.

He heard her call out: 'Ifor! There's a young man with amazing green eyes wants to speak with you.'

How could she have noticed his eyes?

He heard the Boss reply, 'I think I can guess who that might be.'

The Boss appeared: 'Clemo, I thought it must be you. Please come in. My wife will bring us some ale.' He called out for two tankards. 'It might take her a while, I'm afraid. She's badly crippled.'

Clemo had not thought much before about the Boss being married and certainly had not expected the Boss's wife to be so bent and hunched over. If he had thought at all about his boss's domestic situation, he might have pictured the Boss's wife as robust and strong, not a little, shuffling, crippled woman.

She came to the door of the room with a tankard in one hand and her stick in the other. 'I'll go and get the second jar now.' she said and shuffled away.

'So', said Ifor Young, 'what brings you here, Clemo?'

'I am very sorry to trouble you, Sir, but I wanted you to know that my father died last night.'

'Oh no! I am really sorry to hear that. But I had heard he had been improving.'

'He had been, but suddenly he took a turn for the worse. His foot turned black and began to rot, and soon he was no more.'

'I am very sorry, Clemo. That will be a terrible blow for you and your family to bear.'

The door to the room opened slowly. Ifor Young leapt up and reached out to receive the tankard of ale from his wife's gnarled hands. 'Thank you, my sweeting,' he said. Clemo felt embarrassed. He should not have been privy to such a private and loving term, this was the Boss, after all. But the Boss didn't seem to notice Clemo's discomfort. Clemo tucked away the phrase 'my sweeting' and thought that at an appropriate moment he might say it to Laura.

'And when will the Requiem and the funeral be?'

'That's what I have come to see you about, Sir. The Requiem and burial will be on Monday, and I wondered if you might grant me time-off on Monday to attend?'

'Of course, Clemo. It's your duty to be there with your mother and sisters. But I shall expect to see you here on Tuesday. And, by the way, I shall come to the Requiem to represent the Foundry, and I imagine that a few others might want to be there as well but leave that with me.'

'Thank you, Sir. Thank you very much. I am sure my mother will appreciate it greatly if you can be there.'

'Good, Clemo.' Ifor Young put his big brawny arm on Clemo's shoulder and said, 'God bless you, Clemo. Chin up.' It was the affectionate clumsiness of the gesture which brought a lump to Clemo's throat, and thanking the Boss again, he left the house, collected Toby and began the walk home.

He had no sooner left the Boss's garden than he saw Gwyn Evans walking towards him.

'Gwyn! Hello! great to see you.'

'I was very sorry to hear about your father's death, Clemo.' For some reason, Gwyn took his cap off as he muttered the words.

'How on earth did you hear, Gwyn. I've only just told the Boss.'

'It was my father,' explained Gwyn, 'he was in Monmouth early this morning and picked up the news from Dai Parry. Dai is my father's nephew and my big cousin. I bet you never realised that.'

'No, I didn't. But over the last couple of days nothing surprises me anymore.'

'So, what are you doing now, Clemo?'

'I'm going back to Hadnock to have some food and see what else my mother has got lined up for me to do.'

'And how is your mother?'

'Shattered but busy.'

'And your sisters?'

'Well, Joan is Joan, caring and kind, but Issy is taking it very badly.'

'Would you please give Joan and Issy my greetings and tell them that I am hoping to be allowed by the Boss to be at the Requiem.'

'Gwyn, that's really very kind.'

'Not at all. Don't forget to tell Issy that I asked after her and please send her my sympathy.'

Clemo bade farewell to Gwyn and, letting Toby off the chain, watched as the dog scampered fast into the woods that skirted the lane, disappearing from view, but then re-appearing a few hundred yards away further along the path looking back at Clemo to check that he was following. The wonder of watching Toby run was one of Clemo's favourite experiences. The dog seemed to embody absolute freedom, until of course, he was called to heel and was chained to his kennel.

For the rest of the walk Clemo pondered the comparison between his life and Toby's, but like a series of small explosions, in the middle of his thinking, pictures of Laura kept erupting in his mind. He found himself switching mood whenever it happened, from sorrow about his father's death, to delight about Laura. He couldn't understand how his feelings could be so volatile; shouldn't he be constantly praying for his father's soul? Might his thoughts about Laura be a distraction created by the Devil? But, if that was the case, why were those thoughts about Laura so filled with happiness? He could not find a solution, and soon, accompanied by a weary Toby, he arrived at his house.

Although the fire was roaring away, there seemed to be no-one there. He called out. Issy stumbled down the ladder.

'Where's Mam?'

'She's having a lie down,' Issy replied. 'She didn't sleep much last night, and she feels worn out.'

'Anything to eat?'

'It's on the table'. There was a loaf of fresh bread and some cheese.

Clemo sat down. 'Can I have some ale please, Issy?'

'You know where it is, get it yourself.' Issy was obviously in one of her moods.

Clemo ignored her. 'I saw the Boss this morning. He's going to come to the Requiem and burial. And I also bumped into Gwyn Evans. He asked particularly to be remembered to you and sends his sympathy.'

'Oh, does he?' she said, with a certain tone of asperity in her voice, and turned away from Clemo to poke the fire.

'How do you know Gwyn?' asked Clemo.

'You bewilder me, Clemo, you really do. What world do you live in? You don't seem to know anything, except of course, a load of useless Latin, and when to bow in the right place at Mass. Gwyn is Dai Parry's cousin, fathead, so I have met him occasionally in Joan's shop. Does that satisfy you?'

Clemo didn't answer. When Issy was in one of her almost-tantrum moods it was better not to get into an argument. He took a few more bites of the bread. And then said as though talking to himself, 'I was wondering why he singled you out for sympathy, that's all.'

It was the moment for Issy to ignore his remark, but he noticed that she had blushed.

'I'm going out to feed the hens,' she said, slamming the door behind her. Clemo sipped his ale.

The rest of the day passed in relative peace and the following day, Sunday, they went to Mass together.

They were within fifty yards of the church when Issy said to her mother, looking sideways at Clemo, 'I wonder if Laura Davies will be there this morning?'

Her mother did not reply. She was contemplating the ordeal ahead when everyone in church would be offering her their sympathy. She hoped that she wouldn't break down. Clemo kept his counsel but realised that Issy was still chewing over last night's altercation. But why had Issy just mentioned Laura? Did she suspect something?

He went into Mass in the wrong frame of mind. In brief, he was quietly fuming. He knew he should forgive those who sinned against him, but he found it difficult to practice that injunction with Issy. She seemed to have the capacity to put the knife in at exactly the right moment, as she had this morning. He looked across to the women's side of the church where she, Joan and their mother were standing together. And then his eye fell upon Laura. He tried hard to concentrate on what Father Burley was saying, He genuflected in the right places, he raised his eyes at the Elevation and at that precise moment remembered that he had promised to go to Confession on the previous day but had forgotten all about it. What was happening to him? How could he forget something so important? He would have to wait to speak to Father Burley after Mass, apologise, and see whether he might make his Confession then. It was the wrong way round, he realised, but he hoped that Father Burley would understand.

The Mass came to an end with Father Burley pronouncing the Blessing. Clemo went outside and waited for his mother, Joan and Issy to emerge. Dai Parry came out and greeted Clemo; 'Really sorry about your Dad,' he said, and might have said more but was distracted by someone who wanted to speak with him. It looked as though the matter was urgent.

Joan and Laura came out together. They saw Clemo, and Joan said that Laura had something to give him. She then moved to one side whilst Laura gave Clemo his kerchief, washed, dried, and pressed. As she gave it him with an apology for having inadvertently taken it, her fingers brushed his. Clemo thought his heart would explode. He thanked her. But then Issy arrived with her mother, smiled across at Joan and greeted Laura.

'Hello, Laura, haven't seen you for a while. How are you?'

'Very well indeed, thank you, Issy. But I am so sorry about your loss.' Her look of sympathy was directed at Issy but also, under her eyelashes, at Clemo.

At that moment, Father Burley came out of the church. Clemo walked quickly towards him and explained quietly that he had forgotten to come to Confession before Mass but asked if he might make his Confession now. Father Burley agreed and they returned to the church.

As he was saying his prayers afterwards, he heard the latch of the church door lift. He turned and saw Laura standing there. Was she an answer to prayer? Was Providence looking kindly upon him? Or was it the Tempter?

'Oh, I'm sorry to interrupt you, Clemo. Only I felt that I hadn't really thanked you enough for lending me your kerchief.'

He looked at her beautiful face and realised that he would love to kiss her, but dared not do so, especially not in a church, and especially not just after Confession. So, he stumbled a few words of thanks towards her and said that he had to be getting home. They walked together as far as her house, where she said that she would be praying for him on the morrow, and he replied that he would also pray for her. It was, he realised, an inept and inappropriate response, but she didn't seem to mind. He was in turmoil…but what a deliriously happy and dangerous turmoil it was.

He walked home, trying to prepare himself for the following day but actually daydreaming about Laura.

Chapter 9: The Requiem and burial

The morning of the Requiem and burial passed in a daze for all of them. Time seemed to dawdle but also to rush by.

Just after breakfast, Mistress Jenkins arrived with a heavy woollen shroud packed into a large fabric bag with her needles, stout thread and some strips of cloth to wrap around the shroud and bind it in place. It did not take her long to sew the corpse into its shroud and to tie the narrow strips of fabric around it. Agnes stood by whilst Mistress Jenkins worked and when she had finished thanked her for her kindness.

'It is a privilege,' replied Mistress Jenkins and as discreetly as she had arrived, she softly left the house. Clemo, Joan and Issy joined their mother in the bedroom, whereupon Issy, seeing the corpse trussed up ready for burial, burst into loud sobs and was comforted by Joan. 'He looks safely tucked up,' said Clemo, a comment which only provoked a further outburst of sobbing from Issy.

At 1pm there was a scuffling of feet outside the cottage. Clemo looked out. The bier had arrived accompanied by members of the Guild and at their head, wearing a black velvet cap and a black velvet scapula was Giles Thomas. The scapula was embroidered with images of the Five Wounds picked out in gold and silver thread. Issy also looked out and said, under her breath, 'That really is a hideous scapula and it's being worn by a hideous man…look at him, the conceited oaf.'

Her mother told her to be quiet. 'He might hear you.'

'So?' retorted Issy but nevertheless, held her tongue.

Clemo went out to greet the members of the Guild who had gathered around a large wicker basket held by the two youngest members of the Guild. The basket held a collection of tankards, and each member went to collect his own. Clemo thanked them all for being there and then explained that ale would be served immediately.

He rushed into the cottage, and he, Joan, and Issy holding a jug apiece proceeded to pour ale into each man's tankard, whilst their mother poured ale into the silver tankard held by Giles Thomas.

'Good morrow, Mistress Trelawney,' he said, 'It is unfortunate that we should meet on such a sad occasion.' 'Indeed, Master Thomas,' she replied, and moved on rapidly to serve some of the others. Joan, it seemed to Clemo, was studiously avoiding the Guild Master and when Giles Thomas asked if there might be another pot of ale, Issy pretended not to hear and turned away from him. Clemo, anxious that there should be no discourtesy, hurried to Giles Thomas' side and poured ale into the Master's tankard.

'I'd better explain what will happen next,' he said to Clemo. 'Two members of the Guild will collect your father's corpse and tie it safely on to the bier. The Deputy Masters will lay the Guild pall over the corpse, and once I am satisfied that everything is in order, the procession will move off.'

He called the members of the Guild to order and detailed two of its members to go into the house to collect the corpse. When they returned, they placed the corpse in its shroud on the bier. The one at the feet end did not have as tight a grip as he should have had, and the corpse tumbled with a dull thud on to the bed of the bier. Two other members stepped forward and tied lengths of rope around the bier and the corpse to prevent it slipping off. When that was completed Master Thomas called out in a loud voice, 'The Pall!', and the two Deputy Masters stepped forward and laid the heavy black velvet pall over the corpse. It too was decorated with images of the Five Wounds, not in gold and silver, but in red and blue silks.

The Master called out 'Lift!' and four men, two at the front and two at the rear, lifted the bier so that its legs were free of the ground.

The crucifer was at the head of the procession, followed by the Guild Master, then came the bier accompanied by four acolytes, two on each side, and at a signal from the Master, the whole procession moved off. Clemo accompanied his mother; Joan and Dai Parry followed next and behind them was Issy on her own. She looked pale and heartbroken and stumbled as she walked. The procession crossed the wooden bridge. Pedestrians stopped and crossed themselves. There was a pause on the Monmouth side of the bridge for the Master to check that the corpse was still securely fastened. The bearers were able to stretch their shoulders and arms and ready themselves for the next stage down the lane to the church on the west bank of the river.

Clemo could not help looking across at Laura's house as they passed. She was not there. He felt a sting of disappointment.

At the door of the church, Father Burley was waiting to receive the procession. He followed behind the crucifer as the bearers carried the bier the last few paces and set it down with care on the stone-flagged floor.

And there it was, they had arrived. With the four torches burning either side of the bier, the crucifer placed the Processional Cross in its holder behind the altar. Clemo, his mother and sisters took their places, the Guild Master sat in a special chair at the front of the nave, and the Requiem Mass began. Sunlight streamed through the south windows and fell softly on the Pall. Clemo, whilst dreading the burial that would follow, had a strong and comforting sense that his father had come home. Issy continued to sniffle.

Once the Mass had ended, Father Burley headed the procession out of the church, and Clemo noticed, as he and the family followed, that Laura was standing on the women's side of the nave. He dared not look at her but was comforted by her presence. The four bearers struggled across the uneven ground, the bier rocking from side to side, as they moved towards the freshly dug grave. Everyone gathered around and at a signal, Clemo, trembling with nerves, climbed down the ladder into the grave. The sexton, a sinewy man with a thin face, sharp nose and rheumy eyes was already there. At another signal from the Master the two Deputy Masters carefully took off the Pall, then the four bearers stepped forward, untied the ropes, lifted the corpse from the bier and placed it into the waiting arms of Clemo and the Sexton. The weight of his father's body surprised Clemo but he and the Sexton lowered the corpse onto some straw at the bottom of the grave which, Clemo noticed, could not disguise the fact that water was steadily seeping into it forming shallow puddles. As he climbed out, his feet squelched in cold mud. He caught his mother's eye, and she whispered a 'thank you.' Agnes, Clemo, Joan and Issy, at the appropriate moment in the burial service threw handfuls of earth on to the shrouded corpse. The earth landed with a snickering, scrabbling sound. Others, led by the Master did the same, and to conclude the ceremony Father Burley pronounced the blessing.

They walked away from the grave in twos and threes. Clemo noticed Laura standing at the door of the church and went up to her to thank her. 'I wanted to be with you, Clemo,' she said, and for a brief moment rested her hand on his arm. His stomach lurched with joy.

Issy was close behind and also thanked Laura as did Joan, who invited Laura to the funeral meats, and then they formed up in procession again, this time the Master leading, as they wound their way back along the lane to the Guildhall.

Agnes slipped her arm through Clemo's for support, whilst Issy supported her mother on the other side. They said very little but recognised that this was now the family unit.

At the Guildhall, tables and chairs were arranged so that everyone could have a seat. The Master called on Father Burley ('by whose presence we are honoured here today'), to say Grace. Issy stifled a giggle, Agnes glared at her. Clemo was trying to work out how he might find an opportunity to talk with Laura, and he neither heard the Master's comments nor Father Burley's 'Grace.'

The meal began. Wives and sisters of the Guild members brought in jugs of ale followed by hunks of freshly baked bread and a range of cold meats. The Master and the Deputies, seated at the High Table, were served first. Clemo realised, part of the way through the meal, that he would have to make a speech of thanks to the Master and found that his appetite suddenly disappeared. He turned to Issy and asked what he should say, and she whispered back: 'Say how much you loathe the piggy Master because he makes you feel sick but thank the women for the splendid food and drinks ...I dare you'.

At the end of the meal, before the plates and tankards were cleared away, the Master made a speech in which he praised Richard Trelawney as an honoured member of the Guild and a great soldier and iron worker, and declared that although Master Trelawney was a Cornishman, he had upheld the highest traditions of the tin workers craft.' 'See what I mean,' whispered Issy to Clemo, 'he's sneering at our Dad, calling him a soldier. He is so despicable, the fat buffoon.'

Clemo was called on to speak. He stood up. His mouth was dry. He had a sip of ale.

'Father Burley, Master, you have looked after us as a family in our time of grief with great kindness, and we thank you for that. We are deeply grateful that you should have honoured us in this way.

In his speech, the Master called my father a 'soldier'. By which I take it that he was referring to my father's courage, his ability to put his family above all things, and to defend us against all the assaults and wiles of the Devil. My father was, as you will all know, not a wealthy man, nor did he seek to be at the forefront of things. He left that to others who enjoy and revel in their moments in the public eye. He was quiet and unassuming, but he loved us, his family, with a rough tenderness, the memory of which we shall always value and cherish.

As the Master also said, my father was a Cornishman, and just as you Monmothians are proud of your heritage, so was my father proud of his; that he ended up in Hadnock might be thought by some of you to be due to unknown and random chance, but to us who knew him best, it was divinely Providential. Why? Because it was here that he met, fell in love with, and married our wonderful mother. His experience as a young man working in a tin mine meant that he could recognise things of great worth when he found them. He knew when he met our mother, that he had not found tin, but had found the most precious metal of all, pure gold. To have our parents as our parents, as I am sure Joan and Issy would agree, has been and is, for us, the greatest of blessings.

So, on my mother's behalf, and on behalf of Joan and Issy, thank you. Thank you for taking us to your hearts today, thank you for helping us in our loss, thank you to everyone who prepared and served this feast, and thank you for honouring a humble and good man, rough edges, yes, and sometimes, a rough tongue, but a man of the highest integrity. He had courage greater than you may be able to imagine. A man who left his native land (which I know from time to time, he missed terribly), but who found in this new land, my mother, and through her discovered that this too is a special place, a place of blessings.'

He sat down. There was silence for a moment and then the room erupted in applause. To his amazement Issy put her arm around him and hugged him, his mother squeezed his hand, Joan came towards him and planted a kiss on his cheek. He was overwhelmed.

As increasing numbers of people came up to congratulate him on his speech, he felt more and more embarrassed and explained that he didn't know where the words had come from and that he had never made a speech in his life before.

All he wanted now was to go home.

But then he saw Laura. Their eyes met. He excused himself from the well-wishers, went over to speak to her, unaware that all the room was watching and conjecturing. She added her own congratulations, 'Clemo you were wonderful', she said, 'but you should take your mother home now. She will be exhausted.'

He thanked her, promised to see her again ('very soon, I hope') and was then embarrassed by his own forwardness.

On the way to collect his mother, he saw Father Burley waiting to speak to him,

'Congratulations, Clemo; that really was a fine speech; your father would have been proud of you, but…, as your priest, I need to say one thing more. Your boots are covered in the mud of the grave.'

'I'm sorry, Father but I had to climb down into the grave…'

He was interrupted by Father Burley, 'I wasn't referring to your real boots but to the need always to remember this, especially when things have gone unexpectedly well, "Memento, homo, quia pulvis es, et in pulverem reverteris" that is, you are dust and unto dust shall you return… the best human beings know that they always have mud on their boots.'

It was a comment which brought Clemo down to earth. He walked towards his mother in a sombre and recollected mood. It was time to go home.

Chapter 10: An eventful year

When Clemo and the family were back safely in their own cottage, his mother hugged him and thanked him for all he had said. Issy did the same (again!) but added, 'And I hope the piggy Master got the message.'

'Why do you hate him so much, Issy?' he asked.

'You'd better ask Joan', she replied, enigmatically.

Agnes threw some coal and wood on the fire to distract Clemo from pursuing Issy's comment. Clemo decided that he needed to take Toby for a brief walk along the river. As always, the dog was delighted to see him and once released from its chain, chased along ahead of him, looking back from time to time to ensure that he was following.

It was a fine, late-Spring evening, birds were singing, the river flowed softly on its way to the sea. The leaves on the trees were brilliantly green, bursting with the rapture of new life.

Clemo walked as far as the point where he could see Dixton church on the opposite bank. He looked across and hoped he might see Laura, but she must have been indoors. He called Toby to him, knelt and nuzzled him, then stood up, looked again for a long time across the river, and walked slowly back to the cottage.

Issy had gone to her room. His mother was sitting by the fire, her hands in her lap.

'Ah! Clemo, have you had a good walk?'

'Yes, thank you.'

'Now tomorrow, Clemo, life has to begin again, so I imagine that you will want to go to the Foundry. I shall do a bit of dairying at the Farm, and Issy will get out her spinning wheel and begin to work on some wool, but soon she will have to look for other work. Your wages by themselves cannot support three people.'

Clemo agreed but was suddenly hit by a wave of exhaustion. It was time for sleep. He wished his mother a good night, clambered up the ladder, lay on his bed recollecting the events of the day and his brief conversation with Laura, and soon drifted off to sleep.

The following morning, he was up early, grabbed some bread and cheese, pulled on his boots and quietly slipped out of the door whilst his mother and Issy were still asleep. The walk to the Foundry in the early morning sunlight was delicious, and although he missed his father walking beside him, he found that he was content to be moving towards his colleagues again. He looked forward to seeing them. At the entrance to the Foundry, the Boss was waiting to speak with him.

'Good morrow, Clemo. That was a great speech yesterday. I didn't know you were a bard. Where did that come from? Had you practised it before?'

'No, I hadn't realised until the meal had begun that I might have to say something, but somehow the words put themselves in the right order and then just tumbled out.'

'Well. Whatever happened, Clemo, it was a very fine speech. Now, young man, work calls…'

Clemo's colleagues welcomed him and rather shyly congratulated him, but by the time of second breakfast, the event was behind them. Life had to go on.

And for the next few months it did. Clemo continued his work at the Foundry; his mother continued her dairying at Hadnock Farm, and Issy found a job as a servant at one of the large houses in the town. And all the while, it was Laura who was at the centre of Clemo's thinking. He saw her each week at Mass; he managed from time to time to sneak into Joan's shop where Laura was working and snatched a few furtive words with her. Joan was the soul of discretion and left them to talk. She coughed before she came into the shop from the parlour to provide a warning that she was coming through. As the weeks and months passed, and Spring began to merge into Summer, Clemo found himself thinking more and more about Laura. She lit up his life and to his amazement, he seemed to be having the same effect on her. The only difficulty was finding time when they could be together without anyone else being with them. It was an exquisite agony. He ached to be with her. Alone.

It was Joan who recognised that the initial affectionate attraction between Clemo and Laura was blossoming rapidly into love and decided to ensure that the process could flourish. She said one day, whilst Laura and Clemo were talking together in the shop, that she had to pop out for a while to see Issy, and could they look after the shop for her? 'Yes. Mistress Joan,' said Laura demurely, lowering her eyes. Clemo looked hot and embarrassed. Joan left. They were on their own. For the first time. No one could see them. No one could interrupt. Just the two of them.

Clemo and Laura stood facing each other, each unable to speak, each wanting the other to break the silence. Then Clemo, his heart thumping, said very hesitantly, 'Laura, may I kiss you?' Laura replied, 'I don't know about that,' and flung her arms around his neck and kissed him. That first kiss seemed to last for ever. When they finally tore themselves from each other's embrace they looked at each other deeply. Neither spoke, until Laura said that perhaps she ought to tidy the shelves and Clemo announced that perhaps he should go home. They both paused, and then moved hesitantly towards each other and kissed again, their arms entwined around each other's bodies.

'I really must go now, Laura' said Clemo, pulling himself away from her, 'but am I allowed to say one thing more? Only I'm not very good with words...'

'That's not true Clemo, what about your speech at the Guildhall; people talked about it for weeks afterwards.'

'Well, yes, they might have done, but I have never said to anyone what I am about to say to you, and...,' he paused. She waited. 'Laura, I love you.' He blurted the words out and made as if to leave. Laura's eyes shone. 'And do you know what, Clemo?' she replied, 'I love you too...' They kissed again, this time for what seemed to be an eternity. Time stopped, and something more mysterious and beautiful took its place.

And then Clemo, clearing his throat and picking up his cap, announced that he really had to leave because he had to get home and Laura said that he had better go because she really did have to tidy the shelves. At the door, Clemo paused. 'Am I forgiven for kissing you, Laura?'

'What do you think?' she said, and laughing, threw a balled-up kerchief at him.

He walked back across the wooden bridge with his heart singing. He had declared his love. She had declared her love. Could anything be more wonderful?

When he reached the cottage, his mother greeted him, noticed his radiant colour and sparkling eyes and said, 'I imagine you have been to the shop to see Joan?'

'Yes, Mam'.

'And let me guess…Laura Davies was there?'

'Yes, Mam.' He tried not to look in his mother's direction and felt colour rising to his cheeks.

'She is a lovely young woman, Clemo. You could do a lot worse than marry her.'

The blatant suddenness of his mother's statement left him reeling. The fact that he had thought of nothing else for months but marrying Laura must have become obvious to her. How did mothers know? Did they have an extra-special sense?

He stuttered his reply. 'I think she's lovely, Mam…but how did you guess that I was seeing her?'

'Never you mind how I knew…so what are you going to do about it? You're now seventeen, you'll soon be eighteen. It's time to marry.' She bent over and stirred the fire.

Clemo was lost for words and struggled to respond. 'I shall need to think about it.'

'Don't take too long, *cariad*. You know the saying, "strike whilst the iron is hot". Take heed to it. And if you married Laura, we might have two weddings this year.'

'What on earth do you mean?'

'Issy and Gwyn Evans have come to an agreement.'

'Gwyn?'

'Yes, Gwyn. I don't suppose he has ever said anything to you?'

'No. Not a thing.'

'Well, let me tell you, he has almost worn out the path coming up from Redbrook.'

'But I've never seen him in Monmouth.'

'Clemo, you are such a dreamer. Of course, you haven't. He has been meeting Issy in Joan's shop. He's been pretending to come to see his cousin Dai, but really…'

'…he's been seeing Issy.' Clemo finished his mother's sentence for her and sat down heavily in the chair opposite. Sometimes, the ways of people and the world completely eluded him.

'When are they going to get married?'

'Probably in August.'

'And where will they live?'

'Actually, Issy has been very lucky. Gwyn's grandfather had a house and land at Raglan, but when he died, the house and land passed to Gwyn's father, and Gwyn's father is going to let Issy and Gwyn live there.'

'Goodness! I am so pleased for Issy, but she will miss living near you, Mam.'

'And I shall miss her popping in very much…but at least Joan is still close by, and, in any case, Raglan is not many miles away.'

'Everything seems to be changing so fast', said Clemo, resting his head on his hands and staring at the fire. 'But at least I can stay here, can't I?'

'Of course you can, but I want you to promise me two things; firstly, that you will continue learning Latin with Father Burley, and secondly, that you will consider very carefully marrying Laura. She really is a most loving young woman and would make a wonderful partner for you.'

'Alright, Mam. I promise that I shall continue learning with Father Burley. I love Latin, you know, though goodness knows whether I shall ever have a chance to use it. Latin and working at the Foundry don't exactly fit together. And as for Laura…am I allowed to broach the subject of marriage with her?'

'Most certainly. But she won't be surprised when you do…'

'Oh! Mam, why do you think she won't be surprised? I should have thought she would be astonished. In any case, she might turn me down.'

'Don't be so silly, Clemo. Why would she? You're a fine and lovely son and you'll make a fine and lovely husband. Now, it's time for supper.' She creaked her way out of the chair and laid the table with bread, meats and ale.

They said a prayer of thanks and ate in companionable silence, until Clemo spoke.

'Mam, I won't take too long before I speak to Laura, I promise you but there's another question, "Where shall we live"?'

'Well. You can live with me, or I'm sure that Mistress Davies will be able to find room for you in her house. She has slightly more room than I have. And as she's a widow, like me, she'll enjoy your company.'

'Do you know Laura's mother, Mam?'

'Of course I do. She and I have been going to Mass together at Dixton since long before you were born and her late husband was a relative of your Uncle John, Aunt Megan's husband.'

'What kind of relative?'

'Mistress Davies' husband was Uncle John's second cousin. But apart from that and in any case, I see Mistress Davies very often on Market Day and sometimes after Market we call in to Joan's shop together for a chat. I suppose you might say that we are friends and have been for years.'

Clemo could not take it all in. So, in perplexed silence, he finished supper. His mother, knowing how his mind worked said nothing further and cleared away the plates and pots. And then, instead of sitting down with his mother he said that he was going out for a walk with Toby.

Laughing, his mother replied, 'That's a good idea, Clemo but mind you stay this side of the river!'

It had been a tumultuous day. There had been those kisses with Laura in the shop. He could still taste her lips on his, a taste of a sweet, unknown and luscious fruit. And then his mother, out of the blue, had told him that he and Laura should marry. Moreover, it seemed that Issy and Gwyn were going to get married as well. And it also appeared that his mother and Mistress Davies had known each other well for a long time.

He pondered all these things carefully, in his distraction even allowing Toby to wander further away than usual. He looked across at Dixton and said to himself, 'That's where Laura, my future wife, lives'. He turned the thought over and over in his mind, relishing it, savouring it. He felt that he was on the verge of exploding with delight, and looking up to heaven, whispered his thanks to his patron saint, St Clement. And then looked across the river again for a very long time.

On his way back home, whilst still pondering the events of the day, he realised that he felt as if he were caught in a golden, gossamer web. And he asked himself, who had spun it? There were several spinners, he thought; his sister Joan was one, his mother was another and Mistress Davies… was she another? He wondered how long the spinning had been going on. Furthermore, he contemplated whether Laura had been part of that web-making? He found it difficult to believe that she might have been. Surely, she was as innocent as he was? But she was a delightfully astute person, so could she have remained in ignorance of what all those other women were doing?

And what part had he played in all of this? He wasn't just a plaything of others; he really, really loved Laura, and that was his choice; no-one else had made it for him, had they?

Golden web or not, he decided that he revelled at being caught in it. In any case, he said to himself, 'Perhaps I might just be imagining all this subtle plotting.'

When he arrived back at the cottage, the fire had burnt low and his mother had gone to bed, but in the hearth, he saw that she had placed some sticks and coals in the shape of a heart. He smiled and softly climbed the ladder to his room.

Chapter 11: Tintern Abbey

The following day, once Clemo had arrived at the Foundry, he sought out Gwyn to tease him.

'You're good at keeping secrets, Gwyn…all that walking to Monmouth, I wonder what that was for?'

'I've been visiting my cousin, Dai.'

'Of course, and it just happens, by chance, as everyone seems to know except me, that you have been seeing my sister Issy in Joan's shop.'

Gwyn blushed and looked at the floor.

'And I gather that you are planning to marry Issy this year.'

There was a long pause. Then Gwyn shyly admitted that that was true, and he mentioned also that he and Issy were going to live in Raglan.

'So, no more Foundry for you, Gwyn?'

'No, afraid not.'

'Have you got enough land to live off?'

'I have been extremely fortunate; my grandfather owned some land which now that he has died, has come to me. And I can't wait to look out across it from the farmhouse and consider how I might work it.' His eyes lit up. 'I've enjoyed working here but I have come to the conclusion that I'm really an open-air person.'

'I shall miss you, Gwyn.'

'But just think,' said Gwyn smiling, 'you will be my brother-in-law.' He thumped Clemo on the shoulder, and Clemo responded by doing the same in return, 'And just think Gwyn, you will be hitched for life to my lovely, gorgeous, bullying sister…'

It was at this point in the conversation that the Boss turned up.

'Clemo, you will have heard that Gwyn will soon be leaving us. It's a great shame, but the Foundry has to develop, and I want you to explore again the pewter side of things.'

In the weeks that followed, Clemo spent more and more time in the Moulding Shed with Harry Jones, developing and refining the products they wanted to make. Clemo suggested that in addition to plates and tankards they should make Pilgrim Crosses and Medallions of the Virgin Mary. It was agreed that that would be Clemo's speciality, whilst Harry would concentrate on the bigger items, the plates and tankards.

Once Clemo and Harry were satisfied with the quality of their respective products, they had a conversation with the Boss about possible markets for them.

He responded by inspecting their wares with assiduous care and then, having pronounced himself satisfied, said to Harry that he ought to go into Monmouth, get himself a stall and see how sales might go. And to Clemo he said, 'I think you should take some samples to Tintern, Clemo. They get pilgrims at the abbey who might want evidence to take home that their pilgrimages have been properly completed. The next time Evan Prosser comes to the Foundry ask him to take you back to Llandogo with him and you can walk to Tintern from there.'

Clemo felt very excited about the prospect but added that he would not really know what to say once he arrived at the abbey.

'Clemo', said the Boss, 'after that speech at your father's funeral, I think you will find the right words. Trust yourself.'

It was that boost to his confidence that Clemo needed, and the Boss, whether knowingly or not, had provided it.

So, the next time that Evan Prosser turned up, Clemo collected his pewter crosses and medallions in a linen bag and asked if he could be taken on the return journey to Llandogo.

It was agreed that that would be no trouble, and when they set out it was a glorious summer morning. The woods on either side of the valley tumbled down towards the river. In the fields that had been created along the riverbank, sheep and cattle were grazing.

'They lot,' said Evan, beckoning towards the fields, 'belong to the Abbey, the greedy wretches. That abbey has more land than they know what to do with. Why can't they give some to us poor people? That's what I want to know.' He lapsed into a grumpy silence.

At the Llandogo wharves, Clemo said farewell to Evan and strode out towards Tintern. As he left, he heard Evan shout, 'Just ask'em, Clemo, why they keep all the land for themselves.' Clemo waved his hand jauntily in response.

It took him about one hour of walking, and when the abbey came into view as he rounded a bend, the size and glory of the building took his breath away. He stopped and gazed. All that stone piled up and shaped into the largest, the most delicate pointed windows he had ever seen, and arches, and glass glistening in the sunlight, and lead covering the entire roof, from which, in the summer heat, little rivulets of warm air shimmered upwards, distorting the view of the woods on the riverbank opposite.

It made his own church of Dixton look extremely poor in comparison and he couldn't imagine how many monks and servants it would need to keep the whole place in good order. He walked towards it reverentially, quietening his footsteps on the grass verge of the road as it curled down to the gatehouse, and all the while he was awed by its size and its beauty.

He watched for a moment as some travellers ahead of him approached the gatehouse and rang the bell. A wicket gate opened, and a conversation ensued, then they were allowed in.

He took a deep breath and following the example of the travellers, rang the bell. A small aperture guarded by an iron grille in the wooden door, opened.

'Good afternoon, Sir,' he said, 'My name's Clemo Trelawney and I've come from Redbrook Foundry. May I come in?' He shifted the bag on his shoulder.

'What do you want?' asked a disembodied voice the other side of the grille.

'If you would let me in, I could show you.' He eased the bag from his shoulders to the ground.

'What's in the bag?' asked his interlocutor.

'Pewter crosses and medallions which I have made myself at the Foundry. I thought that pilgrims to the abbey might like them.'

'You'd better show me one. Hold it up so that I can see.'

Clemo dipped into his bag, pulled out a simple pewter cross which had a subtle, bluish grey patina, and held it up for the gatekeeper to see. He waited for a comment. None came, but the wicket gate swung open.

'You can come in. I'll call Master Cellarer. He deals with things like this. Wait there.'

Clemo stepped through the entrance. The gatekeeper was a man not much older than himself, thin and scrawny with huge hands and a livid scar across the bridge of his nose.

Clemo waited as the wicket door was firmly locked and bolted and watched as the gatekeeper loped away from him along a stone-flagged passageway. Clemo looked about him. He found himself in a narrow corridor with a strong oak door on his right-hand side. It was a forbidding kind of entrance, and apart from the wooden rafters above his head, did not have the beauty and grace of the buildings he had seen from further away. But he liked its solid simplicity.

He heard the gatekeeper returning. He was accompanied by a small monk wearing a white habit and a black scapula with, on his feet, dark brown sandals. His iron grey hair was shaved in a tonsure. He had a strong forehead, deep-set blue eyes, thin cheeks gouged by deep creases and thin, up-turned lips.

'This young man wants to see you,' said the gatekeeper to the monk, who stretched out his hand to shake Clemo's hand. His grip was firm, the skin hard and calloused. The thin lips parted in a tired smile.

'I understand that you work at Redbrook Foundry and have brought some things to show me. You'd better come this way.' He pushed open the oak door opposite and turning left, led Clemo into a hall. 'This is the Abbot's hall' said the monk, 'but he allows me to use it when I 'm seeing strangers who bring things they think the abbey might buy. There's a table just there. You can put your things on it.'

Clemo opened his linen bag and took out some crosses, and some medallions of the Virgin Mary, and placed them carefully on the polished wooden surface.

'And you made these?' asked the monk, picking up one of the medallions, looking at it carefully.

'Yes, I did,' said Clemo, hesitantly.

'They're rather lovely.' The monk turned the medallion over and over in his hands and then examined one of the pewter crosses. 'So why do you think we might want them?'

Clemo stammered his reply. 'I imagined that you would have pilgrims coming to the abbey and that they might want a reminder of their visit.'

'That's a good enough reason,' said the monk, not looking at him. 'I'm Brother Adam, by the way. Did you know we have a special statue of Our Lady here? It's Our Blessed Lady that most pilgrims come to see.'

'I'm afraid that I did not know that,' replied Clemo, 'but Father Burley has taught me a great deal about the Virgin, and I pray to her every day.'

'Do you really?'

'Yes, I do. My own name-saint is Clement. I'm very fond of him and he helps me greatly through his intercessions.'

'So, why 'Clement'? That's very unusual for someone from these parts.'

'It's because I'm named after him. My name is Clemo. It's the Cornish for Clement. My late father was from Cornwall, so that's how I got my name.'

'You are a very fortunate young man…and it sounds as though Father Burley is teaching you well'.

'He is. He is. He's even teaching me Latin.'

Clemo wondered if perhaps he had said too much, but somehow Brother Adam had drawn it out of him. And then he remembered that he was in the abbey to discover whether they might purchase his crosses and medallions. He tried to bring the conversation around to that by saying, 'I am sure you must have lots of things to do, Brother Adam. I mustn't take up any more of your time.'

'Life in an abbey is never rushed, Clemo. Perhaps you would like to see Our Lady's statue before we talk further, and you leave?'

'I should love that, thank you'.

'Come on then,' said Brother Adam, 'come with me.'

He led Clemo deeper into the abbey precincts and then stopped at the west end of the huge Church. He opened a door and there, created from a clean white stone was a statue of the Virgin Mary holding the Christ child in her arms. The statue was about five feet tall and stood on a solid wooden plinth. Next to it on the floor were posies of fresh flowers, and in front of it on a pricket stand, votive candles were burning. The floor on which the flowers were placed was shiny, worn smooth by the knees of devout pilgrims who had prayed there over the centuries.

The sight of the Virgin glowing white, somehow uniting humility and nobility, tenderness and majesty, in a building which soared above Clemo's head, combined with the flickering flames and the deep stillness of Brother Adam by his side, led Clemo to fall quietly to his knees in prayer. He recited the 'Ave Maria' under his breath, and brought to mind Laura, his mother and his sisters.

He felt he was in a profoundly precious and most holy place, a place where the prayers of ordinary people thronged the air. He looked up and sensed that his prayers were entwining themselves with the prayers of all those other unknown people who had also knelt there, and whose lives of anguish, loss, and suffering had, for a brief moment, in front of the Virgin, found consolation.

He slowly stood up. Brother Adam remained by his side, and whispered, 'She's very lovely, isn't she?'

Clemo simply nodded his assent. He had moved down to a place in his soul beyond words and needed time to come back up to the surface.

As they approached the door to leave, Clemo turned once more towards the Virgin, hoping that through gazing at her, her image would burrow its way deep into his soul.

Brother Adam, sensitive to the moment, waited outside until Clemo emerged into the bright sunlight.

They walked together back to the Abbot's Hall.

'You can see why we get so many pilgrims here, can't you?'

'I can indeed.' Clemo whispered in response.

'So, let's go and look at your crosses and medallions again, shall we?'

'Thank you, but compared with the Virgin they are nothing; they are so poor.'

'Don't put yourself down, Clemo, I think they are very lovely. It is obvious that you have put a great deal of love into them. People will sense that and will want to buy them. What we will do is to place them close to Our Lady; her presence will embrace and infiltrate them so that pilgrims can feel they are taking her home with them. Do you know, Pope John gave us a Bull saying that everyone who worshipped Our Lady in this abbey would receive an Indulgence?'

'Did he? It's no wonder that pilgrims come here, but she is so beautiful in herself that she doesn't really need the Holy Father to give her his approval, does she?'

Brother Adam frowned and decided that he and Clemo should leave their discussion of Our Lady and get down to business.

Clemo was still in a kind of daze and felt that he really did not want to talk of pence and groats and the numbers of crosses and medallions that the Abbey might order. But Brother Adam insisted that they should and soon they had come to an agreement.

Brother Adam said he would take all the crosses and medallions that Clemo had brought with him and handed over some coins as payment.

Clemo, now with an empty bag on his shoulder, and money in his pocket, made to leave.

'Before you go will you promise me, Clemo,' said Brother Adam, 'that you alone will make the crosses and medallions for us, and that you alone will bring each batch to us when they are completed?'

'Of course, Brother, it will be my privilege.' And then, a little to his surprise, he felt emboldened enough to say, 'But I too want to lay down some conditions'

'And what might they be?'

'…that each time I come to the abbey, I might be allowed to say my prayers in front of Our Lady?'

'Done,' said Brother Adam, smiling, and placing his hand on Clemo's shoulder guided him to the gatehouse door and waved to him as he walked up the slope to the lane that would take him home.

Chapter 12: Weddings

Over the next few weeks Clemo continued with his specialist work at the Foundry and each time he went to Tintern kept his promise to pray in front of the Virgin. The abbey had entered very deeply into his being, but despite that, he also spent a great deal of time thinking about his wedding.

He had been to see Mistress Davies to ask permission to marry Laura. The permission had been granted, tho' he was puzzled when Mistress Davies had said: 'We all saw it coming. I know your mother saw it, just as I did. She is pleased as well.' Had Mistress Davies and his mother been talking about the possibility of the marriage? Presumably, they had, so Clemo concluded that he still had much to learn about how families and friendships worked. Gently, but to his puzzlement, his world was expanding.

He had admitted to Mistress Davies that he still had to consider where he and Laura might live, but she had responded rapidly by saying that until they found somewhere else, they were welcome to stay with her.

Dates were fixed. First would be the wedding of Issy and Dai at Dixton. Clemo and Laura saw that event as a practice run for their own great day. Meanwhile, there were wedding clothes to be made; the bedroom allocated to them by Mistress Davies needed whitewashing. Laura made some very pretty curtains for the room and was working on a matching bed cover.

Clemo had never felt so happy. He was deeply in love with Laura and could not wait to begin living with her.

All was going according to plan when suddenly, Clemo and Laura were brought up with a jolt.

They were having supper with Clemo's mother. Laura was still a little shy of her future mother-in-law but was growing fond of her. The supper that evening had gone smoothly enough but Clemo thought his mother seemed worried and pre-occupied. After Agnes, helped by Laura, had cleared the table, and the utensils and plates had been washed in warm water in the large cauldron, the three of them sat down together around the fire.

Clemo asked his mother if she was alright. She replied that she was fine: 'Why do you ask?'.

'Because' said Clemo, 'you weren't your usual self tonight, as though you had something on your mind.'

Laura looked at Clemo, wondering if this might be a Trelawney family matter which she should not know about and therefore quietly suggested that perhaps Clemo could walk her home.

'Don't go, Laura,' Agnes responded, 'You are almost part of the family now, so you ought to stay and hear what I have to say.'

Clemo and Laura looked at each other.

'I've been meaning to tell you this for ages but there doesn't seem to have been the right opportunity, but I suppose tonight is it.'

She sighed, took a deep breath, twisted her fingers together and then began her story.

'As you know, ever since your father died, Clemo, I have been doing a bit of dairying at the Farm. I like it, and when you are out at work it means I have some company. Well…,' She paused, steeling herself to say the next sentence, 'Huw Griffiths at the Farm has been on his own for a couple of years since his wife died. and he has asked me to marry him.'

'Goodness, Mam', retorted Clemo, unable to take in what his mother had said.

Laura interposed with a kindly comment, 'That is lovely news, Mistress Agnes, isn't it, Clemo?

'Yes, it is,' he agreed, but he gazed into the fire for a moment and then continued, 'So, when is it to be?'

'We haven't fixed a date yet; we didn't want to do that until after I had told you.'

'And do Joan and Issy know?'

'Well, yes, I kind of hinted at it when I saw them, and I think they will be happy for me.'

'So that means', said Clemo, trying to adjust to the news, 'you will be leaving here and going to live up at the Farm.'

'Yes. But there is some good news for you two. As you know, Farmer Griffiths owns this cottage. We have rented it from him for years and he has promised me that if you want it, it can be yours.'

Clemo didn't know what to say. He was still trying to take it all in and then said, clumsily, 'But we have just finished decorating a room in Mistress Davies' house. Laura's made it really nice.' He looked across at her proudly and smiled. And then he added, 'Can I keep Toby?'

His mother smiled her assent. That was one decision she knew she would have to make, and in the face of Clemo's child-like exuberance she had made it easily.

Laura interjected, 'I'm sure my mother won't mind if we tell her that unexpectedly a house has come up for us to live in; she will be pleased for us, and, in any case, she can let my room out to a lodger.' Laura was already planning what she could do to the house they were currently sitting in.

'Oh Mam!' said Clemo, getting up from his chair and kissing her on the cheek. 'What an amazing surprise.'

'So, it hadn't crossed your mind, Clemo?'

'No, not at all.'

'And you didn't realise when you found that heart made from sticks and coals in the hearth, a little while back?'

'No.'

'I'm embarrassed to admit it,' said Agnes, 'but, sitting here one night when I was on my own, I was thinking of Huw, so I made that heart and it was only after you had come home, and after I had gone to bed that I realised I had left it lying around. It was stupid. You must think I'm like a giddy fourteen-year-old.'

Clemo didn't answer immediately, trying to come to terms with the fact that he had thought the heart had been left there for him. He turned to Laura: 'What do you think, Laura?'

Laura leaned across to touch Agnes gently on her arm and said, 'I think love is so wonderful it's too precious to be wasted just on us young ones, so I am very, very happy for you, Mistress Trelawney.'

And at that moment Clemo was so proud of Laura that he wanted to hug her. She seemed to know by instinct what were the right words to say.

When Clemo walked Laura home later that evening they discussed what Clemo's mother had said. Clemo admitted that he had been taken completely by surprise, but also expressed the thought that living in the cottage with Laura as his wife made him incredibly happy. He left Laura at her mother's house but only after a series of long and gorgeous kisses. When he needed to tear himself away, he asked Laura to think about what she would do to the cottage. 'I already have,' she replied, laughing, and pushed him in the chest, saying, 'Good night Clemo, my future husband.' She turned and ran into the house.

Clemo slowly walked back across the bridge, paused to look at the river, and when he arrived home, he found his mother still sitting by the fire lost in thought.

He assured her that he was very happy for her and they then discussed possible dates for his wedding and for hers, and for Issy and Gwyn, and concluded that Issy and Gwyn should be the first to marry, then his mother and Farmer Huw should be the next because that would leave the cottage free for Clemo and Laura.

The following weeks were taken up with the preparations for all the weddings. Issy and Gwyn's wedding went really well; they seemed really happy, then Huw and Agnes married, with sober and staid rejoicing as befitted a middle-aged couple, but the after-wedding party was made even happier when Joan announced that she was expecting a baby. Issy looked at her sister with something like jealousy, and Clemo squeezed Laura's hand and whispered, 'Us next?' Laura shushed him but squeezed his hand in return.

Laura soon set about cleaning and organising the cottage. She finished the bedcover she had been making and carried the featherbed mattress across from her old house to the new one. Clemo discovered that he was quite useful with a paint brush and set about whitewashing every room in the house. He even managed to clean the window shutters by scrubbing them with water and vinegar, and made sure that the sheep, hens and cattle in the smallholding were in good shape.

Then came the great day of his wedding. Clemo put on a new white linen tunic, dark woollen trousers, a leather belt, a leather sleeveless jerkin, and a new Monmouth cap which had been dyed a deep blue. On the cap he had pinned a pewter brooch he had made with the entwined initials C and L. He walked across the bridge with his mother and Farmer Huw, feeling nervous and excited and saw his sisters and their husbands waiting at the church porch with Laura and her mother.

Laura was wearing a simple yellow fustian skirt, a white cotton blouse and over it, a bodice of deep red felted wool held together at the front with leather lacing. On her head she wore a white cotton coif but had added a circlet of flowers and was carrying a posy of the same flowers from her garden. All her clothes she had made herself, and as Clemo exclaimed to his mother as they drew close, 'She is so lovely.' His mother agreed; 'Radiant', she said.

Father Burley welcomed everyone at the church door and explained that no-one had objected to the marriage when he had called the Banns on the previous three Sundays. He then listened as Clemo and Laura made their marriage vows to each other. Clemo took from the pocket of his jerkin a gold ring (most of his earnings at the Foundry had been saved for the ring). He placed the ring on the Bible held by Father Burley who blessed it, and then instructed Clemo to take the ring from the Bible and place it on the fourth finger of Laura's right hand. It was a moment Clemo would never forget. It was as though heaven had embraced earth. Father Burley then led the wedding party into the church for a Mass. Clemo and Laura knelt at the altar and towards the end of the service a veil was placed over their heads; Father Burley pronounced the Blessing, and they were man and wife.

They almost skipped down the aisle, thanked everyone for coming to the wedding and led the entire party back to their house where two of Farmer Huw's servants had prepared a meal of meats, cheeses, bread and ale, and a friend from the Foundry was playing a fiddle in the corner.

Gwyn joshed Clemo by asking about the pewter initials on his hat and pretended not to know what they signified. 'Classic Lover' responded Clemo, at which point Laura naughtily added, 'That is yet to be seen'. Father Burley led everyone towards the marriage bed, pronounced another blessing over it and after everyone had left, Clemo and Laura were alone.

He felt strangely shy and apprehensive, and said to Laura that whilst she was getting ready for bed. he would go out to say 'Goodnight' to Toby. The dog, as always, greeted him ecstatically. Clemo knelt down next to him, put his arms around the dog's neck and whispered into the dog's ear, 'Toby. I am the luckiest man in the world.' And having patted him, went back into the house.

The following weeks passed in a dreamy haze. Clemo went off to the Foundry each day; Laura adjusted to running the house and continued her work in Joan's shop as well as joining Agnes at the farm to help with the dairy. She wanted to learn as much as she could about being a housewife, and under instruction from Agnes she also learnt how to brew ale.

In the evenings she and Clemo took stools outside the cottage door and in the summer warmth gazed at the river, watching its lazy whirlpools and the insects that hovered abstractedly over the water.

One evening she asked Clemo to teach her how to write, and he willingly did so, carving the quills for her pen and painstakingly guided her hand as she traced out the letters of the alphabet. She was a willing pupil; he was a willing teacher.

One night a little later, sitting together looking at the river, when the faint coolness of Autumn had begun to steal the summer away, Laura asked Clemo if they could go inside because she was feeling cold. He told her to build up the fire whilst he stayed outside to enjoy the remains of the twilight. It was a time of the day that he loved, the sense that nature was preparing herself for a long sleep, and the sun was sinking down for a rest before chivvying them up from their snug bed the following morning. He looked around meditatively, and slowly went inside.

Laura was sitting by the fire, her hands folded in her lap. He stood looking at her and said, 'Laura, my sweeting, I love you so much, I think my heart is going to break.' And he moved towards her to kneel at her feet.

'Don't say that', she replied, ruffling his hair, 'you are going to need all your heart-strength for when our baby arrives.'

He remained kneeling, looking up at her, his eyes wide with shock. The firelight cast its soft and flickering light on Laura's face.

'What are you saying, Laura? Are you saying what I think you might be saying?'

She placed her warm hands either side of his face and replied, looking down at him, 'Yes, my darling Clemo-of-the-green-eyes, you are going to be a father.'

He was dumbstruck. Words lodged in his throat and would not emerge. But finally, he stammered, 'Laura, you are absolutely amazing. And I must take care of you even more.'

'Clemo,' she replied, 'that is lovely of you, but it won't be necessary. I am not the first woman in the world to have a baby. We shall manage fine, and all we have to do for a while is to carry on as normal. Do you think you can manage that?'

'I shall try,' he replied, 'but it will be hard.'

'What you can do to help me most is to go as often as you can to Tintern and pray to the Virgin that all will be well.'

'I shall do that, my hearts' gleam, and you can be sure that my prayers for you will fill the entire world with longing and love.'

'The world's a bit big,' she replied, laughing, 'just filling Hadnock will do.'

Chapter 13: The dream ends

Joan gave birth to a little boy. She had been safely delivered. The baby was strong. Dai was visibly proud and in the privacy of their home would often cuddle the little one, gazing into its eyes and murmuring nonsense words.

Issy came to visit and brought a wooden rattle for the baby, stayed overnight, and had a long and delicious chat with Joan, mostly about the plans Gwyn had for the farm {'He's taken to farming like a duck to water') before she reluctantly begged a lift back to Raglan from a carter she knew.

Laura, during the last couple of weeks of Joan's pregnancy had managed the shop on her own and had done so with growing confidence and composure. She had talked at length about babies with Joan, all the while resting her hand upon her stomach.

Then, one evening, just after Clemo had returned from work, Laura's waters broke.

'Go and fetch your mother quickly,' she said. Clemo rushed out of the house and ran along the lane to the farm, his mind whirling. He banged on the door. A young maid answered. He told her that he needed urgently to speak with Mistress Griffiths (the name seemed incongruous as he uttered it) because his wife needed her to come to the cottage immediately.

Before he had finished talking, his mother arrived at the door.

'Mam, Laura needs you. Her waters have broken.' He gabbled the words in his anxiety.

'It's what happens, Clemo,' she said to steady him, and tied on a clean pinafore taken from a chair by the door, grabbed a shawl which she threw around her shoulders and picked up a reed-woven bag covered with a cloth.

'You're very prepared, Mam.'

'Of course I am. I knew that she must be getting close to her time, so I had got a few things ready.'

She shouted out to Huw, 'Laura's waters have broken, so I'm going to see her and I'm taking Annie with me, if that's alright with you. We shall need her to run errands.'

There was an answering affirmative grunt from somewhere in the depths of the house.

She called the young maid to her.

'Annie, get your shawl and come with me.'

The little girl, in a mob cap and blue apron tied over her long blue woollen dress, reappeared with her red shawl.

'Right' said Agnes, 'off we go.'

They set off quickly and Agnes explained that Annie would be a real help. She was the oldest of five and was used to babies arriving, 'Isn't that so, Annie?'

'Yes. Mistress Griffith,' answered the girl, looking pleased to have had one of her talents recognised.

Clemo tried to break into a run to get to Laura ahead of them. But his mother grabbed his arm very firmly.

'Clemo, from this moment on, you are not to come into the cottage. This is for women only.'

'But she's my wife,' he expostulated.

'True, but giving birth needs women. It doesn't need men. What you can do is go across to Mistress Davies, tell her what has happened and suggest she comes across, and then you go and stay with Joan.'

'But…'.

'Clemo, no "buts". We'll call you when there's any news. It could be a while yet. We shall send Annie to fetch Mistress Jenkins, the midwife, when we need her, so you should go to the Foundry as normal in the morning.'

His mother's voice was firm. Annie looked at Clemo with the kind of withering contempt that only twelve-year-old girls can muster. 'Didn't he know anything about how things worked?' she thought to herself.

At the door of the cottage Clemo hesitated, said 'Give Laura my love' and walked hurriedly on. He felt hopeless and inadequate, shut out by his own mother...

He ran to Dixton and told Mistress Davies what had happened. She replied that she would go across immediately. She too had a bag ready by the door, and he then made his way to Joan's.

On his arrival he explained all that had happened. Joan was nursing her own baby who was nuzzling at her neck and stretching its hands towards her face. She bent over, held the baby's little hand in hers and kissed it. Dai greeted him and said, 'Welcome to being a man, Clemo. We men can do most things but those of Eve's race know far better than we what needs to be done when it comes to having babies. Now come in, sit by the fire and I'll pour you a glass of Joan's finest ale. It's the best in Monmouth, I can tell you.'

Clemo slept little that night, waking at every sound, wondering if Laura was alright. In the morning, with great reluctance, he set off for work and on his way across the wooden bridge looked towards the cottage to see if there were any signs of life. There were none. He walked along the lane to Redbrook and must have appeared haggard when he arrived because Harry Jones in the Moulding Shed asked him what was troubling him.

'It's Laura, she's giving birth and I've been banned from the house.'

'Just as well, Clemo, leave it to the women. They know what to do. Now, what are we working on this morning?'

Clemo did his best to concentrate but found it difficult. The day passed with agonising slowness. At every moment he expected a messenger to arrive. Harry, sensing his anxiety, said 'Worrying won't bring the baby any quicker, Clemo. Save your strength for later. You'll need it. Becoming a father changes thing more than you can ever imagine, and I've been a father six times.' He paused, 'but only three survived, alas!' It was said in a matter-of-fact way, but the slight tremor in Harry's voice made Clemo realise that the loss of three of his children had bitten deeply into Harry's heart.

They worked steadily that afternoon but half an hour before the usual departure time, Harry looked at Clemo and said, 'Why don't you go back home. See what's happened.'

Clemo thanked him, and with his head hunched down against the beginnings of a heavy shower of rain, walked rapidly back towards Hadnock. Just as he got to the entrance of Hadnock Lane he saw Mistress Jenkins coming towards him. Her head too was down, and she didn't see Clemo immediately.

'Mistress Jenkins,' he called out, 'have you been to Laura? Has the baby arrived?' The words tumbled out.

'Clemo, I'm very sorry. It's not good news,' she said, 'Your little baby boy was almost dead when he came into the world and I'm afraid that he has already passed on.'

Clemo uttered a loud groan, a deep, animal growl of anguish.

Mistress Jenkins stayed with him, waiting for his first grieving agonies to quieten.

He lent on the balustrade of the bridge, watching the oily dark waters flowing past. When he had recovered sufficiently to find some words he said, 'Oh! that's terrible, terrible.' He paused and then added, 'And how is poor Laura?'

'She's resting, but she lost a lot of blood, so when you go in, don't be too alarmed by how she looks, will you?'

Clemo took off his cap and twisted it in his hands. Tears streamed down his face. He sobbed and tried hard to choke back the sound of his crying. He brushed the tears roughly from his face. He knew that there was something that needed to happen but for a second could not find what he wanted to say, but then it came back to him; he asked, 'Mistress Jenkins, did you baptise the baby whilst he lived?'

'I did…'

'And was it in the name of the Holy Trinity?'

It was her turn to cry, quietly. 'Clemo, I did what I could. I am so sorry.'

He could say no more but turned away, left her, and tore down the lane. He pushed open the door. His mother's face told him everything. She said, 'Clemo, my sweetheart…' wanting to enfold him in her arms. But he eased her away, calling out, 'Where's Laura? Where's the baby?' His eyes were red, wild with grief and anxiety.

'She's in your bedroom. Her mother's with her. Please be very gentle when you go in to see her.'

He wanly smiled his thanks, tapped lightly on the bedroom door, and walked in. Mistress Davies was sitting next to the bed stroking her daughter's hand and tenderly bathing her forehead with a damp cloth.

Laura lay propped up by pillows. She was very, very pale. He knelt by the bed, took her hand in his and whispered, 'Laura, it's Clemo.' Her eyelids flickered but she did not open her eyes. Her lips were parted but her breathing was shallow. From time to time, she made little panting sounds and all the while her mother bathed her forehead. Her cheeks were flushed as though she was developing a fever.

Clemo was in despair. This was his most beloved, most cherished, most wonderful wife, but she did not seem to know that he was there.

He whispered again, 'Laura, my sweeting, it's me, Clemo. You're going to be alright…' His eyes looked up into the eyes of Mistress Davies and saw in them a deep and resigned sadness, as though she were already accepting defeat. It was a look of such anguished and embattled maternal love that he knew he would never forget it.

He switched his eyes away and saw in the small wooden cot next to the bed, (the cot which he had so lovingly made) a tiny face, its eyes closed, looking asleep. On his knees he shuffled towards it and let his tears fall on the child's counterpane. It was made from pale blue wool edged with pink ribbon and he recalled how Laura had brought the ribbon from Joan's shop and had created the counterpane during the previous months.

'We were going to call him Jestin,' he said. 'It was my Cornish grandfather's name'. He reached out and lightly touched the baby's head and nose. He bent double over the cot, willing himself not to weep loudly.

Finally, under slightly more self-control, he rose to his feet. Mistress Davies was still batheing Laura's face, but even in the few minutes he had been in the bedroom Clemo thought that Laura looked paler than before, alabaster-white, but her cheeks were feverishly red.

'Thank you so much, Mistress Davies, for all you are doing.'

'She's my daughter,' she said, 'my darling daughter.' She touched Laura's hair, but it had become moist with perspiration and was sticking to her forehead.

'I'll be back in a moment,' he said and tiptoed out of the room.

His mother was waiting for him.

'Mam, is she going to be alright?'

'I don't know, son; she's young, she's strong, but perhaps if God has taken the baby, he might want Laura as well to look after him.'

It was not the kind of thing that his mother normally said, but for the moment it gave him comfort.

'I met Mistress Jenkins on the way home, and she told me that she had baptised Jestin'

'Yes, she did.'

'Well, that's something, though I hope she used the right words.'

'I'm sure she will have done; she is an experienced midwife.'

Clemo felt his mind flicking from one thought to another. 'What about Father Burley, does he know?'

'I expect Mistress Jenkins will tell him'.

There was a long pause in the conversation as they both gazed at the fire.

'Mam, please tell me that Laura will be alright.'

She looked across at him, waited to make a decision, and then said, 'Why don't we send for Father Burley?'

'But the baby's been baptised. Father Burley can't do any more.'

Agnes realised that Clemo had not grasped how sick Laura was and had interpreted her suggestion about calling Father Burley to be about the baby, when really she had meant…

She decided to leave Clemo in his state of bewilderment, but continued, 'I'll send Annie across to fetch him.'

She called Annie who was outside with Toby and told her to go for Father Burley.

'Can I take Toby with me?'

'Yes, of course.'

'And what message am I to say to Father?'

'Just say that Laura is very, very sick, and that the baby has died… he'll know what to do.'

Annie hurried off, holding Toby as firmly as she could on the end of his chain.

Agnes returned to the house and found Mistress Davies in the room.

'I've left Clemo in the bedroom on his own,' she said, 'He needs to be with her.'

She began to weep quietly. Agnes enfolded her in her arms and explained that she had sent for Father Burley. Both women, wordlessly, knew what that meant. Mistress Davies nodded her head, her grey hair slipping out from under her coif.

Clemo emerged. 'I think Laura might be a bit better,' he said, 'I spoke her name and I think she heard me. But I'm going back in to sit with her again.'

The two women looked at each other but said nothing.

A few minutes later Annie came back and said 'Father Burley's on his way. Shall I put Toby outside now?'

'No. He can stay inside as a treat Annie, but you must sit with him in the corner and keep him quiet.' Annie looked as though she had been given the Crown jewels. She took Toby into the shadows and sat on the floor beside him, stroking him and whispering little sounds of endearment.

The dog's ears pricked up at the sound of footsteps outside and he began to growl.

It was Father Burley. He had been accompanied by a young boy carrying the processional cross, and another young boy who was carrying the oils for anointing.

Father Burley spoke quietly to Agnes and Mistress Davies and asked where Clemo was.

'In the bedroom with Laura,' replied Agnes softly, 'but I don't think he realises how gravely ill Laura is. If you could give her the sacrament and anoint her, I think that Clemo might begin to understand.'

Father Burley ordered the boys to accompany him into the bedroom. They both looked frightened.

Father Burley tapped on the door. Clemo opened it and saw the two boys in their robes, one with the Cross, the other holding in his left hand a glass cruet filled with oil and in his right hand, a strip of white linen cloth. Clemo looked at Father Burley and thanked him for coming and said again that he thought Laura might be getting a little stronger.

Father Burley nodded and entered the room. Laura's cheeks looked extremely feverish; perspiration was breaking out across her forehead. Clemo called to his mother and Mistress Davies to join them and with tenderness Mistress Davies wiped the beads of perspiration from her daughter's forehead.

Father Burley gathered himself and said to Clemo,'Laura's been through a very difficult time, and it might be that she is now so tired that all she wants is to slip away and be with her baby, the angels and the saints…'

Clemo coughed to stifle a sob. Tears were slipping silently down Mistress Davies' cheeks. The boys who had come with the priest had never been at a deathbed before and they were pale with anxiety. Father Burley conducted a brief service in which he anointed Laura with Holy Oil, asked the acolyte to pass him the linen cloth, but the boy in his anxiety dropped it and scrabbled down to retrieve it. A brief Mass was celebrated, and Father Burley placed a tiny fragment of the Host on Laura's tongue.

The room was so quiet it was as though time itself had stopped. Finally, Father Burley pronounced the Blessing and then ushered the boys ahead of him into the next-door room where Annie was still sitting in the corner with Toby. A log fell in the hearth, flames suddenly flickered up the chimney and then died down again.

Agnes, Mistress Davies and Clemo came through to thank Father Burley. And Clemo said that he would come to see Father Burley the following day to talk about the baby's funeral.

Father Burley nodded his thanks to them all and accompanied by the boys, who looked very relieved that their ordeal was over, was taken back to Dixton in procession.

Back in the cottage, Agnes suggested that she and Mistress Davies should take it in turns to sleep in what had once been Joan and Issy's room. 'We'll leave Clemo with Laura,' she said, and then she remembered Annie and said to her, 'Annie, you must go back to the farm.' Annie's face fell. 'But you can take Toby with you.' Her face lit up.

Clemo, exhausted and numb, kept vigil at Laura's bedside.

Chapter 14: The end of the vigil

E arly the next morning, Agnes Trelawney climbed down the ladder, poked at the dull remains of the fire, threw on some kindling and waited for it to catch alight before placing some logs and coal on the tiny, uncertain flames. She poured water into the wooden bucket that stood next to the fire for Mistress Davies and Clemo to use for washing, and then quietly pushed open the bedroom door. Clemo was fast asleep on top of the bed, his hand lightly touching Laura's hand. Agnes looked at Laura. All the colour had drained from her face. Her eyelids were almost closed but not quite. Agnes watched to see if she was breathing, but the bed covers did not move. Laura was dead.

She left the room very quietly, climbed up the ladder to wake Mistress Davies and told her as gently as she could, the terrible news. Mistress Davies' hair was unkempt, her eyes unfocussed as she woke, her clothes awry. She looked with bewildered and agonised horror at Agnes, hauled herself up from the straw mattress and followed Agnes downstairs.

Clemo was still asleep, but perhaps sensing that someone had entered the bedroom, woke slowly. He looked across at Laura and then towards his mother and Mistress Davies. He reached out to hold Laura's hand but found that it was cold and then with another anguished look at the two older women, climbed off the bed rubbing his hair and his eyes. He looked back at Laura, his mind struggling to take in what he was seeing.

Agnes said, 'Clemo, my darling, you need to come to the fire. You've done everything you could for Laura but she, poor lamb, is not with us anymore.'

He crossed himself which prompted Agnes and Mistress Davies to do the same and then under his breath and as an ingrained automatic habit, said,' Requiem aeternam dona ei, Domine, et lux perpetua luceat ei. Requiescat in pace. Amen.' He fell to his knees, like one poleaxed and remained on his knees in front of the fire. He kept repeating, very quietly, the words, 'Laura', 'Jestin' over and over again. He didn't cry, he didn't wail, he was in that depth which is beyond the reach of sorrow. His agony was awful.

Agnes and Mistress Davies eventually helped him to his feet, but he was like one who has been suddenly blinded and struck dumb. No words, no sight, nothing except the most agonising pain gnawing at his heart. He moved slowly to the chair by the fire, looked at Mistress Davies and said, 'I am so sorry, Mistress Davies. Laura was the most beautiful daughter that anyone could have, and she was the most beautiful wife...' The words unlocked a stream of sobs, which, after a while, gradually subsided. Although he was with his mother and Laura's mother, he felt alone like he had never felt alone before. He had done something, he believed, which had killed his father, and now he had lost Laura and Jestin to the sharp-edged scythe of death. Their deaths too felt as though they were somehow his fault. He continued to look at the fire and, hunched over, rubbed his face with his hands saying repeatedly, 'I'm sorry. I'm sorry.'

There was a knock on the door. Annie stood there and said, 'I've brought Toby back and I wondered if there was anything I could do.'

Agnes hugged her and said that she was a very thoughtful girl and that there was something she could do; she could run to Mistress Jenkins' house and ask her to come right away.

'Is that all? Is there anything else I should say?'

'No. She will know why you have come but you can also go to Mistress Parry's shop and ask her if she could come here as well...'

'And what about Toby?'

'Just for now, Toby must stay with us, but you'll see him as soon as you get back.'

Although Agnes had placed some bread and cheese on the table, none of them felt like eating. Clemo remained where he was, gazing into the fire but seeing nothing. Mistress Davies asked if she might go and sit with her daughter, to which Clemo gave his nodded assent. Agnes went outside to fetch more coal and wood.

Annie returned, breathless from her errand, and explained that Mistress Jenkins was on her way and that Mistress Parry would be with them shortly. She was then told to run to the farm to see if Farmer Huw needed anything. She scurried away.

A knock on the door signalled the arrival of Mistress Jenkins with her capacious bag, her face careworn and saddened.

Agnes welcomed her and suggested that with Clemo's permission, she should go about her business. 'Is that alright, Clemo?' she asked. The question seemed to stir him out of his numbed despair, and he asked, with a voice dulled by pain, if Mistress Jenkins could tell him what she would be doing.

Her eyes flicked across to Agnes, and replied, 'Well, I shall wash Laura and make her look nice.'

'Thank you' replied Clemo, 'She was the most wonderful wife...' His voice tailed off into a stifled sob. Toby sidled up to him and lay with his body across Clemo's feet. Clemo bent down and fondled Toby's ears. 'How do you know, Toby? How do you know?'

Mistress Jenkins and Agnes went into the bedroom and there the three women, with extraordinary tenderness, washed Laura's body, dressed her in some new nightclothes they had found in a small cupboard, and brushed her hair. Once that had been done, coins were placed over Laura's eyelids and the bedclothes were smoothed out. They looked at the baby and had a whispered conversation about when Mistress Jenkins might return with the shrouds.

They came out of the bedroom and Agnes suggested that Clemo should now go in and look at Laura. He stood up very slowly and moved towards the bedroom. The women stood to one side and closed the door to allow him his privacy, but from beyond the door they could hear his stifled sobs. When he re-emerged, Mistress Jenkins had left, but the door opened, and Joan, having picked up the terrible news from Mistress Jenkins whom she had met as she walked towards the cottage, came in having left her baby with Dai. She went up to Clemo and hugged him tightly, smoothing his hair, and saying, 'O my brother Clemo! O my brother!' And he hugged her in return.

Unexpectedly, he then said, 'I must go to see Father Burley now...' and cramming his cap on his head (it still had the entwined initials 'C' and 'L' affixed to it), he walked out of the door. Joan asked if he would like her to go with him, but he replied that this was something he had to do by himself.

He called Toby to walk with him and shambled away like someone sleepwalking. The dog didn't leave his heels at any point so that when Clemo finally reached the Priest's house and knocked on the door he looked down and noticed Toby, as if for the first time.

Mistress Fielding answered the door. Clemo asked abruptly if she had some string to tie Toby up. She looked puzzled, said 'Yes' and went to fetch some, which Clemo immediately tied around Toby's neck and fastened the dog to a nearby tree. Mistress Fielding watched and Clemo brushed past her walking into the house saying, 'Thank you. Shall I go into Father Burley's room now?'

Looking a little alarmed by his uncharacteristic brusqueness, she went to find Father Burley, explained what had happened and suggested that Clemo might not be well and that without being given permission, he was already in Father's room.

'Ah,' replied Father Burley, grasping the leather belt around his black cassock, 'Let me go to see what might have happened.'

'Clemo!' he said as he entered the room, finding Clemo leafing through a book taken from the bookshelves.

'Father!'

'Did Augustine say anything about death?' asked Clemo, pointing to the book he was holding.

'Um…let's sit down and you can tell me why you want to know what Augustine thought.'

Clemo sat down, still grasping the leather-bound book. Father Burley, looking at him, saw a man in a deep crisis, behaving with uncharacteristic passion. He wondered whether Clemo might be suffering from possession and began in his mind to say repeatedly, 'In nomine Patris, Filii et Spiritus Sancti' as a kind of beneficent and protective charm.

'Father,,,please don't be alarmed…' said Clemo. 'I just wanted to know, that's all. Why won't you answer me?' His voice rose in anger. He placed the book on his knees, rubbed his hands together vigorously, tousled his hair and scoured his face with great force, leaving long red weals. 'Only you see… well, actually you can't see…I know that. You know that. You know you can't see really. You just pretend.' He stood up. The book fell with a thud on the floor. Clemo didn't notice. 'The thing is…,' he looked out of the window, saw Toby, and said, wildly, 'Toby can see. He really can. Do you think it's a miracle, Father? Are dogs, angels? Does the Devil deceive them, like he deceives us?' He sat down again. 'But Father, the river keeps flowing. Where does all the water go? Hey? Answer me that…' He stood up and paced frantically around the room swinging his arms. 'See, Father, you can't answer that, can you? You are so clever, but you don't know where the water goes…Hah!'

He resumed his seat, rested his head on his hands and breathed deeply. Father Burley looked at him and waited, still reciting to himself, 'In nomine…' Clemo's head lolled backwards. His eyes closed for a moment and, looking at the ceiling, he started muttering the 'Ave Maria…' extremely rapidly, his hands weaving backwards and forwards as though he were conducting music.

Outside, Toby barked.

'Oh, poor Toby, I left him tied up…I am sorry. I am sorry. Father, I am so sorry. I am really sorry.' And he burst into tears that shook his whole body.

Father Burley remained attentive, pulled from his cassock pocket a rosary, and with his other hand offered Clemo a handkerchief to dry his tears. Clemo took it, wiped his face and eyes, and then said, 'Father, am I really here with you? In your house?'

'Yes, Clemo, you are.' The rosary beads began to move steadily through the priest's fingers.

'So, why am I here?' asked Clemo, looking bewildered and scared.

'I think,' said Father Burley very quietly, 'that you might have come to tell me about something dreadful that has happened to you.'

Clemo looked down at his hands, then looked up and said, 'Father…I am so sorry…it's all coming back to me now.' He bent down and picked up the book at his feet, gazed at it and said, 'I think this must be yours.' He handed it to Father Burley who thanked him and placed it back on the shelves. He looked at Clemo and thought that the storm in Clemo's mind was beginning to ease. He suggested that instead of sitting in the room they should go for a walk, 'The fresh air will do us good'

Clemo hesitated but then agreed. Outside, he knelt to untie Toby, fondled the dog's head and said, 'Toby understands, Father…I know he does…'

They walked past the church and turned left along the riverbank. Father Burley continued to wonder whether Clemo had suffered an attack by the devil, or whether he needed bleeding by the town's barber surgeon to release the pressure of his choleric humour.

Clemo said nothing for a while but Father Burley sensed that he was stabilising. Perhaps saying 'In nomine…' was helping, and maybe that silent recital, plus the Rosary, had driven the devil away and peace was coming to Clemo's fractured soul. Crossing a lane, they began to climb a hill. Clemo remained silent, but at the top of the hill as they looked over the fields back towards Monmouth, he said again, 'I'm sorry, Father.' It was said with less fervour than previously and so Father Burley asked what Clemo was sorry about.

'Laura,' he replied simply, 'Laura and Jestin. First, it was my father's death and now…' His voice tailed off. After a few moments of recollection, he continued, '…and now Jestin and Laura have died. I am guilty of the deaths of three people, three people I loved…how can God forgive me? I am beyond forgiveness. Purgatory, Father, is here inside me, now, not in some future time. It's here, and I am in it…' He began to cry soundlessly.

Father Burley waited for the tears to cease, and then said, 'We'll walk back to the church now and there I will lay my hands on your head and say the words of the Blessing and God will be with you.'

Clemo stumbled alongside Father Burley as they made their way back down the hill. At the church Clemo made as if to tie Toby up outside but Father Burley said, 'There's no need to do that, Clemo; let him come in with us…'

Father Burley went to the altar, turned to face the kneeling Clemo, said the Pater Noster, and then moved to stand next to Clemo. Laying his hands on Clemo's head he said the Blessing. There was silence for a long while. Eventually, Clemo rose to his feet, urged Toby to get up, and said, 'Thank you, Father. Can we talk about the funeral now?'… which is what they did. They decided that the grave should be as close to the south wall of the church as possible so that the rainwater, having touched the roof of the church, could fall as a gift from God on Laura and her baby. 'It would be.' said Father Burley, 'A kind of perpetual sacrament.'

The idea seemed to further calm Clemo, and so, having organised the funeral and having said his thanks again to Father Burley, he walked slowly and meditatively back to the cottage.

Chapter 15: Decisions

The Requiem and burial of Laura and Jestin took place took place two days later. There were no processions, no acolytes, no candles, no pomp, though Father Burley had arranged that a crucifer should lead the bier from the house to the church. Laura's body, neatly wrapped in its shroud, lay on the bier and Agnes was about to place the baby next to her, when Clemo intervened. He said that he would carry the dead baby himself. The bier, which had been borrowed from the Guild, was carried by four strapping men from Huw Griffiths' farm. It began to drizzle; a soft summer shower falling out of light grey clouds.

The mourners were led by Clemo himself, holding the dead baby, with Mistress Davies next to him and behind were Agnes and Huw, followed by Joan and Dai, Issy and Gwyn. The final member of the party was Annie, who held Toby on his chain. She had asked Clemo's permission to come and he had told her that she could, and when she asked if she could bring Toby as well, he smiled gently and agreed that that was a lovely idea.

At the church, Father Burley welcomed them and the bier was carried in. Clemo placed the baby in its shroud on the bier next to Laura, looked around the tiny congregation and noticed that two of his colleagues from the Foundry were there, as well as the Boss. He was touched and strengthened by their presence. The Requiem began.

Father Burley gave a brief homily and took as his text, words from the Book of Job: 'Dominus dedit Dominus abstulit', 'The Lord gave, and the Lord has taken away'. Clemo did not hear the rest of the homily. It was the words of the text which troubled him. He could see that at one level the words were true. Was not the Creator of the world so powerful and so majestic that he could do anything he wanted, and so far beyond human understanding that men could not grasp his purposes and yet, and yet, he thought, was not that a form of tyranny? Could God not understand that he, Clemo, loved Laura and loved Jestin, so what kind of implacable cruelty was it that could rob him so arbitrarily of all that he held dear?

At the graveside, the Sexton received the body of Laura and placed it in the straw-lined grave. Then Clemo handed him the be-shrouded little body of his only son, and the Sexton placed the baby on Laura's bosom. Some earth fell from the side of the grave as the Sexton climbed out, and, in turn, the mourners, led by Clemo, took handfuls of earth and in silence threw them on to the bodies. Annie with Toby stood a little way off, watching.

Once that had been done, Clemo thanked Father Burley, went across to the Boss and his colleagues, and thanked them warmly for being there. He noticed that their eyes were wet with tears. The Boss put his strong arm on Clemo's arm but said nothing. The gesture was enough. Clemo moved to Annie, knelt down and rubbed Toby's head, then with Issy one side and Joan the other, locking their arms through his, they walked back to the house for the funeral meats which had been prepared by two of Farmer Griffiths' servants.

Agnes gently took charge of the proceedings, whilst Clemo stood silently by the fire. He wanted them to stay with him for ever and at the same time wanted them to go. As the afternoon wore on, first, Farmer Griffiths left ('I need to see to one or two things'), then Issy and Gwyn, ('We've got to get back to Raglan, which will take us a while'), then Joan and Dai, and Mistress Davies said that she ought to be getting home; to his surprise she came to him and kissed his cheek. He raised his hand to thank her and tried to speak but couldn't. Annie was told that she could take Toby as far as the bridge but that she should bring him back afterwards, tie him to his chain and then go back to the Farm. Meanwhile, the servants rapidly cleared away the food, placed everything in four large woven baskets, covered the baskets with cloths, and took them back to the Farm.

Agnes and Clemo were left on their own. The fire needed attention, which Agnes dealt with, and then spoke to Clemo.

'You have been through so much, Clemo, over the last few days… you will now need to rest for what is left of today, but my advice is that you should go back to work tomorrow. I'll come in after you have gone; Annie and I can see to the animals, and we'll tidy up and get things ready for when you get back…and once your first day at work is over, we can talk about how you are going to cope on your own. I can get you your food, so you won't need to worry about that. It will be easy enough for Annie to bring you your supper from the Farm, and I'll see to your washing…but now, as I say, please try to get some rest.'

She came towards him and hugged him. He hugged her back and thanked her. She closed the door as she left. He was on his own. He sat by the fire, staring at the flames, and sobbed until no more tears flowed from his eyes. He went outside. Toby rushed towards him at the end of his chain, his tail wagging. 'Come on Toby,' he said, 'We're going for a walk.' He turned to his right, out of the cottage, walked along the riverbank and stopped to look across at Dixton. He stayed there for a long while, ruminating on the day's events, and then with Toby beside him and the setting sun casting its glow on the river, walked slowly home. Tomorrow would be another day.

He took his mother's advice and walked to the Foundry. It was a glorious summer morning, blue skies, no clouds. At work, a few of the men came up to him to express their sympathy and then he took himself off to the Moulding Shed to create some crosses and medallions for Tintern. Although he felt numb, it was surprisingly calming work. And thus, the weeks wore on, but he was always glad to go to Tintern to deliver the pilgrims' tokens and to have a conversation with Brother Adam.

Something had been brooding in Clemo's mind since the funeral and he waited for whatever it was to emerge. It did, one day whilst he was talking with Brother Adam.

He had prayed in front of the statue of the Virgin but his prayers felt dry and lacklustre, few words had come, but suddenly an idea came into his mind. He should leave home. It was a place that constantly reminded him of his awful loss, so he should leave. Put it behind him. He expressed all of this to Brother Adam who listened attentively and then said, 'Maybe God is telling you something. Remember, he's not in the fire, nor in the whirlwind but in the still, small voice. And if you do leave, remember that there are Cistercian abbeys which will give you a bed for the night.' Clemo blurted out that he might make his way to London. And Brother Adam replied that if Clemo planned his route well, maybe he could stay at Flaxley Abbey on his first night.

Clemo thought about Brother Adam's words about God's Providence all the way home. They made sense. He would not rush his decision but would have a further chat with Father Burley, with his mother, and with Joan, and then come to a decision. His mother said that she thought he was being impetuous but if that was what he wanted to do then perhaps he should listen to the idea and see where it led. Joan said much the same. And Father Burley advised that whichever direction he went in, he should treat it as a pilgrimage, not a running away.

The more Clemo considered the idea of leaving home, the more it shifted from being a vague possibility to a firm and fixed determination. And it was whilst he was walking to Redbrook one day that he finally made his momentous decision. He had looked up and seen swallows gathering, ready for their departure. Where they went at the end of summer, he had no idea. He wondered if the traditional view that they buried themselves in the mud of rivers and ponds was true. He was not inclined to accept it. He had lived next to a river all his life and had never seen a swallow emerge from the mud. But that they left and went somewhere else, there could be no denying. It was the omen he needed. That same day he told the Boss that with his permission he would like to leave within one week. Ifor Young looked surprised but assured Clemo that if that was what he had set his mind on, he would not be too upset, but that Clemo would be sorely missed, he had no doubt. 'And' he added,' if ever you would like to come back, you will be very welcome'.

Over the next days, Clemo made arrangements for leaving. He told Annie that she could take Toby with her back to the Farm and made her solemnly promise that she would always look after him well. With wide-eyed seriousness, she agreed. He discussed with Farmer Huw and Agnes what his plans were. He told them, with more certainty in his voice than he felt, that he was going to strike out for London. Huw Griffiths responded by saying that Clemo could borrow one of the older horses. It was a most generous and selfless gesture for which Clemo expressed his deep gratitude. They came to an agreement that although the horse would be a loan, if Clemo needed to sell the horse at any time he should feel free to do so, but that he should save the money to repay his mother and Farmer Huw when he returned. He also went to see Father Burley to thank him for his support not only over the funeral but for all he had done over the years. When Clemo explained what his plans were, Father Burley wrote on a scrap of paper the name and address of one of his old Oxford colleagues who was the priest of St Mary Bowe and advised that once Clemo had arrived in London, he should seek him out for any help he might need. Then he asked Clemo to kneel, laid his hands on Clemo's head, and said a Blessing.

'Now, off you go, Clemo, on your 'pilgrimage'…and as we shall pray for you, please pray for us.'

Clemo shook Father Burley's hand warmly and walked back to the cottage for his final night in Hadnock.

The following morning, he went up to the Farm to collect the horse (it was called 'Bluey' because it was a dappled grey) and said farewell to his mother and Huw Griffiths. He rode back to the cottage, loaded his few belongings on to the horse, including a thick woollen cloak which he tied behind the saddle, looked around for a final time and urged Bluey to 'walk on'. At the end of the lane, at the point where he was to turn left and make his way up into the Dean Forest, he saw two figures waiting for him. One was Dai Parry who was also on horseback, the other was Annie with Toby. It was Annie's statement of brave and throat-choked good wishes which almost reduced Clemo to tears, but he was relieved to see that Toby was in good hands. He waved at her and promised to take care of 'Bluey'.

Dai spoke to him. 'I thought you might value a bit of company for a while,' he said, as they turned their horses left to ascend the hill out of Monmouth. 'I've got to go to Coleford to arrange to buy some coal. I'm going to start up a new business dealing in coal and iron ore. Joan can look after the shop for the next months, and, if I'm honest, I want this new business to rival Giles Thomas. As you know, he controls all the coal stocks that come to Monmouth, and I'm sick of that. So, I thought, if you don't mind, I would ride with you for the next six miles.'

The horses walked slowly up the steep incline. Clemo looked back just once towards Monmouth and Dixton and then set his face forwards. But he thought that this might be an opportunity to ask Dai about something Issy had once said about Joan and Giles Thomas.

'May I ask you something, Dai?'

'Of course'.

'Why did my mother and Joan and Issy have such a strong dislike of Master Thomas?'

Dai paused and returned with a further question; 'So, you've never been told the story?'

'No.'

'Well. Perhaps I had better tell you. As you know, Joan began work as a shopgirl in the shop which she now runs. It had been owned by Mistress Cooper, (you may remember her), an old and poverty-stricken widow who was a cousin of Giles Thomas. As she became more and more elderly, Joan was left to look after the business. Giles Thomas owned the property and often popped into the shop when Mistress Cooper was resting out at the back. She really was very poorly. Each time he entered the shop he made suggestive and lewd comments to Joan. One particular day he came in. Mistress Cooper, as he knew, was by now bed ridden upstairs. He locked the door behind him and tried to molest Joan. He tore at her bodice, trying to rape her, she screamed, and by chance, at that very moment, a favourite customer tried to come into the shop. That customer was also a member of the Thomas clan. She looked through the window, saw Joan half naked, and then saw Giles Thomas skulking in a corner. Joan rushed to the door and unlocked it and the woman seeing Joan's distress put her shawl around her and took her to her own house. She was a very brave and kind woman.

To cut a long story short, Giles Thomas went to see the woman and at first, he tried to pretend that he had seen Joan being assaulted by an intruder and had rushed into the shop to help.

The woman asked him if he always locked the door behind him when he was apprehending a criminal. At which point he changed his story and because she lived in one of his properties, threatened to evict her if she breathed a word of what she had seen.

She did not reply but sheltered Joan for the rest of the day and when night fell, brought her to your cottage. As you might imagine, your mother and father were enraged by what had happened. Your mother comforted Joan as best she could but your father went out into the night to confront Giles Thomas. It was a very brave thing to do. Giles sent a maid to answer the door when he heard some knocking, but your father did not wait to be invited in. He stormed into the hall and shouted for Giles Thomas to come to him. If your father had had a dagger, I think he would have killed him, but fortunately he was unarmed. He accused

Giles Thomas of being a molester of women, a rapist and a son of the Devil.

At first, Giles Thomas did not respond, because he knew that his wife and his servants would be able to hear all that was being shouted by your father. All he wanted was to get your father out of the house and for everything to calm down. So he said to your father that he would come to an agreement with him about it. He proposed that Joan could have the shop rent free for life when Mistress Cooper died. Your father didn't know what to do. He was poor. He was up against the most powerful man in the town. He said that he would consider it and left the house still red-hot with anger.

He went home. He and your mother and Joan discussed the proposal and eventually came to the conclusion that because Joan had not been completely violated, they would accept the deal being offered, which, of course, explains why Joan and I can afford to live where we do. And what is more, we always have the whip hand. One word from us, and Giles Thomas could be ruined...'

Clemo stopped his horse. He had turned white with rage and threatened to turn back immediately and have it out with Giles Thomas. But Dai persuaded him not to be so rash.

'You must always realise, Clemo, that whilst the situation remains as it is, Giles Thomas cannot touch us. We always have a hold over him. He knows that, which is why he treats the family so warily and with such apparent generosity. Think back to your father's funeral. All that ceremony, all that finery, that was nothing to do with your father being a member of the Guild, it was to keep everyone sweet.'

'May the devil take him,' said Clemo, spitting, and nudged his horse to walk on.

'And that's why I am going to Coleford,' said Dai, 'Because I can break his hold on his control of coal and wood in Monmouth, and he won't dare to do anything about it. What a great outcome that will be.' He chortled as he said it.

And Clemo repeated his curse: 'May the devil and all his demons take him.'

It was not how he had envisaged his first day on the road, but he was grateful for Dai's honesty. And when they parted at Coleford, Clemo again said aloud, 'Giles Thomas, may the devil and all his demons break you in pieces and may you roast forever in hell.'

His anger abated. He thanked Dai for his company, asked that he should give Clemo's love to the family, and, waving a farewell, set the horse to walk eastwards.

Chapter 16: Flaxley and beyond

He hadn't gone many paces when he realised that he had not asked anyone the directions to get to his intended destination. He greeted a couple of women and a man standing on the side of the road and asked if they knew the way to Flaxley Abbey. The man thought it might be somewhere beyond Littledean but he couldn't swear to it. The women said that they didn't know, but they explained that if he wanted to get to Littledean he should take a right fork just out of the town and keep going. Eventually he would get to Littledean where, they advised him, he should ask someone for further instructions.

The road wound up a knoll, flattened out and then descended a long, steep hill, scarred on either side by stone quarries. Heavy trees blotted out much of the light and Clemo wondered if his 'pilgrimage' was sensible. He was on his own. He could easily fall prey to thieves. At the bottom of the hill, he saw two heavily built men in extremely rough and torn clothes, loitering at the cross-roads. They were black with soot and to Clemo they appeared threatening. He wondered if they might be charcoal burners and therefore, he assumed, they would be rugged and even lawless, for that was their collective reputation. With his heart thumping in fear, he greeted them. They responded by gruffly asking him who he was and where he had come from.

'From Monmouth,' he replied, trying to remain as calm as possible.

'So you're a Taff then,' one of them said, sidling up to Bluey and holding the bridle.

He decided not to enter into a discussion about his origins, but to side-step their question.

'I worked in Redbrook, at the Foundry.'

'Oh,' the older one replied, 'at Redbrook Foundry?'

'Yes.'

'With Ifor Young?'

'Goodness, yes,' he said in surprise, 'Do you know him?'

'Yes, I do.' It was the older one who spoke. 'I know him well. He's my mother's cousin. And where are you going?'

'Flaxley.'

'Ah...there's some foundries near there, so you should be alright for a job.'

They let go of Bluey's bridle and wished him well. What Clemo had feared might be a rough moment had turned into a quiet blessing. He was cheered. If everyone he met was similar, perhaps his journey would be a good one. He leaned over and patted Bluey's neck.

The next hill was so steep that he walked up it beside Bluey and at the top, in a glade of beech trees he decided to stop for something to eat. He hobbled Bluey, whispered into Bluey's ear that they seemed to be getting along fine together and thanked him for a good morning. No-one passed, and lunch over, they moved on.

He really was in entirely new territory now. It seemed to be nothing but trees, and the road after a few miles took him down into another valley followed by a steep climb. Towards the top he saw a tumble-down chapel in a field close to the road. He stopped for a moment to look at it, and as he did so, a woman in very poor and ragged clothes came out of her cottage to observe him.

'A stupid woman used to live there,' she announced, loudly. 'She wasn't right in the head, prayed all day, or said she did, then expected to be fed by the rest of us. Nice work if you can get it,' she continued, 'Then she died. We didn't find her body for a week and by that time the smell was terrible. A couple of monks from Flaxley came to bury her. Mad woman. As mad as a March hare. And the monks were as mad as she was, I reckon, so I expect they thought she was a saint. Saint, be blowed, she was off her head. Totally mad...' She moved to go back into her cottage, but Clemo interrupted her: 'So, am I on the right road for Flaxley?'

'Yes. Are you going to stay there? Because if you are, you'll end up as mad as the rest of them, just mark my words.'

Clemo thanked her for her advice but as she had gone back into her dark cottage, she didn't hear him. He and Bluey jogged on and at the very top of the hill he stopped dead. He found himself looking out over a new and astonishing world. There was a large, meandering river in the middle distance, glinting in the sunlight, beyond it lay some hazy meadows and in the far distance, a long low line of blue hills; between the river and the hills, to his left and far away, he spotted a tall Church tower.

Living all his life, as he had, confined, and enclosed by the tree-lined banks of the River Wye and never having travelled further than Tintern, the view in front of him took on a vertiginous, dream-like quality. It was the scale and beauty of it that left him speechless. He sat there for a while gazing out at it, lost in wonder.

A man in his working clothes stained with iron oxide scuffed by and interrupted his reverie.

'First time you've seen it?' he asked.

'It certainly is. What part of the country am I looking at?'

'See that church tower. That's Gloucester, and those hills are the Cotswolds, and the river is the Severn. Ever had elvers?' he asked. Clemo admitted that he didn't know what elvers were.

'You should try some. They're the best.'

And with that enigmatic comment, and before Clemo could ask him where he mined for iron ore, the man had moved on. Clemo continued to sit there, enraptured by the stillness and the view. Bluey ignored him, lowered his head and tore at some tufts of grass by the roadside, but began to ease himself forward. It was the signal to move on.

Clemo thought he had never seen anything so lovely in his entire life, but Bluey plodded on down a hill, through Littledean, and a few miles further on in a small but narrow valley, Clemo caught the smell of woodsmoke. Rounding a corner he saw a small cottage from whose chimney a thin plume of pale blue smoke was drifting. A child was playing in the garden being looked after by an old woman sitting on a kitchen stool.

'Am I on the right road for Flaxley Abbey, Mistress?', he asked.

'You are. Straight on, and you'll see a mill. Turn to your left about a mile further on and you'll come across the Abbey. You can't go wrong… and ask them if they've got any spare plums for me.' She chuckled and waved him goodbye. The child with a grubby, dirt-streaked face just watched him warily.

The instructions were perfect. It was late in the afternoon when he arrived at the abbey. He looked about him. The gatehouse was in poor repair, the bell sagged on its moorings, the gates were askew. No-one was there. He dismounted and rang the bell. Nothing happened. He waited and rang the bell again and from beyond the gates he heard the sound of footsteps moving slowly. The gate creaked open and an old monk in a dirty white habit and a stained scapula looked at him with soft blue eyes clouded with cataracts.

'Yes?' enquired the monk.

'My name is Clemo and I wonder if I could stay the night?'

Bluey stood patiently beside him, tossing his head to deter the flies that had gathered around him.

'You are the first guest we've had for a long, long time. Come in. You'll have to take us as you find us. We aren't so many now.'

Clemo led Bluey through the gateway and into a courtyard where grass was growing between the cobbles.

'I'll go and tell Father Abbot that you have arrived. What was your name again?' He cupped his hand behind his ear to help him understand what Clemo said. 'And I'll ask John to look after your horse. He'll know what to do. Our stables are empty now, but we'll find something for your lovely horse. What's his name?'

'Bluey,' replied Clemo.

'Ah…'

Clemo stood waiting whilst the elderly monk slowly walked away from him, muttering, 'Bluey…Bluey…'

A few minutes later, a man wearing a dark blue apron over a grey shirt and black trousers, who was just a little younger than the elderly monk, arrived. 'I'm John', he explained, 'I'm the servant here… but the way things are going, not for much longer. This place used to be handsome but look at it now. It's falling to rack and ruin.' He moved to Bluey, patted his neck and gently led Bluey away to the stables.

Clemo remained where he was. Compared with Tintern, this place seemed so woebegone. John returned. 'You'd better come with me; by the time Brother Eustace gets to Father Abbot he'll have forgotten what he is there for. Let me take you…' He limped beside Clemo and took him through the cloisters to a door on the east side. Down the staircase slowly stumbled Brother Eustace who, catching sight of Clemo again, said, 'We haven't met before, have we? My name is Brother Eustace,' and with that announcement he walked away, his sandals slapping on the flagstones. Some swallows flew from their nests in the roof of the cloisters, chirping noisily.

Clemo was taken up the stairs by John to meet Father Abbot, a lean, grey-faced man with a growth of silver stubble on his chin, and hands knotted with arthritis. He struggled to his feet and welcomed Clemo.

'You are the first guest we have had in months…so you are very welcome. Thank you for choosing to stay with us.'

He turned to John and asked him to make up a bed in the Abbot's guest chamber and said that he and Clemo would eat together in his room.

Clemo was touched by the abbot's gentle grace and found himself explaining about the loss of Laura and Jestin and his own need to leave his original home because its memories were too hard to bear. The abbot listened carefully, saying very little, and from time to time the conversation lapsed into a companionable silence until Clemo felt moved to say he was struggling to understand what the Book of Job meant when it said, 'The Lord gave, and the Lord has taken away.'

'But it's true, isn't it?' replied the abbot, 'God can do what he likes.'

'Forgive me, Father' said Clemo, 'I understand that, but does it give God pleasure to snatch a woman and a child from the arms of a man who loves them?'

The abbot took a long time to reply and then said, 'God's ways are inscrutable. Inscrutable. Take this abbey, for example. There was a time when it was buzzing with life, but even though we have continued to pray and to say the offices there are hardly any of us left…yet that, though we cannot understand it, must also be God's will… and we poor mortals have to leave it at that.'

A knock on the door interrupted the conversation and John entered, carrying a tray of food and some grey earthenware drinking pots.

'I've chosen the mead for you tonight, Father,' he said, 'because we have a guest. And I shall make up the bed in your guest room in a while.' He bowed and left.

'If you want an example of humble service, don't consider any of us monks, look at John,' said the abbot, 'look at John.'

Clemo smiled and uncharacteristically thought to himself that John at his advanced age would not be able to find work anywhere else, and was then ashamed of his own cynicism.

In the conversation during the rest of the evening Clemo explained that because he was so fond of Tintern he was making his way to London via Cistercian abbeys and asked for directions to whatever the next abbey might be.

The Abbot folded his hands in his lap and explained that the next nearest abbey was Hailes. He spoke of it with a tiny edge of jealousy entering his voice, 'Now, there's an abbey,' he said.' It's much bigger than ours and it has a relic, the Holy Blood, which draws the crowds... we haven't anything like that here, but we do have plums. Lots and lots of plums, beautiful purple plums they are. But you are just one week too late to taste them, unless we might be able to find you some late ripening ones for your journey tomorrow. Now this is the route you must take to get to Hailes.' He walked unsteadily towards a table, took a piece of paper and on it, with his gnarled fingers gripping a reed pen, slowly sketched a map.

'There' he said, sitting down heavily in his chair and handing the map to Clemo.'Now', he continued, 'you must excuse me because I have to say my prayers'. He pointed the way to his guest chamber and there on a straw mattress Clemo lay himself down to sleep. He was much more tired than he realised and soon was lost to the world. He thought he heard a nearby door open and close in the middle of the night as the abbot made his way to the church for Matins.

Very early the next morning, the sun streaming through his window woke him. He found that John had placed some bread, cheese and ale on a small table, and having had breakfast Clemo went down the stairs to find John to ask if Bluey could be got ready for the long journey he planned to make that day to Hailes.

John, as assiduous as ever, said, 'Say a prayer for me when you get there. Now come with me and we'll get your lovely horse ready.' They walked together to the stables. Bluey seemed pleased to see them. John found some fresh hay, which he smelt to ensure it really was fresh, and put it in a rack for Bluey to eat it from. Then he went and collected a couple of leather buckets of water from the Westbury brook which ran through the grounds. Bluey drank, more buckets were filled and brought, and he ate heartily. 'First meal of the day for a horse is the most important', he said to Clemo. 'You look after him and he'll look after you, that's what I always say.' He stood by until Bluey seemed satisfied, then rubbed the horse's neck, fixed the saddle, all the while leaving Clemo to watch. 'Lovely horse, getting on a bit, but a lovely horse, I'll be bound.'

Clemo checked the girth and climbed up into the saddle. 'Now, don't forget, young man, say one for me when you look at the Holy Blood, and good luck to you. Off you go'. He slapped the horse's rump and Bluey started on the long day's journey to Hailes.

The land was flatter when they reached the end of the valley and as Bluey clearly wanted to move a bit faster, Clemo allowed him to trot for a while at his own pace. A beautiful Summer morning, a happy horse, and a day waiting to be explored. The future was promising.

Chapter 17: Hailes Abbey

The closer Clemo and Bluey got to Gloucester, the busier the road became, and on the outskirts of the city Clemo decided to stop for some food. Bluey fended for himself whilst Clemo dipped into his saddle bag for his bread. He found that John of Flaxley had not only provided cheese to go with the bread, but had also provided two plums carefully wrapped in what appeared to be paper from an old hand-written book. Clemo bit into one of the plums. The sweetness was delicious, the juices squirted out of his mouth and ran down his chin.

A man passing by shouted, 'I bet that's good. Come from Flaxley, did it?'

Clemo replied that the man was entirely correct, but then asked, 'How did you know?'

'Plums of that colour come from Flaxley and Blaisdon. They're the best plums in the kingdom. Where are you off to?'

'Hailes,' replied Clemo.

'Long way,' said the man. 'Enjoy the day.' And walked on.

Clemo was tempted to stop to look at the Benedictine Abbey in Gloucester but decided that because his journey was at the limit of Bluey's range, he should gently press on. But he admired the Abbey and St Oswald's Priory. The city seemed to be filled with churches. At the crossroads only two hundred yards from the abbey, following the Abbot of Flaxley's instructions, he turned left and was soon out of the noise and bustle of the city.

From time to time he allowed Bluey to trot but trying to reserve Bluey's strength was his main concern and so, whenever he came to a stream he stopped and allowed Bluey to drink and to nibble the stream's verges.

The day wore on. He himself was starting to tire, but then he saw Hailes. Or rather, he didn't actually see it, but as the road was beginning to be thronged with pilgrims, he thought he must be getting nearer. Some of the pilgrims were footsore, walking slowly as though they had travelled a long way. Some had scallop shells attached to their jaunty hats. One youngish man was hopping along on wooden crutches with rags under his armpits to help bear his body's weight, his face was creased with determination; a blind man was being accompanied by a colleague, and one poor soul was lying on a stretcher being carried by a group of friends. Two others had dreadful facial skin complaints which they did their best to hide with scarves, another had a deformed hand, yet another a hunched back. They were driven by a longing for healing, making their way slowly to one of the greatest of Christian relics. Surely that should bring them relief and ease their pain? At the head of one group, he saw a lord and lady riding fine horses, accompanied by liveried servants. Yet most of the pilgrims were ordinary folk like himself.

And then he spotted amongst the crowd a man and woman carrying a small child. They looked so weary that his heart went out to them. He came alongside them, dismounted, and asked if either of them would like to ride Bluey. They declined his offer, but they got into conversation. Their child was wrapped in a woollen blanket, its pale and sickly face just visible.

'Where are you from?' asked Clemo.

'Deerhurst,' replied the man, 'it's about 15 miles from here.'

'And you have carried your little one all the way?'

'Yes, but if we can get her better it will be worth it.' The child coughed. Tiny flecks of blood sprayed on to the blanket. Her mother leant across and wiped the child's face with a cloth.

'And what's wrong with her?'

'We don't know. She took bad one day and has been going downhill ever since. We think a witch put a spell on her. So, we've come to pray that the Holy Blood will get rid of the evil… We want our daughter back.' The longing in the father's voice was intense.

The crowd ahead slowed down. They were approaching the gates of the abbey where pilgrims were being allowed through, a few at a time. The lord and lady and their retainers trotted past to the front of the queue and were welcomed warmly and immediately let in. The rest had to wait.

By the time Clemo and Bluey and the couple with their sick daughter arrived at the head of the queue, the abbey servants were becoming agitated and losing their tempers. It was clear that they were not expecting so many pilgrims and discussed where all of them could be accommodated. The couple with the sick daughter explained that they were there just for the showing of the relic and would then walk back home. They were let through, though one of the servants looked askance at the little girl as they went past. Clemo asked if he and Bluey could have accommodation for one night. There was a heated discussion but when Clemo explained that he had been sent to Hailes with the support of the Abbot of Flaxley, he was allowed in. Bluey was led off by a boy to the stables and Clemo was taken to the guest accommodation.

It was a huge building, like a barn, filled with pilgrims. The stench of sweat, urine, and suppurating wounds was overpowering. On the floor were some straw-filled mattresses covered with stained woollen blankets. A servant allocated a mattress to Clemo and then shouted to the pilgrims that the Holy Blood would be available for everyone to see when they heard a bell ring five times....'once for each of the wounds of Christ,' he explained. Clemo lay down. He was next to an elderly man who said that he came to Hailes each year on behalf of his sick wife who could no longer walk. 'She's been bound by the Devil for the past three years, but', he went on, 'when I take her a medal from here it seems to cheer her up...and that's the main thing. Except, of course, the Devil isn't letting her go. He's a brute. that one...a horrible, cruel, nasty brute, and I don't mind if he hears me saying so.'

Clemo noticed that the man took hold of a rosary he had in his hands and said a few 'Ave's' just to make sure that no diabolical counter-attack would follow his outburst.

'When will the bell ring?' Clemo asked.

'Oh, I don't know. We just have to wait and be patient. You'll need to get your money ready.'

'What for?'

'To see the Holy Blood, of course. Them monks are a law to themselves. They won't let you in without you put a groat in the plate.'

He turned over on his side, explaining that he was going to have a snooze.

Clemo lay on his mattress, his hands clasped behind his head, and stared at the massive beams of the roof and tried to follow the old man's advice. He would endeavour to be patient; it was, after all, a virtue, but he had a growing feeling that he didn't like this place. Flaxley might have been tumbledown but it was still honest, whereas this place felt as though it was built to rob people. Was it right that the poorest and the sickest people of the kingdom should have to pay so that they could gain some spiritual solace? What kind of arrangement was that?

He must have dozed off, for the next thing he knew was that the old man was shaking him awake saying that the bell had rung.

Clemo stumbled from his mattress and followed the crowd ahead of him. There was a chatter of excitement. This was what everyone had come for. They walked down some stairs and along a footpath. The church ahead of them was massive, soaring up into the sky. Slowly they shuffled forward until they were on the threshold. The chatter died away. People were holding their rosaries. 'What have you brought your rosary for?' Clemo whispered to a woman standing next to him.

'Don't you know?' she replied, 'You place it against the shrine and when you take it back home with you, the power of the Holy Blood will protect you…. and you get years and years off purgatory.'

Clemo wondered if the Holy Blood would ease the purgatory that he felt he carried deep in his soul.

They made their way inside, the crowds controlled by monks at the door holding collection plates. Clemo dug a groat from his leather purse and dropped it on to a plate piled high with coins. He had never seen so many coins before. And he noticed that the plate was not made from pewter but was solid silver.

He moved forward and there it was, on its stone plinth; the Holy Blood of Christ in a glass vial, displayed within a crystal container. People around him were genuflecting, purchasing candles and lighting them, reaching out with their rosaries, kneeling in fervent adoration. He saw the young man on his crutches trying to get close, but he was blocked by the crowd, nevertheless, his face was enraptured. Clemo thought he glimpsed the couple with their sick daughter and prayed that they might have found some peace and that their little girl might have been granted a miracle.

The pilgrims moved slowly along the aisle which channelled them around the back of the relic to altars at the east end of the church, each altar, in its own chapel, ablaze with votive candles; at one of them, a priest dressed in sumptuous vestments made from cloth of gold, was saying Mass. His congregation consisted of the lord and lady kneeling in prayer, plus a sub-deacon who was swinging a thurible sending wafts of incense into the air; no-one else was allowed through the wrought-iron gates which closed each chapel off from the pilgrims' processional route.

He looked above him. The vaulting of the roof was a subtle framework of golden stone and where the ribs of the vault met high up, he could see that there were painted stone roof-bosses portraying scenes from the Bible. The whole place was spectacular. But hadn't he learnt from Brother Adam at Tintern that Cistercians wanted things to be plain, simple, and unadorned, yet here everything spoke of wealth and riches? And yet, despite his misgivings, as he paused and genuflected at the chapel where Mass was being offered, did he not feel a frisson of holiness? Did he not feel that Laura and Jestin were very close? Was God, even in this crowded, money-ridden place, speaking to him?

After a supper of broth and bread he went to check that Bluey was being well looked after and then went back to the church for Vespers. He sat in the nave with all the remaining pilgrims (some had already left) and let the simple music, the candlelight and the stillness bring balm to his soul, and having commended himself, his father, Laura, Jestin and all the family to the mercies of God, he took himself back to the huge Guest Room where he made himself comfortable and fell asleep.

The following morning, he was up early. Perhaps it was the bell tolling for Prime that woke him. He washed, tidied himself and went to Prime where, in the nave, there were fewer pilgrims than at Vespers. Again, he loved the simple music soaring up into the stone roof with the dawn just breaking outside the clear windows. He heard the monks leave but continued to stand there in prayer and then moved forward towards a statue of the Virgin Mary surrounded by flickering votive candles. He said his 'Ave's,' prayed yet again for his family, and prayed too for Father Burley, thanking God for him with the growing realisation of the influence Father Burley had had on him. Not only had he taught him to read and write Latin, but he had also moulded and shaped Clemo's view of the world and its purpose. Even when he had temporarily lost his mind when he was grieving for Laura and Jestin, Father Burley had stood by him, a quietly reassuring presence. It was a moment in that abbey for Clemo of growing self-awareness but he was deeply conscious that he still had a very long way to go before he could be on a spiritual par with Father Burley. He decided, in the cool light of morning in that abbey that he would try to become more centred on God and the Church. Was not that what God might want of him?

He shook himself out of his reverie, walked back to the guest quarters, helped himself to a small breakfast of bread and ale and made his way through the misty morning to the stables. There Bluey was being prepared for the day ahead by one of the abbey's grooms, who complimented Clemo on his horse and asked him where he was travelling to.

'Bruern' replied Clemo. 'I'm hoping to stay there tonight. I gather that I have to make my way to Stow on the Wold first, is that correct?'

'It certainly is,' replied the groom. 'And when you get there you will need to ask your way to Bruern. Best of luck…you'll need it with that lot at Bruern. They are an unruly bunch…'

Clemo nuzzled up to Bluey, thanked the groom for his overnight care of the horse, mounted, and trotted out of the abbey precinct.

Chapter 18: Bruern Abbey

The journey to Stow on the Wold was a delight. The road took him up the Cotswold scarp. Bluey was feeling refreshed and, as before, Clemo allowed him to trot when he wanted to, and with the breeze on his face and the sun shedding its golden, early morning light on everything, it seemed to Clemo that he was being especially blessed.

Yet, as he rode, he continued to ruminate on all that he had seen at Hailes: all those pilgrims, desperate for healing; the heavy silver plate overflowing with coins; the undoubted beauty of the Mass in a beautiful building. What kept running through his mind were some words he had once heard Dai Parry, his brother-in-law, say: 'When Adam delved and Eve span, who was then the gentleman?' Was it right, Clemo asked himself, that the monks should have a separate place in the Abbey, walled off from the pilgrims? Was it right that the lord and lady moved to the front of the queue keeping that man and woman with their sick daughter, waiting? Was society ordered in the way it was by God, with the King at the top and the peasants at the bottom? But if it weren't like that, would there not be chaos?

He arrived at Bruern Abbey late in the afternoon and was met at the gatehouse by a big, burly man who explained that he was the gatekeeper and blacksmith and accompanied the Abbot on his travels. It was a statement about status and preening self-satisfaction. 'In fact,' said the blacksmith, 'when I accompany the abbot, I wear his livery. I'll show you.'

The blacksmith wandered into his lodge and quickly re-emerged carrying his livery. It was a red and blue tabard, adorned with a coat of arms in gold thread. 'See', he said displaying its noble and luxurious qualities and to top it off, he put on a black velvet cap.

Clemo had not yet been given access to the abbey and was perturbed by the way in which the gatekeeper had not asked him about his journey, or whether Bluey needed some fodder or water, or whether Clemo, as a pilgrim-traveller, might need to be shown to the guest accommodation. It was clear that he would have to be suitably amazed by the blacksmith's role and livery before anything so mundane as food, rest, and drink might be offered.

So Clemo expressed pleasure, not to say stupefaction at the blacksmith's attire, and that did the trick. He was allowed in.

'The Abbot's not at home now,' explained the blacksmith, 'but I've not had to go with him this time. He hasn't gone far. And our Prior, Richard, came back from London yesterday, so there might be a bit of delay whilst we get you settled in, but leave things with me. I'll look after you. If you wait here, I'll get one of the servants to look after your horse…isn't he a handsome creature? and then I'll arrange your accommodation, and things like that…'

It seemed to Clemo that the abbey was more in the hands of the blacksmith than it was in the hands of the absent abbot.

A young, dark-haired boy with a tight and narrow face came to lead Bluey away. Bluey snorted; he wasn't happy, but Clemo couldn't immediately see why. The boy pulled sharply on Bluey's reins. Clemo shouted: 'Hey. There's no need for that, treat him properly.' The boy ignored him. Bluey snorted again. Clemo felt uneasy. Might that boy continue to mistreat Bluey once he was out of sight in the stables?

A few minutes later, the blacksmith returned with an ageing, sad-looking monk. 'This is Brother Chad,' he explained, 'he is our Guest Master.'

The Guest Master muttered something inaudible and scuffing along the path with his head down, led Clemo to the accommodation. He didn't speak a word on the way, until he got to the oak door of the lodgings. Then he stopped, turned to Clemo and asked, cagily, 'Are you a friend of Will the blacksmith?'

'No. I've never met him before in my life.'

Clemo wasn't sure that Brother Chad believed him.

'You'll not be on your own this afternoon,' said Brother Chad, 'There's another guest in the room, but that shouldn't trouble you, if you really are a stranger and you don't know Will.'

He led Clemo up the stairs to a small dark room in which there were two beds, two wooden chairs, a large crucifix, and a fire in the grate that was struggling to stay alight.

'Hello,' said the other guest, 'I'm Harry. I'm a friend of Will the Blacksmith and I'm staying here tonight.' Clemo introduced himself ('My name is Clemo') and again wondered about the role of the blacksmith in the abbey.

'Where are you from?' asked Harry. He was a big, strong man with an open, ruddy face. Perhaps a farmer, thought Clemo.

'Monmouth' replied Clemo, 'I'm just here for one night before I go on to Oxford and then I'm going to London.'

'London?' said Harry. 'Never been there myself. I'm from Burford, just down the road. Born and bred there. You wouldn't catch me going anywhere near London.'

'So', said Clemo, 'if you're from Burford, why are you staying here tonight, wouldn't you rather be at home?'

'That I would, but Will wanted me here tonight just to keep an eye on things.'

'What for?'

Harry shifted uneasily. 'Nothing much really, but he thought I might be useful. That's what friends are for, isn't it?' he said, enigmatically, '...to look out for each other. Will and I have known each other for years and years.' And with that he lapsed into silence.

Clemo was puzzled and decided, as he was unpacking his few belongings, that he would try to discover what the situation might be that Harry, the Blacksmith's friend, had been asked to deal with.

He sat on the chair next to the fire opposite Harry, who tried to stir a few flames from the embers.

'Look', said Clemo, 'this is probably none of my business, but what's going on here? Something is, but I can't fathom out what it might be.'

'And you've never been here before?' asked Harry.

'No, never.'

'So you're not a friend of the Abbot?'

'No.'

'And you're not a friend of the Prior?'

'No.'

'Can I trust you?'

'I hope so.'

'Well, then…the problem is the Prior. He's just been released from the Fleet and came back here yesterday, as angry and vicious as a ferret in a sack.'

'What's the Fleet? And what's the Prior so angry about?' asked Clemo.

'The Fleet's a big and horrible prison in London. The Prior's been imprisoned there for almost a year, and he's angry because he believes he has taken the punishment for something which was the abbot's responsibility. It's all about a debt that was owed…money, eh? Love of money is the root of all evil, isn't it? And that grasping Cardinal, Cardinal Wolsey, reckoned that the Prior had also stolen the Abbey's seal. If he had stolen it, of course, that's really serious, but the Prior denies everything. Now, I don't know the rights or wrongs, but some of the monks have sided with the Abbot and some with the Prior. So, you can imagine the atmosphere here today. It's pure poison. And that's why I'm here. If any squabbles break out, it will be Will and me who will have to knock a few heads together.'

Clemo was appalled that a monastery should have sunk to such unholy depths and said so to the brawny, smiling Harry.

'Human nature,' replied Harry, 'it's the same inside the abbey's walls, as it is outside. If you can change mankind, well, you can change the world…but if I were you, Clemo, I should try to lose some of your innocence. The only innocent man in the Bible was Adam and look what happened to him.'

Clemo felt suitably chastened. Perhaps he was too innocent; perhaps he was too unworldly; perhaps this journey was making him grow up a bit? Perhaps, despite losing his father, wife, and son, he still had much to learn?

He thanked Harry for providing the background.

There was a knock on the door. It was the thin and cagey Brother Chad with a tray of sparse meat, a chunk of bread, and tankards only half full of ale.

'What's happened to your hospitality?' asked Harry, biting into the bread,'…stale bread, old meat and half a pot of ale, what is this place coming to?'

Brother Chad lowered his eyes and muttered something through his thin lips about the Prior which neither Harry nor Clemo could hear.

'Now, Brother,' said Harry, 'Don't come muttering at us. We are your guests. The problems in this abbey are something for you monks to sort out, and if you don't, heaven help you. Wolsey will be after you like a wolf let loose amongst lambs.' He laughed, but Brother Chad glared at him and then shuffled out of the door.

'Why would Cardinal Wolsey trouble himself with Bruern?' asked Clemo.

'Oh, my dear young man, you don't know the half about how the world works, do you? Let me explain. If you stood by the road in Burford, you would see cart load after cart load of stone passing by. It's coming from Taynton and Sherborne, and the quarry owners are making a tidy packet, I can tell you. The stone is on its way to Oxford because Cardinal Wolsey is building a huge new College there. It's in honour not of Our Lady, nor of St Peter, but guess what, it's in honour of himself. He's calling it Cardinal College and he's built it on the site of St Frideswide's Priory. He closed that Priory about four years ago and threw out the Augustinians just because he wanted to create a college where the Fellows and students would pray daily for his soul. In my book, that's called Vanity, but maybe I'm wrong; maybe I'm just a simple farmer minding his own business, keeping his head down, ploughing and sowing and reaping.

By the way, I hear that it's not the only abbey he's closed…so, if Wolsey can close a Priory without any fuss being made and take over all their lands and monies, he might cast his greedy little eyes on Bruern, mightn't he? Therefore, if the monks here have any sense, they'll sort out their problems very quickly and not give Wolsey the opportunity to close them down for being rowdy and lawless.'

He sat back in his chair, looked straight at Clemo and said 'I have told you all this because you look like a fellow I can trust but don't breathe a word to anyone of what I have told you. I reckon we are living in dangerous times, so best to keep quiet, eh? Don't want to smell the smoke of bonfires burning heretics, do we?' He slapped Clemo firmly on the knee.

'Now, come on…let's go to see if Will can rustle up some better ale than that pig-swill they've just given us.'

'But I thought I should join the brothers for their prayers,' replied Clemo.

'If I were you, young man, I would stay clear of the lot of them. If you went to prayers with them tonight it would be like stepping on a wasp's nest. Leave them to it. Let them sting each other…better that than sting you. And let me tell you, if any of them break out of their nest and fly towards me or Will, leave us to deal with it. We're used to swatting wasps.' He laughed to himself and Clemo wryly thought that the ascetic, ill-favoured Brother Chad and his fellow monks would be no match for the muscular Will and Harry.

On the way to the gatekeeper's Lodge, Clemo excused himself for a moment. 'I just want to check on my horse' he explained, 'The boy who took him to the stables seemed an unpleasant character …and I don't think that I entirely trust him.'

'Ah…' replied Harry, 'you are losing your innocence…that's good. That whippersnapper is a nasty piece of work. It was the Prior who asked him to work here, but if he has done anything to your horse tell him that Harry and Will will string him up…that's all…string him up by his thumbs…'

When Clemo reached the stable it was empty. Bluey was on his own but whinnied in greeting when he saw Clemo who patted him on the neck. As he did so, he noticed that there were two long weals, half hidden by the horse's mane. The weals had the remains of thorns embedded in them as though someone had used a long bramble-bush cane as a weapon. Clemo shouted angrily for the boy. There was no answer. So, he stormed off to tell Will and Harry what had happened. They were furious and went searching for the boy but couldn't find him.

'I'll give him such a tanning when he comes back,' said Will, 'he won't know what's hit him.'

'I doubt he'll return,' said Harry, 'and good riddance. He's always been a bad 'un.'

Clemo suggested that he would sleep in the stable that night to protect Bluey, and whilst Harry repeated that he didn't think the boy would return, he nevertheless sympathised with Clemo. Will went off to fetch a couple of blankets for a makeshift bed and gave him a pot of salve to help heal the wounds. He handed the blankets and the salve to Clemo and apologised for what had happened.

'It's not your fault', replied Clemo.

'It is,' said Will, 'in my abbey, things like that should not happen. I'm very sorry.'

Clemo thanked Will and Harry for their care and advice and took himself off to the stable where he gently eased the thorns from Bluey's neck and rubbed in the salve. He settled down for the night, mulling over the blacksmith describing the abbey as 'his'. Was this abbey totally out of control?

Chapter 19: Oxford

The following morning, Clemo was woken by Will coming in to the stable with some bread and meat on a pewter plate and a mug of ale.

'Good morning, Clemo. I hope you slept well. How is your horse doing?'

Clemo struggled to his feet and went to look at Bluey's neck. 'The weals have gone down,' he replied and stroked Bluey's face. Will told Clemo to have his breakfast whilst he took a look at Bluey's hooves. He found that one of the shoes was in danger of coming loose and said that he'd take Bluey to his smithy just to tidy up the hoof and replace a broken nail.

'That's really kind of you,' said Clemo, biting into the fresh bread.

'It's the least I can do after what happened last night. That rascal will never work here again. Anyone who mistreats animals deserves to be flogged. How could he do it? I suppose some people are born with a streak of cruelty in them, and that's all there is to it.'

He led Bluey out of the stable, leaving Clemo to finish his food.

Clemo reflected on Will's kindness and could not help contrasting it with Brother Chad's wary and miserable demeanour. Alright, Will might be overly proud of his livery, but underneath the muscle and the bluster there was obviously a warm heart, at least as far as animals were concerned.

Whilst Bluey was being cared for, Clemo made his way to the Guest Room where Harry was just finishing his breakfast. He greeted him. 'I hope you slept well, Harry.'

'I did, thank you, but this breakfast is no better than last night's meagre feast. What makes the monks so dismal? Why can't they just cheer up?'

Clemo did not feel obliged to defend the Bruern monks, but he told Harry about Brother Adam at Tintern and what a lovely man he was. 'In fact,' he said, 'He doesn't know it, but it might be because of him that one day I might become a monk.'

'Really?'

'Yes, really. My wife and son died a while ago and I've begun to think that there must be something I can do with my life to help others in distress, in the way Brother Adam helped me.'

Harry looked at the floor and then back at Clemo: 'Well, that's a noble idea Clemo, but as you have found here, not every abbey is well-organised or even honest. So, don't go rushing at things. Take my advice, take your time. As you know yourself, farming is about the long, slow sweep of the seasons, not about hours and minutes, and it's the same with human life. We have to take time, mull things over, and only then make a move. Talking of which, I must go to see Will and make sure that today's going to be quiet, and if it is, I shall go back to Burford.'

Clemo accompanied Harry to the Smithy where Bluey was looking very pleased with himself. He'd been fed and watered by Will; he had a better fitting shoe and now he was ready for the day.

'So, you're off to Oxford,' said Will, wiping his hands on his thick trousers, 'what do you intend to do there?'

'I'm going to see if there's a Cistercian house that will give me a room for the night, before I head to London...'

Harry laughed.

'You're in luck, Clemo. Will's brother is the Porter at St Bernard's College. He'll see you right, won't he, Will?'

'He certainly will...and if you tell him how you stayed here last night and how sweet and generous and kind Brother Chad was, he will find you the best board and lodging in Oxford. And you can add that you met the biggest rogue in Oxfordshire too, a man called Harry who sends his compliments... and wonders when he's going to receive a haunch of venison from the College's kitchen.'

Will and Harry laughed as they ribbed each other.

'And when you go through Burford,' shouted Harry, 'your eyes will alight on the most beautiful woman in the world…and that will be my wife… give her my love!'

'Don't be taken in, Clemo,' replied Will, 'Harry has never married!! On your way then…and may God bless you.' He raised his huge, work-stained hand in a gesture very like a blessing.

It seemed a surprisingly pious exclamation from Will, but perhaps there was more to him than Clemo had first thought.

He waved them goodbye and set out on the long day's journey to Oxford. Bluey was on good form; the sun was shining, though there was a slight nip in the air, but the ride along the Oxford road was a delight and when he reached the city that afternoon, he was thrilled by all he saw. The stone of the new colleges was glowing golden in the sun, whilst the older colleges looked as though they had grown miraculously from the earth. Carts of Cotswold stone trundled past, moving towards Cardinal College. The road was thronged with students who seemed to Clemo to consist of two types: there were those who were lounging around enjoying themselves, whereas the others were scurrying determinedly towards lecture rooms. Idle play versus dutiful work.

Clemo soon found St Bernard's College where he was met by a tall, thin gatekeeper with well-defined eyebrows and hollow cheeks. He looked stern and unbending.

'I bring you greetings from Wiil, your brother at Bruern,' Clemo called out as he dismounted.

The man's face broke into a toothless grin.

'I stayed with him last night,' Clemo continued, 'and he told me that if I explained to you how sweet, kind and charitable Brother Chad had been, you might give me a room for the night.'

The gatekeeper laughed aloud, in fact, so loudly that one or two passers-by stopped to stare.

'Come in, young man. Come in. With that kind of recommendation, you are doubly welcome.'

He asked Clemo to stop briefly by the door while he called for a boy to look after Bluey. A boy of about thirteen came running up, looked at Bluey and smiled. Clemo patted Bluey and released him into the care of the happy boy.

'That boy', said the gatekeeper, 'is one of the best. He'll spoil your horse rotten. Now, step inside.'

Clemo found himself in a narrow, stone-flagged hallway; on one side there was a door, the top half of which was open.

'That's my little house... My name is George. Will is my older brother. As you can see, we are not very alike, but we visit each other as often as we can.'

'And my name is Clemo. I'm sorry, but I forgot to tell you that Harry asked when he could expect a haunch of venison.' George laughed aloud, a high, rasping laugh that ended with a downward gurgle. A happy man.

'Harry's a card,' he said, 'a real card. Now, young Clemo, how long are you going to stay with us?'

'One night, if possible. My plan is to head towards London tomorrow.'

'London? Evil place. Do you really have to go there?' asked George. 'Because if I were you, I'd avoid it like the plague. It's a nasty, stinking hole, that it is. I went there once. Never again. I couldn't get back here fast enough. Still, it's up to you... Now, let me organise your accommodation. Let me think....ah, yes, St Cuthbert is free.'

Clemo must have looked puzzled because George explained that every room in the College was named after a saint.

'Come with me.'

He turned to bolt the outer door, and then led Clemo past the chapel and towards some simple rooms on the west side. 'Lovely little rooms these,' he said, opening a door for Clemo to go through. 'Make yourself comfortable, and I'll bring you a jug of ale. You'll need it after coming from Bruern. You won't have been given much there.'

The room was indeed small, but it had a bed, a chair, a cupboard, a leather water bucket, and a fireplace in which a fire had been laid but not yet lit.

Clemo felt he could relax; after the vicissitudes of Bruern, this felt to him like a good place.

George was true to his word and was soon there with a jug of ale. He knelt down to light the fire with a steel, flint and tinder, and with the help of some wood shavings soon had the fire blazing.

'Now, sup this ale, and then if you feel like it, you could go for a walk around Oxford before Vespers. You'll hear the bell ring. Just go to the chapel and you'll be shown what to do.'

And with that, George left the room. Clemo sat on the chair and gazed at the fire, recollecting all that had transpired in the previous four days. It seemed more like a month, so much had happened. He felt pleased with all he had achieved, though when he thought of Dixton and the river, he was assailed by a sharp pang of homesickness.

To ease his melancholy, he decided to take George's advice and went out into the City. The smell from a nearby pie-shop close to St Bernard's whetted his appetite and he stopped to buy a gravy-rich meat pie. It was so delicious, so good, that he leaned against the wall just gazing around him, enjoying everything. He had never been in such a big city; never seen such fine buildings, never seen so many clerics and monks in one place. He was just wiping his mouth with his kerchief (he still had the last bits of the pie in his hand) when he turned to walk up the street. At that moment he received a massive blow on the back of his head and fell to the ground, poleaxed. His face hit the road with a dull thud and the world turned black.

He woke up in his room at St Bernard's several hours later where he saw a monk seated beside the fire.

'Hello, Clemo, how are you feeling?'

Clemo tried to move, but his head hurt so much that he winced with the pain.

'What's happened?' he asked.

'Someone tried to bash your head in,' replied the monk.

'I feel grim,' replied Clemo,'Sorry'.

'No need to apologise. It was lucky that George found you. He heard some scuffling and noise outside the gate, and there you were, in the gutter with a crowd of people standing round you. Apparently one of them said he saw your attacker running away with your purse in his fist. A couple of people gave chase, but the thief was faster and more cunning than them and he lost them.'

Clemo felt for his purse. It was no longer there next to his hose. All that was left was its leather strap, neatly sliced through.

'But that was all my money, everything I've got,' said Clemo.

'Look, Clemo, you mustn't worry yourself about that. We'll take care of you. I'm Brother Guy and I'm the Infirmarer here. 'So, take a drink of this.' He offered Clemo a tankard with some liquid herbal mixture in it. 'I've stoked up the fire. That drink will make you drowsy, but I'll be back later to see how you are doing.' He tiptoed out of the room. Within seconds, Clemo was asleep again.

Later that evening, he woke. A couple of candles were burning, their flickering flames revealing Brother Guy seated next to the bed.

Clemo groaned as he woke.

'Any better?' asked Brother Guy,

'I don't know yet,' replied Clemo, who still felt in a daze, but eased himself up slightly so that he could look around him.

'Lie still,' ordered Brother Guy, 'Now that you are awake, I need to bathe your face.'

He took a piece of soft cotton, dipped it into some warm water held in a copper bowl and very gently, with a maternal care, bathed the wounds that scarred Clemo's nose and forehead, and then carefully placed a warm towel on Clemo's face to help the blood begin its healing work.

Clemo felt soothed and asked where Brother Guy had learnt his skills. 'From a brilliant Jewish doctor in London', he replied. 'I always wanted to be an apothecary, but I felt called to be a monk, and here I am. Incidentally, who are Laura and Jestin?'

Clemo was startled by the question. How could this kind stranger possibly know the names of his beloved Laura and his first-born son?

'How did you know their names?' asked Clemo.

'Not a guess, Clemo. When you were brought in here you kept saying their names over and over again. You didn't know you were doing it. It's what often happens when the brain has received a blow, the body shuts down, but what is of central importance to the patient can emerge in repeated statements. In your case, you repeated two names, 'Laura' and 'Jestin' and you did that for a long while.'

Clemo's nose felt swollen. He touched his forehead and felt a large bump. And having satisfied himself that nothing was broken, except possibly his nose, he hesitantly told Brother Guy the story of Laura and Jestin, and about the death of his father.

Once he had finished, Brother Guy stayed very still and then said, 'You've suffered severe grief in your short life, Clemo. It's no wonder you needed to get away from things for a while. Now, continue to rest. I shall bring you some beef soup and once you've had that you will need to sleep again. Be assured that the Brothers in the chapel will be praying for you and for your swift return to health.'

His reassuring words and his gentle manner brought comfort to Clemo and he lay back on the pillow, trying to understand everything that had happened to him. But he couldn't get things in quite the right order and decided that he needed to relax and not worry. Perhaps everything would be alright, even if he was far from home and completely penniless.

Brother Guy returned with some soup which, because Clemo's lips were swollen, he spooned into Clemo's mouth.

Clemo lay back on the pillow and asked if Bluey was being looked after as well as he was.

'I've been to check him myself, he's fine, and the boy who looks after the stables has a real gift with horses, so, don't worry.'

Having thanked Brother Guy for his kindness, Clemo settled back onto the pillow and slept.

He woke early the next morning. He touched his forehead; the swelling had gone down a little. He felt his nose and thought that that too was in reasonable but sore shape. He carefully and slowly hauled himself up in bed and stepped out on to the wooden floor. Holding on to the wall for support he guided himself out of the door looking for the *necessarium*. It was along the corridor and there he found a highly polished metal mirror with which he could look at his face. He was appalled by what he saw: swollen lips, a larger than normal nose enhanced by a deep cut across the bridge, scabs above his eyebrows, a shiny lump on his forehead and two eyes that were beginning to take on the hue of Flaxley plums. In brief, his face was a mess.

Chapter 20: Recovery and after

For the next few days Clemo rested and began to join in the regular life of the College. He also went to see Bluey each day and gave the stable lad permission to ride Bluey whenever he wished.

Clemo, however, was facing a decision. He had set himself the task of going to London, but he had so settled into the life of St Bernard's that he was reluctant to leave. And then there was the problem of what to do about Bluey. His stepfather had told him to sell the horse but Clemo had become so attached to Bluey that he could not bear to think of the horse being sold to a stranger.

He was discussing his dilemma with Brother Guy, who had continued to look after him and had restored him to health, when Brother Guy said that he could not see the problem.

'Why not?' asked Clemo, surprised.

'Because one of the brothers here at St Bernard's is from Tintern. When he has to return to Tintern he could ride Bluey and arrange for your stepfather to collect him from there.'

Clemo was delighted with the idea and asked if he might meet the Tintern brother.

'Of course, I shall have to get permission from Father Abbot for you to come to the Parlour and then I can introduce you.'

Permission was granted and the following day Clemo met Brother Illtyd in the Parlour. They struck up an instant friendship having a love for Tintern in common.

'How well do you know Tintern?' asked Brother Illtyd. Clemo explained that he had made pewter crosses and medals for Tintern pilgrims and that he had had many conversations with Brother Adam.

'No!?' expostulated Illtyd, a short, wiry monk in his early twenties. 'Well, I never. Fancy you knowing Brother Adam. Small world isn't it, butty.'

It was Illtyd's use of the word 'butty', (a local Welsh Borders word for 'friend') which almost decided Clemo to return home. He missed the river. He missed his mother and his sisters. What was he thinking of doing by going on to London?

He said all of this to Illtyd who, to Clemo's surprise, whilst expressing sympathy, said, 'If God has called you to leave home, then leave home you must. You may not be able to see what God wants you to do in the future, but God always moves us forward, never backward.'

It was like a bucket of cold water being poured over his head, but it helped Clemo to remain firm in his resolve, even though the tug of home at that moment was strong.

'What are your plans when you get to the wicked city?' asked Illtyd.

'I don't know, but I have learned a bit about trust over the past days, so I shall see what happens. The only certainty is that I have been told by my priest at Dixton, Father Burley, that I should contact one of his friends from Oxford. See…'. He pulled a piece of paper from his pocket and showed the name and address on it to Illtyd.

'Well, that's good, Clemo, but how are you going to get from here to there?'

'I don't know, do you have any ideas?'

'Yes…I do, but first shouldn't you introduce me to Bluey who, I gather, I am to take back to Tintern? Come on, let's go to see Bluey and we can talk about your journey to London on the way.'

'Are you allowed to go to the stables, Brother Illtyd?'

'I am. What you need to understand Clemo is that St Bernard's is certainly a Cistercian house but life here is necessarily different from living in an abbey. In a word, it is more relaxed. We still say the Offices and go to Mass, but our focus has to be on learning, on books and lectures and conversation; that's how you learn, and I must admit that I love it, but my time here comes to an end next week and then Bluey and I will trot back to the Wye.' He smiled as he said it, and continued, 'You and I, Clemo, will be going in opposite directions. I shall go to Tintern with Bluey, and you will go to London with Brother Anton.'

'And who is Brother Anton?'

'He's a brother from St Mary de Graces right by the Tower of London. I've got to know him here in Oxford, and as we came up at the same time, we have become good friends. He is planning to leave in two days' time. I'll introduce you and you can discuss with him how you and he are going to travel together.'

They walked into the stables where the stable boy was rubbing Bluey down and giving him a treat of bran mash.

'He's a lovely horse, Master Clemo,' said the boy, 'you are lucky to have him.'

'I know,' replied Clemo, 'but he's now going to go back home to Tintern with Brother Illtyd, because I have to go on to London'.

The boy's face fell.

'Sorry,' said Clemo, recognising the boy's disappointment, 'but there will be other horses for you to look after in the future. And you are so good at your job those other horses will love you as much as Bluey does.'

'Especially if you give them bran mash,' interjected Illtyd, smiling,'…but not too much and not too often, it can upset their stomachs.'

Illtyd patted Bluey's neck, as did Clemo, and they left the boy to his tasks.

'No time like the present', said Illtyd, 'let's go to see if Brother Anton is in the Parlour and you can have a chat with him about travelling together.

They made their way across the cobbled courtyard and entered the main precincts of the College. At the Parlour door, Illtyd beckoned Clemo forward. They entered a vaulted room where three other brothers were in conversation. Illtyd called out to one of them, a tall, dark, hunchbacked individual,

'Anton, I want you to meet my friend Clemo. He knows Tintern well, so we've got a lot in common. He's on his way to London. He doesn't know how he's going to get there but I told him that you were the expert and that you might be able to accompany him. He's got a contact at St Mary Bowe, so he won't need to stay with you on Tower Hill. What do you say?'

Clemo felt embarrassed being discussed as though he were a parcel.

Brother Anton turned slowly to face them. Clemo noticed that Anton's back was not only hunched, but it was also quite twisted, so his movements were constrained. It gave him the appearance of an ageing philosopher, and his deep brown eyes sheltered by beetling eyebrows furthered the impression.

'I should be delighted to have company,' he said.

Clemo could not place his accent. It was not one he had heard before.

'I'll leave you two to fix the arrangements,' said Illtyd, 'I'm just going back to the stables to see a horse!' And he left the room.

Clemo and Anton sat on two wooden chairs and proceeded to get to know each other. Clemo explained his own background and Brother Anton said that he himself was not English but was originally from Cologne in Germany. He had come to London as clerk to a merchant who was based at the Steelyard but had gradually felt that he ought to become a monk, and because St Mary de Graces was close by he had gone there to test his vocation. He had been there, he explained, for almost ten years but had been sent to Oxford by his abbot to improve his knowledge of the Early Church Fathers.

Clemo shyly explained that he knew nothing about the Early Church Fathers but that he had been taught to read and write Latin by his parish priest. 'And by trade,' he said, 'I am an iron moulder though I have become very interested in pewter.'

'That's an unusual combination of skills,' replied Brother Anton, 'You should have no problem finding work in London…but now, let me change the subject, how are we going to get to London?'

'I really don't know,' replied Clemo.

'As you can see, ' said Brother Anton, reaching his right hand across his body and tapping his shoulder, 'I'm not built for riding or walking, so I was intending to take a boat. How would that suit you?'

'It sounds good,' replied Clemo, 'But I was robbed of all my money four days ago, so I cannot pay the fare.' His face fell.

'That's no problem,' replied Anton, 'As a monk, I don't have any money either, but my abbot will pay for me and I'm sure that he will pay for you as well.'

Clemo's face lit up but then moved into a frown.

'That would be marvellous,' he replied, 'but I can only accept your generosity on condition that once I have found work in London, I can then repay you.'

'That sounds good to me', said Anton. 'So, we shall meet at the Gatekeeper's Lodge in two days' time, after Prime, ready for our journey.'

He rose slowly and stiffly from the chair. Clemo thanked him profusely. Brother Anton fluttered his hand, saying, 'It is nothing,' and ushering Clemo ahead of him, left the Parlour.

The two days passed with Clemo going to the chapel to join the brothers as they said the Offices. And then, after breakfast on his final day came the moment he dreaded. He would have to go to the stables to say goodbye to Bluey. He steeled himself but was moved by the young boy's care of Bluey. He had so brushed and curry-combed Bluey that the horse looked ten years younger. Brother Illtyd came to the stable door.

'Come on, butty. It's time to go. I shall look after Bluey, I promise you…and just imagine how glad he'll be to be back in Hadnock.'

Clemo hugged Bluey, whispered his thanks and asked him to take his love to all the family. His eyes were damp with tears as he thanked the stable boy profusely. He walked with Illtyd to the outside door of the College where Brother Anton and a cart were waiting. George was there too, holding the horse's bridle.

'God speed Brother Anton', he said, 'and you too, Clemo…and mind how you go in that wicked city!'

The horse and cart plodded slowly to the riverbank where they found a large rowing boat waiting for them, manned by two bluff and hearty young oarsmen. They clambered in, Brother Anton having to be helped, and they were off.

As the boat moved easily through the water, Clemo reflected on his time at St Bernard's. It had been a good place to be, in spite of his robbery and assault and he hoped he might return there one day. They spent the first night at Reading Abbey, and the following day another rowing boat with a fresh couple of oarsmen took them on down the river. The nearer they got to London, the more the flow of the current aided them in speeding up their journey.

When they reached Hampton Court, Clemo was astounded by the size of the buildings with their gleaming new brickwork, chimneys, and lead-capped towers.

Brother Anton, who had turned out to be a man of few words, simply said, 'Cardinal Wolsey.'

'What?' exclaimed Clemo, 'Is that his?'

'It is,' said Brother Anton with a look of derisory contempt, and said no more.

As the journey continued, with the splash of the oars creating an almost hypnotic rhythm, Clemo could not believe that London could be so huge; nor did he expect it to be quite so smelly. The river, as they came nearer Westminster, seemed to be little more than an open sewer. He held his nose.

'You'll get used to it,' said Brother Anton, 'and that,' he said, pointing to his right, 'is Lambeth Palace, and on our left is Westminster Abbey. St Mary de Graces, my home, is sometimes called Eastminster.... but that is just a vain conceit.'

The river was swarming with boats; some crossing as ferries from the north to the south bank; some going from south to north; others loaded with victuals making their way upstream for Whitehall; others going downstream, taking drunken sailors to the larger ships waiting below London Bridge, Clemo was aghast at the busyness of it all...and as he had never seen a bridge on which houses had been built he could not help exclaiming, 'It's impossible...do people actually live there?' And then he noticed the tarred heads of traitors atop pikes at the entrance to the bridge and shuddered with disgust. The phrase 'wicked city' kept ringing in his ears.

The boat gathered speed as they shot under London Bridge, Clemo hanging on to the sides, and just beyond the bridge, it slewed across to the riverbank at the foot of the Tower of London.

'Here we are, gentlemen,' said one of the oarsmen, 'I take it you didn't want to go through Traitor's Gate...' and laughed.

Clemo climbed out, Anton tried to do the same but had to be helped because of his back.

They thanked and paid the oarsmen and climbed slowly up the slope beside the Tower to St Mary de Graces. Clemo was speechless with wonder…the size of the Tower, the noise at the wharves, the hordes of people hurrying, the ale-houses, the timber framed-houses jettying out over the dark streets, the packs of stray dogs, the manure and piles of offal, the slops being thrown out of upstairs windows, the crowds, the shouting, the jostling, the women, the men, the ragged children, the cripples, the priests…it was, in his eyes, a living chaos, a vision of hell. He stayed close to Brother Anton who took him into the abbey where a gatekeeper welcomed Brother Anton home.

The precincts, after the noise outside, were a haven of peace. Clemo's head was reeling. He was so glad of the stillness of the abbey but realised that he would have to go out into the chaos again to find some accommodation. How was he to do that?

Brother Anton suggested that they should go to the chapel to give thanks for their safe journey, and after they had said their prayers, said that Clemo might like a bite of food before going to St Mary Bowe.

Clemo was grateful, not least because it would put off the moment when he would have to venture out into the stinking maelstrom again. In truth, he was scared witless.

Brother Anton explained that he would organise a servant to accompany Clemo on his way.

A young, sandy-haired boy with a mischievous but pinched face and deep blue eyes was ordered by Anton to take Clemo on the final part of his journey.

'Right, Master,' said the boy, grinning, and sensing Clemo's bewilderment, 'where is it you want to go?'

'St Mary Bowe.'

'I'll carry your bag,' the boy volunteered, 'follow me.'

He set off at a brisk pace, Clemo struggled to keep up. But the boy obviously knew his way and said to Clemo as they left the abbey gateway, 'This is Hogge Lane…you'll recognise it by the smell of pigs… then we go through the Postern Gate', (the boy nodded his greeting towards the keepers of the gate. He was obviously well known) 'and once you are in the City, which we are now, the best way to find your way around is to remember the churches. So, this is All Hallows, Barking.' He pointed to a church on the right, at the junction of several roads.

Clemo nodded his head but wondered whether in the confusion even this first instruction might be too much to remember.

'And now we walk along Tower Street and this church is St Dunstan in the East, so we turn left. Are you still with me?' Clemo said he was, but in truth was almost overwhelmed already and asked, 'How many more churches until we get to St Mary Bowe?' The boy stopped, scratched his head, looked thoughtful and started counting on his fingers, then answered, 'About seven or eight. But let's push on.' Clemo noticed masts of ships on the river on his left, and people carrying goods down to the wharves. The place seemed to heave with people, all intent on their work, and the streets stank of fish and sewage.

'This is a street you'll get to know', said the boy, 'it's Thames Street and runs alongside the river...now, we're coming up to St Magnus the Martyr, and as you can tell by the crowds, this street on our left leads to London Bridge.'

Clemo looked down to his left, saw the spiked heads, and felt sick. After a few yards he asked if he might rest for a moment because he felt so nauseous. Against a house wall he bent over taking deep breaths. The boy looked on, a wry smile on his lips. Clemo took a few breaths of the fetid air and then said he was ready to continue.

'This,' said the boy, pointing to a small church,'...is All Hallows the Less and just a few yards further on is All Hallows the Great. Don't ask me why there are two All Hallows...and we keep going....until we get to St Martin Vintry on our right. Remember that, Sir...because it is just here that we turn right up Garl Hill. Not far now.'

The gentle climb away from the river meant that the air was slightly sweeter. 'And on our right is St James, Garlickhythe. I can't stand garlic myself, how about you? It's only fit for the French, the stinkers' He laughed at his own joke.

'Honestly, Sir, not much further, but I must point out to you this church on our right which is St Mary Aldermary, and do you know what street we are crossing now?'

Clemo admitted that he didn't. His head was whirling with so many images and names and landmarks.

'This' said the boy proudly, 'is a Roman road called Watling Street and if you followed it all the way to our left you would eventually end up in Chester; but now, here we are, Bowe Lane, and that is St Mary Bowe. So, I'll hand you your bag and wish you good day.' And with a smile and a laugh he ran back the way he'd come, waving as he went.

Clemo shouted his thanks after him, but guessed that the boy, in all the noise, didn't hear.

He stopped for a moment, took a breath to steady his nerves and found the Parsonage

He looked at the stout oak door, wondering as he knocked, what might happen next.

A servant in a simple blue dress and apron answered the door. She was a girl of about fourteen years of age with a pale, indoor face, and slight, sloping shoulders.

'Good morrow. My name is Clemo, and I have brought a note from Father Burley.' He took the crumpled piece of paper out of his pocket, straightened the creases, and was about to hand it to the girl when he heard a voice booming from inside the house, 'Did I hear the name Burley?' And towards Clemo came a giant of a man. 'I'm Father Mossman,' he boomed, 'And who might you be?'

Clemo explained and said that he brought greetings from Father Burley.

'If you are a parishioner of that old rascal,' he declared in his resonant voice, 'then you had better come in and tell me more about yourself.'

The maid stood shyly to one side but did not fail to notice Clemo's striking green eyes as he walked past her following Father Mossman into the parlour.

Chapter 21: Arrival and the job search

He found himself in a large and handsome wood-panelled parlour and was told to take a seat. Father Mossman rang a small hand bell to summon the maid. She arrived promptly and listened carefully to Father Mossman's instructions but looked swiftly at Clemo as she left the room to fetch a couple of tankards of ale. She loved his eyes. Clemo didn't notice her glance.

'Now, young man, begin your story…'

Clemo told Father Mossman his entire life story and laid emphasis upon the part Father Burley had played during his recent bereavements.

'He's a good man and a marvellous priest,' said Father Mossman. 'Truth to tell, I am nothing like as good a priest as he is.'

It was not the maid who interrupted Clemo's narrative but a buxom woman in her mid-thirties wearing a white dress, yellow velvet bodice, blue apron and a blue cap. She brought in the tankards and slices of meat pie on two pewter plates. She glanced at Father Mossman and then at Clemo as she handed him his plate.

'This is Mistress Blake,' explained Father Mossman, 'she's my housekeeper. I am a lucky man.'

Clemo did not notice the slight blush that infused Father Mossman's face.

'Thank you, Mistress', said Clemo.

She left the parlour, no doubt to discuss Clemo with the maid waiting in the kitchen.

'And what are your plans?' asked Father Mossman, wiping his mouth with the linen napkin that Mistress Blake had provided.

'I must first find somewhere to sleep tonight and then tomorrow I shall start to search for work.'

'Look', said Father Mossman, 'you have had a long journey to get here. You must stay with us this night and then we can think about where you might stay from tomorrow onwards. But don't worry about that now, I already have a plan'. He smiled. 'The City is a big and amazing place, but people know each other, and as I have been here for some years, I know my parish and the City like the back of my hand. Just leave the worrying to me.' The maid entered the room to clear away the plates and was requested to fetch two more tankards. She tried hard not to glance at Clemo, but was tempted, and fell. She hurried out, anxious and delighted to have an excuse to return with fresh drinks.

When she returned, she handed a tankard to Clemo and in doing so spilt a few drops of the ale on his shoes. She apologised, handed the other tankard to Father Mossman and before leaving the room bent down at Clemo's feet and with another blushing apology wiped the few drops of ale from his grubby shoes with a blue kerchief.

Clemo was touched by her kindness and once she had left the room said so to Father Mossman.

'She's a good girl,' he said, 'Mistress Blake has brought her up well.'

He hurriedly changed the subject.

'Your work,' he said, 'what do you have in mind?'

Clemo explained that he was an iron moulder by trade but having grown up on a smallholding was also used to animals, and then added that Father Burley had taught him Latin.

'You are a man of many parts then,' replied Father Mossman. 'It shouldn't be too difficult to get you something whilst you find your feet in the City, but now, look…after a journey like yours you will need to rest.' He rang the bell. The maid appeared. 'Ask Mistress Blake to make a bed ready for our guest, and once you have done that, come back here and make up the fire. I need to go to see a parishioner in a few minutes, and our guest is to stay here until his room is available. Is that understood?'

'Yes, Father.'

Clemo heard her running down the corridor to give Mistress Blake the instructions.

'I have to go now,' said Father Mossman, 'but stay here and then when your bedroom is completed, you can take your things up there and wait for my return. I should be about an hour.'

The maid returned with a bucket of coal, begged Clemo's pardon for interrupting him and deftly placed some coal on the fire. As she turned to leave, Clemo asked her how long she had worked for Father Mossman.

'I'm not sure how to answer that,' she replied, 'You could say that I've been here as long as Mistress Blake.' There was a pause. 'She's my mother, and I have a younger brother. He's ten. He lives here too. He's called Edward.'

'And what's your name, may I ask?'

'I'm Alice,' she replied, curtsied, and left the room with a rustle of skirts.

Clemo gazed at the fire and began to come to terms with where he was. In fact, he spoke aloud, saying, 'I am Clemo and I am now in London.' It was the only way that he could register the enormity of all that had happened to him over the previous couple of weeks.

Alice, having tapped lightly on the door, came in and explained that Clemo's room was now ready.

She took him up a fine, polished oak staircase and opening a door showed him his room. There was a half-tester bed draped with heavy curtains; the bedspread was embroidered, and in the grate there was a new fire burning which Alice bent down to tend.

'This is such a lovely room!' exclaimed Clemo. He walked to the window and looked out.

'That's Cheapside,' explained Alice, anxious to help and trying to find an excuse to stay a little longer. 'It leads up to St Paul's.'

Clemo watched as crowds of people walked by. There was such a mixture, some people in fine and costly garments, others in dirty, work-stained clothes, others in rags. The contrast was striking.

'Thank you, Alice,' said Clemo, 'You may go now.' And as he said the words, he realised that he was already picking up a way of speaking which he would never have used in Monmouth.

He continued to look out of the window and watched as a couple of brown-robed friars joshed with one another as they sauntered up the road.

He lay on the bed. It was so soft; a feather bed more luxurious than any bed he'd ever seen before. He touched the surrounding half tester curtains lightly. The fabric was so rich and beautiful, just the kind of fabric that Laura would have loved. And the air was scented with lavender. The combination of the bed, the fire and the lavender meant that he was soon asleep.

It was a knock on the door which roused him. It was Alice, again. 'Father Mossman has returned and invites you to join him in the dining room for supper,' she said, her cheeks dimpling.

Clemo followed her down the stairs and into another wood-panelled room, in the centre of which was a long oak table piled with food: breads and pies and meats and fresh fruit and jugs of ale, mead and cider. A feast.

'Clemo. We have killed the fatted calf…not that you are a Prodigal Son, but we thought we should have something a little special to welcome a pewter-making Latin scholar into our family. Please sit, and if there's anything more you need, you must tell me, and Mistress Blake will find it for you, I'm sure.'

They tucked in. And soon Father Mossman explained his plans.

'I've been thinking, Clemo. There are two ways of finding work in the City; either you know somebody, or you go to the 'Si Quis' door at St Paul's and pin your requests for work there. But I have used the former method: I have just been to see a parishioner who has contacts with the senior steward of the new Imperial Ambassador, Eustace Chapuys. He lives near Austin Friars, it's no distance from here, about a half mile, and apparently, the Steward is looking for a servant who could help both in the house but also, when necessary, help with the horses. How does that sound?'

'It sounds wonderful,' replied Clemo, a broad grin stretching across his face, 'but do you think I am educated enough to work for an Ambassador?'

'Look, Clemo… unlike most servants, you have Latin, you have a craft, you can handle animals, and you're a friend of Father Burley… could there be any higher recommendation?' His booming laugh filled the room. 'I think we can agree that you should begin there as soon as possible, preferably tomorrow. You will need to take your things because the servants live in…and you will join them. At least it will be a roof over your head and there will be food on the table…it will be tremendous. You'll love it. And if you play your cards right, you will meet some of the most powerful people in the country, even if it's only holding their horses for them. It's amazing what gossip you will be able to pick up. And my advice? Hear everything, say nothing.' He chortled and reached out his hand to ring a bell.

Alice appeared. 'Ask your mother to come here for a moment, there's a good girl.'

Clemo thought that it was an endearing and over-familiar way to treat a servant but followed Father Mossman's advice and said nothing.

Mistress Blake entered the room. 'Marguerite,' said Father Mossman, 'would you mind joining us for a moment?' She sat on a chair on the opposite side of the table, next to Clemo. 'I just want your opinion. Clemo is going to work for the new Imperial Ambassador at Austin Friars, beginning tomorrow. What should he do to make sure he creates a good impression from the start?'

'You must forgive me, Master Clemo, for what I am about to say. But you have been travelling for many days. You will need clean clothes for tomorrow, so give me all your laundry as soon as supper is over and then I will get your clothes washed and dried ready for you in the morning.'

Clemo was amazed by the kindness he was being shown and stuttered his gratitude. But Mistress Blake continued, 'I shall also bring some hot water to your room, and you must wash your hands and face thoroughly, because that too will help, and finish off by rubbing yourself all over with the linen cloth that I shall provide…excuse me for saying so, but the City is a smelly place at the best of times and the smells can get into your clothes and into your skin, but a fresh-faced, sparkling, clean young man coming for a job, will create a good and wholesome impression...'

'Any other advice, Marguerite?' asked Father Mossman.

'Not advice, but a question. How will Clemo find his way to Austin Friars tomorrow?'

'I hadn't thought of that,' replied Father Mossman, vaguely.

'So, it's a good job that I did,' said Mistress Blake. 'With your permission, Father, Alice and I will walk with Clemo tomorrow after breakfast, and I can get some things we need on the way.'

Very early the next morning Clemo woke feeling flutteringly nervous. He found his clothes, clean and freshly pressed, on a chair, and hurriedly dressed. He stumbled down the stairs and found freshly baked bread and cheese already laid on the table awaiting his arrival. Alice was there too and asked if he would prefer ale or mead. 'Ale, please, Alice.'

She left the room and very soon had returned with a tankard. 'I didn't spill any this time,' she said, looking at Clemo anxiously but he was feeling so nervous he hardly replied. 'And as soon as you are finished, we must leave,' she said. It was clear that she had inherited some of her mother's confident and thoughtful character. 'Just call us when you have packed your bag.' Clemo returned to his room, said an Ave and Pater Noster to steady his nerves, and clattered down the stairs, bag in hand.

Mistress Blake and Alice carrying a rush-woven basket were waiting for him.

'I should say goodbye to Father Mossman,' said Clemo.

'He's already at Mass but he said to give you his blessing and good wishes and wants you to know that you can always return here if ever you need anything, So, let's go...it really isn't far'.

They stepped out on to Cheapside where, although it was early, there were plenty of people going about their business, though Clemo noticed that most of them were ill-dressed, and he didn't see anyone wearing sumptuous clothes. It was obviously far too early for that.

Mistress Blake and Alice walked on his right-hand side and set a brisk pace. Within a few yards Clemo noticed a number of servants queuing to collect water from a gushing fountain. 'That's the Great

Conduit,' said Alice, 'it's where I meet my friends when I come to get water for our house.' She waved at another young girl and explained to Clemo that the girl was called Gerlinde, a German, and was a servant for a German merchant in the Steelyard. A little way further on, they passed on their left-hand side, St Mildred Poultry, and at a fork in the road they bore left and came to St Christopher le Stocks.

All the while Mistress Blake had not spoken but clearly, there was something that was troubling her. At the church porch she stopped.

'Clemo, there's something else I need to say to you.'

Clemo looked worried and wondered if he had unwittingly done something to upset her and so blurted out that he had really appreciated her kindness and the way she and Alice had looked after him.

'It has been our pleasure, Clemo', she replied, 'you have been a lovely guest, but you are now going to a different kind of house and I feel I should warn you. You will not know anything about the ways of an Ambassador but what you need to remember is that the Ambassador is here to represent his Master, in this case, the Holy Roman Emperor. It is to the Emperor that he owes his complete loyalty. He will have a large staff and you will be joining them. You may find it exciting, but you must always remember that you are going to live in a nest of spies. I know that Father Mossman advised you that you should hear everything and say nothing. It was good advice, and my advice adds to that. You should wait for a long time before you decide who to trust, and even then, be extremely careful. Remember they are all spies, and you won't know whether they are loyal to the Ambassador, or whether they might be being paid to be loyal to King Henry, or to the Queen, or to one of the great Dukes. I have probably spoken out of turn, but I worked for an Ambassador once, the French ambassador, and it was a nightmare. I was young and innocent which meant that when I met Father Mossman and was asked to work for him, it was a huge relief. I was back in a saner and kinder world. So, that's all. Just remember…a nest of spies.'

She looked at him and saw his green eyes fogged with anxiety. She gently touched his arm, and said, 'Not much further now, and please come back to see us. We would like that, wouldn't we, Alice?'

Alice agreed, and blushed.

At the junction of Throgmorton Street and Broad Street they came to the Austin Friars Gatehouse.

'Here you are, Clemo. We are going to leave you now. Just ask at the Gatehouse for the Ambassador's residence and you will be given instructions. Goodbye and may Our Lady and all the Saints be with you. It's the Ambassador's High Steward you need to see.'

Alice waved and she and her mother turned for Cheapside, leaving Clemo to cross the road and begin a new life.

Chapter 22: At the Ambassador's Residence

Clemo stood nervously on the threshold of the Gatehouse. A man with one eye, a stubbly chin, and a few teeth randomly set behind drooling lips, came out of the adjoining lodge, and spoke brusquely to him.

'Yes?'

The man was wearing a uniform of a dark-blue cap in which was a silver badge, a leather jerkin, also with a silver badge attached, breeches and grey hose. In his belt was a dagger in a leather sheath.

'I have an appointment with the Ambassador's High Steward,' Clemo falteringly explained.

'And your name is?'

'Clemo Trelawney.'

'You're expected. Follow the road to your left; this is Throgmorton Street, and you'll find the Ambassador's house on your right-hand side, close to Master Cromwell's house.' The gatekeeper spat.

'You're new to the City?'

'Yes, I am'.

'In that case, you'd better have a look inside the Friary precincts.' He guided Clemo through the gateway and there ahead of him was a graveyard, and just beyond it, a large church, surrounded by gardens. He guessed that there were other buildings beyond, such as cloisters and dining hall.

'Big, isn't it?' said the gatekeeper. He was a man of few words. 'If you are going to work for His Excellency, you can come in here when you want…but you must check with me whether it's convenient or not.'

And with that he escorted Clemo to the street again.

Clemo passed a very large house on his right-hand side and then came to another imposing building. Above the lintel of the door was a Coat of Arms, two silver lions on a blue background, surmounted by a double-headed eagle. He decided that this must be the house of the Ambassador. He banged on the door with his fist and waited. He heard footsteps from beyond the door and then the great door was opened by a liveried servant.

'My name is Clemo Trelawney and I have come here at the request of the High Steward because there is a job he wants me to do.'

He said the words as confidently as he could, but his throat constricted, and the final words only just made it past his lips.

'You are expected,' said the servant, 'follow me.' Clemo found himself in a hall with a floor made from alternating red and black tiles, the walls were covered with tapestries stitched in green, red, yellow and blue wool. They came to another heavy door on the left. 'Wait here and I will enquire whether you are to see the High Steward immediately.'

Clemo waited, shifting his bag from one shoulder to another, smoothing his hair down under his Monmouth cap.

'Come through,' said the servant, 'The High Steward will see you now.'

A middle-aged man with a stern face and heavy jowls was seated behind a desk. Although there was a chair to the side, Clemo was not asked to sit.

'Good morning. You are Clemo Trelawney,' announced the man, as though he were conferring Clemo's name upon him. 'And you are going to be an occasional groom but mostly a servant for His Excellency, the Ambassador. Your name was given to us by Father Mossman at St Mary Bowe. He commended you. That is good.' The man's accent was thick, guttural, and strong. 'You must understand right from the beginning that your loyalty is to His Excellency. You are not to discuss anything you see or hear in this place outside these walls. Is that understood?'

'Yes, it is,' whispered Clemo, and suddenly an image of the River Wye at Hadnock floated into his mind. He felt a long way from his birthplace.

The High Steward was seated at a desk which was sideways on to a window overlooking the street. Clemo glanced outside; an elderly man and woman shuffled past.

'You will wear His Excellency's livery when you are out in public accompanying him or one of his senior staff, and also when you are serving him in the house. Breakfast will be at 4am from mid-March to mid-September, and 6am from mid-September until mid-March. Dinner will be at 10.30 am, supper at 3pm. The meal-times for other guests and senior staff will be one hour later, after you servants have had your meals and prepared the tables for everyone else. You will be paid every quarter and your contract will be renewed, or not, as the case may be, at Martinmas. Is that clear also?

'Yes, Sire,' replied Clemo.

'Good. Then I shall call someone to take you to your sleeping quarters where you will be supplied with your livery. By the way, my name is Herman Keller and if ever you have any serious concerns you must come to see me. We Swiss, you will discover, are a rigorous and just people…'

There was a polite knock on the door.

'Come,' yelled the High Steward. The door opened and a young servant, aged about eighteen dressed in a simple indoor livery, entered the room. He gave a slight bow.

'This is Clemo Trelawney. He is new. You are to take him at once to his quarters and there you will explain to him the rules of the house.'

'Yes, Master.'

Clemo thanked the High Steward and taking his cue from the servant, bowed slightly before he left, accompanying the servant into the hall.

The servant was English. 'Welcome,' said the young man, 'my name's Tom Saunders.'

They walked through a maze of corridors and emerged into a garden which was bathed in early morning sunlight.

Clemo looked at everything around him and asked the servant how long he had worked for the Ambassador.

'About two years. It's not a bad berth as long as you behave yourself. The High Steward is a real disciplinarian, so watch your step. He has a quick temper and if you get on the wrong side of him, woe betide you. You'll be out on the street before you can say Anne Boleyn!'

Clemo did not understand the reference to Anne Boleyn but decided not to ask who she might be. They came to an outbuilding and climbed some stairs. At the top, Tom ushered Clemo into a room where there were four straw mattresses, four chests with four candlesticks on each one, four chairs, and nothing else. On one of the chairs was a pair of trousers. 'They'll be Hans' trousers. He shouldn't have left them there. He's an untidy slob…. He's a Fleming, so we call him 'Spit'. He doesn't like it, but tough.'

'Which is my bed?' asked Clemo.

'This one nearest the door and the draughts,' replied Tom, chuckling.

'And my livery? Where do I get that from?'

'I shall fetch it for you now. Don't go away.' Tom hastened out of the room and clattered down the stairs. Clemo watched through the window as Tom hurried across the garden stopping briefly to chat with a maid carrying a basket of laundry,

Tom soon returned, his arms laden with the clothes: four linen undershirts and underdrawers, two sets of black woollen breeches, two pairs of pale-grey hose, two dark-grey cloth doublets made from a thick woollen fabric decorated along the arms with contrasting pale-grey stripes and a silver lion embroidered on the left shoulder, a black cloth cap, a linen rubbing cloth, and two white aprons.

'There you are,' he announced, 'That's your lot. Your laundry will need to be put out each day in a basket at the bottom of the stairs, and one of the laundry maids will see to it. You will need to be measured for some black shoes, but they will take a while for the cordwainers to make; so, for the moment, make your own shoes as presentable as you can. You must keep your clothes in the chest by your bed and they must always be folded neatly. And the apron…ah, the apron. You must carry your apron rolled up in your left hand, like this…' He demonstrated. 'Now, you do it, Clemo.' Clemo tried but the result was a lopsided mess. 'Rubbish,' said Tom, 'do it again.' On the third go it was classed as just about acceptable. 'You only wear your apron in the main house; never in the garden, and never when you walk across from here to the house. That's the rule. And you must put your apron out to be washed each night. Don't forget. Dirty aprons are not acceptable to the High Steward…and he is a stickler for things like that.'

'Thank you, Tom,' replied Clemo, overwhelmed by all the clothes he had been given, 'but I thought I was to be a groom as well as a servant. Where do I get my groom's working clothes from?'

'Simple,' replied Tom,'from the Head Groom. I'll take you to meet him in a minute. He's a funny old codger but what he doesn't know about horses is not worth knowing. He's a great man, in spite of being Spanish. He's called Pablo.'

'But now before we do that, I must take you to the sewing room. Bring all your livery…don't forget the aprons…and the girls will embroider your name on everything you wear. Treat the girls nicely, because they are gold.'

As they walked back through the garden, Clemo asked Tom where he was from.

'I was born in Ashwell,' he said. 'Have you ever been there?' Clemo admitted that he did not know where Ashwell was, and so had never been there.

'It's just off the Great North Road, on the top edge of Hertfordshire,' Tom explained, 'It's marvellous corn country. I worked on a farm when I was younger, but my father died; my mother and sisters had to move out and I got this job here. But sometimes I really miss the fields and the views. Still, beggars can't be choosers.'

They reached the sewing room which was on the ground floor with a steady north light. The top half of the door opened once Tom had knocked on it, revealing the bottom half of the door constructed with a shelf across its width.

'This is a new man,' explained Tom, 'he's called Clemo, so could you kindly embroider his name on all his clothes. We'll be back in five minutes, when you've finished.' He laughed, took the livery from Clemo and placed it on the shelf.

The woman who had answered the door swiped at him with a piece of cloth and told him to go away, but as she did so, one of the sewing women shouted, 'Are you Cornish, Clemo…because with a name like that, you're bound to be? I am.'

'Actually,' replied Clemo, 'my father was Cornish. My surname is Trelawney, but I was born in Monmouth.'

'I was born near there,' said one of the other women, still wielding her needle but joining in the conversation.

'Whereabouts?' asked Clemo.

'Dingestow' she replied and Clemo smiled, 'I know it well. I used to live at Hadnock and worked at Redbrook at the Foundry.'

The woman put her sewing down. 'Well, I never. My uncle is Ifor Young. See…, ' she said to the other women, 'I told you I was famous and knew everybody.' They laughed. 'Now Clemo Trelawney, you can come to this door as often as you like so that I can hear your accent. You make me feel homesick, honest you do.' She picked up the textile she was working on and jabbed at it with her needle to cover up the fact that she had tears in her eyes.

Tom announced that they had to go and thanked them all.

'You made a real hit there, Clemo. That woman from Monmouth is called Gwen. She's had a hard life, but it will have made her day to have met you.'

They hurried back across the inner yard and skirting the bedroom block came to the stables.

Pablo was just leading a horse out, a deep black rouncey, its coat shining in the sunlight. It tossed its head, and the light caught the fine, highly decorated cast iron curb bit, and the stirrups created with a similar striking beauty.

Clemo gasped involuntarily. A stunning horse, stunningly equipped.

'Pablo,' shouted Tom, 'this is your new groom, Clemo Trelawney.'

'Pleased to meet you, Sire,' said Clemo.

'Buenos Dias' replied Pablo, 'I'm Pablo de Roma and if you will excuse me for a minute, I just want to walk Profundo around to make sure he's turned out as he should be.' He led the horse in a gentle circle on the yard's cobbles, professed himself satisfied except for a bit of wax needed on the girth and asked them to step inside.

Clemo breathed in deeply: the smell of crushed hay, leather, horse sweat, and manure, it was a heady and evocative mixture.

'Muy buenas,' said Pablo.

'Ignore him!' declared Tom, cheekily, 'he speaks English fluently.'

'And you Maestro Clemo, must ignore Tom. He claims to have grown up on a farm, but all he understands is corn. He doesn't know the back end of a horse from the front.' Profundo, catching the mood, decided at that very moment to dump a load of steaming manure on to the stable floor.

'And that, Tom, is the back end,' said Pablo indicating the horse's rump, and laughing.

Tom explained that this was Clemo's first morning at work and that he had been given his servant's clothes for indoor and outdoor use, but Clemo now would like to know what clothes he should wear in the stables.

'Good point,' replied Pablo and turning to look more closely at Clemo and assessing him for size suddenly noticed Clemo's green eyes and exclaimed 'hermosos ojos verdes' ('beautiful green eyes'), but then felt a bit self-conscious about his comment and led them to a far corner of the stable where several canvas aprons were hanging from wooden pegs. He chose one, told Clemo to try it on and then declared, 'That's good, It suits you. It shall be yours from now on.'

At that moment, a bell on the outside of the house rang.

'Ah', said Tom, 'time for dinner. Thank you, Pablo, we'll see you later.' He put his same through Clemo's arm and walked him briskly towards a stout door at the right-hand side of the house. And as he walked he explained that dinner for the servants was at 10.30am. 'I'll take you in.' He opened the door and pushed Clemo ahead of him. 'Straight on,' he said, 'and on the right is another door, we go through that'. Clemo paused, ahead of him was a long refectory table at which the men servants were seating themselves. There was a buzz of conversation which stopped as Clemo entered. 'Gentlemen,' declared Tom, 'this is Clemo Trelawney. It's his first day here…so be very nice to him… but you can beast him later.' The men laughed. Tom escorted Clemo to a place at the lowest end of the table and explained that the newest men sat there and gradually moved up to the top of the table when they had been there longer. Clemo sat and smiled weakly at everyone. He was feeling overwhelmed with the new experiences and felt that he might not be able to speak. These men were going to be his new colleagues. Who were they? How long had they been in the Ambassador's service? But then he brought to mind Mistress Blake's advice about a nest of spies. Could these men really be spies? Was Tom, who had been so affable, was he a spy? And where was Hans seated? Might he be a spy?

His reverie was interrupted by a fat young man stumbling into the room. As he arrived, the table yelled with one voice, 'Spit, spot, the last to the pot.' Hans apologised and reddened with embarrassment. And then the room went silent as the Deputy High Steward walked in and stood behind his seat at the head of the table. On seeing him, everyone stood, bowed their heads and the house chaplain muttered a Latin grace. 'Amen' chorused the servants.

The first meal for Clemo in the new house, began.

Chapter 23: Horses and family trees

Dinner had been huge, three courses of food: potage, fresh bread, and boiled meats, followed by roast meat and vegetables, with tarts and sweetmeats as a third course, all washed down with ale. Clemo had never seen so much food and after the abstemious simplicity of the Cistercian abbeys at which he had stayed on his journey, it seemed gross. However, he said nothing and observed all. An eighteen-year-old young man next to him explained that the courses were served by the kitchen servants. Clemo nodded.

After the meal, Tom Saunders collected him and said that he would train Clemo in a few of his duties as a household servant, which he duly did. But there was so much to learn and Clemo's mind was spinning.

It was a relief to have another break for a light meal at 4pm. This time Clemo found his own way to the dining room and sat next to the eighteen-year-old. He introduced himself, and the young man explained that he was called Antonio; his parents were Italian, from Venezia, but he had lived in London since he was small.

Clemo had not expected so many nationalities to be working together in one house but politely asked Antonio whether he spoke Italian at home. 'Si, signore,' he replied, smiling, 'Of course. Why don't you learn Italian, Clemo? I could teach you.' Clemo thanked him and said he might well take him up on his offer and explained that he himself had learnt Latin. Antonio was amazed and wanted to know what a man who read and spoke Latin was doing as a servant. Clemo gave him a brief summary of his life, to which Antonio listened with great attention.

'Laura sounds as though she was a bella signora,' and he touched Clemo lightly on the arm, 'ah, but what a terrible loss you have suffered.

Terrible. Oddio. Terrible.' He put his right hand on his heart to indicate his sympathy.

When they rose from table, Tom again accompanied Clemo, and showed him the gardens, and the main rooms of the house. 'How did you get on with Antonioo?' he asked, 'He's a charmer, isn't he? He lives at home with his family and comes in each day, and if you want some cheap fruit, or want to know which is the best ale house, or even the best bawd, he's your man.'

Clemo pretended to be worldly wise and thanked Tom for his advice but then asked what else he had to learn before it was time to make for his bed. 'Nothing,' said Tom, 'you are now free, but you must be in the servants' dining room by 4 tomorrow morning wearing your indoor livery and you'll be given your instructions then.' Clemo was delighted to have a few moments on his own and simply wandered around the garden before making his way to the stables to see if Pablo was there.

He was indeed there, mucking out.

He greeted Clemo. 'Buenos tardes, Clemo. If you like, you can put your apron on and give me a hand.'

Clemo was delighted to do so, it was a routine he knew from home and its steady rhythm soothed his mind.

'Horses are better than hombres,' said Pablo. 'They don't play dirty tricks on you, eh? They don't spy on you and tell tales, eh?' He leaned on his pitchfork and looked at Clemo. 'I don't know how many days you will be expected to work with me, Clemo…you will learn that tomorrow from Tom, or from the Deputy Steward, but I think we might get along well. You seem to love horses, eh?'. He looked at Clemo, ' I'll tell you why I love horses…they don't lie.'

Clemo thanked Pablo for allowing him to help on his very first day. 'No es nada, it's nothing…now go to your bed, tomorrow is another day…'

Clemo climbed wearily to the bedroom and found Hans there, stripped to the waist, his clothes strewn across his bed. There were two others in the room lying on top of their beds, their hands behind their heads. 'Hello,' he said to a ginger-headed young man on the bed next to his, 'I'm Clemo Trelawney.'

'I'm Paddy O'Flynn' he said, 'and you'll never guess where I'm from!'

And laughing, the other one explained that he was called Pierre Caron.

'He's our pet frog,' said Paddy throwing a pillow at him.

Hans was still trying to get his livery in order, which reminded Clemo that he still hadn't collected his from the Sewing Room.

He explained that he would be back in a minute but just had to go collect his livery. 'Give our love to Gwen,' said Paddy. The others, even Hans, laughed.

Clemo rushed across the courtyard and skeetered to a halt in front of the Sewing Room door.

He knocked. To his relief, the half door opened. 'Yes?' said Gwen. '…oh, it's you Clemo, my friend from Monmouth. I've put your name on everything. There you are, *cariad.*'

'Thank you very much, Gwen,' he said, the sound of his mother's '*cariad*' ringing in his ears and began to run back towards the bedroom. He was stopped by an angry shout. It was one of the men who sat near the head of the servants table, 'Hey you! No running in the courtyard, you stupid knave. Now, go back to the house door and then walk to your room.'

Clemo, suddenly seething with anger for being treated like a little child and bristling with the 'foolish knave' insult, did as he was told, but carefully noted the man's face. That man, he vowed to himself, would not speak to him like that, ever again…

When he got back to the room, the others were still lying on their beds. Hans had managed to stuff his livery in his bed-side chest, though the lid would not shut. They asked whether Clemo had found the Sewing Room still open. 'And did Gwen send her love to us?' asked Paddy, and Pierre told him to grow up. Clemo carefully folded his clothes before placing them in his chest, and then lay down on his bed.

'What's up?' asked Pierre noticing that Clemo was looking forlorn.

'I was shouted at for running in the courtyard,' he explained. 'I hadn't been told that it was against the rules.'

'Welcome to the residency of His Excellency, the Imperial Ambassador,' retorted Paddy, 'a house where rules are changed daily, and you can get a beating just for breathing.' Hans said nothing. Pierre hushed Paddy.

'I bet that the shouter was Guillaume la Grande Bouche.' Pierre again tried to quieten him. 'Well, Pierre, my friend,' said Paddy mischievously,' if you will teach me your froggy lingo…' Pierre hurled another pillow at him.

'What do you think, Spit?' asked Paddy, 'Have you noticed that Pierre le frog is bullying me?'

Hans did not reply but climbed into bed and turned his back on Paddy.

The unspoken tensions in the room meant that once Clemo had climbed into bed he could not sleep. Too much had happened. Too much was strange.

The following morning, he was woken early by Paddy who reminded him that it was time to go to Mass.

He hurriedly dressed, walked with the others from the bedroom to the Hall, where a priest had set up a portable altar. All the residents trooped in, including the Ambassador who came in last with the High Steward just behind him. and sat in a chair near the altar. Mass began. The familiarity of the Latin service soothed away Clemo's anxieties and so he went to breakfast at the end of Mass with a lighter heart than might have been expected.

Antonio sat next to him and asked him if he had had a good night and whether he was ready to begin his Italian lessons.

'You are kind,' replied Clemo, 'I would like to accept your offer but give me a week to get used to this place and then I shall have a better idea of how I can manage a new language.'

'After your Latin skills,' said Antonio, 'Italian will be easy. But I must go in a few minutes, I have letters to write for the Chief Secretary.'

'So, is that your job here?'

'Si. Yes…coming from Venice, as my family did, I inherited their love of fine paper and learnt to write, which led to me coming here as an Under Clerk. There's a Senior Clerk, but he is an inky fellow and doesn't have my elegant penmanship…,' he laughed, 'which is how I get to write some of the most important letters for His Excellency. Ciao.' He smiled, and left Clemo to finish his ale.

A hand tapped him on the shoulder. It was Tom Saunders. 'You need to get your instructions now; I'll take you to meet the Deputy Steward.'

They left the Servants' Dining Room and following a long, stone flagged corridor, came to a door covered in green baize. Tom tapped lightly, and hearing a voice calling out 'Enter', took Clemo to meet Nathaniel Johnson. He was tall, about thirty-five years of age, with receding hair, and a look of wily authority.

'Good Morning, Clemo. Now…your jobs for today: firstly, you will spend the morning with the Chief Groom, and after dinner you will find Tom who will introduce you to more of the work you are to do in the house. But before you go. Tell me what skills you have.'

Clemo mentioned his work on the smallholding, his love of horses, his work as an iron moulder and pewterer, and also explained that he could read and write in both English and Latin.

The Deputy Steward said nothing except 'Indeed?' and dismissed Tom and Clemo with a wave of his hand.

Once they were out of earshot, Tom said, 'Be careful with him. He's a Scot. Gives the impression of being firmly in control, but underneath he's scared stiff of getting things wrong and incurring the wrath of Herman the German. Frightened men can be dangerous.'

Clemo said his grateful farewells to Tom and with relief made his way to the stables. Pablo was already at work but greeted Clemo warmly.

'Buenos dias, Good Morning…We are going to have a ride out this morning, but first, your duties.'

He introduced Clemo to all the horses, including the four outstanding blacks, and a haughty grey. 'That's His Excellency's,' he explained. 'To-day he's staying at home, but we shall take Profundo and Noble for some exercise. So, your job is to saddle them up and get them ready, whilst I go to have a bite to eat. I shall be back before long; make sure everything is in order once I return.'

Clemo set to with a willing heart and was just completing his tasks when he saw Hans hanging around at the door, looking nervous.

'Hans,' he said, 'what can I do for you?'

'Just help me to get Paddy and Pierre off my back, can you? They are, how can I say it, bullebak. I think the English word is 'bully,' and I'm tired of it.' He looked rattled and made off as soon as he saw Pablo approaching.

'What did young Hans want? He shouldn't have been here. His job's inside, looking after the textiles and helping with the purchase of fabrics. Not really a man's job, but as he lived in Arras and his father was a textile merchant, he's come here to broaden his experience...but he's not a horseman, so tell him to stay away.' His words were quite forceful.

'Now...let me see, are they ready?' He walked around Profundo and Noble, brushed a fleck of dirt off Noble's coat and then said, as he untied both horses from their tethers, 'We are going to ride up to Shoreditch and maybe, even beyond. We have several fields up there which we use for grazing. Clemo mounted with great agility and was watched by Pablo, who said, 'So, you really do know horses, don't you? Come on.'

They rode the horses side by side into Broad Street and because of the crowds, and the horses and carts lumbering in from the country, were forced to walk the horses for a while.As they they rode, Clemo said. 'Someone last night mentioned Anne Boleyn. I know nothing about her. Who is she, Pablo?'

Pablo put his finger to his lips and whispered, 'I'll tell you later...'

Leaving the City through Bishops Gate, Pablo explained that there was some wasteland on their left, called 'Moor Fields'. 'It was drained about three or four years ago, but it is still a bit wet, so we won't go there. Once we get to Spital Fields we might be able to let these two have their head for a while. They need that.'

They began a gentle trot up Bishops Gate Street, then after a few hundred yards turned right along a narrow lane, and there ahead of them was the green expanse of Spital Fields. The horses pricked up their ears and once on the common, Pablo and Clemo let them have their head... it was such joy to have the wind in their faces, and the horses galloping at full stretch beneath them. 'Yea!' shouted Clemo, Pablo responded with a grin. Eventually, they gathered the horses back to a canter, a trot and finally, a walk.

'So, who is Anne Boleyn?' asked Clemo. Pablo looked around to ensure that they could not be over-heard. 'She is the mistress of the King and wants to be Queen.' He said the words through gritted teeth and with a kind of boiling venom.

'But the King is already married to Queen Catherine, isn't he?'

'He is indeed, but when did that ever stop a king, or a scheming, brazen hussy!'

They stopped their horses, side by side. Pablo looked around him again.

'The King wants His Holiness the Pope to declare that his marriage to Catherine of Aragon was invalid, so that he can marry the Boleyn woman.'

Clemo was struggling to understand, and so asked, 'But once you are married by the Church, that's it, isn't it? How can you persuade people that in spite of the priest marrying you, the marriage is not a proper one?'

'Clemo, the longer you live in London, the more you will discover there are two laws, one for the rich, and the other for the poor. Rich people think they can change the laws because they imagine that they don't apply to them. It makes me so angry.' He paused, as though wondering what he might say next.

He decided to take a risk. 'The lady who I used to serve when I lived in the Low Countries was the Archduchess Margaret of Austria. She was a great and fine woman. It was an honour to serve her. I worked as her under-groom when she lived in Mechelen. She, (may God bless her), was the daughter of the Emperor Maximilian and Mary of Burgundy... are you following me, Clemo?'

Clemo nodded.

'You will need to know these things if you are to go on working for His Excellency...The Archduchess's brother was a man called Philip the Handsome, and he married Juana, the daughter of Queen Isabel of Castile and Frederick of Aragon...Still with me?'

'Just,' replied Clemo.

'Good…well Philip and Juana had a son who they called Charles. Unfortunately, Philip, Charles' father died, and Juana was carted off to a nunnery, and so eventually Charles became the Holy Roman Emperor, Charles V. He has the biggest empire the world has ever known, and His Excellency, whom you are now serving, is his Ambassador. And in case you are now confused, let me confuse you even more. Catherine of Aragon was the sister of Juana, and so the Emperor Charles V is her nephew, and the Archduchess of Austria is Catherine of Aragon's sister's sister-in-law!! Or, if you prefer, the Archduchess is the aunt of the Emperor Charles V on his father's side….. I expect that all is now clear.' He laughed. 'Basically, the Spanish stick together, so the Emperor and his Aunt, Catherine of Aragon are close. Clear?"

'No, not really; sorry, Pablo.'

'Just remember that the Emperor Charles V is Catherine's nephew. That's the simplest way of understanding things. So perhaps it is not surprising that His Excellency is on the side of the Emperor and on the side of Catherine…but he will have to be very canny… come on, time to head back.'

They turned their horses' heads for home, Clemo trying to make a diagram in his head of all that Pablo had told him.

Chapter 24: Change of plan

Once they had returned, Clemo and Pablo rubbed down the horses and provided them with fresh water from the stable well. Then they went to dinner.

It was after dinner when Clemo felt Tom tap him on the shoulder again. 'Change of plan,' Tom said. 'You must go straight to the Deputy Steward. He has something to say to you.' Clemo felt immediate anxiety.

'What's it about, Tom? I thought I was supposed to be working with you this afternoon?'

'Search me!' said Tom, but he was smiling as though he knew what the change of plan was but was not allowed to divulge it.

Clemo hurried to the green baize door, knocked firmly on its soft surface and waited for the call to enter. He pulled his jerkin down to make himself more presentable but could do nothing about the stable mud on his shoes.

'Enter!' shouted a voice.

Clemo pushed open the door. Nathaniel Johnson was seated at his desk, his fingers steepled.

'You told me this morning that you could read and write English and Latin. You will find through that door,' he pointed to a door behind him, 'a desk, some paper and two documents that I want you to copy; one of them is in Latin. I want you not only to copy it but to translate it into English. I shall give you an hour to complete the task.' He signalled Clemo to leave.

Clemo, uncertain of what the Deputy Steward's words implied, pushed open the door and found himself in a light-filled room with three desks; two were already occupied by clerks, the other was empty. Antonio was at one of the desks and grinned as Clemo came into the room. The 'inky fellow', the Senior Clerk, was at the other desk and he told Clemo to be seated at the empty desk. 'You will find on that desk some paper, ink, quills and the documents you are to copy. Get on with it.' Clemo glanced at Antonio who surreptitiously, and with a wink, gave him the thumbs up sign.

Clemo sat down and for a moment gazed at the blank paper in front of him. The sunlight was streaming in from his left-hand side. He took it as a good omen and then, pulling the texts he had to copy towards him, picked up the quill and slowly began to write. He hadn't held a pen since leaving Hadnock and so the first sentences were marked by nervous hesitation, but gradually he got into the flow and the words began to take a firm shape. He soon finished copying the English document. It was about a consignment of wine, and then began copying the Latin text which was about a skirmish between troops loyal to the Emperor Charles V and troops of the Papacy.

It did not take him long, and then he translated the Latin text into English, trying to construct not just a literal translation but one which had its own flowing coherence. He put the quill down and wondered what he should do next.

The Senior Clerk noticed that Clemo had completed his task ahead of time and said, sourly, as he looked over Clemo's shoulder 'Now, translate the English text into Latin.'

Clemo did so. He enjoyed it. It brought back happy memories of having to do similar exercises for Father Burley. He leaned back in his chair and put his arms behind his head. All he had to do now was wait.

He heard the Senior Clerk's chair scrape on the wooden floorboards, and felt him come close, leaning over his work.

'Wait there,' said the Senior Clerk. 'I shall take your work to the Deputy Steward.'

As soon as he had left the room, Antonio was beside him, smiling.

'See, Clemo…this is how the world works. I told the Senior Clerk about your skills in Latin; he told the Deputy Steward…and now, here you are, a potential Junior Clerk.' The door opened, Antonio scuttled back to his desk and continued his letter writing. Clemo stood up.

'The Deputy Steward will see you now,' the Senior Clerk announced in a raspy voice.

Clemo went into the next room. He stood in front of the Steward's desk.

'The first two sentences of the English piece are slapdash, but the rest is quite good,' said the Deputy Steward, looking at Clemo from under meagre eyebrows, 'We need an extra Junior Clerk. So, from now on, you will be working for me and for Master Price, the Senior Clerk. You will be needed only in the afternoons and so, in the mornings, you will continue as a groom. Understood?'

'Yes, thank you, Sire.'

'Right, back to your task. Master Price will tell you what he needs from you during the rest of the day'. He dismissed Clemo with his waving, fluttering hand and did not look up as he did so.

Clemo returned to the sunlit letter-writing room wondering if Nathanael Johnson ever smiled and puzzling over this sudden change in his own life. Antonio, his back to the Senior Clerk, held up his thumb, but continued to write as though concentrating on his work.

'This will be your desk, Master Trelawney,' said the Senior Clerk.' You will be here every afternoon after dinner, and I shall tell you what is required. But for now, welcome to the letter room. Without our work, the Residence could not function.' He gave a thin-lipped, self-satisfied little smile.

That afternoon, Clemo copied into a thick ledger the contents of a number of scrappy documents, mostly connected with the purchasing of goods for the house. It was not inherently exciting or interesting work, but he guessed that it was preferable to being shouted at by the chefs in the kitchen which he is where he imagined he might have been sent.

The desks were arranged in single file so that Clemo sat nearest the door to the Deputy Steward's office. Antonio was behind him, and at the rear, keeping an eye on them both was the Senior Clerk.

Clemo heard Antonio announce that he had finished the letter to be taken to Master Cromwell. 'Bring it here,' said Master Price, 'let me check it.' There was a pause as the Senior Clerk read the letter, and having pronounced himself satisfied, told Antonio to deliver it immediately to the Senior Clerk in the Cromwell household.

'Yes, Sire,' responded Antonio, and holding the folded letter which the Senior Clerk had sealed with red wax, left the room.

'While Antonio is not here, Master Trelawney, let me say that I am pleased to have your help. You must tell me how and where you learnt to read and write.'

Clemo told his story about Father Burley, and the Senior Clerk responded, 'Good priests can be a blessing, but I regret to say that not all of them are.' He sighed. 'Times are changing fast, and who knows what the future will bring?'

He sidled back to his desk. Clemo continued his copying and after a while, heard the Senior Clerk wonder aloud why it was taking Antonio so long to deliver a letter to a near neighbour.

'I have to use the Necessarium,' he said to Clemo, 'my stomach is a little troublesome these days. When Antonio returns, tell him that he must not leave on another errand until I say so.'

Antonio returned not long after Master Price had left and keeping his voice low so that he could not be heard by the Deputy Steward, he congratulated Clemo on being appointed. 'Rapid promotion,' he said, 'a glorious future lies ahead of you.' He thumped Clemo on the shoulder.

Clemo gave him the Senior Clerk's instructions that he was not to leave on another errand until given permission and then asked, 'Where have you been?'

'To the house of the most up and coming man in the Kingdom,' he said, dancing a little jig, 'Thomas Cromwell is Cardinal Wolsey's secretary and legal adviser, and has done very well for himself as a result. It helps to account for his house next door. But Cardinal Wolsey, so the rumours have it, will soon be stripped of all his titles for having failed to achieve the King's divorce from Catherine and is probably going to face some other serious charges. Which means that the clever Thomas Cromwell will have to play his cards right over the next few weeks to make sure that he does not fall at the same time as Wolsey. Oh...it's going to be great fun to watch. And you will see, my dear Clemo, that we shall be very busy writing letters in the next few weeks as His Excellency positions himself to watch and analyse what is going on. Intrigue begins here...'

The door opened and Master Price returned.

'What took you so long, Antonio?'

'I was just catching up on a bit of local gossip, Sire,' he replied, 'Next door is buzzing with rumours about Wolsey.'

'Have you informed the Deputy Steward of these rumours?' asked the Senior Clerk.

'I thought I should tell you first, Sire, to see whether or not you feel anyone else ought to know.'

Antonio's flattery, Clemo noted, was enjoyed by the Senior Clerk.

'Very wise, Antonio…so, tell me…and by the way, Master Trelawney, anything you hear this afternoon must not be repeated outside these four walls. That is an order.'

Antonio gave an account of Wolsey's probable fall and afterwards the Senior Clerk said that he would take the news to the Deputy Steward. A minute later, he reappeared and announced, 'Master Johnson and I are going for a walk around the garden and whilst we are gone, make sure you get on with your work.'

They heard the outer door slam. Antonio immediately came to sit on Clemo's desk. 'Now, Master Clemo,' he said, 'let me give you a bit of background. Are you ready?'

Clemo nodded but was anxious that his copying was not yet completed and would not be, if Master Price re-appeared soon.

'Don't worry, Clemo. When those two go for a walk it means that they will be gone a long time.'

'You might be wondering why the Cardinal is on thin ice. The answer is simple. He was given the job of getting an annulment for the King from His Holiness the Pope. Unfortunately, His Holiness at the moment wants to stay in the good books of the Emperor and so played for time. He sent one of his trusted ragazzi to London to hear the King's case. That ragazzo, Cardinal Campeggio, sitting in Court with Wolsey beside him, decided that the case would take longer than expected and postponed the hearing. The King was furious and took it out on Wolsey believing that he had been failed by him. It's all juicy stuff…and if you keep your eyes and ears open in the City, it doesn't take long to work out what is really happening.'

Clemo sat quietly, bewildered that these political things were going on so close to him.

'Not only that,' continued Antonio, 'But Wolsey has been closing some monasteries to pay for his new College in Oxford and a new one in Ipswich, and that has upset some of the King's household who believe that Wolsey is getting too big for his boots. They want to get rid of him. And do you know who is also working against Wolsey?' He leaned forward and with emphasis said, 'Anne Boleyn.'

Clemo was beginning to get the picture, but it was a picture about which he was uneasy.

'And, if you want to know the other scandal...oh, listen to this. Cardinal Wolsey has two or three illegitimate children... and one of them, his son aged 19, has recently been made Archdeacon of Norfolk.'

'What?' said Clemo, astonished, 'How can a Cardinal have children. Cardinals are supposed to have taken vows of celibacy.'

'Quite right, Clemo...but in their case, perhaps they didn't really mean it when they took those vows, perhaps they became priests and Cardinals to feather their own nests. What do you reckon?'

Clemo thought of Father Burley working quietly and faithfully with his poor flock at Dixton. That's what he believed a priest should be like. He was dismayed and perturbed by all Antonio was telling him.

'But it isn't as straightforward as I have made it seem,' said Antonio. 'You see, Thomas Cromwell is a close friend and colleague of Wolsey, and I think that because Cromwell has been so recently bereaved...his wife died earlier this year of the Sweating Sickness and so did his two daughters...that he can't think straight. All he knows is that his own influence at Court will wane if Wolsey falls, and what will he do then? So, in spite of his personal misery he will be trying to calculate what he should do.'

Clemo immediately felt very sorry for Cromwell, but then realised that whilst he might feel sorrow for a man who had lost his wife and his daughters, (it was not unlike his own aching circumstances), nevertheless, if Cromwell was a friend of Wolsey's then he would have been involved in grabbing more and more power for him. He was not an innocent adviser.

'I saw Hampton Court on my way up to London,' Clemo said,

'Well, then, what does that tell you about Cardinal Wolsey?' asked Antonio.

Clemo did not reply. He recalled the advice he had been given: 'Hear everything. Say nothing'. He picked up his quill pen and settled again to work. But his mind was in turmoil. He had only been in the house for two days and he was having to absorb so much.

After supper, Master Price returned to view Clemo's work and pronounced that it was acceptable. 'You might need to have a break now,' he said, 'Go and change out of your livery and breathe the fresh air of London's streets!'

Antonio, who had also been given permission to leave, said he would wait for Clemo outside and show him some of the sights.

Having changed out of his livery, he walked rapidly through a side door to the front of the Residence and there joined Antonio.

'Right,' said Antonio, spreading his arms wide, 'Allow me to show you the great City of London,' and with a jaunty swing of his hips, they set off.

Chapter 25: Introduction to the City

They had gone no distance when Clemo heard someone calling his name. It was Alice. She came hurrying towards him carrying a basket.

Antonio waited to be introduced and was crestfallen when he saw that Alice had eyes only for Clemo.

'My good friend,' he said to Clemo, 'Perhaps it would be better if we postponed our walk. I can see that this delightful and fair young maiden wants to talk with you. Bellissima,' he said, kissed his fingers towards her, and walked away, smiling.

'Oh, Master Trelawney, forgive me for interrupting you but I couldn't let you go past without just saying 'hello'. Where were you going?'

'I have no idea,' replied Clemo, 'Antonio is a new friend, and he was going to show me some of the sights.'

'Well,' replied Alice, coquettishly, 'I know the City quite well, why don't I escort you, and we can then end up at my mother's and you can have a drink with us?'

'That is most kind,' replied Clemo. 'But are you sure?'

'Of course; it isn't a problem. It will be a pleasure.' They set off.

'Everyone who walks around the City,' she announced, 'and is a long way from their own house should know what I am going to show you now. It's one of the most useful and important places in London.'

She laughed, and Clemo imagined that she might be going to take him to a Merchants' Hall; however, she had other ideas. Walking beside her as she hurried through the narrow streets the thick stench of a sewer wafted towards him.

'See', she said, indicating a building, 'this is the largest toilet in the City. It's known as Whittington's Longhouse and it has 128 sittings, 64 for men, and 64 for women …' Again, she laughed. Clemo held his nose.

'You may find the smell a bit rich,' she said, 'but just think of those poor people who live in the almshouses above.' Clemo looked. Perched above the Longhouse were six alms-houses. He could not believe what he was seeing or smelling. It was appalling.

'And poor people live there?' he asked.

'Of course,' said Alice, 'where else are they to go? The drainage ditch is washed out by the Thames when the tides rise and fall. The Longhouse has been there for over 100 years…. but come on, let me take you now to somewhere much nicer.'

They hurried along Thames Street, avoiding the crowds of people, turned up Lambeth Hill and at the top, suddenly, despite the houses in front of them, the huge bulk and the soaring spire of St Paul's Cathedral loomed over them.

'Come on', she said eagerly, and took him in through the west entrance. The scale of the place, the vibrant colours of the stained glass, the pilgrims pushing towards the tomb of St Erkenwald, aristocrats and merchants sauntering in their finery up and down the central nave, people selling their wares, beggars holding out their hands for alms, the rank smell of human sweat, the noise of hundreds of voices echoing off the walls; the hubbub was overwhelming.

'And this,' said Alice, 'is where Prince Arthur married Catherine of Aragon.' She swept her hand around in a proprietorial fashion, as though making a comparison between the chaos of this day's experience and the regal splendour of a wedding.

Clemo fitted that piece of information into his newly forming mental map and decided that he would need to ask more about Catherine of Aragon when he returned to Austin Friars.

'But,' he asked Alice, 'Where is the *si quis* door? I have heard about it from someone.'

Oh, that,' she replied, 'it's the place at the west end of the nave where anyone can put up notices asking for information or jobs or things like that.'

He stood to one side of the huge nave gazing around in a kind of stupefied and horrified wonder. How could a place be so beautiful and so frantic at the same time? In the cacophony what he longed for was a place where he could find some stillness.

'Excuse me, Master Clemo, but what are you thinking?' asked Alice, as a beggar pushed past, and she grabbed Clemo's arm to make sure that no pickpocket could get near him.

'I just find London such an extraordinary place,' he replied. 'It's all the contrasts, from the largest house of necessity I have ever seen, to the Cathedral which also is the largest I have ever seen, and churches jostling each other on every corner, and alehouses, and the crowds and the smell of fish and bloodied meat, and the packs of stray dogs …You have to realise Alice, that I have only been here for two days, and before that I was living in calm, green countryside alongside the River Wye. But what about you, Alice? Have you always lived here?'

'Yes, I was born here. This is my home, and I love it…'

She suggested that it was time to go to meet her mother. 'St Mary Bowe is only just down the street,' she said, 'Come on.' It struck Clemo that she always seemed to be in a hurry, but so was everyone else. Everything seemed to be based on noise, smells, and anxious speed.

He had one last look around St Paul's and then followed Alice out into the churchyard where booksellers were clearing away their goods at the end of the afternoon. He stopped for a moment admiring some of the books still on display but was then moved on by Alice.

'My mother and Father Mossman will be so pleased to see you again,' she said. Her enthusiasm and ebullience were infectious. Somehow, thought Clemo, even though she knows so much about every aspect of this city, the worst bits, and the most amazing bits, she is still gloriously herself. He admired her boundless energy. A remarkable young woman.

When they arrived at the Parsonage, Clemo was ushered in by Alice who called out, 'Mother, look who I have found.'

Mistress Blake, to Clemo's surprise, emerged from the room which he had thought of as being Father Mossman's study. The booming voice invited Clemo in.

'My dear Clemo, it's good to see you. How is your work going?'

Clemo explained that he had become a part-time groom and a part-time clerk and that he was gradually getting used to things. Mistress Blake came in with a tray of tankards, with Alice just behind her carrying a plate of sweet meats.

Mother and daughter served Father Mossman and Clemo, and then sat themselves down as though this was their usual habit. And Clemo thought of the angular Mistress Fielding at Dixton who knew her place…and everyone else's. London was so different.

'So…' boomed Father Mossman, 'I guess that young Alice has been showing you around the City?'

'She has' replied Clemo, 'and a marvellous guide she is. First, she showed me Whittington's Longhouse…' At which point, Mistress Blake chided and teased her daughter, and Alice looked up at her mother with loving delight. '… but then,' continued Clemo,'she took me to St Paul's. What an amazing building. I have never seen anything so large and so beautiful, but it was heaving with people; hundreds of them.'

'It's *the* meeting place for the City,' explained Father Mossman, 'everyone goes there to meet their friends. If the weather is bad, where else is there which is so large and where anyone can get shelter?'

'Bur Alice told me that it was the place where Prince Arthur and Catherine of Aragon were married. You must forgive me, but coming up from the country, I am not so well acquainted with the royal family as you must be. Excuse me asking therefore, who was Prince Arthur and who is Catherine of Aragon?'

Father Mossman explained that Prince Arthur was the elder son of King Henry VII, and Catherine of Aragon was a Princess from Spain…but the Prince had died in Ludlow only a few months after the wedding, and Catherine was left a widow, aged 16.

'Poor girl,' said Mistress Blake.

'Then eight years afterwards she was married to Prince Arthur's younger brother, Henry, now King Henry VIII.' He paused and cleared his throat, 'All seemed to be going well with the couple, but unfortunately, Catherine did not produce a desired and living male child, though she did give birth to the Princess Mary…' Mistress Blake sniffed, and again muttered, 'Poor girl.' '

'And that is why King Henry wants the marriage annulled, because he believes that something must have upset God which would account for him not having sired a male child, and of course, only a living male child can inherit the throne.'

Alice, under her breath said, 'The Duke of Richmond.' Her mother smiled at her.

'Well, yes,' continued Father Mossman, patiently, 'King Henry is the father of an illegitimate son, the young Duke of Richmond, and that gives the King added reason for laying the blame on Catherine. If another woman can give birth to a son by the King, then clearly Henry is, as it were, in the clear. The real fault must therefore lie with Catherine and especially with the validity of the marriage.'

'Thank you for explaining,' said Clemo.

'But,' added Mistress Blake, 'there is also the small matter of Anne Boleyn.'

'I think perhaps we have said enough,' replied Father Mossman, his patience having run out, 'I imagine it's time that Master Clemo returned to Austin Friars. Can you find your way back on your own?'

'I think so'.

Alice butted in, saying, 'I could go with him,' but her mother stated that Alice had things she should be doing in the house and that she had spent enough time gadding about the City.

Clemo thanked them for their kind hospitality and made his way back to the Ambassador's residence via some mistaken and confusing detours. But he felt that some of the landmarks were now falling in to place and he had enlarged his understanding about Catherine of Aragon. It was a small triumph, but at least it was a triumph.

He made his way to his bedroom feeling in need of a rest but found Hans lying on his bed.

'Hello, Hans.'

'Hello, Clemo.'

'Sorry about this morning, but I was so fed up with Paddy and Pierre I didn't know where to turn. Sorry.' Hans looked woebegone.

'Why do they bully you?' asked Clemo.

'I don't know…but there might be two reasons; the first is that they just enjoy bullying; the second is…' He looked at Clemo wondering whether he should say any more.

'And the second is…?' asked Clemo, gently.

'Please don't let this go any further, will you?' Clemo promised that he believed in keeping confidences.

'Only I'm not very good at seeing what is really going on and passing things back to my betters.…and somehow Paddy and Pierre know that. They are much cleverer than me.'

'I'm not certain that I can follow what you are saying Hans, but let me ask you directly. Who are your betters, as you call them?'

'My job for His Excellency in this house is to look after the fabrics, but I am also supposed to report what goes on here and in London to my bosses in the Archduchess's house in Mechelen…and I don't know exactly what they want to know. So, I pass on to them how much has been spent on the textiles, but that isn't what they want; they want gossip, and stuff like that, and because I don't have any friends here, it's difficult to know what the gossip is.' He looked thoroughly miserable. 'I feel an absolute and complete failure and I'm so lonely.'

'Hans,' said Clemo, 'it must be very difficult for you.'

Clemo was also a novice in this spying world and so had little advice to offer. But he tried to find a way forward.

'As I understand it, the Archduchess of Austria is Queen Catherine's aunt, isn't she?'

'Yes.'

'And His Excellency is on good terms with the Archduchess?'

'Yes.'

'So, why do your bosses in Mechelen want you to spy for them? Can't they get what they need, directly from the Ambassador?'

'I have asked myself that…but what if my bosses in Mechelen are not quite what they seem? Suppose they want to know whether the Ambassador is doing his job as he should? It makes me feel like a traitor to the Ambassador to tell tales about him. And the fact is, he's new and I'm new and the only thing I've been able to pass back is…' He paused. '…Promise you won't tell?'

'I have given you my word.'

'Well, the Ambassador is a priest, but I have heard that he has an illegitimate son called Cesare who is probably living in Annecy where the Ambassador originally came from. I passed that back to Mechelen because I thought they would be interested but they already knew it... oh, I don't understand this scheming world at all. Why can't they just let me deal with things I do know about, like fabrics and textiles...'

Clemo could sense Hans' frustration and anxiety but simply did not know what to advise and so asked, 'How do Paddy and Pierre fit in to this?'

'You won't know this yet, but Paddy is a genius with figures. He works for the House Treasurer...so I asked him one day how much the Ambassador had spent on textiles and he guessed that I was not really interested in that and must want the information for some other reason... and he told Pierre and they guessed that I was fishing for news that I could pass on. It didn't take them long to work out that as a Fleming I would probably have contacts at the court of the Archduchess...and ever since, they have been teasing and bullying me telling me that a roll of cotton thread had been purchased by the women in the Sewing Room and would I report that to Mechelen? It is absolutely horrible, Clemo, I hate it and I am beginning to hate myself.' Tears sprang to his eyes. He mumbled his thanks to Clemo, turned on his side and pretended to sleep.

Chapter 26: Hans' disappearance

Later that night, whilst everyone in the room was asleep, Clemo woke and saw Hans stealthily getting out of bed and dressing in his livery.

'Hans', he whispered, 'are you alright?'

'Yes,' Hans whispered back, and muttering the words 'House of Easement', slipped out of the room. Clemo assumed that Hans had a stomach upset but then wondered why he would have dressed in his livery just to go somewhere to relieve himself. He tried to put the idea from his mind but when he woke several hours later noticed that Hans' bed was empty. He waited for Paddy and Pierre to wake and when they did so, asked if either of them knew where Hans might have gone.

'No idea', said Paddy, 'he's a strange one, Hans. He lives in his own world. Who knows what he might have been doing?'

Pierre shrugged his shoulders and offered the view that Hans might have a secret girlfriend.

'Don't talk rubbish, Pierre,' retorted Paddy. 'Who would want to kiss that fat slob?' He laughed and Pierre joined in the bantering merriment. Clemo was uneasy. Where might Hans have gone? But being so new in the residence, Clemo felt that perhaps his concern was not justified. Nevertheless, after all that Hans had told him last night…

He dressed and went to Mass and fortunately, at the end of Mass, saw Gwen leaving.

'Gwen?'

'Oh, Clemo from Monmouth,' she grinned. 'Lovely to see you *cariad*, but you're looking worried. What's the matter?' He explained about Hans' disappearance.

'He's a bit of a lonely character,' replied Gwen 'He doesn't seem to have made any friends since he's been here. He's an unhappy boy, a really unhappy boy. But I'll ask the girls to see what any of them might have heard.'

Clemo went to breakfast and had almost finished, when a young servant girl came to him asking him to go immediately to the Sewing Room. Gwen was waiting for him. She looked deeply concerned.

'One of the girls coming in to work this morning saw a couple of men carrying a corpse up from the river. She looked away because she was frightened, but then when she looked back recognised the livery the corpse was wearing. The men asked her if she knew who the corpse might be, and she admitted that she did. It was Hans. Oh, the poor boy, the poor boy. And the girl is in a real state, I can tell you.'

'Have you told the High Steward?'

'No, sorry, I wondered if you might do that…I must go back to the Sewing Room to comfort the poor mite. She's only been here a few weeks. Oh, life can be so cruel…' She hurried away.

Clemo went straight to the Clerk's room. Antonio was already there and greeted Clemo cheerily. Clemo responded by explaining that he needed to speak to the Senior Clerk or the Under Steward urgently because there had been a tragedy involving one of the household's staff. Antonio's face fell.

They heard the outer door open and Antonio suggested that it signified the arrival of the Under Steward. Clemo went through into the Under Steward's office and apologised that he was not in his livery but that he needed to convey some tragic news.

Nathaniel Johnson sat at his desk and looked at Clemo with hard, grey eyes. He leaned on the desk and steepled his fingers.

'And?' he asked. Clemo told him some of the story of Hans having been found drowned but avoided implicating Pierre or Paddy. That could wait.

'Are you sure it was Hans?'

'One of the young Sewing Room girls coming to work this morning passed two men carrying a corpse they had just fished from the river. The corpse was clothed in our livery, and when the men asked her if she recognised who the corpse was, she affirmed that it was Hans,' replied Clemo.

'Thank you for telling me.' The Deputy Steward looked deeply worried. 'We must deal with this very carefully. We don't want bad gossip and evil rumours associated with this Residence. Leave it with me. Now go to your duties.' The instruction was curt.

Clemo left and made his way to the stable block.

Pablo was there ahead of him but was bending over, examining the cobbles of the stable yard.

'Look, Clemo. Someone has pilfered several of our cobbles. What an odd thing to do.' He pointed to a gap where four large cobble stones had once been buried in the earth.

Clemo looked and began to draw a morbid conclusion. 'I think I might know what has happened,' he said, 'but I can't say any more until I'm sure.'

He heard footsteps approaching hurriedly. It was the young servant girl again, her face pale with worry.

'Please, Master Trelawney, the High Steward has asked me to tell you that you are to go to his office straightaway.'

'Thank you,' he replied, and turning to Pablo, apologised, explaining that he might soon have an answer about the missing cobbles. He strode away, asking the maidservant to guide him to the High Steward's office.

As they walked towards the house, the young girl looked up at him and said that she was a friend of Alice Blake's. 'She told me you were working here.' Clemo smiled. Perhaps this great City had something in common with his hometown after all.

When he arrived, a clerk was waiting outside the door to intercept him. 'The High Steward says you are to wait here until he calls you.'

The door to the office opened and Paddy came out, looking a little sheepish. He avoided Clemo's eye and said nothing.

The door was closed by the clerk. Clemo waited. And then, at the sound of a tinkling bell, the clerk beckoned Clemo forward and told him to enter.

The High Steward was seated behind his desk with the Under Steward standing next to him.

'We know that you are very new in the Residence, Master Trelawney,' said the High Steward, 'but you shared sleeping accommodation with Hans and two others, one of whom I have just interviewed. He claims that as soon as you arrived here, you picked on Hans brutally and frightened him, and that that might have caused Hans to commit self-murder. What do you say?' His voice was barely under control.

'Sire,' replied Clemo, his rage about the lie boiling within him, 'Nothing could be further from the truth.'

'So, you deny it?'

'Of course, Sire.' He decided it was time to get the truth out into the open. 'In fact, Hans had told me, a complete stranger to himself, that he was being bullied by Paddy and Pierre and he didn't know how to handle it. What is more, he also told me last night that he was deeply unhappy about some of the work he had been asked to do here. He explained that he had no friends and felt in absolute despair. I heard him get up last night and asked him if he was alright. He said he was, and he explained that he was going to the House of Easement.'

'Ah…' The High Steward looked at the Under Steward. 'So, you completely deny being the cause of Hans' terrible decision.'

'Sire, I do. Completely.'

He waited. It was time for the Under Steward to speak. 'And do you realise that we have interviewed Pierre and he has corroborated Paddy's story?'

'I did not know that, Sire…but it was I who reported Hans' death to you. Would I have done that if I had been the cause?'

There was a further pause. The tension in the room was palpable. Clemo waited. There was a knock on the door. A young man entered, his face red from running.

'I have just come from making enquiries down by the river, Sire, as you instructed me, and I have located the place to which the body was carried. It's in the Charnel House of St Martin Vintry. I made enquiries there and the Sexton confirmed that a body dressed in our livery was lying on a slab. He took me to see it…and it was Hans. The Sexton also showed me something odd. Apparently, Hans had stuffed his pockets with four large cobble stones to ensure he was pulled under the water and would not resurface'.

'May I speak?' asked Clemo.

'No', retorted the High Steward, 'you may only speak when I give you permission to do so.'

He and the Under Steward went to a corner of the room and conferred with each other. Clemo remained silent and tried hard to control his emotions. He felt that he could easily become the victim of an injustice.

The High Steward returned to his desk. 'You do realise the seriousness of the situation, Trelawney?'

'Yes, Sire, I do...but I am innocent.'

'I did not ask you for comment,' he snapped back.

'The Under Steward and I have come to a decision...you are not to go to the Stables this morning. Instead, you are to go back to your sleeping accommodation and speak to no-one until you are called. Now, get out of my sight.'

Clemo bit his lip and left the room.

In the bedroom he found Pierre and Paddy chatting easily together.

Clemo walked up to them. They fell silent.

'So...Paddy, you obscene toe-rag,' Clemo bunched his fists. 'You have accused me of bullying Hans.' He moved closer to Paddy, his face set. Pierre moved to one side.

'Stay where you are, Pierre,' Clemo ordered, his voice taut, brimming with anger. 'If neither of you admits to bullying Hans and defaming me, you will find that your teeth will be smashed down your throats. I need to tell you that whilst you were both pushing pens at a desk, I was working in a foundry and on a farm, so, you vile wretches, you will be no match for me.' He moved closer to Pierre, who sensed the mismatch between himself and Clemo, and began to back away.

Out of the corner of his eye, Clemo saw the flash of a bright dagger, which Paddy had drawn from beneath his doublet.

Clemo grabbed Pierre and used him as a shield, ready to take on Paddy.

'If you have any sense in that stupid head of yours, you loon,' said Clemo softly, 'you will put that away.' He continued to hold Pierre in a vice-like grip, crushing his ribs.

'You have two options, Paddy; either you can attack me, but in doing so you will probably kill your friend, or you put the dagger down and we talk. Which is it to be?'

'If Pierre is killed, so be it,' snarled Paddy, 'he is as useless as a crushed frog... It was his idea in the first place to have a go at Hans. He should take the blame... not me. He led me on.' Clemo felt Pierre writhing with anger at Paddy's statement.

The door of the room suddenly smashed open. Antonio and the Under Steward plus four retainers were standing there.

'I'll take that dagger, Paddy,' said the Under Steward in a voice as cold as ice. Paddy lunged towards him, the dagger pointed forwards at chest height; the four retainers and Antonio sprang forward, wrestled Paddy to the ground and held him firmly, prising the dagger from his grip. 'Oh dear,' said one of the retainers, 'I do believe I might be breaking his fingers.' There were two audible cracks. Paddy screamed.

The Under Steward spoke: 'Once we have dealt with this villain, I shall need to see you, Pierre, in my office. Until then, you are to stay here. One of my men will remain with you in case you consider bolting for a ship bound for la Belle France. Trelawney, you are to come with me.'

To Clemo's surprise, the strange and dishevelled procession, with Paddy held firmly by three retainers, made its way to the front of the Residence, turned left and marched into the Friary. There, greeted by the gatekeeper, the Under Steward explained that he needed to have the use of the Friary prison for a while.

'Of course, Master Johnson, of course.'

The gatekeeper produced a huge bunch of keys and accompanied them to the prison. And there, once the outer door had been unlocked, Paddy was lifted from his feet and thrown down the stone stairs, landing with a thud at the bottom, where he whimpered in pain.

'Allow him to cool off, Gatekeeper,' ordered the Under Steward, 'Only water…He is to see no-one until tomorrow at the earliest.'

'Now, we shall return to the Residence,' he announced calmly, 'where, no doubt, Pierre will want to change his story.' Clemo admitted to himself that the Under Steward was effective and reluctantly began to admire him.

As they were walking back, the Under Steward apologised to Clemo, 'Sorry for the misunderstanding earlier, but I'm afraid you were sent back to your room as a decoy. It worked. I heard everything. Again, my apologies. And you are not hurt?'

'No. Sire'

'In which case, I suggest that you and Antonio go to dinner and try to put this unfortunate episode behind you.'

'Thank you, Sire', replied Clemo, as he and Antonio made for the servants' dining hall.

'Clemo…you were very brave. I was worried that you might have been injured taking on Pierre and Paddy. It was just as well that we arrived in time.'

'I don't think of myself as brave,' replied Clemo, 'but I was mad with those two telling such lies about me. If you hadn't turned up when you did, I don't know what might have happened.'

At dinner they were served potage. Clemo picked up his spoon to eat the broth but found that his hand was shaking so much he couldn't raise the spoon to his lips.

'Stay there,' ordered Antonio. 'I'll be back in two seconds.'

Clemo sat looking at the broth feeling queasy.

Antonio re-appeared with a goblet. 'Drink this,' he said, 'it will steady your nerves. You've had a bad shock. Orribile.' Clemo sipped the drink.

'What's this?'

'Brandy…now drink it as fast as you can…'

Clemo grimaced but the brandy soon brought a warm glow to his stomach and the trembling eased.

'What will happen to Pierre?' Clemo asked Antonio.

'They'll frighten him so much that he will turn.'

'What do you mean?'

'I suspect that he was planted in this house by the French Ambassador, so the High Steward will offer Pierre a deal. He will tell him that he can keep his post here but will have to provide information from the French to us without the French realising. If he refuses that offer, he will be thrown into the same prison cell as Paddy.'

'What do you think he will do?'

'Oh, he will turn. He is not a brave man. But it will remain a nightmare for him for the rest of his life, because if the French ever suspect that he has become a traitor, he will be put in a sack with a few rats and chucked in the river.'

'Grim,' said Clemo, trying to comprehend the scale of the wiliness and complexity of the Ambassador he was now working for. Gwen had said earlier that it was a cruel world. Clemo could not but agree.

After dinner, he briefly went to the bedroom. It was empty. Someone had already taken Hans' clothes away, Pierre's bed was unmade, but Paddy's had been stripped and all his possessions taken.

Clemo decided to lie on his bed for a moment. He mulled over the previous couple of days. They had been tumultuous. Then, into his mind came a vivid image of Laura sitting outside their cottage on the banks of the Wye. He was assailed by burning pangs of grief combined with the after-effects of shock, and holding his kerchief over his face to quell any sound, he sobbed.

Chapter 27: More secrets

The days and weeks that followed fell into a steady pattern which, after the grim experiences of Clemo's first days in the Ambassador's residence, was a comfort. The mornings were spent with Pablo and the horses. He loved that. And the afternoons were spent as a Junior Clerk. Again, the steady and undemanding rhythm of copying documents was soothing. But perhaps his greatest comfort came from being at the daily Mass. There was something about the pattern of the service, the genuflections, the incense, the candles, the half-darkness, and the murmured prayers which brought him deep solace.

Pierre had returned to the sleeping accommodation and had apologised profusely to Clemo but otherwise seemed to become lonelier and more troubled. Clemo could guess the cause but said nothing. Two new young men took the places of Hans and Paddy, but they too were quiet and self-contained. Clemo wondered whether they might have been sent to keep a careful eye on Pierre and as one of them spoke French, that seemed a likely possibility.

In the early days of October, the residence was abuzz with gossip about the fall of Wolsey. Some said, with a certain amount of glee, that he had already been sent to the Tower; others claimed that he had not but had retreated to his house at Esher. Then came the news that he had been stripped of the Great Seal and was no longer Lord Chancellor and had been replaced by Sir Thomas More. In the Residence, and in the City, there were ripples of excitement, and for some, great delight that such a greedy and avaricious prelate had been brought down to earth. There was much talk of Fortune's wheel and repeated tellings of the story of Icarus.

Whilst these political earthquakes were of interest to the Under Steward and the senior members of the Ambassador's staff, they did not impact directly on Clemo. He simply carried on with his duties, though he was thrilled to be asked to accompany Pablo, the Ambassador, and several other aides on a visit to Catherine of Aragon. Whilst the Ambassador was ensconced with the Queen, Clemo and the others waited outside with the horses and when, after a couple of hours, the Ambassador re-emerged, Clemo overheard him say that he would do as much as he could to support her. But Clemo was more interested in the Ambassador's obvious discomfort as he mounted his horse. He winced with pain. 'Gout,' said Pablo, under his breath.

Clemo had become increasingly attuned to the subtle atmospheric changes in the Residence and soon was able to sense when some major political problem in the outside world was about to erupt. In early November, gossip began to increase saying that there appeared to be much more direct contact between the Ambassador and his neighbour, Thomas Cromwell.

Antonio was Clemo's main source of gossip and he, on the second day of November, regaled Clemo with the news that Cromwell had galloped from Esher to London the previous night to try to curry favour with the senior Lords who surrounded the King. 'It is reported,' said Antonio, in a conspiratorial whisper, 'that Cromwell said the purpose of his journey would be to make or mar. He's always been faithful to Wolsey, but he faces a serious problem now that Wolsey is on the downward slope. How can Cromwell retain his influence? Will people see him as so linked with Wolsey that he will have to fall as well. But I can tell you Clemo, Master Cromwell is amazingly adroit. He'll think of something. You just watch.'

Clemo later learned that Cromwell had organised a seat for himself in Parliament as an MP so that he could keep a careful eye on the proceedings and observe who was in the ascendant and who was failing to receive the King's approbation. But he had also made a speech in favour of Wolsey and in the circumstances, as Antonio explained, where Anne Boleyn wanted Wolsey to be denied any access to the King, that was a clever move.

'Clever?' asked Clemo, surprised.

'Absolutely,' replied Antonio, 'Clever, but risky. Cromwell knows that the King admires loyalty and so, whilst he might not have approved of what Cromwell said, he certainly approved of Cromwell's loyalty to Wolsey. Just keep your eyes peeled, Clemo. There's more to come, of that I am certain. He and the Ambassador are supping together this evening, perhaps I shall learn more after that. Let's see.'

At breakfast the following morning, Antonio regaled Clemo with what he had learnt: that there might soon be a Peace Treaty between the King and the Emperor.

'The Ambassador is very pleased with everything he has done to achieve that. It's a beautiful feather in his velvet cap,' said Antonio, 'and it just proves that Wolsey really has left the field of play, because Wolsey was always in favour of an alliance with France.'

Clemo was innocent of these geopolitical manoeuvres but was prepared to listen to Antonio's excited talk about what was happening.

'Keep your eye on Pierre,' Antonio continued, 'He'll be quietly mad that his native country has been bested…but won't be able to say so now that he's working for our side. He'll be in agony but will try not to show it.'

It was a prophetic statement because when Clemo saw Pierre that same evening he seemed more morose and locked away inside his own mind than ever.

Clemo greeted him but only received a cursory greeting in return.

The following morning, Clemo learnt from Antonio that there was something going on beneath the surface in Parliament. 'It seems,' Antonio whispered to Clemo, 'that Parliament is wanting to clip the wings of the Church.'

'What do you mean?'

'Some of the most powerful members in the Commons are hoping to adjust the fees that the Church receives for taking some services and are promising to banish the custom that Bishops and Canons and Vicars can hold more than a certain number of offices at any one time. Usually, those offices involve a good income…so, the reformers are cutting the Church down to size. I bet that those very same people are the supporters of Anne Boleyn. She,' he whispered, 'is a Reformer. She wants to bring the Church in England more in line with things in Germany and Switzerland but, of course, her lover the King is a traditionalist…so they are all having to watch their steps'. He giggled, 'Do you know, Clemo, I love working here. You can pick up so much about what is going on. It's great, isn't it?'

'I suppose so,' replied Clemo, 'but I'm worried. If Parliament interferes with the Church, anything might happen. Parliament doesn't have the right to interfere, does it?'

'Ah,' replied Antonio, 'but what if Might is Right? What then? What if the King should decide that he wants to be the boss of the church as well as the kingdom, is there anyone who would dare to defy him?'

'There are bound to be some,' replied Clemo, hesitantly.

'Maybe, but where will they get their support from? From France? From the Emperor?'

'From His Holiness,' replied Clemo, confidently.

'But what military power does His Holiness really have? His own armies are small. It's only if he can persuade and pay the Emperor or the French to fight on his behalf, that he can achieve anything.'

Clemo looked hard at Antonio. 'How do you know all this, Antonio?'

The reply began as a burst of laughter.

'I am a Venetian, my friend…and we Venetians drink politics with our mother's milk. How do you think we have survived for so long? I will tell you. It's by observation, by skill and by cunning, that's how. And when you live upon the sea, as Venetians do, these things matter.'

'What do you mean?'

'Oh, Clemo…do you not know that we Venetians live in houses built on timbers sunk into the sea- bed? We don't have any roads. We just have boats. So, if I want to see a friend, I don't ride a horse, I take a boat.'

Clemo was open-mouthed. 'I had no idea. Are you fooling me?'

'Not at all, Venice is the most beautiful city in the world. It really is. We call her, la Serenissima. She makes London look like a third-rate slum. And, let me add, she is one of the greatest trading nations in the world. You should see the ships in our harbours. They come from everywhere and sail to everywhere.'

Clemo was downcast. He felt that there was so much he still had to learn. He had learnt to be an iron-moulder, and of that he was proud, and he could even write and read in Latin and English, but these much bigger things seemed so difficult to grasp. He felt that Antonio was much more agile, much more attuned to the way of the world than he was, much better informed. And as that thought entered his mind there arose a tiny flicker of doubt. Might Antonio have secret sources of information?

It was no more than a flicker and he tried to dismiss the idea, but it had lodged itself and proved that it could not be easily removed.

As an antidote to such imaginings, he sometimes walked to the Parsonage at St Mary Bowe where he would talk with Father Mossman. On one of these occasions, he spoke of his unease about Hans' death.

'Hans was terribly despondent, in the depths of despair, and he was being bullied, so when he told me, on the night he died, that he was going to the House of Easement, I wonder if he had in mind the ease he would find in death? He was in such a state that he could see no other way out. Yet, if I understand correctly, as he committed self-murder he would not have been buried in consecrated ground. Is that true?'

'Yes, it is,' replied Father Mossman, looking down at his feet.

'But Hans was not in his right mind. He was not in control of what he was doing. How could a proper Christian burial be denied him?'

Father Mossman cleared his throat. 'The Church has always taught that life itself is a gift from God and is therefore absolutely precious. So, we are forbidden from committing self-murder because that is contrary to the gracious gift we have been given.'

Clemo paused. 'But we are also taught by the Church that killing is wrong, yet we still go to war. So, that is allowed, but 'self-murder' isn't. What's the difference?'

'In going to war we are following someone else's orders, and in self-murder we are giving our self the orders.'

Clemo looked worried by the answer but decided he needed more time to think through the implications of what Father Mossman had said.

The door burst open. It was Alice.

'Sorry, Father, I didn't know you had Master Trelawney with you.'

Father Mossman smiled indulgently. 'Don't leave, Alice. Are you doing anything else this afternoon?'

'No, Father'

'In that case, perhaps you could ensure that Master Trelawney can find his way home.'

A bright smile lit up her face. 'I should love to do that,' she said.

'I somehow guessed you might.' He laughed.

Clemo and Alice walked along the roads to the Residence.

On the way, Alice was quieter than usual, as though something was troubling her, and after a short while she asked Clemo to stop. 'Can you keep a terrible secret?' she asked, earnestly.

'I hope so.'

'Promise me by the Holy Mass that you won't say a word to anyone?'

'I promise.'

'I think my mother is in love with Father Mossman.' She looked into his eyes.

'Why do you think that?'

'I saw her once, kissing him. And she didn't know that I had seen her.'

'Perhaps she just likes him,' replied Clemo. 'It might have been entirely innocent.'

'But what if he loves her, as well? It takes two to kiss like they were kissing, doesn't it?'

She stood very close to Clemo, seeking his advice and secretly longing for him to take her in his arms and sweep her off her feet. Her eyes were bright, too bright.

'I think, young Alice, you should not spy on other people and you certainly should not have told me what you saw…but I gave you my solemn promise, and I won't tell a soul.'

She pouted but walked him back to the Residence and said, as they parted, that she hoped she might see him again before too long… 'Just to check that you have really kept your promise.' She laughed, touched his arm, and ran away.

He did not return to the bedroom as light-hearted as Alice seemed to be. Might she actually have seen her mother kissing Father Mossman?

Or was that a not very subtle way of declaring her infatuation with himself? If only life could be simple.

Chapter 28: Diplomatic manoeuvres

Antonio, over the next months, duly kept Clemo abreast of political developments. Apparently, the King had sent Thomas Boleyn on an embassy to Bologna to meet the Emperor and the Pope to persuade them to annul Henry's marriage.

'Stupid move,' said Antonio, 'What was the King doing, sending his Mistress's father as his envoy? But he is so in love with La Boleyn that reason doesn't enter his head. Even after that mission had failed, he sent Thomas and George Boleyn to negotiate with the King of France seeking support for an annulment, and the Boleyns also tried to persuade the University of Paris to come out in favour of the annulment. Well, they refused, and that is no surprise. They are French, after all.' He laughed. 'And what will all this do to our friend, Pierre? He won't like hearing that the French are being difficult, but I suspect he will be ordered to tell the French Ambassador that Henry is cosying up to the Emperor again. It might not be true, of course; the King is probably still trying to strengthen the links with France…but to hear that the Emperor is still in the frame will cause the French some sleepless nights.'

Clemo sighed deeply. Everything in this diplomatic world seemed to be composed of distorting mirrors. And then, one day, Antonio announced that he'd heard that Wolsey was trying to obtain a pension from the Spanish. He laughed aloud. 'The cheek of the man. He was arguing only a few months ago that Catherine of Aragon should divorce the King, and he failed. So, what is he doing sounding out our Ambassador asking him to organise a Spanish sweetener? Oh, Clemo…sometimes human nature baffles me! But I'll tell you this, our Ambassador is on the war path now. He has written to the Emperor begging him to tell the Pope that Henry should be ordered to put Anne Boleyn away. He can try…but Henry is absolutely besotted. He's like a youth in love, in spite of being almost forty and growing fatter by the day. Oh heavens, what a world. The great thing for us, dear Clemo, is that we are paid to live through these fascinating times. There are many people who would give anything to know what we know…'

Clemo could not understand Antonio's delight in all the intrigue. All that he wanted was simplicity, a glimpse of the River Wye, trees tumbling their branches and leaves down towards the riverbank, ordinary things, like Toby the dog licking his hand, or the fabrics in Joan's shop, even Issy being tetchy. He understood that world, but this London world left him deeply uneasy. It was like standing on what seemed to be solid earth but all the while you could sense miners underneath your feet digging away, trying to bring everything crashing down.

Antonio told Clemo a few weeks later, that the Ambassador was convinced that unless the Emperor and the Pope between them could bring about the annulment, Henry and Parliament would declare independence. It was an alarming prospect. Christendom itself was at stake. The Turks had already expanded into Hungary and were threatening further incursions. If that happened, as Antonio explained, and either Venice or Vienna fell, the risk to European unity would be immense. The underground miners, whoever they might be, would have achieved their goal. Henry's marriage problems could cause disruption on a far bigger scale than most English people realised. 'The English think it's about the King's marriage problem, but In Europe they see it differently. They see potential international breakdown.'

Antonio's explanation left Clemo feeling small, despondent, and insignificant. His mental map was being re-drawn, and he didn't like what was happening to that map one tiny bit. He explained his distressed incomprehension to Antonio who was sympathetic but concluded that the real problem was that the English did not understand Europe. 'Probably never have, and perhaps never will,' he said, 'and just to add to the discomfort you are feeling Clemo, you should also be aware that there are religious forces at work in Germany and Switzerland which are threatening everything you and I believe in.'

'Please stop, Antonio. I'm feeling giddy with all that you are telling me. I just want to go to Mass, that's all. Perhaps I'm not suited to London life. It's too much for me to grasp.'

'But living as we do in an Ambassador's Residence, perhaps because of what we know, Clemo, we can play our part, even if only a small part, in shaping the new world that's coming.'

'Maybe you can, Antonio, but at the moment, I think it's not for me. Now, if you will excuse me, I just want to wander into the Friary garden, find a tree to sit under and say my beads...' He strolled slowly away; his head bowed. And holding his beads in his right hand, even before he left the Ambassador's grounds, he began reciting his rosary.

Antonio felt for him. Obviously, Clemo did not want to be a man of the world. He didn't enjoy intrigue and gossip. He was a sweet, innocent person, concluded Antonio, but if he disliked the way the world was, what future could there be for him in London? Perhaps the time might come when Clemo would have to make up his mind about his own future?

Unsurprisingly, similar thoughts were going through Clemo's mind as he sat beneath a tree. He tried to draw up a mental list of what he liked about his new life. That list consisted of the horses and Pablo, Antonio, whose vivacity was enchanting, the household of Father Mossman, going to Mass, and occasionally his conversations with Gwen. And what didn't he like? He detested the noise, the smells and the feverish rush of life in the City, he disliked the fact that people in power seemed always to be seeking ways to do each other down whilst climbing higher themselves. Above all, he hated the fact that he really did not know whom he could trust.

He tumbled the rosary beads through his fingers, seeking a way to resolve his problems. Eventually, he came to a decision. He would give himself one more year and then come to a firm resolution. He stood up and felt a degree of relief that he now had a plan. It gave a kind of shape to what he was doing, and, as a result, ironically, he found the next few months much easier. Antonio continued to keep him informed about life on the political stage, who was up and who was down. As Antonio said, 'Fortune's wheel seems to be spinning faster than ever.'

To Clemo's surprise, he loved the Christmas dinners and the fun of the Twelve Days in the Residence as life relaxed and the pace slackened. He was able to talk with Tom Saunders (they talked about farms and farming) and with Gwen, and even managed to raise a smile on the face of the normally grim-faced Under Steward. And he had

211

spent a couple of evenings with Father Mossman and Mistress Blake, Alice and Edward. There was a great deal of laughter and banter in the Parsonage, and Alice dared to tease Clemo suggesting that he needed to laugh more often. He thought that she might have hit a nail on the head, for he realised that since arriving in the City, laughter had been mostly absent from his life. Accompanying Clemo back to the Residence she expanded on her observation. 'You have such beautiful eyes, Master Trelawney, that it would be a sin not to let laughter shine through them more often.' Her mischievous and seductive remark loosened his inhibitions for a moment, and he told her that now she was 16 she could call him 'Clemo'. She blushed and thanked him as her heart turned somersaults within her. She returned to the Parsonagewith a spring in her step and a smile on her face that her mother did not fail to notice.

But once those days of merriment were over, life returned to normal. There was a moment when Antonio told Clemo that the King had charged all the clergy in the kingdom with *praemunire.*

'What's that? asked Clemo.

'It means that anyone who has sought legal help from beyond the shores of this kingdom is guilty of a form of treason. It was the charge the King brought against Wolsey… and look what happened to him.'

'So, people can't appeal to His Holiness anymore?'

'Correct. But the King let the clergy off when they promised to pay him a collective fine of £100,000.'

'What!' exclaimed Clemo, 'That's money that the faithful have given to the church. How can the King claim that it should be his?' He was appalled. It seemed to him that the King was behaving immorally but, of course, did not say so. He was learning discretion, even if the injustice of the King's behaviour left him furious inside.

That was soon followed by the news that the King had declared himself the Protector and Supreme Head of the Church in England. To Clemo it was a sign that the underground miners were now breaking through the surface, for he could see that His Holiness and the Emperor would regard the King's behaviour as an act of foolish hubris.

'Ah, but…' said Antonio smiling, 'Archbishop Warham has managed to persuade the King to add a clause to his claim.'

'And what is that?'

'Archbishop Warham said he could live with the King's description provided the King added the words, 'as far as the Law of Christ allows'.

Having considered that for a moment, Clemo said, 'The King must have been delighted with that. He's got his £100,000 plus a new title and can treat the Archbishop's words as no more than the pestering of a fly.'

'Hooray,' shouted Antonio, 'you are beginning to understand the way that power works. It's a breakthrough, Clemo.' He laughed and gave Clemo a hug. 'It's taken a while, but you're getting there.'

Clemo grinned but inside was ashamed by his apparent delight in being congratulated.

'And let me tell you two other things, Clemo. Firstly, our Ambassador went to see the King recently and found himself being taken to one side by His Majesty. They were deep in conversation when our Ambassador looked up, and above his head saw an open window framing none other than Anne Boleyn. She had listened to the entire conversation and the King had manoeuvred our Ambassador so that she could hear what they were taking about. What does that tell you?'

'That Anne Boleyn is a minx, and her lover is completely devious.'

'Sh', said Antonio, 'you mustn't say such things, or else if someone hears you, you'll find yourself cooling your heels in the Tower'. He laughed aloud, seeing a look of consternation falling across Clemo's face.

'And the other thing Clemo, is that I have heard that the Pope is going to threaten the King with excommunication if he doesn't put Anne away.'

'Really?'

'Yes, really, but of course if the King now sees himself as having absolute jurisdiction over what he and others are calling his 'empire', the King won't be much bothered by the threat.'

Although Clemo had been congratulated by Antonio for his increasing awareness of national politics, he determined not to let it sully his normal life. The horses still needed exercising and riding; Pablo was still a stalwart friend, and life in the Under Steward's office was pleasant enough...though there was an unforgettable moment when the door to the office burst open one day and a clerk rushed in with the news that at a dinner given by Bishop Fisher, at which one of the guests was Sir

Thomas More, several guests who had eaten the soup had been taken violently ill. More and Fisher had declined to eat the soup and they were fine, but 'two people had died,' announced the breathless clerk.

Even ordinary social occasions, it seemed to Clemo, could be fraught with danger. 'Had the soup been poisoned?', he asked. 'The general view,' replied the clerk, 'is that it was an assassination attempt; the cook had confessed, no doubt under duress, and for his crime had been lowered slowly into a vat of boiling oil. His screams could be heard for miles.' Clemo shuddered. It was a reminder of what had happened all those years ago at the Foundry. He couldn't get the screams of the cook or his father out of his head. It was intensely distressing, and worse still, the cook might have been innocent.

He had not told Antonio the story of his father's own accident but when Antonio was laughing about the cook being fried alive, as though it were a joke, Clemo snapped. He told Antonio he was being heartless. 'Think of that man's agony. Think of his wife, what will happen to her? Think of his children? It is not a matter for laughter. It's too awful…'

Antonio felt duly chastened but said to Clemo, 'You will have to develop a thicker skin, my friend, if you are going to survive in this City, but let me change the subject…there have been some new developments. I have heard that there is a group of Reformed Princes in Germany who have begun a League to defy the Emperor. Europe, which seemed completely stable only a few years ago, is developing some ominous cracks… and I guess King Henry will send embassies to them seeking their support for his divorce.'

Clemo was not interested. He kept thinking of the cook. Servants, it seemed, could be slaughtered at the whim of their masters; what kind of world was it where such injustice could happen?

And then, a month or two later, Antonio informed Clemo that King Henry had now abandoned Catherine of Aragon and had gone on one of his royal tours taking Anne Boleyn with him. 'Our Ambassador is in a real temper about this,' he said, 'He's a great supporter of Catherine but it looks as though Henry has now reached the end of the road with her. And our Ambassador is mad because the Emperor will not intervene to save his aunt from humiliation.'

'Fortune's wheel,' said Clemo, deliberately echoing what Antonio had said to him a while back. And although it sounded worldly-wise, in his heart he was close to despair. Those people and institutions he had always considered stable and devoted to the good of the country, patently were not. All that Henry wanted, it seemed, was to live with his mistress, and hang the consequences.

He said as much to Antonio, who replied, 'But don't forget, dear Clemo, Henry wants a legitimate male heir, and he can't achieve that with Catherine of Aragon, so he hopes that Anne Boleyn will solve the problem. That will bring stability to the realm. Without a male heir the country could fall apart. So, I have a question for you, Clemo. Isn't it Henry's duty as King to keep the country safe and strong and stable, even if it means ditching his wife?'

Clemo did not answer.

Chapter 29: A New Year

At the revels to mark Christmas and the Twelve Days, Clemo reminded himself that the new year would be one in which he would have to make up his mind about his own future. It was not a consoling thought, but it felt important. He decided that whilst Antonio was a good and lively friend, because he was so unsure, he needed to approach older and wiser heads to help him in his thinking.

He went to the Parsonage of St Mary Bowe to talk with Father Mossman. As before, the priest, his housekeeper and her family were delighted to see him. Clemo was invited into the parlour where a fire was roaring away. Perhaps it was the warmth, or perhaps it was the mead he had been offered by Alice, but he felt so at home with them that he relaxed. He explained his dilemma.

'I confess, Father,' he said, addressing Father Mossman, 'that I have set this year of our Lord 1532, as one in which I have to make a major decision.'

Alice's eyes were downcast hoping that they would not reveal anything of what she imagined Clemo might say.

He continued, 'I have loved getting to know you and Mistress Blake, Edward and Alice. You have been immensely kind to me. But I have to admit that I do not enjoy London, and whilst I can tolerate my work at the Ambassador's Residence, I feel that I should not continue there for too much longer.'

Alice's face fell.

'I am not sure what I am going to do next, or where I am going to go.' He hesitated, plucking up the courage to find the right words. 'But I am seriously wondering whether I should explore becoming a Cistercian.'

The logs continued to blaze. Outside, people continued to wander past. The world was still turning on its axis. Yet for Clemo, the divulging of what had been kept secretly in his heart for several months, felt of earth-stopping significance. But now he had said it, it was a great relief. He leaned back in his chair.

Mistress Blake jumped into the silence whilst Father Mossman was contemplating how to answer.

'I think, Clemo,' she said quietly, 'that that would be a complete and utter waste. Forgive me for saying so, but the world needs people like you in it to keep it sane. You are such a good man, what use will that goodness be to the rest of us if you lock yourself away in a monastery?'

'My dear,' said Father Mossman, 'do you not think that praying is a way of keeping the world sane?'

'Perhaps,' she replied, 'but you can pray anywhere. You don't have to shut yourself up in some damp and gloomy cell, and live off the fat of the land in order to pray. Doesn't God listen to my poor prayers in Cheapside as much as he listens to the Latin mumblings of monks and nuns?'

Alice rose from the stool on which she had been sitting, excused herself, and hurried from the room, tears streaming down her face.

Clemo was discomfited and surmised that something he had said must have upset her.

'She'll get over it,' said her mother. 'It's better that she is left on her own for a while, and then I'll go to see her.'

Edward, looking bored by what he termed 'grown-ups' talk', asked if he might leave the room as well.

'Yes, you may, Edward...but leave your sister on her own.' Edward left, smirking.

'Clemo,' said Father Mossman, 'tell me more. Why has this thought about the monastic life entered your soul?'

'I really am not certain, but when I look back over my life and ask myself where I have felt most content, it's been with my late wife and baby son, with Brother Adam at Tintern, staying overnight at Flaxley, at Mass, and saying my rosary. And if I ask myself where I have been unhappy, forgive me, it's been here in London. The noise and rush and stink assault me so that I can hardly bear it.'

'But is not the City, with all its faults, also held within God's providence?' asked Father Mossman, gently.

217

Clemo shifted uneasily in his chair. He had not thought about it like that. He had seen his old life as idyllic and his current life as nightmarish, and therefore had felt drawn to a life that would contain more opportunities for the idyllic and fewer opportunities for nightmares. He remained silent whilst he mulled over what Father Mossman had said. Was he perhaps, just being self-indulgent?

And then he said, 'But the other thing I can't stand is that in the Residence I don't know who I can really trust. I knew nothing about diplomacy and politics and international goings-on until I came here… but now…,' he paused, '…everything seems twisted out of its proper shape. People lie and cheat and clamber over each other to reach the top…and from what I see of the top, that seems pretty rotten and putrid as well.'

'Ah…,' said Father Mossman, 'but do you not think that this is what all human beings are like, whether in a monastery or in the King's Palace? Are you perhaps failing to see the propensity that is in all of us not to be entirely straightforward?' He glanced at Mistress Blake, willing her not to speak.

She stood up and said that she ought to go to see how Alice was, and quietly left the room.

Clemo looked at the fire and then at his hands. 'Perhaps that is true,' he said, sighing. Maybe what other people were always calling his 'innocence' was really his unwillingness to recognise his own weaknesses and fragility? Maybe he was being self-centred? Maybe he still had a long way to go in growing up?

He expressed gratitude to Father Mossman for helping him. 'Not at all,' said the priest. 'You are welcome here whenever you like…and Alice would be so upset if you never came here again.' He paused, and then said, as he placed his arm on Clemo's shoulder, 'She's head over heels in love with you, Clemo…you do realise that don't you?'

Clemo nodded, saying he had wondered but that now he ought to leave.

He made his way back to the Residence in a sombre mood. There was so much to think about.

He was greeted at the door by the ever-ebullient Antonio.

'Guess what I've just heard, Clemo. The Queen sent the King a golden goblet for a New Year present. But he was so mad, he sent it straight back. Isn't that amazing?' Clemo dipped his head and excused himself, he really did need time to think things through about his own life, and much as he loved Antonio's company, now was not the time for gossip. But he felt curmudgeonly in doing so and apologised, saying that he had many things on his mind and that he would speak to Antonio later.

'How was Alice?' enquired Antonio, with a mischievous laugh, but Clemo waved his hand in the air and walked away.

Over the next few weeks, other political news was brought to Clemo's attention by Antonio. He was told about a new and special procedure proposed by the House of Commons called 'The Supplication against the Ordinaries'

'Now translate that into simple English,' said Clemo, laughing.

'Easy,' replied Antonio, 'It's another attempt to clip the church's wings and specially to limit the legal powers and privileges that the Church has.'

Clemo looked solemn. 'So, the Commons are also attacking God's Church?'

'In a word, yes. But you need to realise that the civil lawyers around the Commons don't like the grip that the Church has on the Law. They want to limit the Church, so that they can get their own hands on more of the legal lucre!'

'Can't they leave things alone?'

'You might want to ask our neighbour that question.'

'What do you mean?'

'I mean Cromwell…he's up to his cunning eyes in all of this, burrowing away, altering a phrase here, changing a phrase there, making himself indispensable, surreptitiously trying to increase the power of the King and decrease the power of the Church…. And by the way, have you noticed that there is a lot of building work going on next door?'

'I have.'

'That's Master Cromwell extending his property. Always a sign of a man on the make. He's not only a Royal Councillor now, but he has also become the Master of the Jewels.'

'So?'

'So, my dear Clemo, he is now in charge of all the jewels and plate that the King holds under lock and key in the Tower. Which means that when necessary, Cromwell, with the King's permission, can always sell stuff that is surplus to requirements. And thereby satisfy whatever is the King's latest whim. And just in case the King needs to replenish his supply, there's another bit of legislation which ensures that the Annates paid to Rome are to be cut in half. The other half, the King will get...'

Clemo, hearing the news, felt depressed. He expressed his dismay that the Church's power was being whittled away.

'So, you would rather that His Holiness had the money, would you? Money, let me remind you Clemo, which was earned in this country. As an Italian, I am very happy that English money is going to Italy...you should see the glorious buildings being created in Rome... but I can also understand that Cromwell and the King believe that much of that money should stay in England. Isn't that fair?'

Clemo remained bewildered. Antonio was a great guy, but he seemed to have the capacity to put both sides of an argument, leaving Clemo to come to his own conclusions. Clemo was floundering. He wasn't used to thinking in that way. He had been taught that there was only one way of approaching any subject, and that was the one the Church provided. It made life simple and Clemo was all in favour of simplicity. Was this yet another stage in growing up, that he would have to learn to think for himself? His brain ached.

He explained his problem to Antonio who said, 'Clemo, after dinner today come to the office and I will arrange for your education to be developed further.'

'What do you mean?'

'I'm not going to explain. Just be there.' He laughed as he sauntered away.

After dinner, Antonio found Clemo and said to him, 'Come with me. I have two letters to deliver to the Cromwell household. I shall give one to you, and I shall hold the other. Cromwell himself is away at the moment, and that means I can ask my contact to let us in.'

'But I shouldn't come with you. It's not allowed.'

'Oh yes, it is!'

'Who says so?'

'I say so.'

Clemo was handed a sealed letter and walked hesitantly beside Antonio who was, as always, brimming with confidence. On arriving at the door of the Cromwell house, Antonio explained to the doorkeeper that Clemo was learning the ropes as a junior clerk at the Ambassador's residence and had been brought along to meet some of the staff just in case Antonio was ever indisposed.

They were invited to enter and walked along a corridor to the Clerks' room.

'Hey!' shouted one of the clerks as they entered, 'It's Antonio, and who is this you have brought with you?'

'A colleague,' explained Antonio, 'he's called Clemo.'

'Welcome,' said the clerk breezily, gripping Antonio lightly by the shoulder.

'I've a favour to ask,' said Antonio. 'Clemo has not seen the new portrait and as Master Cromwell is away, it seemed a good opportunity to show him what it's like. I'm educating him!'

The clerk laughed and said to Clemo, 'If this man is educating you, heaven help you. He knows a lot, I grant you that, but what he doesn't know, he makes up!' Antonio ruffled the clerk's hair good naturedly.

'Right,' said the clerk, 'follow me. We're having some work done, as you can see, and so the portrait is not yet hung, but here we are.' He ushered them into what was clearly Cromwell's private study. On the table, carefully wrapped against the builder's dust was a painting. He unwrapped it.

'Brilliant!' said Antonio. 'A true likeness. Look Clemo, this is a portrait of a man who knows what he is doing and where he is going. He's not shy. He is exact, he is careful, he is calculating, and wily. Don't you think?'

Clemo thought it better not to answer but said, hesitantly, 'Who painted it?'

'The King's own painter, Hans Holbein,' the clerk answered, with a proud flourish. 'Nothing but the best for our master.'

Clemo looked at it again, and then cast his eyes around the rest of the room. He spotted a book on a shelf and noticed that it was by William Tyndale. He asked about it. 'Oh that,' said the clerk, 'that's nothing, just an old book...but you should not have seen it. Sorry. That was my fault.' He was flustered. 'For goodness' sake, don't tell a soul that you saw it, otherwise I shall end up swinging from a rope.' His face drained of colour.

He carefully re-wrapped the painting and hurried them out of the room. 'Please promise me you will keep this a secret,' he said anxiously.

'Of course, we promise,' said Antonio and Clemo together.

When they left Cromwell's house, Antonio stopped and put his hand on Clemo's arm. 'I wanted you to see the painting,' he said, 'but we should not have seen that book. It's incredibly dangerous for all of us that we saw it. So, not a word to anyone.' He was surprisingly forceful in his words.

'Alright. So, why did you want me to see the painting, Antonio?'

'Because it shows you the kind of world we are living in. Cromwell is a bit of a mystery man. He was born up-river in Putney. He spent time in Italy and joined the Frescobaldi banking family in Florence; then, after a spell working in the Low Countries, when he came back to England, somehow, he joined Wolsey's household, and now he is getting closer and closer to the King. What a man!' Antonio was clearly an admirer. 'He helped Wolsey to disband several monasteries to pay for his new Colleges in Oxford and Ipswich...and you might have heard that earlier this year Cromwell was behind the dissolution of a few Augustinian houses, including one here in London. But this time, the money didn't go to the King, it was used to reward the King's favourites. The monasteries are treasure houses, and the King loves treasure. It's as simple as that. We haven't seen the last of the dissolutions, Clemo. Not by a long way. You mark my words.'

Clemo felt even more disconsolate. The places he loved were being plucked from trees like ripe plums.

'So, was it money from the dissolutions that paid for the painting?'

'It might have been. But Master Cromwell is not above receiving a bribe or two to oil his way forward.'

For some reason, it was the painting and the devious self-satisfaction of the sitter, which helped Clemo to determine his way ahead. If the world was as wicked as it seemed to be, was there not a place within it for people who would intercede with God to improve and save it? Because, for sure, if it were left to human beings alone, the result would be chaos.

Chapter 30: Coming to a decision

Over the next few weeks, Clemo continued with his work as a groom and a junior clerk, but his mind was thinking about little else except becoming a monk. It was like a compulsion. It would not let him alone. So, after much deliberation, he decided to go to see Brother Anton at St Mary Graces thinking that he might have some insights about the Cistercians and perhaps, some advice. Accordingly, he walked to St Mary Graces, retracing the journey he had made on his first day in the City.

At the gatehouse, he asked if he might be allowed to see Brother Anton. Permission was given and he was asked to wait in the courtyard whilst a message was sent. A monk in white habit and black scapula soon came across the courtyard to meet him.

'I gather you want to see Brother Anton,' said the monk. 'I am sorry to say that he is not well and so has not been able to greet you himself, but I shall take you to him. When did you last see him?'

Clemo explained that he had first met Brother Anton at St Bernard's and had had the pleasure of travelling to London in his company.

'So, you're that young man. He has often spoken of you. He used to say that one day you would come to see him, and here you are. He will be very pleased.'

Clemo was taken to the Parlour and there was Brother Anton seated in a chair by the fire. He had lost weight and was more hunched over than he had been when Clemo had first met him. The skin on his hands looked paper thin and a wasting sickness had emphasised the stark protuberance of his nose and highlighted his cheekbones, but his eyes were deep and compassionately lively.

The other monk left them.

'How good it is to see you again, Clemo. I knew that I would see you one day. I have been waiting for you.'

His voice was almost a whisper, quiet but intense. Clemo thought that Brother Anton might not have many more weeks to live and felt guilty that he had not come sooner. He began to apologise.

'There's no need for that. I just knew you would come. Now, tell me why you are here.'

Clemo explained that he had not been able to fully settle in London, despite making some good friends, and that, although he mostly enjoyed his work, especially his time as a groom, and felt privileged to have seen diplomatic life from the inside, he found the world of politics deeply disturbing. And he concluded by saying that something seemed to be missing from his own life. 'It is,' he said, 'as though there is something waiting to be discovered...but I don't know what that something is or where it might be found.'

Brother Anton held out his hands to the fire. Then he turned slowly and stiffly towards Clemo and said, 'I think that there is perhaps something you are not telling me. What is it?'

'I am sorry, Brother Anton. I have not told you the idea that has been going round and round in my mind because it seems presumptuous to do so. And perhaps, in any case, I am fooling myself.'

'Look, Clemo,' replied Anton, 'As you can probably see, I don't have many more days left on this earth, but if you felt able to reveal to me what it is that has been going on in your head, maybe I could help.'

Clemo took a minute or so to frame his reply. In the presence of Brother Anton, he felt so inadequate, so unconfident, so gauche. Here was a man who seemed the exact opposite of the Cromwell portrait. A man who had nothing, and yet in his nothingness seemed to have everything.

So then, plucking up courage, he said, 'I wonder if I ought to become a Cistercian.'

It was Brother Anton's turn to take time to weigh up his response. His hands went out to the fire again, shaking slightly. And then he said, 'Well, Clemo, if it is God who has put these ideas in your head, you should see where they might lead, shouldn't you?'

'But how can I know for certain that it is God?'

'None of us can ever know that for sure. It's a case of walking in the direction that God seems to be showing you…and if it is God who is working within your soul, you will find the destination that is right for you…but, let me add this, that destination itself will probably change as your life goes on.'

'Thank you, Brother…' Clemo almost choked on his words. 'Will you please pray for me?' He had never said such a thing before but felt that it was somehow necessary. He knelt in front of Brother Anton who placed his thin hands around Clemo's face.

'I shall, Clemo but before I do, allow me to say one thing more. I really don't know how long our Order is going to last in England. Things seem to be changing so rapidly, none of us can tell what is likely to happen. But …the very first Cistercian house founded in England is Our Lady of Waverley. It might be right that you should test your vocation there, where it all began. Yes…that is what you should do. Now I shall say the words of God's blessing.' He moved his hands from around Clemo's face and placed them on the top of Clemo's head. He stayed silent for a while, and then said, 'The blessing of God Almighty, the Father, the Son and the Holy Ghost be upon you, and remain with you, this day, and for evermore.'

Clemo rose to his feet. Brother Anton slumped in his chair, completely drained of energy. Clemo thanked Brother Anton (who was too exhausted to respond) and walked slowly and quietly to the door; as he opened it, the monk he had met at the gatehouse was standing outside. Clemo explained that he had been really helped by Brother Anton. 'He's been waiting to see you for so long…' replied the monk. 'Now, I'll go in to see how he is and if you wouldn't mind, could you find your own way to the gatehouse?'

'Of course, I can, and thank you.'

He walked slowly away. It felt that his destination was now clear. It was the combination of hesitancy and certainty in Brother Anton's answers that he had found so helpful. Brother Anton had not given him clear and unequivocal answers but had pointed him in a potential direction, and, for the moment, that was enough. It brought a sense of peace to his soul. Out of his confusion, a pattern was beginning to emerge.

He decided that he would walk back along Thames Street and then go up towards St Mary Bowe before finally making for the Residence. It seemed fitting that the path he had taken when he had first arrived in London, should be the same one he should choose now.

He recalled with amusement how anxious he had been on that first day, whereas now he could actually enjoy the sight of the river, the ships unloading their wares, the wherries scurrying from one bank to the other; even the smells did not seem so bad as he remembered. And walking past St Mary Bowe he gave thanks that he had met, and been welcomed so warmly, by Father Mossman, Mistress Blake, Alice and Edward.

He had just turned into Cheapside when he heard footsteps scampering behind him and a frantic voice calling out, 'Clemo! Clemo!' He turned around and saw Alice running towards him, her right hand holding her cap on her head, her dress and apron dishevelled and awry. Her face was white.

'Oh Clemo, thank God, thank God,' she gasped. 'I've just had a terrible shock.' She grasped his arm, 'Quick' she said, 'before my mother comes looking for me.' Her breath was coming in short gasps. She looked wild and frightened.

'Alice, what's happened?' Clemo asked.

'I can't tell you here out in the street. Let's go to St Paul's and I'll tell you when we are there. Oh, I am so shaken. It's terrible, terrible.' She thrust her arm through Clemo's and almost dragged him along beside her.

At St Paul's there was the usual throng but at least they could find a corner where they could have a discreet conversation. She pulled him towards one of the chapels on the north side of the nave. It was dark but there were a couple of stools on which they could sit.

Alice put her head in her hands. She was shaking, and choking sobs emerged from her mouth as she tried to control herself. Clemo waited until she was a little calmer and then gently said, 'Alice, please tell me what has happened.'

'My mother and I have had a terrible row. It was all about nothing; it was about whether or not I had upset Father Mossman by spilling some ale on the carpet, and in the middle of it I shouted at her, and

I don't know why, I shouted, 'You have never told me anything about my father. What's the big secret?' She slapped me across my face…see,' she pointed at a red mark on her cheek. 'She's never done that before. I was so angry and frightened that I didn't know what to do. We've never had a row like that before, never, but she then gripped me by my wrists and said that I should never raise the question ever again. 'Your father is dead', she said. And I said, 'But who was he? I have a right to know,' and then her face seemed to contort with rage and fear. It was terrible. And, because I was so frightened, I decided to hurt her more. I don't know why I wanted to do that, but at that moment, my anger took over and I told her that I had once seen her kissing Father Mossman. She turned very pale and said that I was telling lies. I said that I was not, and I insisted that I had seen them kissing, and said to her, 'I saw you giving him long, long kisses, in the hall when you thought that Edward and I were asleep.' And then she crumpled, turned away from me, and started to cry.'

Clemo waited for the rest of the story. Alice looked around to see if anyone might be listening to what she was saying. When she thought it safe to do so, she continued: 'I put my arm around her (I do love my Mother, honestly, she has been the most wonderful mother to me and to Edward), I put my arm around her to comfort her and to tell her that I was sorry for upsetting her, and gradually she stopped crying. She then asked me to go with her to the parlour, where we could sit down. Once we were there she said, 'Well, I suppose you are old enough now to be told the truth.'

I thought she would tell me about the dark and handsome man who I always imagined had been my father, (I often told myself stories about him when I was small… in my head I always imagined him as kind of story-book hero who had died in a sea fight defending our country against the Spanish) but she didn't say that.'

'What did she say?'

'She started crying again, and then quietly she said, "You have been living with your father for years". I couldn't work out what she meant…and then the light dawned. When I had seen Mother and Father Mossman kissing, they were kissing because they were lovers. Father Mossman was my father. And he was Edward's father.' She began to cry, silently. 'And they never let on. Can you imagine my shock? My world has been turned upside down.'

'And does Edward know?'

'I asked my mother that and she said he wasn't old enough to be told. Which is when it all became too much for me. I tore out of the house…and then I saw you…and here we are…' She took her kerchief from the pocket of her apron and began to wipe her face.

'Alice' said Clemo, who was himself wrestling with everything she had told him, 'What are you going to do now? We can't stay here. Do you feel up to going back home to see your mother?'

'I don't know,' she said, her eyes cast down to the floor. 'I just don't know. I hardly know who I am any more, let alone what I ought to do. She has deceived me, Clemo. My own mother, the person I love best in all the world, has deceived me…and so has Father Mossman. All the time I have been living with them and acting as a servant, they have kept this secret from me. I hate them. I absolutely hate them. How could they do this to me…and to Edward? How could they?' She began to sob again.

The crowds in the Cathedral were beginning to thin out; darkness was falling.

'Alice…we shall have to leave very soon,' said Clemo with as much gentleness as he could, 'Let's just think for a moment about your mother. She too has been carrying this secret all her life and right now she will be beside herself with worry. She will imagine all kinds of terrible things might have happened to you…she's probably down by the river right now, asking if anyone has seen you and when they say that they haven't, her worries will be awful.'

'And what about me? Aren't my worries awful too?'

'They are,' replied Clemo, 'but if we go back to your home, at least she will know you are safe. You said that you love her…isn't the best thing to do to go home, and spend some time together? Even in your anger and confusion, the fact of your love for her and her love for you might be a starting point for a conversation…hard and difficult though it might be…Come on, let me walk you home. I'll stay with you and make sure you get there safely…' He stood up, put his arm around

Alice's shoulders and guided her out from the Cathedral and towards Cheapside.

He felt very confused himself and completely out of his depth in such a harrowing situation, but thought that if he simply walked alongside Alice, that might help. At the very least, he was saving her from doing something terrible. He thought of Hans and shuddered inwardly.

As they neared the Parsonage, Clemo saw Mistress Blake rushing towards them along Cheapside, her arms outstretched, her face distorted with worry and sorrow. She called out, 'Alice! Alice!'

On seeing her, Alice clung more firmly to Clemo who gently released her and said as Mistress Blake embraced Alice. 'Alice, you must go with your mother now but if you want me to call round', he looked at Mistress Blake, 'I am willing to do so. You have been so good to me, the least I can do is to help you.'

The two women were locked in each other's arms, their tears mingling. Clemo walked away, completely bewildered by all he had been told, and headed for the Residence.

Chapter 31: Major changes afoot

He lay awake for a long time, thinking over all that had happened during the day. The elation of realising what he should do with his life had been snuffed out by the grim situation in the Mossman household. Since his arrival in London, Clemo had come to learn that powerful people such as Cromwell did not seem to live by the rules that ordinary people kept, but now he had stumbled across the secrets, deceptions and agonies kept in a priest's house. It was difficult to comprehend; however, he did understand Alice's turmoil, and hoped that once she and her mother had talked and perhaps, once Father Mossman had also unburdened himself, some kind of normality could be resumed. But if the situation in the Parsonage ever escaped into the air of the outside world, what might happen then?

The following morning, he went as usual to the stables. Being with horses brought him peace; he was soothed by the ordinariness of things, the smell of hay, the touch of leather, the shine of the horses' coats, the sound of their hooves on the cobbles. He was brushing his favourite horse, Noble, when he saw a young maid servant coming towards him. It was Alice's friend.

She apologised for interrupting Clemo's work but said that she had a message to give him. She pulled a piece of paper from her apron pocket and handed it to him. He broke the seal and read it whilst she watched. It was from Father Mossman. It was a heart-breaking letter in which Father Mossman thanked Clemo for caring for Alice on the previous day, expressed profuse apologies about what had occurred and humbly asked if Clemo could spare some time either later in the day or on the morrow to go to see the family. 'Please,' the letter concluded, 'pray for us and if you can, forgive us.'

The maid servant stood waiting. Clemo asked if she could run to the Parsonage and tell them that, work permitting, Clemo would see them later that evening.

As the girl was leaving, Clemo saw Antonio bearing down on him. He quickly stuffed the letter in his jerkin pocket.

'How's Alice?' asked Antonio with a wink and a grin. 'It must be getting serious if she sends letters to you. 'But,' he paused, putting his forefinger to his chin, in a theatrical manner, 'the question is, can Alice write? And if she cannot write, who might have written the letter you have just received...ah, the scheming, sweet duplicities of love.'

Clemo did not answer but began to brush the horse's coat vigorously.

'I come, dear Clemo, with some more news from the world outside the walls of this Residence. Now, this is a really juicy bit of gossip. You may have heard that Thomas Cranmer has been appointed Archbishop, but...but...rumour has it that whilst he was in Nuremberg on the King's business, he had a bit of private business to transact himself. Can you imagine what that might have been?'

'No, I can't,' replied Clemo. He tried to make his irritability about gossip clear, by turning his back on Antonio and continuing to brush Nobile.

'Rumour', said Antonio, warming to his subject, 'is saying that Thomas Cranmer married a wife whilst he was abroad...'

Clemo hurled the brush he had been holding back into the stable.

'Clemo, I'm sorry if I have upset you, I didn't know you would feel so strongly about such matters.'

Clemo half bent over to wipe his hands on his breeches and when he stood upright, looked straight at Antonio, and said, 'Look, Antonio, I am sorry. But I have had my fill of gossip, I can't be doing with it anymore. The world seems to have gone mad...and I don't want to spend much more time in its greasy clutches. It is just unbearable.'

Antonio was taken aback by the outburst and asked bluntly whether Clemo's response meant that he was contemplating 'doing a Hans'. 'Because if you are,' he said, 'I shall do everything I can to stop you.' He had become very stern. His usual vivacity had given way to a solemn seriousness.

Clemo turned to face him and decided to take him into his confidence. 'Antonio, you are a great friend. You have made my life in the Residence bearable, even when I frequently felt that I had made a dreadful decision in coming to work here. I enjoy your jokes; I envy your sheer love of life...but my own life seems to be going in a direction which will be very different from yours. I was not entirely expecting this to happen, but it is.'

'So, Alice is the lucky girl, is she?' asked Antonio.

Clemo laughed. 'Antonio, you are incorrigible. You have only two things on your mind: women and gossip.'

'That's about right. What gives spice to the world? What brings joy and pleasure? Answer, a lovely woman and juicy gossip. Nothing wrong with that, is there?'

'No,' replied Clemo, 'but I think that there might be more to life than even that.'

'Such as?' asked Antonio.

'I am going to be absolutely candid with you, Antonio. I shall ask you to keep what I am about to say, under your hat, though I know you will probably not be able to do so...'

'That is an outrageous slur on my upright and honest character,' replied Antonio, laughing. 'So, what are you now going to tell me?'

Clemo swallowed. 'I think I am going to become a monk.'

'Oddio,' said Antonio, sighing deeply, 'you are not being serious with me, are you? Promise me that this is some kind of English joke.'

'It's no joke. I am truly serious. I believe that that is what I ought to do...'

'But do you know what monks and nuns are like these days? Nobody has a good word to say about them: people see them as greedy wastrels, buffoons, ignoramuses, and fat, lascivious fornicators.'

'I know that that is what some people say, Antonio, but when did you yourself last visit a monastery?'

'Not since my family left Venice.'

'So, everything you say is not based on any personal experience, it's gossip, Antonio, just gossip...' Clemo chortled.

'But some gossip is connected with the truth, like the rumour about the celibate, potential Archbishop of Canterbury getting married. That suggests to me that either he is very headstrong, which I doubt, or he knows which way the reforming wind is blowing in England. And if the Archbishop is as astute as people say he is, it implies, my dear Clemo, that becoming a monk is unlikely to have much of a future. Don't forget what Cromwell and the King did to those small Augustinian houses. A married Archbishop and an avaricious and ruthless King…the signs are there in front of your nose, Clemo. Don't ignore them.'

Antonio walked away and Clemo continued to brush Noble.

Later that day, once his work as a junior clerk had been completed, Clemo asked permission from the Senior Clerk if he might miss supper because he had an appointment to see the parish priest at St Mary Bowe.

'If your tasks are all finished, Clemo you may go.' And then he added, with a knowing smile, 'Please give my greetings to Alice Blake.'

Clemo stared hard at Antonio who had his head down copying a long document and avoided looking up, but Clemo heard him sniggering. Gossip was the currency of the Residence, it would seem. Clemo said nothing as he left.

Arriving at the Parsonage, he knocked on the great door. It was Mistress Blake who opened it. She looked gaunt and careworn; there were dark circles under her eyes.

'Clemo, thank you for coming to see us. I am sorry that you have been caught up in all of this. Father Mossman is desperate to see you and has asked that he might talk to you on his own.'

'And how is Alice?' asked Clemo.

'I think she is recovering from the shock, but it will take her a long time before she can come to terms with it.'

'And Edward?'

'He doesn't know yet.'

Clemo was not convinced that Edward had not read the emotional temperature of the house but kept that thought to himself.

'Let me take you to Father Mossman,' she said, and she led him to the parlour.

'Father,' she said, trying hard to play the housekeeper, 'Clemo Trelawney has arrived.' She ushered him into the room and left the two men looking at each other.

'Thank you for coming, Clemo,' said Father Mossman, his voice softer and less booming than usual. 'Marguerite and I are very grateful to you for the way you looked after Alice yesterday. Please sit down. I shall come to the point immediately, I think that will be best, don't you?'

His voice had developed a slight tremor. He coughed to clear his throat and then leaned forward in his chair, his hands grasping each other as though he was praying.

'Marguerite came to be my housekeeper about twenty years ago. She was a demure and lovely young woman who had lost both her parents to the sweating sickness a few months before. She was a delightful housekeeper and knew exactly what needed to be done. My house had never been so well organised. And that is how it went on for about ten months. But the fact is, I was becoming more and more fond of her. And I guessed that the same could be said for her. However, there came a day when after much agonising on my part, I blurted out my feelings and apologised as soon as I had done so. I was a priest, I had vowed celibacy and I felt torn in two, from head to toe. It was agony. And yet I could not deny that I had fallen in love. But when I told her... I can see her now. She stood and looked at me and apologetically admitted that she was also in love with me and then said that she would leave immediately. I begged her not to. I couldn't imagine life without her. I held her in my arms and said that we could probably find a way through.' He paused. 'We talked about little else for days and days and then I suggested that if she could pretend to be my housekeeper, I would ensure that I would not mention our love for each other to anyone. Well, our love grew and grew and led, as you know, to the birth of Alice. We had a careful plan. During her pregnancy Marguerite, like all housekeepers, wore voluminous dresses and aprons, so her pregnancy didn't show. When it came time to give birth to Alice, she went to her cousin in the country and returned here as soon as she had been safely delivered. We told people that Marguerite had been asked to care for her baby niece because the mother had died in childbirth. And, fortunately, that story was believed...though I guess some might have wondered whether the story was true.

Edward's arrival was a bit trickier. Again, Marguerite went to her cousin's, was safely delivered, and returned with Edward, explaining that Edward was a foundling and she had been asked by a desperate young woman to care for him. That story pushed the boundaries of credulity, I admit. But we kept up the pretence for years and gradually any rumours there might have been subsided…until yesterday. We'll come to that in a moment. But I want to assure you that I love Marguerite profoundly. She is a blessing to me. She really is my helpmeet, my joy, and my crown. I love her now, more than ever. And then yesterday happened. We are desperate for Alice. We love her very much indeed. She is a fine young woman, and we did not intend to deceive her and had agreed that one day we would have to tell her. But that day never came…and now it has.'

He remained leaning forward, looking at the floor.

'I am so sorry, so sorry.' He choked back a sob. 'I just want you to know that Alice and Edward are not the result of a couple of mistimed fumbles or human lust. They are the children of parents who love them more than life itself. But Marguerite and I do not know what to do now. We have wondered if perhaps we might stay and brazen it out but have come to the conclusion that we shall probably have to leave and continue our lives elsewhere. But how we shall earn our living is a matter of terrible worry and concern. We are still trying to see what we can do…but for the moment, whatever you may think of us, we didn't want you not to know the truth. We felt we owed it to you. Now, would you mind if Marguerite joined us?'

Clemo sat quietly, stunned by all he had been told. He himself had made his confession to Father Burley often enough but didn't imagine that he would ever himself hear the confession of a priest. It was, he felt, the wrong way round, yet despite all his misgivings, (weren't Alice and Edward the real victims of this deceit?) he could not but respect Father Mossman's honesty, remorse, and humility.

There was a gentle knock at the door. Marguerite Blake entered. Father Mossman looked at her and said, 'I have told Clemo everything, my dear.'

She drew up another chair and looked directly at Clemo. 'We are so grateful that you happened to walk past yesterday when Alice tore out of the house. If anything in this sad mess can be described as providential, that can. We can never thank you enough.'

'And where is Alice now, and what about Edward?'

'Alice has gone to see a friend. I think you know her. She works at the Ambassador's residence. They have been friends since childhood. And Edward has gone out to play with some friends down by the river. So, we have a little while before they return. We have decided that we should have a family conversation, the four of us, in which all the secrets that Alice uncovered yesterday should be known by Edward as well. I expect he will be terribly upset, but if we are to set out on a new life, we can only do so on the basis of honesty.' She reached across to hold Father Mossman's hand. 'We are agreed on that, aren't we?' He nodded. 'And we think that once Father Mossman has seen the Archbishop and has resigned, we shall have to find somewhere else to live. That is not going to be easy, but we have some money saved up for a rainy day. And now is the rainy day. So…we shall be leaving.'

'I shall miss you dreadfully' said Clemo. 'You have been a lifeline for me, and I thank you… and, as you know, I shall be leaving the City before too long myself. Nothing is yet carved in stone, but the signs are beginning to form a recognisable shape. And I need to thank you Father Mossman, for helping me to make this decision.'

'Ironic, isn't it?' replied Father Mossman, 'that apparently, I have been able to help you whilst being in a complete mess myself.'

'But may I ask one thing more?' said Clemo, 'You said just now that you would be seeing the Archbishop. Why is that? Should you not go to the Bishop of London?'

'No,' replied Father Mossman, 'St Mary Bowe is what is known as a 'peculiar'; in other words, it comes under the jurisdiction of the Archbishop and not the Bishop and has done so for centuries. But as there is no Archbishop in residence at the moment…he is on his way back from Italy…that makes things a bit trickier for me. But I shall definitely go to Lambeth tomorrow. That is my firm intention.'

Chapter 32: Making the break

The Ambassador was in a foul temper. The King, accompanied by Anne Boleyn (who had been created Marquess of Pembroke in her own right two months earlier) had gone on a royal visit to France, surrounded by over three thousand retainers. It was intended to be a statement of English Royal magnificence. The French Ambassador was cock-a-hoop that he had managed to devise this rapprochement between England and France, but the Imperial Ambassador was less pleased. It meant that all his efforts to achieve an alliance between England and the Holy Roman Emperor had failed. He was, therefore, not part of the entourage which had crossed the Channel. In brief, he had been snubbed. And because everyone in the Residence knew it, they were all behaving circumspectly. Not putting a foot wrong. It meant that Clemo did not feel it would be the right moment to divulge his own monastic plans. They would have to wait until after Christmas and after the return of Cromwell and all who had accompanied the King.

The Christmas and Twelve days celebrations went ahead, but they were much more muted than in previous years. And the mood did not get very much better in late January when the rumour mill started up again. It was believed, 'on good authority', said Antonio, that the King had married Anne Boleyn.

Clemo was no longer surprised by anything that happened, and although he quietly expressed his concerns to Antonio ('How can a man marry, when he is already married?'), he largely kept his thinking to himself. In any case, his mind was moving towards his own future. He had decided that, if he could receive permission, he would set out for Waverley Abbey on February 2nd, the Feast of the Presentation. It seemed to be an auspicious day. He was now offering himself to God, in the way that Jesus had been offered in the Temple. What could be more appropriate?

He decided in mid-January that he would formally tell the Senior Clerk and the Deputy Steward about his sense of vocation and ask permission to leave. Neither interview went quite as he imagined they might have done. The Senior Clerk said that he thought Clemo was mad to even consider becoming a monk, particularly as he had done so well in the Residence and was in line for promotion. 'When Antonio leaves in March, I had it in mind to ask you to take over from him. But if you are going to be utterly foolish... I suppose we shall have to do without you. What a waste. What an absolute waste.' Clemo was taken aback by the news about Antonio but said nothing.

The reaction of the Deputy Steward to Clemo seeking permission was altogether more eirenic. He said that he had sensed that Clemo had never been entirely happy in the Residence and even speculated whether lying behind that unhappiness was a growing vocation to the religious life. Clemo had no inkling that the Deputy Steward might have been so sympathetic but was grateful for receiving permission to leave. 'There is only one thing I ask of you Clemo,' said the Deputy Steward, 'and that is that you must come to see me the day before you leave. That is an order.'

Clemo left the interviews bemused but was angry that Antonio had kept his own plans secret. He immediately searched him out and found him lounging around in the small room where documents were sealed and stored.

When Clemo entered, Antonio smiled. 'So, is the deed done, my good friend?'

'If by that you mean, have I asked permission to leave, then yes, the deed is done. But why didn't you tell me that you were planning to leave as well? That was probably the only secret you have ever kept to yourself. Where are you going?'

'Next door,' replied Antonio, 'Master Cromwell has heard of my amazing brilliance and erudition and as he only employs brilliant, erudite people, he wants me to join his staff.' He laughed loudly. 'Clemo... I offer you some Venetian advice: always try to decide who is on the up, and then make yourself indispensable to them. ...but it's pointless offering you that advice, because you have already decided to do the exact opposite. You are going to make yourself indispensable to an institution that is on its last legs. I respect and admire you, I really do, but I think you are making a terrible mistake. But, come on, it's time for dinner...let's go and celebrate the turns of Fortuna's wheel with a slap-up meal of cold potage...!'

They left, with Antonio's arm draped around Clemo's shoulders.

Now that permission had been granted for his departure, Clemo had two things he had to do. He had to tell Pablo, and he had to tell Father Mossman and the family.

Accordingly, after dinner he went to the stables. Pablo was leading Noble out into the yard.

Clemo called out to him, and walked up to Noble, patting the horse's neck. 'Pablo, I have some news for you.'

'If it's news that comes from Antonio, I don't want to know it.'

'No, this time, it's directly from me.'

'And what might that news be?' Pablo looked at him across the horse's shoulder, whilst with his left hand he was stroking the horse's head.

'I'm afraid that I shall be leaving here at Candlemas.'

Pablo stopped stroking the horse and said, 'Oh, Clemo, that can't be true. That is terrible news. You are the best groom I've ever had. You can't leave. You really can't. What will Noble do?' He slapped the horse's rump.

'I shall miss you very much, Pablo. You have been the best of friends, and I have learnt so much from you. And I shall miss the horses too, especially Noble, he is so beautiful, but I am leaving to become a monk.'

'Really?'

'Yes, really.'

'Which monastery are you going to?'

'Our Lady of Waverley. It's a Cistercian house in Surrey.'

'I'm devastated Clemo...you'll have to forgive me, but at my age, young friends are so important, and we have had some really good times together. If you go into a monastery, I shall never be able to see you again'.

'But I shall pray for you, Pablo.'

'That's kind, but it's nothing compared with actually seeing people. Prayer is all very well, but people matter more than anything… well, perhaps not as much as horses…'. He chuckled and wiped a rough hand across his eyes. 'Candlemas, you say… but that's only a few days away. How are you going to get to Waverley Abbey?'

'I haven't really thought about that,' replied Clemo.

'Well, Noble and I can't let you just walk out of the gate on your own. How about we come part of the way with you?'

'Pablo, that would be wonderful. Thank you.'

'Don't thank me, thank Noble. He whispered the idea in my ear…!! Now, let's be serious. If you are leaving at Candlemas, I shall get the horses ready and you will need to be packed and ready to go by 7 o'clock. How does that sound?'

'That sounds really good,' replied Clemo, 'Pablo, thank you very much. You are amazingly kind.'

They confirmed the arrangements for two days hence, and Clemo went to see the Mossman family. As he was walking through the streets that had become so familiar to him, he began to realise that he would miss the noise and bustle much more than he had initially thought. His own inner contradictions puzzled him. Might he be making a terrible mistake? Might he be running from the frying pan into the fire? Might he do better to stay in London longer? Yet, at the same time, he recognised that inner pull in himself towards a serener future in an abbey where he could pray and think and not be distracted by the political pressures of London.

When he arrived at the door of the Parsonage, Edward was emerging. His hair tousled. 'She's inside,' he said, with a wide grin, and ran off.

Alice met him. She looked so much better than the day when he had found her in such distress. 'Please come in, Clemo. Everyone will be pleased to see you…but what have you come for?'

'Alice,' he replied, as gently as he could, 'I shall be leaving here at Candlemas and I wanted to see you and your mother and Father Mossman to say a proper goodbye.'

'But Candlemas is only two days away. Oh Clemo, can't you change your mind? Please? Come and live with us if you are fed up with the Residence. You don't have to become a monk.' She tried to be brave, but her troubled eyes were brimming with tears. 'Please don't go, Clemo.'

'I'm sorry, Alice, but somehow I feel that this is what I ought to do, that God is calling me.'

'But what if you are deceiving yourself? What if the still, small voice is your own and not God's?' she replied. It was the kind of searingly honest statement that he had come to expect from Alice, and he loved her for it. He almost hugged her but held back because it would not be fair on her.

'Alice, you could be right,' he said, 'but I shall have to take that risk.'

She bowed her head and led him into the parlour.

'Clemo,' boomed Father Mossman. 'It's really good to see you. What news?'

Marguerite was seated on a small stool doing some needlework and beamed up at Clemo.

'I have come to tell you that I shall be leaving for Waverley Abbey at Candlemas.'

'Tell him he is making an awful mistake,' said Alice.

'I can't do that,' replied Father Mossman, 'God knows these things better than we do.'

Alice looked away.

'And I have some news for you, Clemo. You will remember that I told you that I would be going to Lambeth Palace to report my situation. Well, I did that, and I can tell you I was worried sick. Of course, the new Archbishop was not in residence, so I had to meet one of the Lambeth legal officers. I explained my circumstances and expected him to dismiss me on the spot. But he told me that he had no legal authority to take any action until the Archbishop was consecrated and enthroned and that until that happened, I should stay put. And then he said that he thought the Archbishop, according to rumour, would be likely to understand the situation. "After all," said the legal officer, "clergy were allowed to marry from the earliest times and celibacy only became the rule from about the 11th century. It therefore might give the Archbishop some latitude."

The officer did not exactly wink, but I could see what he was trying to convey. So, until I see His Grace, we stay here and perhaps we can stay for longer than I had originally thought. It's a kind of reprieve.'

Clemo was pleased that the family were not about to be turfed out of their home, and having worked in the Residence, he had learnt how words were used to convey more than one meaning, so perhaps, he thought, the family would be safe for the time being.

The conversation moved on, and he told them why he had chosen to explore his vocation at Waverley, and they reminisced about his time in London, but then he felt it was time to leave. It was a parting he was dreading but steeled himself. He stood up, thanked them warmly for their loving-kindness but as he moved to the door, Alice threw her arms around him. He kissed her chastely on the cheek and assured her that she and the family would be forever in his prayers. As he walked out into the street, he could hear Alice sobbing.

The next day was spent saying goodbye to friends in the Residence, including Gwen who he informed that he was going to become a monk. 'You lucky man', she said, to his surprise, 'Are you going back to Tintern?' 'No', he replied, 'I took advice, and it was suggested that I should go to Waverley and test my vocation there'. 'In that case, I am not going to wish you well,' she said, teasing him, 'Now, if you had told me that you were going to Tintern I could have understood it. Anyway, *cariad*, it's been lovely knowing you. Please pray for me. Maybe, if life is kind, I might see you one day back in Monmouth.'

Next, he went to see the Under Steward, who welcomed him into his office.

'Thank you for coming to say goodbye, Clemo. I have something for you to remind you of the time you spent with us.' He opened a drawer in his desk and pulled out a small package carefully wrapped in silk fabric. He handed it to Clemo and said that he would be pleased if Clemo opened it immediately. Clemo duly obeyed and pulled from the fabric envelope a rosary made of red glass beads, interspersed at regular intervals with polished stones, and hanging from it a tiny silver medallion on which were the Ambassador's coat-of-arms.

'It's so beautiful,' said Clemo,'thank you very much.' He moved towards the Under Steward and shook his hand. 'Thank you again.'

'Having worked here Clemo, you will realise that there is always a catch… In this case, the catch is that we would ask you to pray for us daily when you reach your abbey. Pray for Queen Catherine, pray for His Excellency, and pray for us, that despite everything, truth and peace will eventually prevail.'

Clemo was taken aback by the warm emotions that flowed through the Under Steward's words and promised that he would always treasure the rosary and would indeed pray for them all. He quietly left the room, overwhelmed.

In the darkness of the next morning, hefting a large leather bag containing his few belongings, he made his way to the stables. And there was Pablo, and there was Noble, saddled and waiting patiently for him. He was so moved that Pablo was allowing him to ride Noble that he was unable to speak. They clattered through almost empty streets, crossed London Bridge and made their way down the Portsmouth road just as the sun was creeping up over the horizon.

At Esher, Pablo left him. They embraced; Clemo thanked him for his friendship, and tears filled his eyes as he watched Pablo on his own horse, and Noble now on a leading rein, clatter away.

He soon found a carter heading for Guildford and begged a lift from him, then, having stopped at Ripley for some bread, cheese and ale, the last few miles were rapidly covered. On leaving the carter, Clemo was asked where he was making for.

'Waverley Abbey,' he replied.

'It's a great walk along the Hog's Back. Enjoy the views; they're probably the last good thing you'll see for a long time. Monks, indeed. Got no time for them, the lazy sods…' He laughed and Clemo set off on the last stretch of his journey.

Chapter 33: Arrival at the Abbey

In response to the ringing of the iron bell, a wooden flap was opened in the Abbey's oak door. The flap was defended by an iron grille and in the gathering darkness Clemo could not see who his questioner might be. All he had heard was the question, 'Who are you?'

'My name is Clemo,'

'Is that your only name?'. The voice was gruff and untrusting.

'No. My other name's Trelawney'.

'Not from round here, then', replied the voice.

It was raining, a cold February rain that fell steadily out of low clouds. Clemo's hair under his hood was plastered down on his forehead.

'No,' replied Clemo, 'but can you please let me in?'

'Depends'. The flap began to close shut.

'On what?'

'Depends what you want.'

The rain continued to pour down. Clemo shuffled his feet on the wet stones. He decided that a forthright answer might gain him access.

'I want to become a monk.'

'That's what they all say'. The flap closed a little further.

'But it's the truth. I have come all the way from London because I want to join this Abbey'.

Silence from behind the door.

'In this rain?'

'Yes, and I am getting soaked through.'

'How did you hear about us?' asked the voice.

'You are famous,' replied Clemo. 'Everyone knows of Waverley... but they were wrong about one thing.'

'What's that?'

Clemo took the risk: 'The abbey is known for welcoming strangers and people in need.'

'That's good to hear', replied the voice. The flap opened a small way. 'So, I suppose I'd better let you in.'

There was the noise of iron bolts at the top and bottom of the door being eased. Slowly, the huge door was pulled back.

'Are you carrying anything?'

Clemo could only see the outline of the gatekeeper in the gloom.

'Just a few spare clothes in my bag.' He lifted his cloak to one side and showed the leather bag he was carrying.

'Take it off,' said the gatekeeper, 'and lay it on the ground, and then step forward so that I can see you properly.'

With some effort Clemo did as he was bidden. Behind the gatekeeper, on a bracket on the wall was a lighted, wooden torch. Its flames, guttering up from the tar wrappings, gave enough light for Clemo to be more clearly seen, but beyond was darkness.

'So,' said the gatekeeper, who was dressed in a grey woollen tunic with a cap pulled down over his ears. 'You want to become a monk?'

'Yes, very much...'

'Well. More fool you, that's all I can say. I'd better see who I can find to look after you.... you're wet... you'll catch your death standing there in the draught. Move, whilst I shut this door.'

The gatekeeper heaved on the door until it was firmly closed and bent down stiffly to shoot the lower bolt. Then he levered himself upright, his hands braced on his knees, stretched upwards with a groan and slid the upper bolt into its housing.

'You can't be too careful,' he said, turning slowly towards Clemo. 'You never know who's coming...and in weather like this you could have been anybody.' Clemo didn't quite follow the man's drift, but as the trickles of rain continued to stream down his face, he managed a wan smile.

'You certainly can't', he said, 'but I can assure you that I am genuine.'

'We'll soon see if that's the truth,' said the gatekeeper morosely and called to a child to come to help him. Out of the darkness ran a small boy about nine years of age.

'Jack, go and tell Master Cellarer that I have got a guest for him to see to.' The boy looked at Clemo, watching the water that was easing out of his cloak and puddling around his feet.

'Yes, Grandpa,' said the boy and ran off towards some nearby buildings.

The gatekeeper continued to look at Clemo, trying to weigh him up. 'Never heard the name Clemo afore,' he said ruminatively. 'Never. Are you foreign?'

'In a manner of speaking. My father was Cornish, and my mother was Welsh.'

'Ah' said the gatekeeper, scratching his straggly grey beard, 'I thought there was summat about you…you never can tell. We live in strange times…' Again, the meaning eluded Clemo, but the gatekeeper beckoned Clemo to move nearer the torch so that he could be better observed.

'Now, let me look at you'. He walked around Clemo as though he were studying a wounded animal and having finished his perambulation, he drew his face closer to Clemo's. There was a smell of garlic on his breath. 'I knew I'd never seen you before…I've never seen eyes like yours in these parts. They're too green to be from hereabouts. Where did you get them from?'

Clem's eyes were often commented upon. They were a pale sea-green with a thin navy-blue line encircling the iris and, staring out as they were from under the shelter of his dark hood their brilliance was all the more striking.

'I suppose I got them from my parents. My father's eyes were the same colour.'

'Ah. I expect you did then. I can tell a lot by a man's eyes.' The gatekeeper was becoming positively loquacious. 'When you have spent as many years as I have looking out through that grille, you get to notice every visitor's eyes because that's mostly all you can see. Oh yes, I can tell a lot about people just by their eyes…'

At that moment, the little boy came rushing up and announced that the Cellarer was on his way. 'Only I can run faster than he can', he added proudly, looking towards his grandfather and Clemo for approval.

Out of the darkness a tall monk arrived in his white habit and black scapula. He had a thin, bony face and a pronounced nose. The gatekeeper stood his ground. 'This young man has just arrived,' he announced, pointing to Clemo,, 'and says he has come here because he wants to be a monk.'

Not a muscle moved in the Cellarer's face. 'Well. You'd better come in,' said the Cellarer, 'but first we must get you a place to stay. Rufus', he said, addressing the gatekeeper, 'is the fire lit in the Guest Chamber? '

'It is… as it always is.' There was a hint of aggression in the gatekeeper's response.

'Very good. I shall take you there myself. By the way, what is your name?'

'Clemo Trelawney'.

'Come on then, Clemo', he said, and bending down to pick up Clemo's leather bag, he strode across the glistening cobbles towards a small, stone-built house. Clemo followed.

They climbed up a steep stair, the door was flung open by the Cellarer who, with a wave of his arm, said, 'This is all yours. Make yourself comfortable. There's water there; the bed is made up, and', he said, pointing to the fireplace where a couple of logs were struggling to give out any heat, 'the fire is lit, the water in the cauldron should be warm enough for you to wash. Do you have any dry clothes?' He pointed to the bag he had carried into the room before placing it on the floor.

'Yes, thank you.'

'Good. I think you ought to get out of those wet things as soon as possible. I shall be back after Vespers, and then we can have a proper talk.' He strode out of the door. A man of few words, but Clemo already rather liked him.

He looked around the room. There was a wooden bed with a blanket covering the coarse linen sheets, next to it a simple table, and close to the table an upright wooden chair. A small cupboard stood in one corner. There was a fireplace with an iron cauldron in which water was warming; close by was a wooden water-bucket, and to Clemo's surprise, a large wooden chair like a throne which had carved lions on each side at the top and a plump velvet cushion on the seat. A stone shelf set into the wall held a bowl and a block of coarse soap, and hanging on a hook nearby was a linen towel. At the far end of the room was a Prieu-Dieu and above it, a crucifix. A window looked over the courtyard.

It was plain and simple, but after his long journey, Clemo was delighted to be there. He shrugged his cloak from his shoulders and let it fall on to the wooden floor. Next, he pulled his tunic over his head, then his undershirt and his hose and braes. He stood in front of the fire, threw on another log, and prepared to wash.

When he had finished, he pulled from his bag a pair of braes and was just tying the cord around his waist when he heard a knock at the door.

'Come in,' he shouted and was surprised to see Rufus hobble in carrying some more logs. 'I thought you might need these', he said, placing them in a reed basket near the fire. 'And I've brought you some candles. The one's in here are almost done.' He gesticulated towards a couple of candles which were giving out a little light.

Clemo continued to dress. Rufus stood by the door watching him. 'So, are you feeling drier now?'

'I am indeed, thank you. This fire is just what I needed.'

'Ah' said Rufus, 'and because you are our guest, I brought you some ash logs and some apple wood…but if you are going to be a monk here, don't expect this kind of treatment every day, because you won't get it. And you certainly won't get any Castile soap…' As far as Clemo could tell, the soap he had washed with was the usual mix of fat and gritty ash. 'No, you won't get any of that fancy Castile soap, though we had a Lord arrive a couple of weeks ago who insisted on using his own Castile soap…show-off'.

He turned to go. 'And you won't get a room like this again until you're an abbot, so make the most of it.'

He limped slightly as he left the room and closed the door. Clemo, warmed through, felt like a King. He continued to smile...what a brilliant place to spend a night...and with that thought he eased himself into the cushioned throne-chair next to the fire and gazed around the room. Bliss. He had arrived. First stage over.

Perhaps he had dozed because the next thing he heard was a knock on the door.

'Come in,' he shouted. The door eased open and Rufus was there again, carrying a wooden board on which was a bowl of vegetable broth, a hunk of bread and a tankard of ale. 'Somebody must have known you were coming because, if I'm not mistaken, there might even be some meat in this potage.' He placed the board on the table and pulled a spoon from his tunic pocket and placed it beside the bowl. 'It's from the kitchen,' he said, by way of explanation.

'My poor old legs,' he exclaimed and seated himself in the throne-chair to watch Clemo eat. 'If you don't mind, I'll just wait here until you've finished...and that'll save me another journey.'

Clemo sat down at the table, said a prayer of thanksgiving under his breath, and spooned the broth to his lips.

'So,' said Rufus, 'you've come from London. What were you doing there?'

'I was a groom and a clerk,' replied Clemo, 'in the City'.

'Oh...where, exactly?'

'Near Austin Friars.'

'I think I've heard of it, but if you worked for the friars you won't have made any money. Did you have your bait on the way down here?'

'Yes. I stopped at Ripley and had some bread,'

'I used to know Ripley a bit. I was a carter many years ago and we used to trundle through Ripley from time to time. Good ale there.'

Clemo decided that it was time for him to ask a few questions: 'Were you a carter in Farnham?'

'Where else? Never been far. Except once when I had to take the cart from the Castle to His Lordship's house in Southwark. What a noisy, stinking hole. I couldn't get home fast enough.'

'So, you didn't like London?'

'I did not, there's no mistake. And I was beazled by the time I got home, completely beazled.'

'Were you born in Farnham?'

'Of course. Best town in the whole of England, I'll be bound.'

The fire and the warmth in the small room seemed to be loosening Rufus' tongue. 'Best town in England. I met a French man once in the Borough. He'd come up from Portsmouth and he said the same.'

A log shifted and settled in the fire; a couple of sparks flew lazily up the chimney. Clemo finished his meal and Rufus struggled to his feet to take the board and dishes away… 'Yes. Best town anywhere…So I'll wish you a good night…'

'Thank you,' said Clemo, feeling satisfied by the meal, 'I am really grateful.'

'What did you say your name was?

'Clemo. Clemo Trelawney'.

'Never come across that name in Farnham. No. Never…'

And with that, Rufus limped out of the door and made his way slowly and heavily down the stairs.

Once he'd gone, Clemo threw another log on the fire, then took his wet clothes and spread them in front of the fire to dry. He was content; at least, his body was, but his mind did not match his body's ease. He still had Master Cellarer to meet before he could stretch out on the bed and lose himself in sleep. He had gained access to the Abbey. He was pleased about that, but what might follow?

Chapter 34: Master Cellarer

A soft tap on the door.

Clemo opened it. The Cellarer was there. Somehow, he seemed taller than before and with the firelight from the room flickering across his face, the underlying bone structure of his skull was even more distinct.

'May I come in?' His voice was deep and warm, and his manner courteous.

'Of course.'

'Where may I sit?'

'I think you should take the lion chair.'

'Lovely piece of furniture, isn't it? It was given to us by someone many years ago. Now…', he said, folding his arms so that his hands were hidden by the wide sleeves of his white robe, '…tell me about yourself…'

Clemo was not expecting such a question immediately, and whilst his mind whirled furiously, he parried by replying, 'I left London early this morning. I rode with my Head Groom as far as Esher, a carter gave me a lift to Guildford, and I walked from there.'

The Cellarer smiled, 'That wasn't quite what I meant. Tell me your life story… Begin from the very beginning. I've plenty of time…'

The fire cast shadows around the room. Clemo stood up, threw another log on the fire. And decided how he should reply.

'I was born in a place called Hadnock, near Monmouth, on the banks of the River Wye. My father worked at Redbrook in an iron foundry. I have two sisters. They are both older than I am. Isabel is twenty-six and Joan is about twenty-nine.'

'And how old are you?'

'Twenty-four'

'Are your sisters married?'

'Yes, both are… one of them is married to a Monmouth man, and the other is married to a man from Raglan. Between them they have four children, three girls and a boy…'

'And what about you? Were you ever married?'

'I was, but sadly, my wife and our little boy called Jestin, died in childbirth.'

'I am very sorry to hear that,' replied Master Cellarer. 'It will have left wounds in your soul.'

Clemo nodded. He could not have found the words to answer without choking.

'And your mother?'

'She is called Agnes.'

'That's a lovely name. Do you know what it means?'

'No'

'It means 'pure' and 'holy'…and you haven't told me the name of your father…'

There was a slight pause which the Cellarer noted. Clemo looked at the floor. 'He was called Richard'.

'So…he was called Richard Trelawney…and therefore came from Cornwall… How did he fetch up in Monmouth? It's just a few miles from there to Tintern, isn't it?'

At this point Clemo had to make a swift decision. Was the Cellarer trustworthy? Could he afford to tell him the entire story of his father's life? Might it be dangerous to do so? The Cellarer waited.

Clemo shifted in his chair. He decided that he would have to recount his father's story. There was little point in hiding it, but he would play for time.

'How do you know Tintern?' Clemo asked.

'It's our sister house and it was where I tested my vocation as a young man.'

'Did you really? It is so beautiful. When I used to take a boat down the river from Monmouth, I always longed to catch my first glimpse of Tintern.'. A sudden pang of homesickness hit him. He coughed to cover his embarrassment.

'We'll talk about Tintern another day,' said the Cellarer, smiling, 'but for now, go on with the story about how your Cornish father came to live near Monmouth. It sounds as though it might be unusual.'

'How long have we got?' asked Clemo.

'All night, if necessary'. The Cellarer was sitting quietly, attentively. His face was set. The warmth had disappeared from his voice for a moment.

So, Clemo thought, this isn't just a chat… he twisted in his chair as if to make himself more comfortable.

'My father certainly was Cornish. He was born near Perranporth and was a tin miner. But like many tin miners…' Clemo paused, wondering whether he should continue. The Cellarer looked at him. The fire flickered.

'…like many miners in Cornwall he had a very hard life…'

And he continued slightly hesitantly by recounting the story of the march from Cornwall to London, the battle and the rout, the way in which his father had had to flee for his life, how he arrived in Bristol where he had paid to be a passenger in a trow carrying tin ore to Llandogo, and how his father found work in a foundry in Redbrook.

'And we know what happened after that battle at Blackheath, don't we?' said the Cellarer. 'Hundreds of Cornish men were slaughtered. The leaders were captured and were hanged, drawn and quartered at Tyburn.'

'It's always the poor,' said Clemo, feeling anger smouldering within him,.'It's always the poor who are beaten. Those miners were up against an army; an army with better weapons and better training, an army that had not marched over two hundred miles. But my father didn't speak much about it afterwards. The experience scarred him for life. He wasn't injured, thank goodness, leastways not in his body, but the scars went deep into his mind. And sometimes at night, as a child, I would wake when he was having nightmares and screaming in terror.'

'That must have been terrible for him, for your mother, for your sisters and for you.'

'It was…and the truth of it was kept secret from me until I was nine.'

'And did anything else happen to you in your childhood and youth?'

The Master Cellarer seemed to have the ability to release in Clemo a series of stories. So Clemo told him about learning Latin with Father Burley and about his father's death.

He found the process of re-telling the stories to this stranger surprisingly cathartic.

But then the Master Cellarer said, easing out his long legs,'Clemo. You will be tired after your journey and after telling me so much about yourself. I suggest that we stop now, and you can have a long sleep. But we will pick up some more of your story tomorrow.' He stood, bowed slightly, wished Clemo a good night and silently left the room. Clemo, relieved that his first interview had taken place, prepared himself for sleep, took the red-bead Rosary from his pocket and kneeling by the bed said his prayers before tumbling exhausted into bed, where he slept soundly.

Early the next morning it was still dark, but the clanging of the abbey bell had roused him. He stumbled out of bed, used the *necessarium*, washed and put on his clothes from the previous day because they had now dried.

He could only wait to see if some form of breakfast would arrive. Slow and heavy steps on the stair soon announced the presence of Rufus. The door latch was lifted and in came the morning meal, a hunk of bread, a small piece of cheese and a pot of ale.

'Sleep well?' asked Rufus.

'Yes, thank you.'

'Good... I understand from Master Cellarer that after he has come to see you once you have finished breakfast, you will have a free day. What are you going to do with it?'

'I think I shall walk into Farnham and have a look around.'

'Ah...and which way will you go?'

'I shall retrace the steps I took yesterday. I came along by the river.'

'Ah...but...', said Rufus, 'there's more than one way to get into Farnham from here.'

255

'Is there?'

'Yes, there certainly is'. Rufus looked radiantly satisfied with his display of local knowledge. He stood by the fireplace smiling, as Clemo tore off a piece of bread and cheese and ate it.

'Good bit of cheese that,' said Rufus. He was not a man of many words. 'Comes from Forde.'

'And where's Forde?' asked Clemo, assuming that it was the name of a nearby farm.

'Oh…a good way from here. It's near Chard, in the West Country, and the abbot of Forde sends us a cheese now and again.'

'That's good of him,' replied Clemo, for want of anything better to say. He continued to chew in silence. Rufus watched him.

'And this fire…,' said Rufus, indicating the cold ashes in the fireplace, 'I have to clean it out once you have seen Master Cellarer … but I shan't light it until a bit before you come back in. No…I shan't light it until then…'

Clemo ate the rest of his breakfast in silence. Outside a dull, grey dawn began to break. Rufus still stood there, impassive, watchful.

'So, which way should I take to get to Farnham?'

'Depends,' retorted Rufus, 'depends on where you might be going but today being Thursday is market day. So, if I were you, I'd go by the Mill…' He seemed to have the capacity to link two ideas together which bore no real relationship to each other. Clemo was puzzled but remained patient.

'Well, thank you, Rufus, for breakfast. I'll see you a bit later I expect.'

'I expect you will,' came the reply, 'I expect you will. If I hear the gatehouse bell ring, seeing as it's you, I might even answer it… on the other hand, I might not…'

Clemo assumed that this was Rufus' idea of a joke and was relieved when Rufus had taken away the breakfast board and left the chamber.

He sat down in the lion chair and pondered his day's programme. He would have to wait for the Master Cellarer to arrive and after that had been completed, he could just gather up his things and leave for his walk.

He looked out of the window at the abbey church and saw some activity in the yard, but life did not seem to be being lived at any great pace. After London, it was a relief. And the air down here in the meadows by the river was sweet, which was a blessing in itself. It confirmed that he really did want to explore becoming a monk.

At least, he thought he wanted to become a monk, but after his experience of the interview last night, tiny bubbles of doubt had begun to trouble the surface of his mind. He knew for certain that he wanted a simpler life than the one he had had in London, but would it be here? Questions gently wandered around his mind. He sat contemplating the cold ash in the fireplace and began to feel chilled. A knock on the door signalled the arrival of the Master Cellarer.

'Good morning, Clemo. I trust you slept well?'

'I did indeed, thank you.'

'But Rufus has not laid the fire, that is very remiss of him. We can't have our guests sitting in their rooms shivering. Shivering and prayer don't go together. I shall ensure that the fire will be lit very soon. So, I won't keep you for long. Now', he said, 'Carry on from your account last night. Tell me why and how you left Hadnock. I have immensely happy memories of Tintern, but we can reminisce about the Wye Valley on another occasion. So, tell me. You were working at Redbrook Foundry and your father had told you that it was time for you to leave home. Sadly, he died. You continued at the Foundry. You met Laura and fell in love with her. You were married but she and your little son tragically died. Which left you on your own. So, why did you leave everything and everyone you loved?'

Clemo had often asked himself the same question and found it difficult to put his answer into words.

'I think that I wanted a fresh start. There were too many sad memories in Monmouth.'

'I understand that, but our memories are not located outside ourselves, are they? They are always within us. We think we can get away from things, but the reality is, we cannot. Our memories have helped to make us who we are, for good or ill.' The Master Cellarer looked carefully at Clemo, who shifted uneasily under the Master Cellarer's gaze.

'I hadn't really thought of that,' he replied, 'but now you say it, it is true. All the time I was in London, I kept thinking of Laura and Jestin, and my mother and sisters, and Father Burley.'

'So, why did you choose London as your destination?'

'Because it was so far away and was so different. I travelled there by staying at Cistercian houses and found much in them that I admired. Perhaps they sowed a seed.'

'But not all abbeys are alike, are they? Some you will have loved; others will have left you feeling despondent. Tell me which of the abbeys lifted your spirits, and which left you troubled?'

Clemo was not certain how to answer the question because he did not know whether Cistercian abbeys knew each other well, so if he blamed one and praised another, might the news of his descriptions get back to the houses in which he had stayed?

The Master Cellarer intervened. 'Clemo, honesty, honesty...'

So Clemo praised Flaxley, expressed his unease about Hailes, and said how kind the gatekeeper at Bruern had been and how, despite being robbed just outside its walls, St Bernard's Hall had been one of the high spots.

'Well, then Clemo, you did not find a single abbey which was perfect?'

'No,' he sighed, 'I did not.'

'Do you think Waverley is perfect?'

'I don't know, I have never been here before.'

'Quite so. I can assure you that it isn't. Like all monasteries it's made up of fallible and sinful humanity and whilst some bits of our life are wonderful, there is a great deal that is humdrum and there are lots of difficulties. As you know, we live in perplexing times. But let me pose one final question, and then you must go for your walk.

You haven't mentioned once that you believe that God is calling you. You have told me a great deal about what you wanted to leave behind: you wanted to leave Hadnock behind, you wanted to leave London behind, but you have said nothing about whether God might be involved in calling you to be a monk. Don't give me your answer now. Think about it, and when you have returned from your walk you can tell me what your answer might be. Meanwhile, I shall get Rufus to light the fire…' He smiled and left the room.

Clemo felt deflated. And decided that a walk might clear his head.

Chapter 35: Walk by the Wey

He waited until it was a little lighter outside and then, wrapping his cloak around him and lifting his bag on to his shoulder, he made for the Abbey Gatehouse. The door was firmly bolted but the wicket gate appeared to be open. He was about to step through when he heard a voice from behind hailing him. It wasn't Rufus; instead, a younger monk appeared. Dressed in his white habit and black scapula he greeted Clemo warmly and with a broad grin.

'Look, I'm not supposed to speak, but Rufus is somewhere else as usual, and you seemed a bit lost. Can I help in any way? I'm Brother John. Who are you?'

'My name is Clemo and I'm a visitor, but I saw Master Cellarer last night and again this morning, and he suggested that I might want to walk into Farnham today.'

'Good idea,' replied Brother John, 'but if you spent last night and this morning in conversation with the Cellarer, I guess you weren't discussing the price of wool…?'

Clemo was wary of the question and decided to say little. 'No, but it was interesting.'

'As I would expect. The Cellarer was Novice Master here a few years ago, so he tends to get to know people quickly. But don't be put off. He means well. Enjoy the day. We might meet again later.'

And with that, Brother John turned and walked back towards the main abbey buildings.

Clemo stepped through the gate, turned right, crossed a narrow bridge, and then walked along a path that bordered the river. Decaying wet leaves littered the ground. A few leaves still clung on to the branches and one or two drifted down in front of him. He kicked them, in a remembrance of childhood, and hoped that no-one was watching his child-like antics. He looked behind. No-one; so, he kicked a few more leaves; perhaps the day would prove to be good after all. A ray of weak sunshine came through the clouds and splashed the path ahead of him. His spirits lifted, but it could not distract his mind from the questioning he had endured the previous night and earlier this morning. Did he really want to become a monk? What was it that had grabbed him and pushed him in that direction? Was his thinking really about running away from things, rather than facing them? He was bewildered by his own confusion.

The walk along the riverbank did nothing to ease his self-questioning but when he arrived in the town the market was in full swing and he was distracted by it: there were stalls selling cheese and butter; others selling fabrics; yet others selling knives and scissors, and, to his relief there was a stall next to a glowing brazier where slices of bacon were cooking on a griddle. He ordered a slice and watched as it was slapped on to a hunk of fresh bread by the stallholder. He sat at a nearby table to eat it. The food was so delicious and so nourishing that it lifted his spirits. He watched people sauntering about. Some were chatting to friends; others were intent on buying things from the market stalls. He looked at their clothes. They were better than the clothes worn by his people in Monmouth but not as lavish as clothes he had seen in London. It felt safely ordinary, and that pleased him.

He noticed, quite close by, the low central tower of the parish church and decided to go there to see what it was like. He walked up a narrow, cobbled lane, along the path to a door on the north side and went in. It was much bigger than he had imagined, filled with light; a smell of incense drifted through the air and statues of the saints delighted his eye. Several had candles burning in front of them. He found a side-chapel and went into it to pray. Pulling his Rosary from his pocket he began to tell his beads. The rhythm eased the tensions from his mind but though the tensions eased, the question posed by the Master Cellarer continued to tug at his soul. He really was puzzled by his own motives, perhaps becoming a monk was not such a good idea after all? But if not that, what?

He walked out of the church and an elderly man greeted him; he found his way to the main street and up to his left saw a dominating castle. He wondered who lived there and asked a passer-by. 'The Lord Bishop of Winchester owns it,' said the man. Clemo could not tell whether the reply was said with pride or disdain. 'But', the man continued, 'in the Borough we have our own freedoms, thank goodness.' He walked on, leaving Clemo gazing up the hill. The castle was a building which spoke of the power and authority of the Church, and the parish church of the town by its very size also spoke of dominance, yet from the cleanliness of the church and the flickering votive candles, he judged that it was loved by the townsfolk. He contrasted its size with the tiny church at Dixton. His mind tried to make sense of it. So, he thought to himself, the town has a very large parish church, and it also has a huge Bishop's castle, and Waverley Abbey is also massive. It too, no doubt, owns and farms hundreds of acres. And that thought sent his mind back to the few small meadows at Hadnock. Was it right that there should be such a gap between the wealth of the Church and the rest of society? Or was this the way God had ordered society so that everyone knew their place?

He decided that it was time to stroll back to the Abbey and hope that the questions which had erupted in his mind might settle before his next meeting with the Master Cellarer.

Rufus was waiting for him. 'So, what do you think of Farnham?'

'I had delicious bacon and bread in the market.'

'Good, that will have been Mistress Fry. Best bacon in the country I reckon. Good woman, she is. Yes, a good woman. Known her all my life. Master Cellarer asked me to tell him when you were back. You're in for another grilling, I bet.' He chuckled to himself. 'If I were you, I'd go straight back to Mistress Fry and ask for another round. It would put off the evil day.' He laughed aloud. 'You go to your room. I've laid and lit the fire and now you must wait for the Inquisitor to come. Oh yes, the Inquisitor…that's what I call him, the Inquisitor.'

Clemo thanked Rufus for letting him in and went to his room. There was indeed a fire, but it was a meagre one, more smoke than flame. He felt cold and apprehensive. Might the next interview determine his whole life?

There was a knock on the door. Rufus stood there with a tankard of ale. 'After Mistress Fry's bacon, this will go down a treat. Oh, yes.' He handed Clemo the tankard and then limped out of the door and clumped down the stairs. Clemo waited.

He did not have to wait long, The Master Cellarer arrived. Clemo felt butterflies in his stomach. And, despite the ale, his mouth was dry.

'So, Clemo,' said Master Cellarer seating himself in the lion chair, 'was it a good walk? Did it clear your mind?'

'I am sorry to say that though the walk was good, I feel more confused than ever. I really don't know what to do, and I am certainly struggling to answer the question you posed me.'

'Excellent', replied Master Cellarer, 'That's exactly what I hoped I would hear.'

The response surprised Clemo. He had expected that, because he could not give a definitive answer, he would be thanked for coming and then shown the door.

'But I thought you would want me to give you a clear answer', he said.

'Not at all. The fact that you are unclear shows that you are not in the grip of some absurd fantasy, and if you had told me that God had spoken to you on, let us say, a week last Tuesday, telling you unequivocally that you had to become a monk, I would have suggested that you were in the wrong place. The fact is, trying to discern whether God is calling you is a life-long process. It does not happen in an instant, despite the story of St Paul. He was the exception. Most of us struggle, we really do, and even when we have become monks, the struggle continues. Trying to discover what God wants us to do is a daily ordeal. And sometimes we can go weeks or months without being aware of God at all. Does that shock you?'

'It does a little. I had thought that once you became a monk, everything would be clear and serene.'

'Don't misunderstand me, Clemo, there are moments when, as you say, things are indeed clear and serene. Those moments are a grace; they are like sunlight breaking from behind the clouds and you know that you are in the right place, but they are a grace. In fact, Clemo, it is all grace. That's what it is. All grace. So, what do you want to do?'

'I am not sure. I think that I should like to stay here for a while and try to discover whether God really is calling me to this life.'

'Good. That's very encouraging. So, let me explain what will happen. You will spend a few weeks as a postulant; that is, you will make no promises, and neither shall we, but you will join in the daily life of the abbey and see how you get on. If at the end of that time you want to leave, that will be fine. But, if at the end of that time you feel you want to stay and explore further then you can seek the permission of the community to become a novice. That is a really serious step. There will be vows and you will wear the habit. And only after a year of being a novice will you come to your final decision (and so shall we) whether you should enter the religious life. How does that sound?'

'It sounds exactly what I need', replied Clemo, 'one step at a time.'

'What I suggest then, is this. You can stay in this guest room for one more night, then tomorrow the Novice Master will come to see you. He will take you to meet Father Abbot and afterwards will show you where you will be sleeping and eating and will tell you about the times of the services.

Good. That's excellent. I am so pleased. Enjoy the rest of the day, and don't forget to pray. Pray like you've never prayed before. Rufus will look after you and that will keep your feet firmly on the ground. He's a miserable old codger but his heart is in the right place. So, good day.' He stood up, smiled at Clemo and left.

Clemo moved to the lion chair, threw another couple of logs on the fire, and breathed a sigh of relief. A decision had been made, and it could always be changed. He still had the possibility of freedom.

He gazed at the fire for a while and thought affectionately of his mother and sisters and Father Burley, and then rehearsed all that had happened to him since he had set out from Hadnock all those years ago. It was pleasing to be able to daydream, but he wished he had real news of his family and could contact them to let them know how he was faring. Perhaps someone would be travelling from Waverley to Tintern and he could send and receive messages in that way. He thought too of Father Mossman and his family and smiled when he thought of Alice. He realised that she was in his thoughts more frequently than anyone else. He loved her positivity, the sense that nothing was beyond her capacity, but then remembered the sobs he heard when he left the Parsonage. He hoped that her heart would soon heal but then, with a start, was aware that actually he missed her more than anyone else. He put another log on the fire and then knelt at the prieu-dieu to say his prayers. They did not come easily; somehow, the daydreams and the prayers became muddled together, so he prayed, with a frown, for more single-mindedness.

Dinner and supper were supplied, and later he went to sleep.

The following morning, after a breakfast of bread and ale brought to him by Rufus, who seemed to know that Clemo would be meeting the Novice Master later ('Not a bad bloke, but talks too much'), he spent another hour just waiting. And then there was a knock on the door.

'Good morning, I'm the Novice Master. Sorry not to have been here when you first arrived but I have only just returned from a meeting with all the Novice Masters in the South of the country. We had a good time, but it was a bit depressing because not many potential novices are coming forward. Yes, it's really disappointing. But we must stay optimistic, mustn't we? So, you are Clemo and you have spent the past few years in London and before that you lived and worked near Tintern. Beautiful abbey, Tintern, one of my favourites. It was originally founded from L'Aumone, just as we were. Ever been to France? I don't suppose you have; I haven't either, but I should like to go to Citeaux one day. Yes, I certainly would… Now…let's have a talk, shall we?'

Clemo felt that Rufus had been entirely correct in his assessment of the loquaciousness of the Novice Master. He was a small man, tubby, round-faced, and lacked a few teeth. As he talked, he had the habit of sucking the inside of his cheeks, so that he reminded Clemo of a wheezy pair of bellows.

And before Clemo could say anything, the Novice Master launched into another long monologue about what his work entailed. 'You can have no idea of how busy I am. There's always something cropping up. The day before I left for my meeting, I had to help repair the precinct wall. We can't get servants anymore. Then I had to return a book to the Armarium and when I was doing that, I realised that one of the tiles on the cloister roof on the west side had slipped, so I found a ladder and bodged a repair. Well…now, about you. I know where you have come from and I know you want to become a monk, but…oh! dear, that fire has burnt low, why don't we put a log on?' He bent down and threw a log haphazardly against the fire back. 'Never was good at throwing things, don't know why, but there we are, we all have our little crosses to bear, don't we? Now, where was I? Ah, yes…'

Clemo still had not said a word. The Novice Master seemed like the personification of inconsequence and distraction.

'So, where were we? Ah, yes...you. And you are to become a postulant, is that correct?

'Yes', replied Clemo.

'Good, in that case I shall introduce you to the Abbey, help you to find your way around. You have met Rufus, and the Master Cellarer (he's called Brother Jacob, by the way), and I am Brother Romuald. Not 'Ronald' but 'Romuald' with an 'm' and a 'u'; he was the founder of the Carthusians. Oh! dear, what am I saying? My mistake. I meant the Camaldolese Order in Italy. He was a great and holy man, a hermit; I shall never become like him, but I can try... now, let's go to see the abbey and I shall introduce you to Father Abbot and then we can have another talk, how's that?'

Clemo thought that the prospect of silence after such a cascade of talk would be a relief. He duly followed Brother Romuald out of the door, down the stairs, and into the courtyard. It was raining.

Chapter 36: Tour of the Abbey

Having shown Clemo where he should stand in the abbey church during the Offices---it was in the nave, with the other lay servants, Brother Romuald then took him to the grounds at the eastern end of the abbey. 'I've shown you where your life in this abbey will begin,' said Brother Romuald, 'now you should see where it will end.' Clemo could see a number of humpy graves between the abbey itself and the river.

'It is such a comfort to me to know that this is where I shall lie when I am dead; don't you feel the same? I remind myself every day that I am dust, and unto dust I shall return. It keeps everything in perspective. Mind you, it won't be so comfortable when the river floods, and it does, you know, not often, but it has been known to flood the Monk's Dorter, and then it's damp and cold for years, but there we are, we are not supposed to have life easy, 'Take up your Cross' as our Lord once said. I love this place, garden one side, graveyard the other, Garden of Eden, if you like, and the Garden of Paradise. All that's missing is the Tree of Life.' Romuald laughed at his own weak joke, and continued, 'I love the grass, it's so green and mellow and this place is always hushed. Even when we monks are gardening, we are not allowed to speak, unless, of course, one of us puts a fork through his foot, then we can speak, but quietly not to disturb the others. It happened once, you know, poor old Brother Aelfric, his sight was going but he loved gardening and missed the right place to break up the soil with the fork and instead put the prongs of the fork right through his foot. Not a nice sight, and he died as a result. But what could be lovelier? Out here in the sunshine one minute, a few days later buried just yards away from his accident. What a blessing that must have been for him, though some said they had never heard him swear until he speared his own foot. Mind you, there was another occasion when…'

Brother Romuald continued to talk but Clem found that he had to switch off. It was simply too much. However, he walked beside

Romuald until they neared the door leading to the Abbot's own quarters and he heard Brother Romuald saying,'…of course, originally the abbot was supposed to sleep with his brothers in the Dorter, but that has not happened for years, and our abbot wouldn't like to be so close to the rest of us. He cares for us, of course, but, well…I must not keep talking. So, here we are. Once Father Abbot has finished seeing you, I'll see you in the Parlour.' He knocked lightly on the door and walked away, leaving Clemo to meet Father Abbot.

The door opened slowly, and in the doorway stood a very little monk, with a grey, raggedy tonsure, a deeply lined face and a mouth that was almost devoid of teeth.

'Ah…come in…come in…' He walked ahead of Clemo until they reached a small parlour where a fire was flickering in the hearth. 'Please sit down.' He gestured to a stool on which Clemo sat but seated himself in a larger, wooden chair which had padded arms of fading and threadbare red velvet. His feet just touched the floor. He reminded Clemo of a diffident mouse.

'Now…you want to be a postulant; that's right, isn't it?' And then, in a voice that was mellifluous but quiet and without pausing for breath, he asked, 'Why?'

Clemo tried to explain that he was not absolutely sure that he was called to be a monk but was grateful for the opportunity to test his vocation in the way that the Master Cellarer had outlined.

'Ah…'replied Father Abbot. 'My name, by the way, is William. I agree with Master Cellarer, it's exceedingly wise to take these steps slowly. Once they have been taken, there can be no going back into the wicked ways of the wicked world. Yes, the world is wicked, and seems to be getting wickeder by the day. You've heard, I expect, that the King has married Anne Boleyn?'

Clemo explained that he had heard and went on to explain that having worked in the Residence of the Ambassador of the Holy Roman Emperor, he had heard lots of political tales but was now looking forward to leaving all of that behind.

'So, have you heard the latest rumour? It seems that Master Cromwell is planning some legislation for the King in which the King will be declared to have even more powers than he has at present, probably including absolute power over God's most Holy Church?'

Clemo replied that he had not heard that rumour, but he did know Master Cromwell's house and some of the staff who lived and worked there.

The abbot's mousey face lit up. 'Do you indeed? Well, that might be very useful to us…oh! that's good, really good. Sometimes the ways of God are deeply hidden but then break through the surface and surprise us all.'

They talked for another half an hour about Clemo's early life and the journey he had made to London.

'Now…before you leave me, tell me, what are the names of the people you know in Master Cromwell's house?'

It was not a question that Clemo was expecting, nor did he want to answer it explicitly just in case Antonio might get into trouble as a result.

He hedged. 'I had a good and close friend there but if you will forgive me, Father, I do not want to divulge his name. I learnt, when I was in the Ambassador's service that in diplomacy it is important only to relinquish information as and when necessary; otherwise, the rule is to keep quiet.'

He watched the Abbot carefully in case he had overstepped the mark.

'Well spoken, young man…' The voice hardened and took on an unpleasant whine, 'but if you become a Novice here, one of the things you will have to do is to promise complete obedience to your abbot… do you understand me?'

'Yes, Father.'

'So, think carefully about whether you can do that, because I sense that the wickedness of the world has burrowed more deeply under your skin than you may realise.'

'Yes, Father.' Clemo looked carefully into the abbot's eyes and saw cunning and weakness hiding there. It left him feeling uncomfortable. He wondered if the mouse was actually ruthless, or whether, in the event of the rumour of a cat arriving, the mouse would be more likely to dash for the safety of its own nest regardless of the safety of his fellow mice.

He was dismissed and made his way to the Monks' Parlour where Brother Romuald was waiting for him.

'How did you get on?'

'Fine, I think.'

'Good...he's a wily old thing, but we do respect him, partly because he's our abbot, and partly because through these complicated days he has held us together. You see, there are probably reformers amongst us, though we cannot be certain. We have our suspicions, but that's what they remain. Martin Luther lit a candle that no-one seems able to blow out, and our Cistercian brothers in France are very worried. Will the disease spread like a contagion? That's what everyone is secretly asking, even inside these walls. We go on as usual, of course, but the uncertainty out in the world has a way of infecting us in here, and even though we are mostly silent (except me, because I am given a dispensation to talk with the postulants and novices, which I love) we can tell what each other is thinking. And I am sure that there are some hot-headed radicals amongst us...of course, that does not include you, unless you tell me otherwise, which I guess you would be unlikely to do, having served in an Ambassador's residence. It is an honour for us to have you amongst us, it really is...but look, I am talking too much again. I have just two other places to show you.' He strode off. 'Let's go to what we call the Lay Brother's refectory. We still call it that, but we've had no lay brothers for well over a century; that is where you will take your meals as a Postulant. And then I shall show you the Lay Brother's Dorter; that's where the servants sleep and where you will sleep.

Now, as a postulant you will be expected to follow the services in the Church as though you were a monk, but the rest of the time we shall allot you tasks so that you can see how the abbey works... Come on, let's go and see what is happening in the Refectory, it's almost dinner time, so perhaps you ought to stay there for dinner and afterwards I shall take you to show you your sleeping quarters. Yes, let's do that. You will be hungry...but that's a good thing. It's what we monks feel much of the time, though we do get used to it, but sometimes we lust after meat, yes, we lust after it.' He laughed and took Clemo to the Lay Brother's refectory where a small group of servants had gathered ready for dinner.

'Gentlemen,' announced Brother Romuald, 'This is Clemo Trelawney who has come to be a postulant with us, so give him a warm Waverley welcome.' He gave a wave and left.

The oldest of the servants, stooped and grey, came slowly towards Clemo. 'Hello, I'm Richard,' he said with a soft growl, 'I'm the boss here'.

'You wish,' shouted one of the younger servants, laughing.

'Ignore that pip-squeak,' said Richard, 'come and join us for our sumptuous repast. The food, such as it is, is brought from the monks' kitchen, so it's often cold before it gets to us, but what does that matter; we're only servants. Isn't that right, lads?' he asked of the others seated at the table. 'Agreed,' they replied, as though this was a routine, rehearsed response. 'Come and sit next to me...and we'll try to persuade you not to come here.' He chortled.

Bowls of soup were brought in. The soup was tepid. The accompanying bread was hard.

'Why do you think I should not come here?' Clemo asked.

A middle-aged servant just across the table from him, replied, 'Because it's finished. There's no future for this abbey. I reckon, we shall only be here for a few more years, and then we shall probably have a new master...so maybe, the devil you know...' He bent his head and continued to slurp his soup.

'That's not true,' said another middle-aged man, 'the abbey will survive. I'm sure of that. All this fuss that's going on in London won't affect us. We're too far away.'

'I don't agree,' intervened a younger man. 'My father goes up to London regularly as a carter and he says the place is buzzing with rumours. He says that the King will get his way, and Queen Catherine will be sent packing.'

'And what's that to do with us?' asked another.

'Everything,' replied an older man, 'The King will want money... he's just spent a fortune going to France, and he'll need to refill his coffers. He'll look around and say to himself, "These abbeys have got far too much land. They don't need all of that. They can pray without getting fat, so I think I shall 'borrow' money from them",and the abbots will say "Yes, Sir, we agree." and they'll get pensions, and we shall be left to find whatever work we can. You watch. I bet the plans are being made already.'

The table went silent.

'So, your advice to me,' said Clemo, 'is that I should not become a monk.'

'That is up to you…but all my friends here,' said Richard, 'keep their ears to the ground, and I think that what they are saying, with a few exceptions, may well be right. Times are changing. You can smell it in the air.'

'And with a nose the size of yours,' laughed one of the men, pointing at him, 'you should know.'

They began to leave the table, but Richard stayed seated and asked Clemo to wait behind for a few minutes.

When they had all gone, he said, 'They're a good bunch of lads, Clemo. When most of them began here, like me, we thought we would have jobs for life. Not much money, admittedly, but plenty of work, and a roof over our heads. But what you have just witnessed is a bunch of men who are worried; they are becoming more and more uneasy. And this isn't just idle talk. Because some of our number often have to go with the Master Cellarer on his journeys, we pick up the news in ways that the monks cannot. The monks think we are just servants, and that, of course, is what we are, but we are a darned sight better informed than they are.'

He stood up and explained that he had to go to fetch some timber from the woods, 'though I'm getting too old for these jobs', and walked away, one hand rubbing his back.

Clemo also left and found Brother Romuald waiting for him.

'I hope you had a good dinner. Now I am going to take you to your sleeping quarters.'

He walked quickly to the Lay Brother's Dorter. It was a long room with about ten beds on either side.

Clemo saw that his leather bag had been removed from the Guests' room and was lying on top of a bed next to the entrance door. His cloak was next to it.

'It looks as though Rufus has decided where you are to sleep. It's a good choice. When you wake for Matins you can leave the room without waking anyone else. So, let me remind you of the times of the Offices…Matins is at 2am, Lauds at 5am, Prime at 6, Terce at 9, Sext at 12 noon, None at 3pm, Vespers 6pm, Compline at about 8pm…and then you can sleep until 2 the next morning. So, the next Office is Sext. I shall see you there. Bye.'

Clemo looked around the room. It was bare except for a cupboard and a chair by each bed. This was to be his home for the next weeks.

He unpacked his bag, checked to ensure that his Dixton book was still there and was delighted to find that his Rosary was in its proper place as well. And by the time he had unpacked, it was almost Noon. He left the room and went across to the church. Just a couple of the most elderly servants were already there. He took his stool in the nave, placed it against a pillar and waited for the service to begin.

Its sound was ethereal. He could hardly believe that amongst the monks making such beautiful music was the mousey Abbot, Brother Jacob, and the talkative Brother Romuald. Despite his morning's interviews and dismal conversations in which his doubts had grown, once the worship began, he felt wonderfully at home. Perhaps becoming a postulant was the right decision?

Chapter 37: The Letter

He had three hours to fill before the next service. Brother Romuald suggested that he should help Richard, the oldest servant, in the woodshed and pointed him in that direction.

Clemo could hear the noise of a saw rasping slowly, and saw Richard bent over a sawing-horse, struggling to complete the cutting of a small piece of timber.

'I've been sent to help you,' Clemo announced as he arrived.

'Damn that Brother Romuald. He's always interfering; now I shan't be able to take my time.'

'Sorry,' replied Clemo, 'But I'll tell you what. You sit down and I'll get on with the sawing. You can tell me when to stop and then we can have a chat.'

Richard pronounced himself grumpily satisfied with the offer and made himself comfortable on a chopping block whilst Clemo continued to saw the wood for the abbey fires.

'Good to see a young man properly occupied,' said Richard. 'You know, I could work as fast as you once, but not any longer. I'm too old now and I've got the screws.'

'How long have you worked here?' asked Clemo.

'Most of my life, but I shan't be able to go on much longer. There were more monks when I began, but there aren't so many now.'

'How many are there?'

'Fourteen, virtually all of them are old, and two of them are ill. There's one younger one, Brother John. There are no novices and no postulants except you, so I reckon it can't go on for many more years. Sad, but there it is.'

Clemo's mind flipped back to the service he had just attended. The sound of the music was still echoing in his soul. How could that beauty be created by twelve elderly men? It was astonishing.

He continued to wield the saw and then Richard said that he should chop some of the logs into kindling. 'I'll get off this chopping block, and let you get on with it. 'Oh! I do love watching other people work,' he laughed.

'And how many servants work here?' asked Clemo.

'About half!'

Richard was pleased with his joke. 'Actually, just over twenty; some of us live in, but all the others live in Farnham, Elstead or Tilford, and come in every day.'

The rhythm of the sawing and chopping took Clemo's mind back to Dixton and his family and then on to London. He wondered what Alice would be doing and what mischief Antonio might be getting up to, and whether, with all this talk about the decline of the abbeys, Antonio might be involved in plotting their demise. It was a melancholy thought.

Just before three o'clock, when the five-minute bell rang to announce that None would be starting shortly, he thanked Richard for letting him help and went to the Abbey. Again, the music, the murmur of Latin, the pools of silence, the simplicity of the building. It felt as though the monks and the building itself were part of the music and silence of eternity. He heard the monks leave after the service but stayed behind for a while in the majestic space to say his Rosary, and then at four o'clock he had supper with the other servants. As darkness began to set in, he went to the church again, this time for Vespers, and rested afterwards before returning to the church in the candle-lit darkness for Compline, the final service of the day.

He returned to the Lay Brother's Dorter where some of the servants were already asleep and lay awake turning over the events of the day in his mind. He dreaded not waking up for the 2 o'clock service and, of course, as a result, hardly slept but must have drifted off briefly, for the next thing he heard was the five-minute bell. He stumbled quietly out of bed and made his way to the church through the darkness for Matins. Concentration did not come easily to him at that hour of the morning, and it seemed the same could be said of the monks, for in the choir beyond the nave the chanting was ragged.

For the next few weeks Clemo followed the same daily pattern, a mixture of prayer and work. 'Laborare est orare' Brother Romuald said to him one day when Clemo admitted that he was finding the work easier than the services. He enjoyed the pattern; it gave shape to each day, but he continued to wonder whether his idea of becoming a monk was the right one.

And then in the second week of April he received a letter. It was Rufus who brought it to him. 'Probably from a lovely woman,' he said, grinning.

Clemo was startled to receive the letter, took it into the woodshed where he knew no-one would be working, and opened the seal carefully, his heart thumping. It was from Antonio.

'My very dear Clemo,' it began. 'I hope you are enjoying your new life. You are much missed here. But I thought you would be interested to know some of the news. Master Cromwell has been made Chancellor of the Exchequer, (see, I told you to hitch yourself to a rising man) and Convocation has declared that the marriage of King Henry and Catherine was null and void. So, we now await the legal proceedings. But, most important of all, Mistress Alice (what a beautiful woman she is becoming) is still pining for you and talks of little else. If you could write to her, it would help her greatly.

Your true friend, Antonio.'

Clemo was surprised by his own reactions to receiving the letter. It was, he felt, as though a canon ball had crashed through the abbey walls, leaving smoke and dust and confusion in its wake. He was bewildered. He had just about reconciled himself to his new life and had put aside his misgivings. He had tried to put his past life behind him and was beginning to think very seriously about entering the novitiate, but now the letter disrupted everything. There was no-one with whom he could discuss it, which, he realised, was significant in itself. It made him suddenly aware that he had not made any friends since arriving at Waverley and, in any case, the Novice Master had told him that if he became a novice and a monk, close personal friendships would not be allowed.

He sat on the chopping block holding the letter in his hands and read it several times. It was innocuous enough, but because it reminded him that he had no friends and reminded him too of Alice (about whom he had so frequently thought) and because it somehow brought a vivacious breath of air from his previous occupation, it led him to wonder yet again whether he was really called to monastic life. True, he loved the worship, and he loved the pace of life at the Abbey, but it didn't make up for the loss of friendship, and it didn't do anything to assuage his growing feelings for Alice. How could he spend the rest of his life without friends? How could he ignore the feelings that Alice so obviously had for him? Was this denial of some of the loveliest things of human life really what God wanted? The letter had released in him thoughts and fears which, until that moment, had been unformed but which now erupted with unexpected force.

He stood up slowly and saw Brother Romuald coming towards him.

'So, what are you doing skulking in there, Clemo?' he asked. The fact that the question was phrased in a humorous manner could not disguise the fact that behind it lay a real desire to interfere and to curtail Clemo's freedom.

'I needed to read a letter I received and to do so in private,' answered Clemo, with more forceful briskness than usual.

'Ah! You will discover once you become a Novice that you will have no privacy. Your life will be devoted totally to God, and nothing must get in the way of that. After all, that is what being a monk is: total service of God. Do you feel like a walk and a chat?'

Clemo reluctantly agreed to the proposed walk sensing that it might be used to entrap him further. With no other potential novices in the Abbey, Brother Romuald's reputation was at stake.

They began to stroll around the precinct walls.

'I think Clemo, that we ought to bring your postulancy to an end quite soon, so that you can progress into the novitiate. You have been with us since Candlemas, which means you have been here for almost ten weeks. Do you feel you have come to understand the abbey and how we work?'

Amazingly, Brother Romuald did not go into one of his interminable rambling speeches.

Clemo paused, wanting to give an honest answer.

'Please, Brother Romuald, let me say this: until I received this letter a short while ago, I was beginning to think that I might indeed be being called into the novitiate. But I am now very uncertain. Please don't misunderstand me: you have all been astonishingly kind. I love the worship, I love the sense of order and calm, and I have come to love this setting in a way that has amazed me. It's not the Wye Valley, but it has its own gentle loveliness.'

'But you are now troubled by doubts?' asked Brother Romuald. 'It happens to all of us, Clemo. We all have to spend time in the wilderness. It's where we are tested by Satan. It is a spiritual battle which, we pray, the Devil does not win. He can be so seductive, so appealing. Look, all of us in the monastic life say much the same: the closer you get to making a life-time decision, the more the Devil will be after you. He hates to lose and will twist you this way and that to try to ensure you come to his decision, not God's. Maybe the letter you have just received is one of Satan's tricks…I suggest that you should take that letter, go into the church, and lay it in front of Our Lady. Say your prayers in front of her, look her in the eyes and allow her to look at you, and then ask her for her help. That way you will repel the Devil's advances, at least for a while.'

Clemo found Brother Romuald's words subtly irritating but appealing, so he walked towards the church and there, in front of Our Lady of Waverley, he placed the letter and begged for her guidance. The votive candles flickered, the atmosphere enveloped him, and he looked steadfastly to her for help. He waited. But nothing happened. Was her silence, he wondered, assent for his move into the novitiate, or was her silence approval of how the letter was affecting him?

He came out into the precincts of the abbey deeply mystified. The letter continually rustled in his jerkin pocket. He took it out again and read it. It was so warm and humane and filled with promise. Surely that was the way he should go…towards ordinary life with all its joys and sorrows. Would not God be with him there, as much as He was with the monks at Waverley? Had not Mary herself been living an ordinary life in Nazareth when the angel came to her? She was not in a convent, was she, when the Annunciation happened? Perhaps her holiness and humility had been found in ordinary things?

In his meditative mood he paused, as other questions pounded against the citadel of his mind. If he chose not to enter the novitiate, would this be another example of his constant running away? On the other hand, might God be helping him to see by the arrival of the letter, that the novitiate was not for him? Was it an example of Abraham being asked to sacrifice Isaac but being reprieved by God at the last minute? In other words, God had tested him; he, Clemo, had obeyed but was now being told not to complete the mission?

For the next few days, he went through an agonising spiritual struggle. He could not come to a strong and stable decision, but then, a shaft of light broke through his anguish: suppose what some people regarded as running away, was nothing of the sort? Why should it not be seen as running *towards*? It was a consoling thought and one which began to shape his decision-making. And then another thought hit him. Instead of becoming a novice, why didn't he offer to stay at the abbey as a servant, at least for another couple of years?

He decided, once he had reached these conclusions, to seek out Brother Romuald and tell him his decision.

It was one of the most difficult conversations that Clemo had ever had with anyone. He explained, as courteously as he could, that he felt God was not calling him into the novitiate.

Brother Romuald reiterated his view that the Devil was at work. But Clemo found himself resisting that line of thinking, and instead, argued that God did not create the world and humankind only to ask humankind to reject the world he had so wonderfully created; to do so, argued Clemo, was perverse.

Brother Romuald could not tolerate such an argument and asked whether the clay had the right to question the potter.

'But what if the clay,' responded Clemo,'needs the potter, and the potter needs the clay? And if that is the case, the act of creation is a mutually respectful activity, isn't it?' It was an idea that only formed in his mind as he said it. He realised that it was a very raw thought and needed further refinement. Images of his work at Redbrook Foundry sprang to mind...the trial and error, the mistakes, the discipline of the craft, the humility needed by the craftsman in the presence of his materials. With an apology for having challenged Brother Romuald so unkindly, Clemo explained how his work in a foundry had helped the idea to take shape.

They had further discussion, and then Clemo suggested a way forward: 'I would be delighted to stay on at the abbey as a servant, if you would allow that, and to come as often as possible to the services, and to assist you and the Brothers in any way I can. Might that be a solution?'

'I shall have to talk about this further with my brothers and with Father Abbot,' Romuald replied, before he walked off. Clemo could not imagine the thoughts that might be going through Brother Romuald's mind, but he felt huge relief at having been able to express what he truly felt. As he too walked away, he noticed that the precincts and the Abbey looked prettier and more inviting than ever.

Chapter 38: The sorrow of the servants

Clemo was going back towards the Lay Brother's Dorter after his discussion with Brother Romuald when he saw Richard ahead of him, walking very slowly in the same direction. He noticed Richard put a trembling hand to his head, stop, and then collapse to the ground like a tree being felled. Clemo rushed forward and tried to move him. But there was no response from Richard, just a low groan, like breath being expired, which then ceased. There was no-one else around. Clemo shouted loudly for help. In the stillness his shout echoed and bounced off the nearby buildings. Rufus came limping towards him calling out and asking what had happened. Brother John also came hurrying towards Clemo who was kneeling on the cobbles next to Richard. Between them they managed to roll Richard on to his back, but he was obviously dead. Brother John said a prayer under his breath and softly touched Richard's forehead making the sign of the cross as he did so. He stood up, told Rufus to fetch a sheet from the Dorter and asked him to arrange for someone to alert the Master Cellarer about what had just happened.

Soon, a few of the servants had gathered round, looking anxious. The Master Cellarer arrived and took charge. The sheet brought by Rufus was placed beneath Richard's corpse, three other servants were asked to join Clemo in taking a corner of the sheet each. With some difficulty they hoisted Richard from the ground. 'Take him to the Infirmary,' said the Master Cellarer. 'Brother John, you will say prayers and I will join you in a moment.' The ungainly procession set off, Brother John leading and reciting aloud the Pater Noster and the Aves.

Clemo, despite the sad weight of Richard's body, felt privileged to have been invited to carry Richard away from the courtyard. At the Infirmary there was some straw on the floor, and they laid Richard gently there. Brother John continued to recite Psalms as the others stood around looking dejected and saddened. He said some words from a Compline antiphon: 'Media vita in morte sumus quem quaerimus adjutorem nisi te, Domine, qui pro peccatis nostris juste irasceris?' Clemo found himself automatically translating for the benefit of the servants: 'In the midst of life we are in death; of whom may we seek for succour, but of thee, O Lord, who for our sins art justly displeased?' Brother John looked at him in astonishment, as did the other servants. 'Sorry', said Clemo, 'I learnt Latin when I was younger and I thought that, as Richard was our servant brother, we should all know what Brother John has been saying.' Brother John graciously and warmly thanked Clemo. The Master Cellarer arrived and told the servants to leave but asked Brother John and Clemo to stay.

'Thank you, Clemo, for your presence of mind when you saw Richard collapse. He has been a faithful servant of this Abbey all his life, he really has, and our community will be the poorer without him. But forgive me Clemo, even at this particular moment I wonder if we might have a conversation, and Brother John, will you please organise a Requiem for Richard this evening and see to all that is needed. I guess that he will be buried either tomorrow or the day after.' He stood looking down at Richard, said a prayer, shook his head gently from side to side in sadness and beckoned Clemo to join him.

As they were about to leave, Brother John apologised for interrupting them and explained to the Master Cellarer that Clemo had translated 'Media vita in morte sumus', after he had recited it, so that the servants could understand what was being said. Clemo hung his head with embarrassment. 'How wonderful,' replied the Master Cellarer, 'And not just wonderful, but very thoughtful, thank you.'

He and Clemo left.

'I understand from Brother Romuald that you will not be proceeding to the novitiate,' the Master Cellarer said to Clemo, 'I am sorry to hear that; you would have brought intelligence and grace to our community, but so be it, so be it. I just wanted to assure you that I can imagine how difficult that decision must have been for you. I was very like you, years ago. I too faced a similar decision; then, in the shadow of Tintern, I felt it was right to go ahead…but sometimes, even now, I wonder whether it was the right judgement to have made. That's all I wanted to say, so, whatever you do, may God be with you.'

Clemo was deeply touched by the Master Cellarer's sympathy and understanding and thanked him. He went on to explain that he hoped to stay at Waverley as a servant, but that depended upon the permission of Father Abbot.

'It would be good if you could be allowed to stay. After the sudden death of Richard, we need some younger people around us. And if you stay, I have a particular project I should love you to undertake. But that's not my decision, that is Father Abbot's responsibility.'

He walked slowly away, his hands enfolded in the sleeves of his robe, his head bowed as he sorrowed for Richard.

Clemo had been so caught up in the shock of seeing Richard collapse, and then in the practicalities of carrying him to the Infirmary that he now felt dazed. He wandered down to the river and watched the water ripple and meander slowly past. It was the only way that he could come to terms with the reality of it all. Later that same night, he and many of the servants, including Rufus, attended the Requiem. In the Dorter afterwards, everyone was silent. Death had come calling. They were now a member short in their small servant community.

The following morning, Clemo was summoned to see Father Abbot.

'Ah, Clemo. Thank you for all you did for Richard last night. He was a good old thing, and we shall all miss him dreadfully.' The Abbot looked out of the window and as he did so, continued speaking, 'I have asked to see you because I believe you have decided not to continue as a postulant. Is that correct?'

'It is.'

'Can you tell me why?'

Clemo explained his reasons, just as he had to Brother Romuald. After he had finished there was a long silence.

'I am not going to try to persuade you to change your mind,' said the Abbot, 'but you would have made a fine monk.' Again, there was a long silence and then the abbot continued, 'I understand that you would like to stay here as a servant. That is highly irregular; however…' He looked out of the window again, '…with the death of Richard, and because people no longer come to us asking for a position, I am content that you should stay, but it is on one condition…that you remain obedient to my authority.'

Clemo understood that this was the nature of being a servant but uttered a version of the phrase he had heard that Archbishop Warham had said to the King, 'I am content, as far as the law of Christ allows.'

The abbot looked at him carefully. 'Thank you…but there was no need to repeat the words of the Archbishop.'

Clemo apologised and explained that he had said the words half in jest.

'So, welcome to being a servant at Waverley Abbey.'

The abbot stood up and went to a table near the window and said, over his shoulder, 'I have a job for you to do tomorrow as soon as the funeral for Richard is finished.' He picked up a sheet of paper. 'I want you to deliver this letter to Master Cromwell. You can take a horse from the stables for the journey. You should stay overnight at Chertsey with the Benedictines. It is an important letter which I will keep in my rooms here, and you are to collect it, deliver it, and wait for a reply. Is that understood?'

'Indeed, it is,' replied Clemo, who was finding it difficult to restrain his happiness. It meant that he could see Antonio, Alice and some of his old friends again. What a marvellous outcome.

He thanked the abbot, left the room, and almost skipped through the abbey grounds on his way to the stables where he explained to the groom what his requirements were for the morrow. He was shown a horse, a deep chestnut in colour with a white blaze on its nose, and asked to see it being walked. The groom reluctantly obliged. It seemed alright but looked a little stiff and slow.

'I have to go to London tomorrow. Will the horse be up to it?'

'Of course. He hasn't been out for a while, so he will enjoy a day or two away from here.'

Clemo hardly slept that night. He kept imagining what Antonio's response would be when he turned up. And he thought of Alice and the Mossmans and hoped that they would be pleased to see him.

After the funeral and burial which were held early the next morning, Clemo collected the sealed letter from Father Abbot and then ran to the stables. The horse, called Sunny, had been saddled up and was waiting impatiently. Fixing his leather bag across his shoulder and ensuring that the letter was safely stowed away, Clemo set off. It was a beautiful Spring morning, so the journey along the Hog's Back was startlingly beautiful. Not a cloud in the sky, bright sunshine, and four days of being answerable to no-one. It was bliss and helped Clemo realise that he had made the right decision.

The overnight stop in Chertsey was uneventful, though he much admired the large and ornate tower of the abbey and enjoyed being introduced by one of the Chertsey servants to some of the quirkier floor tiles that decorated the transepts.

'On! On! Sunny,' he shouted, the next day. London was within striking distance and although he could have taken a boat down the Thames he decided to ride instead, for the sheer pleasure of being free.

Some hours later, he crossed London Bridge, made for Austin Friars and walked Sunny into the yard. The noise of the hooves on the cobbles alerted Pablo who threw up his arms in delight. 'Clemo! Clemo!' he shouted and told one of the junior servants to go to the sewing room and tell Gwen that there was someone in the yard waiting to speak with her. She came bustling out, her skirts flying, looking anxious. Then she spotted Clemo. 'Oh! Clemo, *cariad!* Clemo, *bach.'* She flung her arms around his neck and hugged him. 'I thought I would never see you again, and here you are.' She was soon joined by her sewing colleagues who could not resist wondering who it might be that had come for Gwen. Clemo's welcome was delightfully warm, and they insisted that he should have dinner with them. He asked Pablo if Sunny could stay in the stables overnight. 'Of course, and we'll get him properly fed, brushed and polished up for you!'

Clemo went with Gwen to the Servants' dining hall but insisted that for courtesy's sake he should go to see the Under Steward.

'That isn't possible', said Gwen.

'Why not?'

'He has left. Apparently, he was caught passing unauthorised messages to Scotland.'

Clemo's face fell. 'But he was good to me.'

'I know,' replied Gwen, 'But there we are. It's the way of the world.'

Dinner was a boisterous affair. So many people wanted to greet Clemo and ask him what it was like to be a monk.

'I've decided against it,' Clemo explained, 'and part of the reason is you. I discovered that I could not do without friends...' They all laughed.

After dinner he went next door to Master Cromwell's house and tapped on the main door. When it was opened by a young servant, Clemo asked if he might deliver a letter from the Abbot of Waverley. The servant invited him to step inside. In a nearby room there was a shout, a clatter of chairs being pushed aside, a peal of laughter, and Antonio arrived. To the servant's astonishment Antonio hugged Clemo and kept saying, 'Mio caro! Mio caro fratello!' He dragged Clemo by the arm into the house and for the next hour they talked incessantly and agreed to have breakfast together in an ale house the next day. Finally, Clemo handed Antonio the letter from the abbot and explained that he had to take a reply back to Waverley the following day. Antonio understood and promised that the response would be ready.

Clemo then, with an excited and beating heart, made his way to St Mary Bowe. It was Edward who opened the door in response to Clemo's knocking. He looked at Clemo in surprise, and mischievously announced in a loud voice, 'She's inside. I'll see if she wants to see you.' He called out to Alice who, on coming to the door, almost fainted with surprise and joy. She hauled Clemo in, and there was much rejoicing on the part of Father Mossman and Mistress Blake. They exchanged news and insisted that Clemo should stay with them that night.

It was a wonderful evening, not least because, as it was getting dark, Clemo shyly asked permission to take a walk with Alice. Permission was laughingly granted.

They sauntered up Cheapside towards St Paul's, and there, in the shadow of the cathedral he told her how much he had missed her and how he had longed to see her again and then he kissed her, a long, lingering, slow kiss that melted his heart and left them both breathless.

He apologised for his forwardness and she replied that there was nothing to apologise for, so he kissed her again and slowly, very slowly they walked back to the Parsonage, oblivious of everyone around them.

His farewell to Alice and the family the following morning was marked by sorrow. He didn't want to leave. Alice did not want him to leave but he explained that he would write and would do his best to come to London again before long. Her mother gently peeled Alice away from the door and Clemo walked to the tavern where he and Antonio had agreed to meet. Over bread and cheese Antonio brought Clemo up to date with all that had happened in the past few weeks.

There was the Bill of Restraint of Appeals, which Antonio explained he had helped to draft, though it was Master Cromwell who had had the final say and the Bill had become law in April.

'But what is it about?' asked Clemo.

'Can't you guess from the Title? It grants the King power to prevent anyone from appealing for legal help to the Pope. In effect, it declares that the King and Parliament are supreme in all things.' He looked around the tavern to ensure that no-one could hear what he was about to say. He whispered, 'And I have heard, (but keep this under your hat) that the new Archbishop, Thomas Cranmer, and his colleagues will hold a Court at Dunstable Priory very soon, and my guess is that they will declare the marriage of Catherine and the King to have been null and void.'

Clemo could not help being pleased that he was being so well informed about these things but was saddened by the turn of events. It was clear to him that the Church's ancient rights were being brutally curtailed.

They walked together back to Austin Friars where Antonio handed Clemo the letter for the abbot. 'Take great care of it,' he said, 'It took me a long time to write'. Clemo laughed but wondered whether there might not be some truth in what Antonio had said.

They said farewell. Clemo collected Sunny who, indeed, had been brushed and groomed until his coat shone, and the saddle and harness had been polished to perfection. He clasped Pablo by his shoulders and thanked him for such a generous and hospitable welcome. He promised to return before too long and rode Sunny out into the street heading for the journey home.

Chapter 39: Sheep and Merchants

Once he was back at Waverley, Clemo took the letter from Master Cromwell to the Abbot and then went to the Dorter to wash and change his clothes. He lay on his bed for a few minutes, thinking of nothing except Alice.

One of his fellow servants came to find him, 'Master Cellarer wants to see you.'

Clemo , still feeling a little stiff from four days riding, went to the Cellarer's office.

'Clemo, it's good to see you. I hope you had a good journey. I should like to make a proposal to you, which, of course, now you are a servant, you are not allowed to refuse.' He smiled. 'Being used to country ways, you will know that shearing will begin in the next couple of weeks. Our system is that once the fleeces have been graded, some Italian merchants will arrive and we shall come to an arrangement with them about how the fleeces are to be shipped, but most importantly, we shall discuss what they are worth and how they are to be paid for. I shall head up the negotiations, but I want you to be with me. After everything you have told me about your friendship with Antonio, you might have learnt some subtle ways of understanding Italian merchants. Good, that is all…and thank you.'

The sheep gathering process began a couple of weeks later when the abbey's own flocks of sheep were herded by their shepherds into the river to clean the fleeces. It was a complicated task in which Clemo and the other shepherds, aided by their dogs, had to manoeuvre the sheep into holding pens. Hurdles were placed in the river to create a passageway across, then the passageway was connected to the holding pens using even more hurdles, and finally, gates were used to control the sheep so that one at a time, they left the holding pen and went down into the river where the shepherds were waiting to wash them. The shepherds standing in the river had to be hardy and astute to control the struggling animals before allowing them to scramble out of the river up on to dry ground on the other bank. Each day was long and demanding.

For the abbey it was also a challenging time: the abbey had to feed and arrange sleeping quarters for the shepherds and shearers. As some of the shepherds only met on this one occasion each year, the noise level in the precincts, especially following the consumption of large quantities of ale, was high. It was one of the busiest times of the year for the Master Cellarer who had to purchase large quantities of food and drink to cope with the noisy influx and, in addition, had to ensure that each person knew what his particular job was to be.

Once the washing had been completed, (and the same process was undertaken by the tenant farmers with their flocks on their own land), life became quieter for a couple of weeks to allow time for the sheep's fleeces to dry in the May sunshine. And then the fun began. Long, wooden shearing benches were set up, onto which each sheep was lifted. Once on the bench, the sheep was laid on it and the shearers, sitting at one end of the bench, could begin to cut off the fleece with their metal shears. It was heavy, smelly work. When the fleeces were completely taken from the sheep, servants carried the fleeces away. As a result of being sheared, each sheep looked vulnerably naked, and Clemo noticed that some of the sheep had been nicked by the shears of those who were less skilled. The wounds were dressed immediately with tar or a broom salve. The fleeces were collected, graded, tied into rough bales, and weighed. It was Clemo's job to keep accurate written records of the weight of each bale and to ensure that the fleeces, according to the way they had been graded and sorted, were not muddled up. And whilst the sheep nearest the abbey had their fleeces weighed and sorted, the same process had to be completed when the tenant farmers brought their bales of fleeces to the abbey's communal barn. Clemo was given charge of this task and was a little daunted by the responsibility.

And then, after the annual feast at the abbey for all the shearers and shepherds, Clemo and the Master Cellarer waited for the Italian wool merchants to arrive. There were only two of them and they appeared on beautifully groomed horses. Clemo, seeing them at the Gatehouse, was most impressed, not only by the horses but by the elegant demeanour of the merchants. He welcomed them and took them to meet the Master Cellarer. The Master Cellarer, after greeting the guests, introduced Clemo to them and for a few minutes whilst pleasantries were being exchanged, nothing seemed out of the ordinary. But then Clemo mentioned during the conversation that he had a good Italian friend who worked near Austin Friars. The merchants' faces lit up. They asked who Clemo's friend was. He explained that his friend's name was Antonio and before he had added the surname, one of the merchants shouted out, 'di Venezia! Certo, I know him well, and I know his parents. Lovely people…for Venetians.' He laughed. 'Me? I'm from Florence. The best city in Italy, better than Rome, better than Venice. Si. Si. Better than anywhere else on earth and the Duomo, bellissima, bellissima…oddio, so you know Antonio? He's a friend of mine, and that means, Clemo, you are now my friend as well.' He shook Clemo's hand warmly.

The Master Cellarer looked on, smiling, and calculated that Clemo's presence might have ensured that this year they would get a good price for the wool.

The two merchants inspected the bales of wool carefully. They took handfuls of wool from the bales; felt the texture with their fingers, and then tried to tug the wool apart to gauge the length and strength of the wool fibres. There was much frowning, rubbing of chins and scratching of heads. At one point, the merchants excused themselves and went into a corner out of earshot, and there, with much gesticulation, they began to formulate the price they would offer. They returned to stand opposite Clemo and the Master Cellarer, and with long faces explained that this had not been a good year for English wool, that the taxes they had to pay to ship the wool to the Low Countries had risen, and that transport costs in England had also increased. So, bearing that in mind, they offered a price.

The Master Cellarer thanked them and explained that he and Clemo also needed a conversation. Taking Clemo by the arm he steered him into a darkened corner of the barn. 'Now, Clemo,' he said, 'That's not a bad price they have offered but I'm going to see if I can get them to raise their bid. This is all a game really. They will not be surprised when we go back to them and explain that we think their offer price is a bit on the low side. So, I shall suggest that if they could raise their price by 10% we would accept. They won't agree to that but will offer us perhaps 5% and we shall look disappointed, but appearing reluctant, we shall seal the deal. So, in a minute we shall return, but let's make it look as though you and I are disagreeing, because they will be watching us to see if they can split us apart. Don't forget, it's a game, but if we can go back to the Abbey with their offer increased by 5%, I shall be extremely happy. Now, look as though we are disagreeing.' Clemo enjoyed the play-acting and entered into it wholeheartedly.

They went back to the merchants and after some haggling the 5% price was eventually agreed upon by both sides. They all shook hands and the two merchants said that when they returned to London, they would tell Antonio that they had met Clemo. They smiled and laughed as they left. 'Arrividerci,' they shouted, 'We're now going to see some of the Bishop of Winchester's wool, and we shall find a suitable price to disappoint him!!'

'See Clemo, your presence made the difference!' exclaimed the Master Cellarer. And to forestall any doubts Clemo might have had, he said, 'What did Our Lord say? "Wise as serpents, innocent as doves," It's the favourite text for all Master Cellarers.' Clemo acknowledged that but felt inwardly saddened that his views of the life of monks was having to be so frequently recalibrated.

After the noise and bustle of the shearing season, the rest of the year seemed to go quietly by. But the Master Cellarer had seen a willing and able pupil in Cleo and used him increasingly in the business of purchasing goods and materials for the abbey. He gradually extended Clemo's understanding of finance so that by the time Christmas arrived, Clemo was being trusted to negotiate some deals on his own with outside purveyors. Meanwhile, he was able to send and receive letters from Alice and promised that in the New Year he would return to London to see her.

The Master Cellarer, recognising Clemo's desire to see his beloved, allowed him a five-day holiday after Christmas. It was a time of bliss for Alice and Clemo; they could wander around the City and could begin make plans for their future together.

It was on one such happy day when they had strolled as far as the Tower, that Alice told Clemo that the Tower now held a famous prisoner, the Maid of Kent. For some years she had been the talk of the City having received numerous visions and uttering prophecies. 'Even the King,' explained Alice, 'has met her.'

'So why is she now in the Tower?' asked Clemo.

'Because once the King had divorced Catherine and had married Anne, the Maid of Kent prophesied that the King would soon die. And as you might guess, the more she prophesied the King's death, the more enraged the King became. She was arrested last November and now lies over there.' Alice pointed to the Tower.

'And what will happen to her?' asked Clemo.

'It's anyone's guess but she has a number of supporters who believe that her visions and prophecies come directly from God. The King also believed her prophecies whilst she was supporting his tirades against Martin Luther, but now…well, I guess it will depend on what the King and Master Cromwell decide. But she must be very lonely and frightened in that place.' She looked hard at the Tower. 'It's strange to think that we are free out here, whilst she is held fast in there. It gives me the creeps. Come on; let's go, and think of happier things like, for instance, us…' She took Clemo by the hand and led him away.

They were watching the wherries criss-crossing the river when she said, 'Clemo, I can't bear that we are parted for such long times, so I have had a thought. If I could get a job as a servant with the Bishop of Winchester in his residence across the River, perhaps I could then find a way of getting transferred to Farnham where he has his Castle…and then we would be much closer. What do you think?

'Alice, it's a wonderful idea, but I am not sure. Bishop Gardiner is a powerful man, and you might find that in working for him you could be caught up in all kinds of political troubles. I would hate you to put yourself at risk. And, because it will be a household made up almost entirely of men, I wouldn't want you to be reduced to becoming their washerwoman.'

She looked saddened. 'I thought it was a brilliant idea,' she said.

'It is, it is,' replied Clemo, 'But as I discovered, being with people at the centre of political and diplomatic life can be difficult. In any case, you can read and write, why don't you see if you can work for an apothecary. It's a growing profession and you would be brilliant at it. And then, you could set up as an apothecary wherever we live… Farnham, for instance.' Alice smiled and kissed him. 'Leave that idea with me,' she said, and twirled around him in a way that made him love her more deeply than ever. He was a very happy man.

Chapter 40: The Maid of Kent

It was Clemo's good fortune that messages from Father Abbot to Thomas Cromwell and to the Abbey of St Mary de Graces seemed to increase during the new year. As the most trusted messenger, he was therefore able to see Alice and Antonio more often than he had expected.

In early February, through contacts of Father Mossman, Alice obtained a job as a servant with an apothecary in Bucklersbury, and when Clemo saw her later in March she was able to tell him that her boss was already allowing her to prepare some of the herbs and spices. It meant, she said, that if she learnt quickly, she might be ready to leave London in a year's time and then she and Clemo could marry. They could begin to make plans, which Clemo said he regarded as a 'delicious prospect'.

On his messenger visits to London, he also had long conversations with Antonio who kept him informed about the way political life was going. 'Earlier in March,' Antonio explained, 'there was a new Act passed by Parliament called An Act in Restraint of Annates.' He rolled the phrase around his tongue, rejoicing in the legalistic formulation of the Act's title. Clemo suggested that this was yet another of Cromwell's wily plans. 'Yes, it is,' agreed Antonio, 'but it was only partially successful. It was intended that the monies forbidden to be passed to Rome should be paid instead to the King…but there was an uproar from the Upper House, so although the Act was passed, none of the monies came to the King. Cromwell lost that battle, but he is a great tactician. You see, Clemo, he might have failed in part of his plan, but he had another idea which he had attached to the Act and that was to ensure that from now on, it is the King alone who can appoint Bishops.'

'What?!' exclaimed Clemo.

'Well, in theory, the Cathedrals have a voice in the appointment of bishops. They are allowed to protest if they do not like the bishop who has been chosen, but they can't overturn what the King has decreed. If they try to do so, they will be accused of praemunire. It's neat, isn't it?' He grinned.

'But that means that the King has more and more power over the Church.'

'Exactly…but which would you rather have: the Pope, hundreds of miles away in Rome, making the decisions, or the King in London?' Clemo decided that he would not answer the question but raised a quizzical eyebrow. Antonio laughed at his response.

'You're learning, Clemo. You aren't the innocent country boy anymore. And, by the way, I hope that you and Alice will be really happy…!'

Clemo had to take messages to London in April, and as had become his custom, he stayed with Father Mossman and the family. All the talk on the first evening was about a rumour spreading through the City that the Maid of Kent was to be executed the following day.

'What does that mean?' he asked.

Father Mossman looked at the floor, and replied, 'It means that she will be paraded through the streets tied to a hurdle pulled by a horse, with her head close to the road. She will not be alone. Five of her supporters will also be with her, each in a separate part of the procession. Two of them are Benedictines, one is a priest, and two are Franciscans. They will be taken to Tyburn where they will be hanged…and then who knows if any other terrible things will be done…' His normally strong voice failed. He continued to look at the floor, his hands together.

Clemo felt sick. 'Do you really mean that the authorities will hang a poor woman?'

'Sadly, yes. It is said that she confessed that she had lied about the visions and messages she claimed to have had …but it did not save her. It is alleged that she and some colleagues conspired against the King and, as you will know, conspiracies against the King are held to be acts of treason.'

'Might she have been the dupe of others? Might she be mad? Would not her trial have discovered that?' asked Clemo.

There was a long silence and then Father Mossman answered, 'But there was no trial.' He repeated the words, 'There was no trial. She was condemned by an Act of Attainder passed in Parliament.'

Clemo was appalled by the injustice but decided that it would not be sensible to express any of the views he might hold. He kept silence, though his silence spoke loudly.

The rest of that evening was spent in a sombre mood. Clemo kissed Alice good night and made his way slowly to his room. He slept only fitfully.

In the morning he noticed from his window that crowds of people were gathering on the street outside, laughing and jostling.

'What are those people doing out in the street?' he asked at breakfast.

'They are waiting to see the Maid of Kent and her supporters dragged past. It's a day out for them,' said Alice, bitterly. 'It's one of the few amusements they will get all year. One day they rush to see a pig being killed; the next day they rush to see a woman hanged. What a terrible City this is.'

As they ate, they could hear the noise of shouting growing louder. Edward burst into the room, 'Come and look everyone, the Maid of Kent is on her way to Tyburn.'

'I think you ought to see this, Clemo,' said Alice dolefully, 'just to remind you how bestial and horrible people can be. Think of it as part of your moral education.'

They walked upstairs and looked out of the window. The noise was increasing, and then they saw an officer on a horse riding down the centre of the roadway. He was followed by a priest, and soldiers carrying pikes walking in line on either side of the road. Behind them came a carthorse dragging a hurdle over the rough ground, jolting the woman tied to it from side to side. As she passed, the crowds hissed and booed, and threw rotten fruit and stinking fish at her, but kept some back for the other prisoners roped together walking behind, their monastic habits covered with garbage and stained with filth. And behind them came another detachment of pike-carrying soldiers.

As the procession passed the window, Clemo looked down at the face of the woman on the hurdle and saw in her eyes a look of terror and despair. It was an image that would haunt him for the rest of his life.

His face lost all its colour. He crossed himself. Alice took his hand and said, 'Sorry, Clemo, but you really did need to see that. Because that too is part of the City's life. At times like this, I hate the City and I hate humanity, and I cannot understand God at all. How can God allow such awful things to happen? It appals me. And some of the wealthier people out in the street today, jeering and hissing and shouting, will be in my shop tomorrow asking for something for a tiny headache. It's their souls that need healing, not their bodies.' Clemo put his arm around her shoulder as she sobbed quietly. He had no words of consolation nor answers to her question but experienced a stunned anger.

Later that day, Edward rushed into the house and shouted that the Maid of Kent's head was about to be paraded past on a pole to be exhibited on London Bridge. 'Come and see!', he shouted. Alice slapped him hard across the face, 'Do you not have any human compassion, you ignorant, malicious, ugly toad!'. Edward tried to reply but his mother intervened. 'Don't look to me for sympathy, Edward…you got all you deserved.' He ran upstairs in a furious sulk.

Clemo left for Waverley the following morning, glad to be away from the horrors he had witnessed but saddened that he might not see Alice again for another couple of months. He rode to Chertsey in a heavy, despairing mood, and even attending Mass that night in a side-chapel of the abbey did nothing to counter his worries and questions. God seemed to have become appallingly absent.

When he eventually rode slowly into Waverley, he felt pleased to be home, until Rufus said to him, 'I guess you saw the Maid of Kent going to be hanged a couple of days ago. What was she like?'

'Pitiful,' said Clemo, the image of her still fresh in his mind, and wanting to avoid any conversation. But the news of her hanging and beheading and the hanging of the monks and a priest had somehow arrived ahead of him, and some of the servants in the Dorter that night raised the question again.

Clemo lost his temper. 'You are ghouls,' he cried, 'ghouls…That was a woman who had not had a trial, who was paraded through the streets like an animal and whose head was stuck on a pole on London

Bridge. No woman has ever had that happen to her before. Can you not see how appalling a thing that is? I can only hope that Our Lady prayed for her soul. Perhaps she can understand why human beings can be so evil, but I certainly cannot. Now, good night.'

The room fell silent. It took him hours to get to sleep. All he could see in his mind's eye was the woman's face as she was dragged to her death surrounded by a howling mob.

The next morning, he had a conversation with the Master Cellarer about all he had seen, but even from that wise man he could find no source of balm. The Master Cellarer paraphrased Augustine about human nature being twisted by the Fall and therefore being in need of a divine physician to bring healing. It was an idea, at that moment, that was too calm and too lucid to meet Clemo's innermost despair. All he could do was to keep repeating the words of the Kyrie Eleison, hoping that the sound of the words would ease the anguish he was suffering.

But the Master Cellarer came to the rescue by forcing Clemo's mind to move away from his awful experience. He ordered him to think about the forthcoming shearing season. 'Work will ease your pain, Clemo,' he said.

They began to rehearse the plans they would have to make to cope with the shearing. But then Master Cellarer announced that for part of the season he might be required by Father Abbot to offer his expertise to some of the other Cistercian houses. 'And if that happens, Clemo, I shall rely on you to look after Waverley's interests. '

Clemo was stunned by the request and apprehensive about carrying so much responsibility. 'It might not happen, Clemo…but it probably will, knowing my luck.'

The Master Cellarer's prognostications were entirely accurate. He was at Waverley for the first couple of days but then had to leave. Clemo was anxious but wanted to do a good job, and by a mixture of hard work, skill and charm the shearing went extremely well. In fact, so well, that at the Feast, the shearers gave him three cheers. When he wrote to Alice the next day the glow of pride made itself felt through every word of the letter.

However, although all the fleeces were safely stowed in the barn, he still had to deal with the Italian merchants. And then they arrived. Not two of them this time, but three, and the third was Antonio.

'Ciao, Clemo,' he shouted, as Clemo met him and his two companions at the gatehouse.

'Antonio, what on earth brings you here?'

'I have been given some days off to recover from a brief malady, and my friends here suggested that some fresh country air would do me good…so, here I am.'

'By my troth, it's good to see you…but I must see if the Guest Room might be available to you. If it is, you will be very welcome.' He had a word with Rufus who assured Clemo that the Guest Room was indeed free, so Clemo arranged for Antonio to be taken there by another servant. 'Have a rest. I have to talk with your merchant friends and then I'll be back later.'

He apologised for not greeting the merchants with proper respect, but they were all smiles, recognising what an unexpected shock it had been for Clemo to see Antonio arrive with them. But he also had to tell them that the Master Cellarer was away on business and he had been left in charge.

'Very good,' they replied, 'That suits us fine.'

After a breakfast they were taken to the barn to see the fleeces.

They handled the fleeces, tried the wool for strength and length, and pronounced themselves delighted with the quality of the fleeces. 'And now, my friend, the price…' They conferred with each other and then offered a price that was higher than the previous year. Clemo was inwardly delighted but didn't show it. Instead, he bartered with them until they had come to an agreement that provided the abbey with a large bonus on top of the price offered.

'Time for dinner,' he said, and took them to meet Father Abbott whilst he himself went to the Guest Room to find Antonio and invite him to dine with the servants.

Antonio was asleep but when he awoke was immediately cheerful. And with Clemo's arm over his shoulder he was taken to meet the other servants.

Clemo made an announcement in the Servants' Refectory introducing Antonio and asked everyone to treat Antonio with courteous respect because he was an important clerk in the household of Master Cromwell.

There were some welcoming cheers, though they were quite muted. It seemed that Cromwell's reputation had spread more widely than might have been expected.

'Now, Antonio,' said Clemo, 'tell me why you have really come to visit me.'

'Because I wanted to see you, of course, but also to get a feel for the lie of the land.'

'What do you mean?'

'You may not be aware of it, Clemo, but there is an influential and wealthy family living in Farnham, the Whites; they own a good deal of property and one of the sons, John, is up and coming in the City. People speak very highly of him, and I thought, out of sheer curiosity I ought to see where his family comes from. You never know, it might be useful.'

'What you mean is, useful to Master Cromwell.'

He grinned at Clemo but did not answer. Instead, he changed the subject. 'I plan to walk into Farnham later this morning and see what I can find out. By the way, I shall only be staying tonight. Tomorrow my merchant friends will call in again to see you, (I think they might have something to discuss) and once your conversation with them is finished we shall ride slowly back to London...but now, Farnham here we come...' Having asked Clemo the way, he strode off, whistling. Clemo was left wondering what the merchants might want to see him about on the morrow.

He and Antonio were able to spend some pleasurable hours together later that same day, but Antonio was not willing to divulge what the merchants might want to talk to Clemo about. He teased Clemo by saying, 'It might be to your advantage,' but then changed the subject to the politics of London.

'I have a suspicion', he said, 'that Master Cromwell might be planning a large piece of legislation on behalf of the King. Perhaps something to do with the King's future status, but nothing is entirely clear. However, the house has become increasingly busy with lawyers recently, but no details have yet come my way.' Clearly, Antonio knew more than he was letting on but would divulge no more.

The following morning, after breakfast, the merchants arrived and over a tankard of ale, with Antonio present, they gently began their discussions with Clemo.

'Clemo', they said, 'it is clear to us that you learn quickly. You handled the negotiations with us yesterday with subtlety and skill. We were impressed. So, allow us to ask you: what are your plans for your own future?'

'I hope to be married next year.'

Antonio interrupted him by exclaiming that Alice was a beautiful woman, and the merchants concurred, 'Si. Si. We know Alice Blake. She is bellissima, really beautiful. You are a lucky man. But that means you will need money. No-one can marry without money. Yet here you are, working as a servant in an abbey. How can you afford to marry on what you earn?'

'I expect we shall manage,' replied Clemo, defensively.

'That's not a good enough answer,' they replied. 'You will need more money than you get here. Look. We'll be honest with you.. It is obvious to us that you have the capacity and skills to help us. We should like you to consider this proposal: next year after the shearing here at Waverley, or at the outside, in two years' time, why don't you join us in purchasing fleeces from other landlords in the area? Would you be interested? You could be our agent.'

Clemo was astonished. Such an idea had never occurred to him. He responded in a hesitant fashion, 'But I have little experience. I would have to learn.'

'Of course, but the Master Cellarer is already teaching you well, and in a year or two you will be ready to go further. Between now and when we next meet, you must learn as much as you can about the wool trade--the best breeds of sheep, the differences in their fleeces, the way cloth is prepared, the processes of dyeing, the varieties of cloth. Whilst you are doing that (and we are serious about how much you will need to learn) think about our offer, and via Antonio, in due course you can let us know what you think. But we believe that you would love the challenge and the work is really interesting. You could buy Alice some nice things, if you joined us. She would be very proud of you.'

The merchants and Antonio left, and Clemo returned to his abbey duties. He had come to love Waverley and therefore the thought of one day leaving it left him disconcerted. He decided to put it to the back of his mind until he had an opportunity to discuss it with Alice, but he also decided that he would follow the advice of the merchants, and would set himself the task in the coming months and years to learn as much as possible about the wool trade.

Chapter 41: The vice tightens its grip

When Clemo next saw Alice in the Summer he talked with her and with the family about the proposal made by the Italian merchants. He explained that he had already had many conversations with shepherds, fullers, weavers and cloth men in Farnham and the neighbourhood, and was enjoying the challenge of learning about the wool trade. Alice was impressed by his enthusiasm and determination but thought it was worth exploring further until he had convinced himself that he really did want a change of occupation. She suggested that perhaps Clemo should wait until after their marriage to make a final decision. 'By then I shall perhaps be ready to begin some apothecary work,' she said, 'and that might change the picture.' Her mother smiled, recognising that what Alice was really saying was that she would hope to be having a baby as soon as they were married. But Clemo did not interpret Alice's words in that way.

Meanwhile, London was abuzz with news about the Observant Friars of Greenwich being turned out of their Friary for supporting Catherine of Aragon. In a conversation with Father Mossman, Clemo discovered that many of the Friars had been sent to prison in other friaries and over thirty of them had died of illness, ill-treatment, or starvation, including two who had been held in Newgate. Clemo found the news deeply troubling and when he saw Antonio expressed his concern.

'Ah', said Antonio,' but the King is the King, and he is one who must not be defied. He has married Anne Boleyn; the Church in England has declared that that marriage is valid…and so anyone who supports Catherine is automatically regarded as subversive and treacherous.'

'And do you believe that Antonio?'

'What I believe is determined by the fact that I work for Master Cromwell.'

'So, you have no opinions of your own?'

'I didn't say that. I simply stated a fact--- that I work for Master Cromwell, that's all.' He smiled and suggested that they should find an alehouse where they could talk in peace and quiet. When they had found a private spot where they could not be overheard, Antonio hinted to Clemo that in the Autumn it would be likely that clarity would be brought to the matter of the King's status. When Clemo asked for further details, Antonio explained that he had probably said too much already and could say no more.

'I wonder,' said Clemo in response, looking hard at Antonio, 'whether we servants gradually take on some of the salient characteristics of our masters?'

Antonio retorted with the suggestion that the merchants had talked with Clemo earlier in the year because he had become increasingly like the canny Master Cellarer. Clemo smiled and said, 'Touché.'

It was in November of that year that Clemo recalled his conversations with Antonio when Parliament passed the Act of Supremacy. It declared that the King was the only Supreme Head on Earth of the Church of England.

In Waverley, news of the Act caused consternation and sharp exchanges of views amongst the monks. Some felt that only the Pope could have the title of Supreme Head, others said that if the King had been appointed by God then whatever happened he had to be obeyed. The Father Abbot asked that all conversations in the Monk's Parlour and within the Precincts of the Abbey should remain confidential. 'Otherwise', he said, in a rare display of controlled anger, 'We could be putting ourselves and our beloved Abbey at risk if anyone thought we were unhappy with the King and with Parliament. So, brothers,' he said, 'I beg you, nay, I order you to remain silent on the subject from this day forward. And I need to remind you that as your Abbot, I shall be called upon to take the Oath of Supremacy... therefore, I ask for your prayers, your understanding, and above all, in this abbey, for a sense of unity. Remember Psalm 133, *Ecce quam bonum et quam iucundum habitare fratres in unum* ("Behold, how good and pleasant a thing it is when brethren dwell together in unity.")

The brothers were chastened by the abbot's words, recognising that whilst they might have the individual right to keep their own counsel, the abbot had to wrestle with his conscience and would have to think not only of his personal well-being but of the safety and continuance of the abbey in anything he said or undertook. No-one envied him the heavy responsibility. The abbey, in the weeks of Advent, felt weighed down by uncertainty and by the changes that were being forced upon it.

The uncertainty did not stay within the walls of the cloister; the servants, including Clemo, noticed and understood the subdued atmosphere, and although Christmas was marked by the traditional rejoicing, the abbey seemed to have subtly changed. It had become watchful and apprehensive about what the future might bring.

The news from London in January did nothing to relieve the gloom. If anything, it added a touch of anger. It was the Master Cellarer who was the first to pick up the story. Master Cromwell, he announced one day, had been promoted to a new post: Vice-Regent in Spirituals. In other words, he was given total control of the Church. Father Abbot, the Prior and the Master Cellarer met frequently in the Abbot's lodgings to discuss what the likely outcome of such an appointment might mean.

'I'm afraid, it's simple,' explained the Master Cellarer, 'he will be after money. Greed and power are an entirely unhealthy mix.'

And when the notice arrived at the Abbey, informing the Abbot that there was to be an assessment, the Valor Ecclesiasticus, of the assets of all the abbeys and churches in the country, the mood at Waverley became deeply uneasy.

Clemo was asked by the abbot to take a letter in response, directly to Thomas Cromwell. 'This letter is of great importance to our future. Do not let it out of your sight until you hand it over to Cromwell. And at the same time, you must give him this.' He lifted the lid of a heavy oak chest and drew from it a small linen bag. 'This bag,' he explained, 'contains £50.00. It is a gift for Cromwell. Make sure he receives it. It might buy us his favour.'

Having handed the bag of coins to Clemo, the abbot sat down wearily in his chair. 'I am sorry to involve you in all of this, Clemo. It is a dreadful situation and one which weighs heavily on my conscience and on my soul. I pray that you will not become contaminated by having to act as my messenger. What I have said to you, and the money I have entrusted to you, must remain a matter between you and me. Now, kneel in front of me, and let me give you the blessing of God.' Clemo knelt and felt the hands of the abbot upon his head. He was invited to stand. 'God speed, Clemo. Please take great care, not only of the letter and of the money, but most of all of yourself. We live in desperate, unholy times. May God have mercy on us all.'

Clemo left the room, and as he left, heard the abbot quietly sobbing.

His journey to London was uneventful but all the talk at Chertsey Abbey was of Cromwell and his machinations. The mood there was, as it was in Waverley, anxious and angry.

He walked his horse into the Ambassador's residence and had a long chat with Pablo but then made his way to Cromwell's house.

At the door, the servant recognised him and invited him in. Antonio, as always, was delighted to see him but seemed more preoccupied than usual. Clemo handed over the letter and then took the bag of coins and gave it to Antonio.

'Make sure that Master Cromwell knows who has sent this gift to him.'

'I will indeed. Similar bags are appearing daily. My Master is delighted.'

'One more request, Antonio. Where can I wash my hands?'

'I'll show you.'

Clemo didn't move. Antonio looked at him and then realised the deeper meaning of what Clemo had said. Under his breath he whispered, 'Sorry.'

They arranged to meet later that night in their favourite tavern. And in one of the darker corners of that ale-house Antonio explained that the Valor Ecclesiasticus was requiring complicated administrative arrangements. 'Can you imagine, Clemo? The abbots and clergy will each have to assess what their landholdings are worth and then report them with a sworn statement to the Commissioners, and it is all supposed to be completed by May. That's impossible, of course, and it might be the early Summer before everything is done, but Cromwell is determined to have the final tally in front of him as soon as possible.'

Clemo stared into his tankard. 'Let me ask you a question, Antonio. Why do you work for him? Can't you see the despair he is creating in monasteries across the country. These monks have devoted their lives to prayer for our country and they are being treated like milch cows. How can you do it?'

'Let me ask you a question in return. Did not our Lord tell the young man to give away all he possessed? And have not the monasteries of our country been acting as trading houses for most of their lives? Aren't they rich beyond the dreams of ordinary people?'

Clemo had to acknowledge that there was much truth in what Antonio had said.

Antonio continued, 'And if you could see the wealth of the churches in Rome, would you not be appalled that for centuries the poor people of England have been taxed to pay for them?'

Clemo admitted that he did not know what the churches of Rome were like.

'Well...just think of Cardinal Wolsey. Was he not as rich as Croesus?'

'But Cromwell worked for him.'

'Indeed, he did, and I sometimes wonder whether in his heart of hearts, Cromwell's ideas about reforming the church aren't a reaction to all the avarice and greed he witnessed whilst in Wolsey's service.'

'But, judging from the building works going on in his own house, perhaps he has been mortally infected by the same greed...'

'It goes deeper than that, Clemo. I believe he has some sympathies with the reform movements in Germany. I think he would like to take power and control from priests and abbots and hand it to the people.'

'Perhaps,' retorted Clemo, sardonically, 'whilst keeping the cash for himself and the King and the King's friends.'

They were silent for a moment as they tried to understand the deeper and murkier depths of the contemporary political and religious situation.

'Let me lighten the mood, Clemo. You met my fellow-Italians last year. What are your thoughts now? Will you join them in their venture?'

'Alice thinks that it might be right for me to have another conversation with them to see what they have in mind before I come to a final decision.'

'Spoken like a married man! And the good news is that I can pass that message on to them. They will be delighted. They are good men, and you will do well to join them. I am wondering if I might do the same myself one day.'

Clemo made his way to Cheapside where he and the family spent much of the late evening discussing what Cromwell was up to, but more happily they also discussed dates for the wedding and finally decided that it should take place at St Mary Bowe on the Saturday after Easter. Alice fizzed with excitement and was delighted that Clemo wanted a wedding ceremony at the church porch followed by a priestly blessing, rather than doing what some of her friends had done which was simply to make their vows in front of a witness. But she then asked Clemo whether he had found anywhere for them to live.

'Not yet.'

Alice took his arm and linked her arm through his, giving it a squeeze.

'And what if I told you that I might well have found somewhere...'

'Alice, what do you mean?'

'Let me tell you.... I was in my master's shop a few weeks ago when an important man walked in. I was out at the back but then my master asked me to come into the shop. "I want you to meet John White", said my master. "He is a good friend of mine and I have been telling him how you, Alice, are due to marry a young man from Farnham and that you hope to live there..."

John White asked me what my plans were, and then said he owned several houses in Farnham, including one in the Borough, the main street in Farnham. He explained that the house would soon be vacant and went on to say that it has a small shop at the front which would be ideal for a young apothecary... and then asked me if it might be suitable for us.

I could not believe what I was hearing. I remember curtseying to John White and thanking him profusely for the opportunity and promised him that once you and I had had a chance to talk, I would give him my answer. Clemo, isn't it wonderful?'

Clemo was speechless.

'Alice, my dearest sweetheart, you are the most wonderful woman in the world. And I love you.' He leaned across to kiss her.

For the rest of that evening he and Alice laid plans, and, to cap it all, Father Mossman said he would pay the rent on the house for a year as his wedding gift to them.

It was only whilst he was lying in bed too excited to sleep because of all that had happened, that he realised the only reason Father Mossman could make such a generous gift was because he collected so much in annual gifts and rents from his parishioners. He, Clemo, and Alice were therefore the beneficiaries of other people's donations to the Church. Did that mean, from a moral perspective, that the money was pure, or was it somehow tainted because it resulted in Father Mossman becoming relatively rich whilst many of the parishioners were poor? He turned the question over and over in his mind but could not solve it. However, in the end he resolved to accept Father Mossman's amazing gift because it meant that he and Alice could begin their new life together without undue anxiety. He decided that this was a moral solution that quietened his conscience and therefore, he was eventually able to sleep, but his dreams remained troubled.

Chapter 42: Endings and Beginnings

Clemo returned to Waverley in good spirits and realised, with some anxiety, that he would have to ask the Master Cellarer for permission to marry and live in the town. He encountered the Master Cellarer as he was leading his horse to the stables.

'You look very happy Clemo. What's the cause?'

'So much has occurred since I left a few days ago; firstly, Alice has agreed to marry me, and secondly, she has found a house for us in The Borough.'

'Goodness! How did she do that? She lives in London and has never been to Farnham. She must be a well-connected woman.' He smiled.

Clemo explained that she had met a man called John White, and as soon as the name 'White' was mentioned, the Master Cellarer laughed. 'You, my dear Clemo, have fallen on your feet. The White family are the most powerful and the most wealthy family in these parts. So, I guess you want to ask me for permission to live in Farnham once you are married, and come here to work each day? Is that correct?'

'I am afraid that it is,'replied Clemo, feeling a little crestfallen, and wondering whether permission would be granted.

'Look, Clemo…you are my right hand man. I cannot do without you; so, if you wish to marry and live in the Borough, you have my permission. But it is on condition that you continue to work alongside me here in the Abbey…whilst there still is an abbey.'

'What do you mean, Master Cellarer?'

'Clemo, I share my thinking with you in confidence. But you *must* see the way the wind is blowing. The Valor Ecclesiasticus is not an innocent and idle game. Once we have handed in our figures to the

Commissioners, Cromwell will look at them and see that there is a large amount of money locked up in the monasteries of England. When he worked for Wolsey he helped the Cardinal to close some abbeys to pay for his Colleges. Well, he has that experience behind him and he will use it to close us all down, I'm certain of it.'

'But that is stealing,' repled Clemo.

'That is maybe how you see it, but others will probably talk of liberating resources so that they can be used in a more productive way… and you and I will be out on the street, begging for our bread. Now, once you have seen to your horse, please join me in my office. Father Abbot has delegated to me the task of valuing all our property and land, and I shall need your assistance as I get to grips with the task. I shall have some ale waiting for you…'

Over the next two weeks, Clemo and the Master Cellarer were closeted together drawing up an inventory of all the Abbey's possessions. When it was completed it was handed to the abbot so that he could report the results to the Commissioners.

Father Abbot was ill-at-ease as the days drew closer for him to present the inventory. He was seen praying in front of the statue of Our Lady in the church more than was his usual custom. His mood was echoed by all the other monks. The offices continued as usual but the voices of the monks had become subdued. The servants continued to go about their several tasks but they too felt depressed. Even the food from the kitchens seemed to have lost its savour.

Clemo, recognising all the signs, had to work hard not to appear ebullient. Inside, however, he was bursting with happiness. He had been given the name of John White's steward and had taken time to walk into Farnham to see him and to arrange everything for his and Alice's arrival in the second week after Easter.

Everything looked good. He was given permission to ride to London for his wedding at St Mary Bowe. And there, nervously waiting at the church porch with Antonio, who was his witness, and with Father Mossman wearing his best cloth-of-gold Easter vestments that glinted in the sunlight, he saw Alice arrive with her mother and Edward. Alice was wearing a simple white dress and around her head was a circlet of gold wire interlaced with myrtle. Passers by stopped and smiled, and Clemo could not help bringing to mind his first wedding at Dixton, and his mother and sisters. Mixed emotions flickered across his face: old bereavements jostled with new-found happiness.

After he and Alice had exchanged vows they were led into the church by Father Mossman for the final prayers and blessing. They heard the church door open behind them, and when he and Alice turned to walk down the aisle, they saw Gwen and Pablo standing next to the door looking shyly pleased, and near them was Alice's boss from the Apothecary, and to Clemo's amazement, so was the Master Cellarer.

They were all invited back to the Parsonage afterwards for meats, pies, bread and ales. It gave Clemo the chance to thank Antonio for being with him, and to express his amazed delight that the Master Cellarer had turned up. 'Ah, my dear Clemo, I had to be here to make certain that it all happened. I didn't want you having second thoughts about becoming a monk...Now, I shall leave you. I am staying with the brothers at St Mary Graces, and am looking forward to seeing them all.' He turned to Alice, 'I hope that you and Clemo will be richly blessed in your new life and as a near neighbour when you live in Farnham, I shall come to see you, that is, if you can tolerate the presence of an old moth-eaten monk!' He walked away, his shoulders slightly bowed.

Alice had arranged for a carter to take them and their few belongings to Farnham. Their possessions were few, an oak chest which was Antonio's gift to them (he had been given it by Cromwell), a feather bed, and linens given to her by her mother, her own clothes in a large linen bag and, carefully wrapped in straw and blankets, some apothecary jars given by her master .

The cart, with Clemo's horse tethered to it, rumbled slowly across London Bridge and headed out of London along the Portsmouth road. They stopped in Esher for the night, Clemo sleeping with the other male travellers in one room and Alice with the female servants in another, and the carter bedded down in the cart to protect it from thieves. Clemo longed to be with Alice, and years later they would joke about their first night as man and wife being spent in a flea-ridden ale house in separate rooms.

At first light, the cart trundled on towards Guildford and when they stopped there, Clemo was so anxious to show Alice the delights of the Hog's Back that he told the carter he and Alice would ride his horse to Farnham and they would wait for the carter at their house.

Clemo helped Alice to sit behind him, told her to put her arms around his waist (she needed no encouragement) and the horse walked briskly towards Farnham. Alice exclaimed that she had never seen anything so beautiful as the views from the Hog's Back and although the ride was a bit uncomfortable, just being with Clemo was enough to distract her, and Clemo imagined that he was a knight bringing his bride to an enchanted castle. The reality, of course, was that the house in the Borough was small with a narrow shop front, a back parlour, a narrow garden and outhouses; upstairs, there were two bedrooms and an attic room. Alice thought it was heaven, and so did Clemo. 'And it's all your doing,' he exclaimed, as they waited for the carter to arrive, and talked with John White's steward who had welcomed them and handed them the keys.

The following morning, Clemo set off on the horse to ride to Waverley, leaving Alice to arrange their few things. But she was most anxious to ensure that the shop looked good. She scrubbed it until all the surfaces shone, and then, having washed and dried the apothecary jars she placed them on the shelves and stood back to admire what she had achieved. Her London Master had generously supplied a number of herbs and potions with which to begin her work but she realised that she would very soon have to go to the market to see what herbs she could find there, or go on foraging expeditions herself. Having arranged the shop to her satisfaction, she went in search of bread and ale and a pie for their first supper together. It was, she thought, one of the happiest days of her life, as though the sun's rays had entered and warmed her very soul.

Their lives thereafter, settled into a pattern. At first, trade in the shop was quiet but gradually, as word spread, so more and more people came to seek her advice.

Clemo contrasted the mood in the shop with the situation in the Abbey, where Father Abbot, having handed over the accounts to the Commissioners, had withdrawn more and more into himself. A couple of servants had left and were not replaced which meant that Clemo had increased responsibilitiues.

In the second week of May, news reached the Abbey that three Carthusian priors, a Bridgettine monk, and a priest had been hanged drawn and quartered at Tyburn for refusing to take the Oath of Supremacy to the King. The image of the Maid of Kent came into Clemo's mind as he and the other servants joined the Abbot and the monks in church. The Abbot explained at the beginning of the Requiem that the Mass was for all those who had died, but was careful not to mention either the names or the occupations of those who had been executed at Tyburn. The Requiem was a sombre affair and Clemo noted that the Abbot celebrated the Mass with intense feeling and with a profound sadness.

Just one week later, the Italian merchants rode into the Abbey ready for their annual bartering over the price of the fleeces. As they inspected the fleeces, with Clemo accompanying them, they raised the question of whether he was going to join them. He explained that he had spent the past twelve months trying to learn as much as possible about the wool and cloth trade, and now, although still having much to learn, he expected to be able to join them the following year. He said that he owed the Abbey and the Master Cellarer about nine months more work.

One of the merchants laughed,'You have just about hit the date spot on.'

'What do you mean?' asked Clemo.

'Of course, we are not privy to what is going on in the high politics of the monarch's court, but our contacts in that world have hinted that there will be more reforms involving abbeys, of an even greater magnitude than the ones we have already experienced.'

'So, you really do know Antonio well!', retorted Clemo, with a laugh.

'Perhaps we do, perhaps we don't! Have you heard of another Antonio, Antonio Bonvisi, he's a great man . We know him extremely well, as does your friend Antonio di Venezia. Antonio Bonvisi lives in Crosby Hall in Bishopsgate and is the flower around which all we lesser Italian bees hover. He is the most important banker and merchant in London, and in due course, Clemo, you will need to meet hhim. But now, for the next nine months, continue your learning, and keep your beautiful green eyes alert to all the shifts in the wool and cloth trade. This time next year you will become our agent.'

Clemo thanked them for putting such trust in him. They replied that being a merchant depended, in essence, on whether people could be trusted. And they repeated that they had faith in him as a Christian gentleman.

Clemo was bowled over by being referred to as a 'gentleman,' and later that evening told Alice about it.

'To be a gentleman, Master Trelawney, is not about your parentage. It's about your integrity...so, Clemo Trelawney, give me a kiss for flattering you!!'

He continued his learning about wool and cloth, and began to feel that he was in a position where he could now distinguish between different qualities of wool and cloth and could price them accordingly. The Master Cellarer was impressed by Clemo's desire to explore the subject and was complimentary. But there came a day in June, when his mood darkened.

'Clemo,' he announced, as they sorting out bills in his office, 'we are in for a rough time. Cromwell not only knows how much the Abbey is worth; he is now turning the screws even harder. He has hand-picked a few reformist men who have been given the task of inspecting every monastery in England to see if our morals and our religious practices are of the highest standard. We have nothing to fear in Waverley but Cromwell's orders to his men to seek the 'highest standards' are designed to make each abbey fail. What institution does not have flaws? What institution could not do better? Is any human being perfect? And we all know that this is the man behind the execution of the Carthusians, and I heard only yesterday, that Bishop John Fisher has been executed. Cromwell is utterly ruthless. And so is the King...and of course, if you ever reported to anyone that I had said that, I too would soon be hanging from a gibbet. So, Clemo, my dear friend and companion... what a terrible and fearful age we are living in.'

In July, news came to the abbey that Thomas More had been executed.

'It's like a drum beat, all these killings,' said the Master Cellarer, 'a drum beat which is getting louder and louder, and closer and closer... Clemo, my friend, pray with all your heart and soul for this Abbey, for Father Abbot, and of your mercy, pray for me.' Clemo thought of the Master Cellarer as a tough man, and had never heard him speak with such anguished feeling. His voice choked and he rubbed his eyes with his hands brushing away the tears.

He cleared his throat, and said, 'I must pull myself together, Clemo; forgive me for that outburst. Now, let's get on with these bills...'

The drums did indeed beat louder, and they did indeed come closer. One day in September, a man on horseback turned up at the gatehouse...

Chapter 43: Finale

Rufus greeted the man warily and received in return, an order.

'Take my horse and get someone to take me to the Abbot.'

Rufus, disliking the man's peremptory tone, pretended not to hear.

'Do you know who I am, churl? I am Dr Richard Layton and I am here on behalf of the King. Now, do as you are bidden.'

Rufus spat on the floor, took the horse, and called his grandson to find Father Abbot and ask him to attend the gatehouse. The young boy rushed away. Rufus still held the horse's bridle, and waited alongside the impatient man until he saw his grandson return with Father Abbot.

'I think you might have been expecting me, though from the attitude of your gatekeeper, it would seem that he had not been warned of my arrival. I am Dr Richard Layton. I am here on behalf of His Majesty.'

'You are welcome,' replied the Abbot, his voice carefully controlled, as he tried not to reveal his anxiety.

'I have had a long day. Take me to my lodgings and when I am ready, I shall come to your rooms, Abbot.'

The Abbot bowed slightly, asked Rufus to show the man to the Guest Room, and walked slowly back to his Lodgings. On the way, he passed Clemo.

'Clemo, Dr Richard Layton has just arrived to inspect us. Can you please ensure tomorrow that all the servants go to collect firewood out in the woods for most of the day, and I shall instruct the brothers to do the same'. Clemo looked puzzled by the instruction.

'I shall explain later,' said the Abbot.

That evening, after supper with the Abbot, Richard Layton described what his duties were.

'I am to give you these Injunctions, Abbot. You can read them now and I shall wait whilst you do so.'

Father Abbot took the parchment and by the light of a flickering candle read the document slowly and carefully. The Injunctions ordered him to ensure that the brothers were taught and would uphold the Royal Supremacy and the Succession. It stated that the Bible was to be read for at least an hour each day and that monks were not to leave the monastic precinct. As there were over thirty detailed instructions, it took the Abbot a while to read and re-read them.

'Well?' said Layton, once the abbot had completed his reading, 'Do you understand what you are now required to do?'

'I do, but many of these injunctions are ones which we keep already.'

'But not with sufficient rigour,' replied Layton.

The Abbot looked at his adversary, and then said, 'I cannot quite see how you can know that we are not obeying these instructions rigourously when you have never been to Waverley before.'

'Father Abbot, since August I have visited abbeys, priories and monasteries throughout southern England and I have seen how lazy and immoral you all are.'

'All of us?'

'Indeed. All of you. Don't claim to be the exception, Abbot, because I shall not believe you.'

'Ah…'

'What do you mean by "Ah"?'

'Just a little verbal habit of mine, but I think it meant that if you are inspecting us but you know what you are going to find before you actually look, that inspection might determine outcomes which you have already decided upon. Am I correct?'

'Less of your impertinence, Abbot. Do not forget that I am here as the representative of His Majesty and Master Cromwell.'

'So I understand…but I see you are holding another set of papers, are they for me to read as well?'

'They are.' He handed the papers to him. 'I shall not wait whilst you read them. They are questions to which we are seeking answers. I shall come to you again after breakfast and shall expect you to have read and answered them all, but now I shall return to my rooms. Fetch a servant to take me there.'

'Forgive me, but before I do so, I need to be clear. Are you expecting me to have answered all your questions by the morrow, because if you are, I shall probably have to miss Compline and Matins and, as you will know, my duty as abbot requires me to offer prayer to the Almighty eight times each day.'

'I expect the Almighty will manage without your wheedling prayers, Abbot. Now, where is the servant?'

'I shall ask him to attend us.'

'You don't "ask", Abbot, you order.'

'Ah.'

Richard Layton was taken to the Guest Room where the fire in the hearth had burnt low and gave out little heat. He undressed and sank into bed feeling exhausted and irritated by his encounter with the abbot. Was the abbot playing him like a fish, or was the abbot the fish that he himself would catch? It took him no time at all to determine which of the two options was the most likely. He smiled and slept, but woke in the morning feeling cold. The fire had gone out and there was no sign of a servant coming to rekindle it.

He opened the door and shouted for a servant. Rufus heard him but decided to respond to the call, slowly.

Layton called out again. Rufus climbed the stairs one step at a time carrying wood shavings, twigs, coal and logs. He knelt down to create the fire.

'Don't you know that you need to clean the hearth first?' thundered Layton.

'Do I?' responded Rufus,'Well, I never. There's always something new to learn every day.' He took a small brush from his capacious pocket and began painstakingly to sweep the hearth.

'For goodness' sake, don't bother with that. You're too slow. It's so cold in here you could use it as a store room. Just light the fire. You can clean it out tomorrow.'

Rufus took an age to lay the fire and made several attempts to strike a flint but eventually the shavings caught.

'Now…who is going to bring my breakfast?'

'I am, Sire. I shall not be gone long.' Rufus hobbled slowly down the stairs smiling to himself, and muttering imprecations under his breath.

Layton was in a foul mood when he saw the Abbot again, and asked if the Articles of Enquiry had been completed.

'Indeed, they have been,' replied the Abbot, 'but I was up much of the night doing so.'

'I make no apology for having inconvenienced you. These are important matters. And I suspect that the Almighty might agree with me.'

The Abbey had seemed unusually quiet when Layton walked across to the Abbot's Lodging. He asked where all the brothers and servants were.

'Out in the woods gathering firewood in readiness for the winter. It's an ancient Waverley tradition which we keep, close to the Feast of Saints Cosmas and Damian. As we gather the kindling, we meditate on the wooden arrows which assailed them.'

Layton did not know whether to believe the Abbot. Was he being strung along, or was this another example of absurd devotions being given to mythological saints? Unfortunately, it annoyed him even more.

The following day he wrote a peevish letter to Cromwell accusing the Abbot of not being very bright and stating that there was a breakdown in discipline in the abbey. He laid the responsibility for this at the feet of the abbot, a man he described in his letter as 'honest, but not one of the children of Solomon'. Father Abbot asked if he could write a letter to Cromwell in defence of the Abbey. 'Of course you can,' replied Layton, 'and you can send it to Master Cromwell with the other papers you have completed. That way we shall be certain that neither your letter nor your answers will go missing.' It was a sneering response.

When Layton had gone, Father Abbot asked Clemo to come to him and requested him to carry his letter and the sealed Articles of Enquiry to Cromwell.

'I shall certainly do that for you, Father,' replied Clemo, 'but may I ask why we all had to go into the woods yesterday?'

'I didn't want anyone to be cross-questioned by Dr Layton, it was as simple as that. But I told him that it was an ancient Waverley tradition that we always set aside a day close to the Feast of Cosmas and Damian to gather wood. And he believed me.' The Abbot chortled.

In London, Clemo had an opportunity to see the Mossman family and assured them that Alice was flourishing and that he himself was the happiest man in the world.

He also paid a visit to Antonio.

'I hope, Clemo,' said Antonio, 'that you are seriously looking at working with my merchant friends, because, allow me to warn you, I am currently working with Master Cromwell on some legislation which might result in the ending of many abbeys, including Waverley, by the middle of next year.'

It was not news that Clemo wished to hear but he was no longer surprised by the machinations of the King or Cromwell, and promised faithfully to Antonio that he would not breathe a word of what he had been told. His ride back to Waverley through cold and driving autumnal rain matched his mood.

At Waverley, whilst the services continued to be offered during the succeeding months, and the daily routine of the abbey was little changed, over everything hung a miasma of uncertainty and fear. What would happen next? No-one knew.

In March, with an Act of Parliament, the final death knell was sounded: all abbeys with an income of less than £200.00 were to be closed. Waverley fell into that category. The monks were to be given the choice of moving to a bigger monastery, or of leaving with a pension. The servants, of course, were offered nothing.

In May, the Italian merchants arrived. Clemo and the Master Cellarer greeted them and dealt expeditiously with the financial transactions. Clemo promised that as soon as the abbey had finally closed he would join them and begin his new life as one of their agents.

Meanwhile, meetings of the monks were held, and subdued and miserable conversations took place. Some of the monks decided that they would go elsewhere, including Father Abbot. He arranged to go to

Beaulieu Abbey, in order, as he said, to keep his monastic vows of prayer and simplicity of life. Two of the priest-monks were offered curacies in nearby villages. Others were assured that if they left and renounced their vows, no harm or hurt would befall them. Gradually, the abbey emptied.

Clemo had long discussions with the Master Cellarer and asked him what plans he had.

'In truth, Clemo, I do not know. I shall stay here as long as possible, and trust that whoever is given the abbey and its lands will need a Steward to oversee the place. Perhaps they will take me on.'

The walk that Clemo made each day to Waverley was increasingly sad. When he arrived at the abbey he would be told about each monk and each servant who had left. Some of the servants followed the example of the Master Cellarer and decided to offer their skills to the new owner, so, they stayed on, looking thoroughly woebegone.

There came a day when, of the monks, only the Master Cellarer was left. He cut a forlorn but courageous figure. Clemo helped him with the final accounts which were due to be offered to the new owner. At the end of the day, Clemo put down his quill on the desk and looked across at the Master Cellarer.

'Please don't say anything, Clemo,' said the Master Cellarer. 'You have a new life awaiting you but I am resolved to stay here. I shall continue to say the offices on my own in the church until such time as that is forbidden. So, off you go to your lovely wife… and may the rest of your life be richly blessed.'

They hugged each other tightly and said their farewells. And, as Clemo walked towards Farnham along the river bank, the same way he had originally arrived, he heard in the shimmering summer air, a single bell tolling in the abbey.

Printed in Great Britain
by Amazon

67445601R00183